INDEPENDENCE DAY

INDEPENDENCE DAY

Dean Devlin & Roland Emmerich
and Stephen Molstad

HarperPrism

HarperPaperbacks *A Division of* HarperCollins*Publishers*
10 East 53rd Street, New York, N.Y. 10022

HarperPaperbacks may be purchased for educational, business, or sales promotional use. For information, please write: Special Markets Department, HarperCollins*Publishers*, 10 East 53rd Street, New York, N.Y. 10022.

Printed in the United States of America

Designed by Lili Schwartz

HarperPrism is an imprint of HarperPaperbacks.
HarperPaperbacks, HarperPrism, and colophon are trademarks of HarperCollins*Publishers*.

Special thanks to
Elizabeth "Little Bit" Ostrom
and Dionne McNeff
for their invaluable assistance.

THE SEA OF TRANQUILLITY was an eerily still wasteland, a silent crater-shaped outdoor tomb of ashes and stone. Two sets of footprints were etched into the powdery gray soil surrounding the landing site, each one as freshly cut as the day it was made. On the horizon, a curved sliver of the bright earth was rising into the sky, the vivid blue of its oceans a stark contrast to the colorless valley. Hammered into the lunar surface were the sensor rods of a seismometer, a square box capable of detecting the crash of a sea-sized meteor at a distance of fifty miles, and on the far side of the camp, an American flag waving proudly in a nonexistent breeze. The entire site was littered with debris: scientific experiments and the cartons which had carried them, the unused plastic bags used to gather soil samples, and a handful of commemorative trinkets. This equipment, carelessly scattered around an area the size of a baseball infield, had been imported by the astronauts of Apollo 11, the first two humans to set foot on the moon. When they left, they jettisoned everything deemed nonessential for the ride back home. Armstrong and Aldrin had taken one giant step for man, and left behind a ton of garbage for moonkind.

Their decades-old footprints marched fifteen paces out toward the horizon in every direction before turning back to the center of the camp. Seen from high above, they formed a pattern in the sand like a large, misshapen daisy. At the eye of this flower stood the gleaming Lunar Landing Platform, a four-footed framework of tubes and gold foil which looked like a jungle gym on a hastily abandoned campground. Marooned deep in a sea of silence, the spot had the creepy aspect of a long-ago picnic which had come to an abrupt and terrifying end, as if there had been no time for the visitors to pack up their belongings. Only enough time to turn and run for safety. Nothing, not a single grain of sand, had moved in all the years since the earthlings' departure.

But something was beginning to change. Gradually, an infinitesimal churning began to engulf the area. For many hours, it was nothing more perceptible than the disturbance caused by the fluttering of a moth's wings at a distance of a thousand paces. But it grew steadily, inexorably, into a tremble. The electric needles inside the seismometer skittered to life. The machine's sensors shot awake and began to scream their warning to the scientists on earth. But the moon's extremes of heat and cold had disabled its radio transmitter within days of it first being planted. Like a night watchman with his tongue cut out, the small device struggled hour after hour to sound the alarm as the rumbling grew. A single grain of sand tumbled down the edge of a footprint, then another, and another. As the quaking blossomed into a deep rumble, the stiff wire sewn into the bottom seam of the American flag began to wobble back and forth. The footprints began to shake apart and disintegrate in the vibrating sand.

Then a vast shadow moved across the sky. It passed directly overhead, eclipsing the sun and plunging the entire crater into an unnatural darkness. The moonquake intensified as the thing moved closer. Whatever it was, it was much too large to have been sent from earth.

THE ROCKY FLATLANDS of the New Mexico desert could feel as alien and inhospitable as the moon. On a dark night when the moon was new, this was one of the quietest places on the planet: a thousand miles of blood-red desert, its clay hills baked hard and smooth. At one o'clock in the morning on July 2, jackrabbits and lizards, drawn by the warmth of the pavement, were gathered on a thin strip of asphalt in a valley where a dirt road snaked its way out of the foothills and down to the main highway. The only discernible movement came from the incredible profusion of insects, a thousand species of them that had adapted to this harsh environment.

Where the dirt road ran up toward the crest of some hills, there was a wooden sign half-hidden in the sagebrush. It read "NATIONAL AERONAUTICS AND SPACE ADMINISTRATION, SETI." Those who followed the road—with or without permission—to the top of the rise were rewarded with a spectacular sight. On the other side were two dozen enormous signal-collecting dishes, each one well over one hundred feet in diameter. Precision-built from curved steel beams painted white, these giant bowls dominated a long narrow valley. Because the moon was new, the only light on them was the red glow of the beacon lamps attached to the collector rods suspended over the center of each dish. The beacons were a precaution against curious or hopelessly lost pilots hitting the equipment with their planes and tangling themselves into the steel beams like flies caught in the strands of a spiderweb.

SETI, the Search for Extra-Terrestrial Intelligence, was a government-funded,

NASA-administered scientific project and the field of giant radio telescopes was its primary laboratory. Far from the noise pollution that blanketed the cities, scientists had erected this mile-wide listening post to search for clues that would help solve a riddle almost as old as human imagination: Are we alone in the universe?

The telescopes picked up the noise emitted by a billion stars, quasars, and black holes, sounds that were not only very faint, but mind-bogglingly old. Traveling at the speed of light, radio emissions from the sun reach the earth after a delay of eight minutes, while those coming from the next nearest star take over four years. Most of the cosmic noise splashing into the dishes was several million years old, with a signal strength of less than a quadrillionth of a watt. Taken together and added up, all the radio energy ever received by earth amounted to less energy than a single snowflake striking the ground. And yet, these giant upturned steel ears were so exquisitely sensitive they could paint detailed color pictures of objects far too dim and distant for optical telescopes to perceive. They twisted slowly in the moonlight like a field of robotic flowers opening to the faint moonlight.

Tucked between these giants was a pre-fab three-bedroom ranch house which had been converted into a high-technology observatory. A skyful of data was gushing down into the telescopes, zipping along fiber optic cable into the house where it was sliced up, sorted, and analyzed by the most sophisticated signal-processing station ever built. All of this technological wizardry operated under the control of a master computer monitoring the entire system, which meant guys like Richard Yamuro had very little to do.

Richard was an astronomer who'd made a name for himself with his work on "the redshift" phenomenon associated with quasars. Six months out of graduate school, he'd landed a position at the prestigious Universita di Bologna in northern Italy. When SETI called two years later to offer him a job, he'd leapt at the chance to exchange his swank downtown apartment for a tiny cabin in the arid backcountry of New Mexico.

SETI was founded in the early sixties by a handful of "crackpots astronomers," who just happened to be some of the world's top research scientists. Their idea was simple: radio is a basic technology. It is easy to send and even simpler to receive. Its waves travel at the speed of light, effortlessly penetrating things like planets, galaxies, and clouds of gas without significant loss of strength. If an advanced civilization were attempting to communicate with us, these scientists argued, they would never be able to cross the infinite distances of the universe. The only realistic way to establish communication with earth would be to send a radio message. After years of lobbying in Congress,

SETI won the funding for a ten-year exploration of the skies over the northern hemisphere. Under the guidance of NASA, the small staff had set up two other installations, one in Hawaii and the other in Puerto Rico. If intelligent life existed somewhere in the universe, the small band of SETI astronomers were the people most likely to find them.

Richard had pulled the overnight observation shift, which in most jobs would be the least attractive, but among the handful of scientists stationed in New Mexico, it was the most sought-after time to work. At four A.M. the night-watch commander could override the scanning system and use one of the large telescopes for his or her own projects. Which meant Richard still had two hours to kill before he had anything interesting to do. In the meantime, he was brushing up his golfing skills. Going down to one knee, he pictured himself lining up his birdie putt on the eighteenth green at Pebble Beach.

"The entire tournament comes down to this one final shot," he whispered like a television commentator. "Yamuro's left himself twenty feet from the hole. Normally, that would be no problem for a golfer of his amazing skills, but he'll be putting across the roughest, most wicked section of turf, the uneven stretch of green called 'the walkway.'"

"That's exactly right, Bob," he murmured, becoming the second announcer, "it's an almost impossible shot. The pressure is really on Yamuro at this point. It's a make or break situation, but we've seen him come through situations like this a hundred times before. If anyone can do it, he can."

At the far side of a room jammed with expensive electronic gadgetry, he'd laid a crinkled paper cup on its side. The golfer got to his feet and took a series of practice swings as the huge imaginary crowd looked on in perfect silence. Then he lifted his eyes to survey the scene. He glanced toward the tall narrow machine nicknamed "The Veg-O-Matic" for its ability to slice and dice the random noise of the universe into computer-digestible morsels. In its place, he saw his family biting their nails as the tension mounted. His mother, a grim expression on her face, nodded her head to show her son she believed in his ability to sink the putt, thereby bringing honor and glory to the Yamuro name. The golfer looked behind him and spotted a familiar face. "Carl," he said solemnly to an autographed photo of the popular astronomer Carl Sagan mounted on the office wall, "I'm gonna need your help with this one, pal."

At last, Yamuro stepped up to the ball, brought his club back, then, with a crisp and confident stroke, sent the ball sailing toward the hole. It moved unevenly over the worn spots in the office carpet until it reached the paper cup and clipped the edge of it before rolling off to one side. He had missed the shot! The golfer collapsed in agony to the floor. He had failed himself, his army of fans and, worst of all, his mother. While he was down on both knees, clutching at his heart and trying to find the words which could express his feelings of sorrow, the red phone rang.

The nightwatch commander's heart jumped into his throat. The red phone was not an outside line. It came directly from the master computer and was the signal that something unusual had been picked up on the monitors. Leaving his club on the floor, Yamuro snatched up the phone and listened carefully to the computer's digitally sampled voice reading off a string of coordinates. Blinking red lights began erupting all over the main control board.

"This isn't really happening," he muttered as he wrote down the time, frequency, and position coordinates of the disturbance onto a pad of paper. When the red phone rang, which it very rarely did, it meant the computers in the next room, the ones sorting through the billion channels of shrill, random bursts of space noise, had detected something out of the ordinary, something with an intentional pattern. With a sense of dread and a rising pulse rate, Yamuro slipped into the chair at the main instrument console and reached for the headphones. He slipped them over his ears and listened, but heard nothing unusual, only the usual hiss and crackle of the universe. Protocol, at that point, called for him to alert the other scientists, some of them sleeping in their cabins scattered around the grounds. But before he became a member of SETI's False Alarm Club, Yamuro wanted to check it out more carefully. It was probably nothing more than a new spy satellite, or a lost pilot calling for help. He punched some numbers into the keyboard of the computer and took over manual control of dish number one. Reading the input data, the scope swiveled back to the exact position it had been in when the disturbance began.

Then he heard it. Startled by the sound, he jerked backward in his chair, eyes the size of pancakes. Over the usual popping, fizzling background noise, he heard a tonal progression coming through loud and clear. The resonant sound oscillated up and down inside a frequency window known as the hydrogen band. It sounded almost like a musical instrument, an unlikely cross between a piccolo and a foghorn, and vaguely like a church organ in dire need of a tuning. It was like nothing he'd ever heard before, and he recognized it immediately as a signal. Slowly, something like a shocked smile crossed his lips and he reached for the intercom.

Ten minutes later, the small control room looked like a high-tech pajama party. Sleepy astronomers in robes and slippers crowded around the main console, taking turns with the headphones, all of them talking at once. By the time SETI's chief project scientist, Beulah Shore, came stumbling through the darkness from her cabin, her staff was already convinced they'd made contact with an alien culture. "This is the real thing, Beul," Yamuro told her.

Shore looked at him dubiously and plopped herself down in a chair below a poster that read "I BELIEVE IN LITTLE GREEN MEN," which she herself had posted. "This better not be one of those damned Russian spy jobs," she grumbled as she slipped the headphones on and listened with no visible change of expression. Two things were running through her mind: *This is it! We've found it!* There was no mistaking the slow rising and falling of the tone for anything accidental. But at the same time, her scientific training and her need to protect the project forced her to be skeptical. There was already a buzz of excitement among her co-workers and she had seen the ruinous effects of disappointment set in after previous false alarms.

"Interesting," she allowed, poker-faced, "but let's not jump the gun, people. I want to run a source trajectory. Doug, get on the phone to Arecibo and feed them the numbers."

Arecibo was a remote coastal valley in eastern Puerto Rico, home to the largest radio telescope in the world, one thousand meters in diameter. Within five minutes, the astronomers there had shut down their own experiments and wheeled their big dish around to the target coordinates. On a separate telephone line, high-speed modems transferred the data feed instantaneously. As the results of the Arecibo scope came over the line, the normally polite scientists jostled one another for a first look at the print-out as it came spitting out of the machine.

"This can't be right," one scientist said, puzzled and somewhat frightened.

Yamuro tore the page from the printer and turned to Beulah. "According to these calculations, distance to source is three hundred eighty five kilometers," he said in confusion. Then he added what everyone in the cramped room already knew, "That means it's coming from the moon."

Shore walked over to the room's only window, pulled back the curtain a few inches and scrutinized the crescent moon. "Looks like we might have visitors." Then, after a moment of reflection, she added, "It would've been nice if they'd called first."

JUST ACROSS THE Potomac River from the White House, the Pentagon was the largest office building in the world. The giant five-sided structure was home to the byzantine bureaucracies of the United States Armed Forces and was a small city unto itself. Even two hours before sunrise, when its workforce was reduced to the few thousand souls who pulled the graveyard shift, it was a bustling place. An armada of semis were lined up near the building's loading docks to deliver everything from classified documents to restaurant supplies, while dozens of trash trucks hauled away the previous day's mountain of waste.

Speeding across the southern parking lot, an unmarked late-model Ford sedan was headed directly for the building at seventy miles per hour. A second before it rammed into the side of the edifice, it broke into a long skid and fishtailed perfectly into the parking space closest to the front doors.

Seconds later, General William M. Grey, commander in chief of the United States Space Command and head of the Joint Chiefs of Staff came up the steps into the lobby, the steel taps on the soles of his shoes clicking an angry rhythm across the tiled floor. Forty-five minutes earlier, he'd been dead asleep when the phone rang. Nevertheless, the stocky sixty-year-old arrived at the office looking every inch the five-star general, all spit and polish. Without breaking stride, he was joined by his staff commander, Colonel Ray Castillo. The lanky young science officer followed his scowling boss to a fleet of elevators and opened a set of doors with a swipe of his identity card. The doors swooshed open and the two men stepped inside. The instant the doors were closed, the men knew it was safe to talk.

"Who else knows about this?" the general demanded.

"SETI out in New Mexico phoned about an hour ago. They picked up a radio signal at approximately one fifteen A.M. The thing is emitting a repetitive signal, which we're trying to interpret." Castillo answered nervously, trying to sound professional. He knew how little tolerance Grey had for sloppy work.

"They tell anybody else? The press?"

"They agreed to keep quiet about it for the time being. They're afraid of losing credibility if they announce anything prematurely, so they're going to run additional tests."

"Well, what is this damn thing? Do they know?"

Colonel Castillo shook his head and smiled. "No, sir, they're clueless, even more confused than we are." Grey swiveled his head around and impaled his assistant with a disapproving grimace. The men and women who worked for the United States Space Command, an autonomous division of the Air Force, were not permitted to be confused about anything, not while Grey was running the show. Their job was to know all of the answers all of the time. Castillo winced and studied the stack of papers he was carrying. "Excuse me, sir."

The doors opened onto a clean white basement hallway. Castillo led the way down the corridor and through a thick door. He and the general stepped into a plush, cavernous underground strategy room, with a big screen computerized map dominating the main wall. Designed and built in the late seventies, the room was a large oval space with the primary work area, sixty radar consoles, sunk three feet below a 360° perimeter walkway. Three dozen high-security-clearance personnel were down in the pit monitoring everything that moved through the sky: every satellite, every reconnaissance mission, every commercial passenger flight, and every moment of every space shuttle mission. In addition, a network of specially dedicated surveillance satellites kept an eye on each of the thousands of known nuclear missile silos worldwide. With its thick carpeting and colorfully painted wall murals of space flight, it always reminded Grey of "a goddamned library," as he had called it on more than one occasion.

"Take a look at these monitors," Castillo said, pointing to a row of ordinary televisions tuned to news broadcasts from around the globe. Every few seconds, the picture quality would suddenly disintegrate into a rolling blur, different from any sort of picture distortion they'd seen before. "Satellite reception has been impaired. *All* satellite reception, ours included. But we were able to get these shots."

He led the way to a nearby glass table which was lit from below and showed Grey a large photographic transparency. Taken with an infra-red camera, it showed a blotchy, orb-like object set against a background of stars. The image quality was too grainy and distorted for the general to make either heads or tails of it. Several members of the Space Command staff joined them at the table. Grey, the only non-scientist in the group, wasn't about to start asking a bunch of asinine questions. Instead, he glowered down at the blurry image for a moment before announcing his opinion.

"Looks like a big turd."

Castillo was about to laugh when he realized his boss wasn't trying to be funny. He continued his presentation by laying down a second, equally turd-like photo of the object. "We estimate this thing has a diameter of over five hundred and fifty kilometers," he explained, "and a mass equal to roughly one-quarter of the moon's."

"Holy Mother of . . ." Grey didn't like the sound of that. "What do you think it is? A meteor, maybe?"

The entire clique of officers glanced around at one another. Obviously, Grey hadn't been completely briefed about the nature of the object they were looking at. "No, sir," one of the officers piped up, "it's definitely not a meteor."

"How do you know?"

"Well, for one thing, sir, it's *been* slowing down. It's *been* slowing down ever since we first spotted it."

Grey's trademark scowl melted temporarily into one of bewilderment as the implications of what he was being told began to register. If it was slowing down, it could only mean the object was being controlled, piloted.

Without a moment of hesitation, he marched to the nearest phone and called the secretary of defense at home. When informed by the man's wife that he was sleeping, Grey barked in to the receiver, "Then wake him up! This is an emergency."

THOMAS WHITMORE, forty-eight years old, was one of the first people awake in a city of early risers. Still in his pajamas, he lay on top of the covers with a pair of bifocals perched at the end of his nose thumbing through a stack of newpapers. It was a sweltering, muggy night in the District of Columbia, and even with the air-conditioning running, he was too uncomfortable to fall back asleep. The phone rang at a few minutes past 4 A.M. Without lifting his eyes from an article about international shipping policy, he reached over to the nightstand, picked up the receiver, and waited for whomever was calling to begin speaking.

"Hello, handsome," a female voice purred into the phone.

That captured his attention. Recognizing the voice, Whitmore tossed the paper to one side. "Well, well. I didn't expect to hear from you tonight. Thought you'd already be asleep. How may I assist you?" He smiled.

"Talk to me while I get undressed," she replied.

"I think I can help you with that request," Whitmore said, arching an eyebrow. He didn't get an invitation like that every day. He glanced around the sumptuously appointed bedroom, making sure no one was around except the small figure beneath the sheet at the other side of the bed. Glancing up at the clock, he noticed, "It's past four in the morning here. Are you just getting in?"

"Yes, I am." She didn't sound too pleased.

"You must want to strangle me."

"That possibility has crossed my mind."

"Honey, federal law specifically prohibits attempts to cause me any bodily harm," he informed her. "Why are you so late?"

"The party was out in Malibu and they closed the Pacific Coast Highway. The waves were crashing all the way up onto the highway. They think there must have been an earthquake somewhere out at sea. Anyway—"

"So, what did Howard say?" Whitmore asked anxiously. He had sent her to Los Angeles on a not-so-secret mission, hoping to recruit Howard Story, a super-rich Hollywood entertainment executive with a Wall Street background, to join their campaign.

"He's on board," she reported.

"Excellent! Marilyn, you're amazing. Thank you. I'll never ask you to do this kind of thing again."

"Liar," she crooned with a smile. One of the things Marilyn Whitmore loved the most about her husband was his inability to lie. She shut off the light in her hotel room and slipped into bed. She hated those glitzy West Coast movie people and their lavish garden parties, everyone trying to impress everyone else with their name-dropping and tedious descriptions of their next big project. She'd rather have been in bare feet and jeans hanging around "the house."

"In that case, I have a confession to make," Whitmore told her. "I'm lying in bed next to a beautiful young brunette." As he said this, the small figure on the other side of the bed stirred slightly, vaguely aware she was being talked about. Whitmore pulled back the sheet to reveal the sleeping face of his six-year-old daughter, Patricia, who had graced her pillow case with a tiny drool mark.

"Tom, I hope you didn't let her stay up watching TV all night again."

"Only part of the night," her husband admitted.

Patricia recognized something in her father's voice and, without opening her eyes, lifted her head off the pillow. "Is that Mommy?"

"Uh-oh! Somebody's waking up," Whitmore said into the phone, "and I think she wants to talk to you. When exactly are you flying back here?"

"Right after the luncheon tomorrow."

"Great. Call me from the plane if you can. I love you. Now, here's the wee one."

He passed the phone to his daughter and found the remote control for the television. He turned the set on and surfed through a few channels until he ran across a political talk show, a panel of pundits pontificating on politics. The first thing he noticed was the picture distortion. Every few seconds, the screen split into vertical bars which then rolled and collapsed to the side. Although it was distracting, it didn't prevent him from listening to the crossfire argument.

"I said it during the campaign and I still say it today," a bald man in suspenders declared, "the brand of leadership the president provided during the Gulf War bears no relationship to the kind of savvy insider politics needed to survive in Washington. After a brief honeymoon period with the congress, his inexperience is catching up with him. His popularity numbers continue to decline in the polls."

A woman with smart hair and a sharp tongue waved her hand in the air, dismissing the bald man's ideas. "Charlie, you remind me of a broken clock— you're only right twice a day. But this is one of the few times I agree with you. The current administration has gotten bogged down in the swamp of D.C. deal-making. In recent weeks, the president has waded into the murky waters of pragmatic backroom politics, only to find the sharks of the Republican party biting at his ankles."

Whitmore rolled his eyes at the overwrought prose. "Where in the world do they find these people?" Simultaneously disgusted and entertained, he got out of bed to see if he could adjust the set. As he began working the knobs, the channels began flipping by one after the other. He stared at the set confused until he turned around and discovered that Patricia had picked up the remote control he'd left behind. After saying good-bye to her mother, she was hunting for the morning's first cartoons. Every station had the same picture distortion.

"Honey, it's too early for cartoons. You need to go back to sleep for a little while."

"Yes, I know, but . . ." The little girl paused to think, hoping she might be able to negotiate a compromise. Then she tried a different strategy. "Why is the picture all messed up?"

"It's an experiment," her father informed her. "The people at the television stations want to see if they can make little girls watch really boring shows all night so they miss everything fun during the day."

Patricia Whitmore wasn't buying any of it. "Daddy," she tilted her head to one side, "that's preposterous."

"Preposterous?" Whitmore chuckled. "I like that." Nevertheless, he switched off the television and put the remote out of reach. "Get some sleep, sweetheart." He put on his robe, gathered up his newspapers, and slipped out the door.

In the hallway, a man in an expensive suit was sitting on a chair reading a paperback novel. Startled, he snapped the book closed and jumped to his feet. "Good morning, Mr. President."

"Morning, George." Whitmore stopped and handed him a section of the newspaper. "I've got one word for you: the Chicago White Sox!"

"They won again?"

"Read it and weep, my friend."

In truth, neither man cared very much about sports, but both of them paid enough attention to give them something to talk about when they were together. George was from Kansas City and Whitmore from Chicago. Last night's victory put the Sox half a game ahead of the Royals in the pennant race. George, the Secret Service agent who protected the president from midnight to six, pretended to study the paper until Whitmore was a polite distance down the hallway. He then pulled out his walkie-talkie and whispered a message to his fellow bodyguards, alerting them that their workday had begun.

The breakfast nook was a cheery room decorated with yellow wallpaper and antique furniture collected by Woodrow Wilson in the early years of the century. At the long table in the center of the room was an attractive young woman in a white blouse and tan skirt. Her shoes were sensible and her hair was perfect. She'd already finished her breakfast and was elbow deep in a mound of newspapers and press releases by the time her boss joined her.

"Connie, you're up early."

"This is disgusting, reprehensible," she growled without looking up, "the lowest form of bottom-feeding scum-sucking journalism I've ever seen."

She was beautiful, intelligent, and always ready for a fight. Constance Spano, President Whitmore's communications director, had started out as a campaign staffer during his very first run for political office and, over the years, had developed into his most trusted adviser. The two of them had reached the point where they could finish each other's sentences. Although she was in her late thirties, she looked much younger and was a very visible symbol of Whitmore's "baby-boomer" presidency. She made it her job to aggressively defend her boss against an increasingly hostile and irresponsible press. The object of her wrath this morning was the editorial page of *The Post*.

"I can't believe this crap," she said slapping the paper with the back of her hand, "there are a hundred bills before Congress right now and they devote their Friday op/ed column to personality assassination." Without looking up, she cleared some room for him at the table.

"Good morning, Connie," her boss said again pointedly, as he poured himself a cup of coffee.

She looked up from the paper. "Oh, right, sorry. Good morning," she said before launching off once again on the crimes of the city's conservative newspapers. "Tom, they've spent all week taking cheap shots at your health care and energy proposals, but today they're attacking your character outright. Just listen to this: 'Addressing Congress . . . '" She paused long enough for the butler to serve the chief his omelet. "'. . . Addressing Congress earlier this week, Whitmore seemed less like the president than the orphan child Oliver holding up his empty bowl and pleading, "Please sir, I'd like some more."'" Connie stared across the table, outraged. "Am I missing something here, or is that just old-fashioned mud-slinging?"

Whitmore, an unusual politician, never took the papers too seriously. He left that part of the job to Connie, knowing that before the day was done, she would strike back at anyone who had dared to attack him. "He deserved it," the president said between mouthfuls.

"Who did? Deserved what?"

"Oliver. A hungry kid asking for a second helping of gruel from the stingy master of the orphanage. I think it's kind of flattering."

Connie disagreed. "The point is, they're attacking your age. Trying to spread the idea that you don't have enough experience or wisdom. And the only reason it's working for them is because of the perception that you've hung up your guns, set aside your ideals. When Thomas Whitmore is fighting for what he believes in, the media calls it idealism. But lately, there's been too damn much compromising, too much you-scratch-my-back, I'll-scratch-yours business." She shut up and reached for her coffee, realizing she'd overstated her case. But somebody, Connie thought, needed to have the guts to say it out loud.

Whitmore stabbed another bite of his omelet, chewing it thoroughly before he responded. "There's a fine line between standing behind a principle and *hiding* behind one," he said calmly. "I can tolerate some compromise if we're actually able to get some things done around here. The American people didn't send me here to make a bunch of pretty speeches. They want results, and that's what I'm trying to give them."

As far as Connie was concerned, he was missing the point. Real accomplishments, she believed, weren't born from a spirit of muddling through. She feared Whitmore was losing his fire, his vision. Until recently, everything about his presidency had been different. They'd campaigned on the themes of service and sacrifice, an "Ask not what your country can do for you . . ." message that all the experts and operators told them was sure-fire political suicide. They said nobody wanted to hear about doing more and having less. But in Whitmore's awkward-charming way, he'd made the message real to millions of Americans, and he had easily beaten his Republican opponent. In his first year, he'd introduced major legislative initiatives to reform everything from the legal system to health care to the environment. But for the past few months, the programs had been stalled in committees, held hostage by lawmakers who all wanted something on the side for their districts. Against the advice of Connie and many of his advisers, the young president had spent most of his time and energy shepherding his bills through the process, allowing himself to get bogged down by first-term representatives he could have steamrollered. All of them were willing to cooperate, but only in exchange for one favor or another. In the meantime, his prestige and popularity were down among the voters. Connie considered Whitmore not only her boss, but her friend and her hero. It killed her to see him bleeding from the thousand small wounds inflicted on him by other politicians, and the summer session was only beginning.

"Speaking of getting something accomplished," Whitmore grinned, showing her the front page of the *Orange County Register*, "I've been named one of the ten sexiest men in America! Finally, we're getting somewhere on the *real* issues." That broke the mood and both of them enjoyed a laugh as they began reading through the article.

They were interrupted by a young man who poked his head in the doorway. "Excuse me, Mr. President?"

"Alex, good morning," he said to the staffer. "What is it?"

"Phone call, sir. It's the secretary of defense with an emergency situation," he reported nervously as Whitmore made his way to the breakfast room phone.

"What's going on?" Whitmore asked. For the next two minutes, he listened, walking over to the window and peering outside. Whatever it was, Connie already knew from the expression on the chief's face that it was serious. Serious enough to change the day's whole schedule.

ONE OF THE amazing things about humanity is how often and how effortlessly we ignore miracles. The strangest, craziest, most sublime things happen around us all the time without anyone taking much notice.

One such miracle used to take place at Cliffside Park in New Jersey. For a few glorious moments every summer morning, as the sun began rising out of the Atlantic, great slabs of light sliced between the skyscraper canyons of Manhattan, mixing with the mist coming off the Hudson. It was a scene made famous on postcards and television commercials, but the men who gathered in the park every morning before dawn almost never gave the sight so much as a quick glance. They were mostly older gentlemen who had come to play chess on the long rows of stone tables near Cliffside Drive. For every man playing a game, there were three others standing about watching. In hushed murmuring voices, they exchanged gossip and news, announced the births of grandchildren and the deaths of long-time friends. Except for their sneakers and sweatshirts, they could have been the ancient Greeks conferring in the agora.

The largest group of these men were gathered loosely around two expert chess players, David and Julius. They seemed to be unlikely opponents. David was tall, gaunt, and intense, with a mop of curly black hair. Although he was in his late thirties, he played with the concentration of a child building a house of cards. His fingers smooshed his face into strange expressions and his long limbs coiled around one another at odd, uncomfortable looking angles. Completely focused on the game, he was totally unaware of looking like a human pretzel. He knew he needed to concentrate if he hoped to beat a wily opponent like Julius.

Julius, on the other hand, had only one way of sitting. At sixty-eight years old, he often said, his ass was too fat to squiggle around like David's. Once he had plopped himself down, that's how he stayed. His legs, stuck straight out, were barely long enough to rest his heels on the ground. His meticulously ironed slacks were jacked halfway up his calves, exposing the white socks he didn't think anyone could see. Under his windbreaker, he wore one of the two dozen white shirts he got from his brother-in-law when he retired from the garment business five years ago: *Hey, why not? They fit perfect!* To complete his look, the old guy was working a half-smoked cigar around the side of his mouth.

These opponents had faced one another many times, usually drawing a sizable crowd. This morning's match had begun with a flurry of standard moves until the older man, a speed player, began a blitzkrieg with his bishops. Since then, David had had to think about every move very carefully. Julius, always a showman, went to work on David psychologically, loud enough for everyone to hear. "How long are you gonna take? My social security will expire and you'll still be sitting here."

David pulled his fingers slowly across his face. Without looking up, he said, "I'm thinking."

"So think already!"

Still thinking, David lifted his queen's knight and moved it tentatively forward. The moment his fingers lifted off the piece, Julius responded like lightning, pushing a pawn forward to challenge. David glanced up for a moment, genuinely puzzled, before looking down to study his options.

"Again he's thinking," Julius announced, reaching into a carefully folded paper bag to retrieve a Styrofoam cup full of coffee.

David shot him a disappointed look. "Hey, where's the travel mug I bought you?"

"In the sink, dirty from yesterday."

"Do you have any idea how long those things take to decompose?" David reached across the table to take the cup, but Julius drew back, protecting his caffeinated treasure.

"Listen, Mr. Ecosystem, if you don't move soon, *I'll* start to decompose. Play the game."

Disgruntled, David countered the challenging pawn with one of his own. Then Julius really gave him something to think about. Without hesitation, he slid his queen into the middle of the battle. "So," the old man leaned in over the board, "if I am not mistaken, a certain someone left a message on your answering machine yesterday." Julius sat back and took a sip of his coffee.

David merely grunted. "Furthermore, I understand that this person is single after an unfortunate divorce, that she has no children, that she has an interesting career, that she's educated and attractive. All good things."

"You're doing it again," his opponent complained with a growl. At some point, Julius would invariably bring up something uncomfortable, some emotionally-charged issue that made it difficult to continue with the match. David was pretty sure there was no malicious intent, that the old guy was just worried about him, wanted to see him happy. Then again, maybe he was just trying to win at chess. He protected his bishop by advancing his king's knight.

"So did you call her back I'm wondering," Julius said, casually advancing another pawn.

"Look, I'm sure she's a beautiful and sophisticated woman, but she invited me to go country line dancing. I can't really see myself doing that, and besides, I'm convinced those tight cowboy jeans can do permanent damage to one's reproductive organs."

"What, so you can't even call the poor girl back and spend five minutes on the phone? After she worked up the chutzpah to call you, you can't just maybe be polite and call her back?"

"Dad, I'm not interested," David said flatly. "Besides, I'm still a married man." He held up the wedding ring on his finger to prove his point. He pulled one of his bishops back to safety.

Suddenly, Julius felt embarrassed by the presence of the crowd, the old-timers who were his friends and confidants. They knew the whole sad story of David's broken marriage and his refusal, or inability, to let it go. He glanced around at them, hoping they'd take a hint and make themselves scarce. Not a chance. They were more interested in the conversation than in the game. As he usually did, Julius went ahead and said what was on his mind anyhow. "Son, I'm thankful you spend so much time with me. Family is important. But I'm only saying, it's been what, four years? And you still haven't signed the divorce papers?"

"Three years."

"Three, four, ten, what difference? The point is, it's time to move on with your life. I'm serious—this is not healthy what you're doing." As if to prove his point, Julius reached across the table and captured a knight with his queen.

"Healthy? Look who's talking about healthy." He pointed at the old man's cigar and coffee. "We're exposed to so many carcinogens in our environment and you make it worse by—" The frantic chirping of David's pager interrupted him. He glanced down at the number display and saw that it was only Marty calling from the office for the third time that morning.

"That's about six times they've called you. Are you *trying* to get yourself fired? Or maybe you've decided to get a real job." David moved his bishop to take one of the pawns guarding Julius's king.

"Checkmate," he announced matter-of-factly. "See you tomorrow, Dad." He untangled his limbs, hopped up, and planted a kiss on his father's cheek, then grabbed his fifteen-speed racing bike.

"That's not checkmate," Julius roared, "I can still take your . . . but then you can . . . oh." He yelled across the park as David began to pedal away, "You could let an old man win once in a while, it wouldn't kill you!" But secretly, Julius Levinson loved the fact that his son could swoop in whenever he felt like it and beat almost anyone in the park.

A RUSH HOUR jam session was underway. Grumbling across the George Washington Bridge, blaring bumper to bumper traffic mingled its noise with the honking and screeching of ten thousand hungry seagulls to produce an early morning orchestral cacophony over the Hudson, the whole mess pouring itself into Manhattan. David, on his bike, shot through the gridlock and hung a hard right onto Riverside Drive. Five minutes later, he turned onto a street full of old warehouses and coasted to a stop in front of an aging six-story brick building. Foot-high stainless steel letters anchored into the bricks spelled out the name of the site's present occupant: COMPACT CABLE CORPORATION. Outside the front doors, a man with a picket sign was marching back and forth, protesting.

David dismounted and wheeled the bike over to the man. "Still planning to shut us down, huh?"

"You got that right, brother," the man answered. King Solomon was a slight, hyperalert black man in his fifties. As usual, he was dressed up in a crisp suit and a bow tie. His sign read, "Unchain the Airways, Cable Companies have NO RIGHT to charge you."

"Haven't seen you for a couple of months. Everything all right?"

King looked both ways then leaned closer, conspiratorially, "Been at the library, doing research. I found a ton of good stuff for my show." King had a half-hour slot on the public access channel where he went head-to-head with the giant communications conglomerates like AT&T. In addition, he'd been picketing around town for years, explaining his idiosyncratic theories, a mix of socialism and anarchy, to anyone who would listen. "Hey, Levinson, you got a minute?"

David pictured Marty stomping around the office in a ballistic frenzy over some minor technical glitch, pulling his hair out. "Sure, I got a minute."

"Okay, the subject is phone calls, but it applies to the legalized extortion of the cable television companies as well, 'cause both move through satellites. Because you guys control these satellites, you can charge little guys like me outrageous prices to do things like watch a football game or make a call to my lady friend who lives in Amsterdam, right? Now the same thing was going on in England way back in the 1840s. The government was trying to regulate communication so they could make extra money. If somebody wanted to send a letter, they had to go to the post office and hand it to a clerk. The farther the letter was going, the more this clerk charged you. Long distance rates, see? The whole thing was so expensive and such a damn headache, nobody wrote letters. Then this one dude came along, I forget his name right now, who figured out all the work, all the labor, was done at the beginning and the end of the process, sorting out and then delivering the letters. All the costs along the way, the shipment, remained the same whether there was one letter or a hundred. So this guy goes to the king and says, 'This is bullshit, baby. Let's have one low price for all letters, wherever they're going.' The king said okay, and do you know what happened?"

"Everybody started writing letters?"

"Exactamundo, mon ami. All over Europe folks started expressing their feelings and communicating scientific ideas, and shazam! we had the Industrial Revolution. That's why I'm out here every day. If y'all would quit monopolizing the satellites sent up there at taxpayers' expense, I could be on the phone to my lady friend in Amsterdam and my show could be seen in China. The common people could have a renaissance, an information revolution. Whaddaya think?"

Somewhere in the middle of King's speech, David's pager had buzzed again. This was absurd, even for the eternally panicked Marty. He began to think something serious might be happening. "As usual, King, you're convincing. Have you ever played on the World Wide Web, the Internet?"

He hadn't. Didn't own a computer. David told him where to find a public terminal and suggested that he check it out. It was the closest thing he knew to unrestricted communication. Then it was time to go into work and face Marty.

INSIDE THE REVOLVING doors was a completely different world. Compact Cable's front lobby was a graceful, marble and mahogany environment with a ceiling three stories tall. A swank, low-slung reception desk stood in the middle of the room guarding the entrance. With his bike hoisted onto one shoulder, David strolled past the receptionist and into the main office space, a beehive of partitioned work areas with a huge bank of television monitors mounted to the southern wall. The minute he walked in, he knew something big was up. The room was much louder than usual, the activity more frantic. Before he could put down his bike, he was confronted by a one-man electrical storm. Marty Gilbert, a heavyset man with a lascivious goatee, blasted out of his office, waving his arms and shouting.

"What the hell is the point of having a beeper if you never turn the damn thing on?" Steaming mad, Marty stopped in the middle of the room waiting for an answer. He was armed with his two favorite weapons: a can of diet soda in one hand, a cordless phone in the other.

"It was turned on," David explained matter-of-factly. "I was ignoring you."

"You mean to tell me," Marty screamed, "you got every one of those pages and you didn't call in? Did it occur to you that maybe, just maybe, something critical was going on?"

David was used to Marty's apoplectic, foot-stomping shit fits. He had one every couple of days and they usually lasted about ten minutes. The man lived in a perpetual state of high anxiety. He was constitutionally high-strung and had compounded his problem by taking on the incredibly stressful job of operations manager for one of the largest cable providers in the nation. His job was, in his words, "to be in charge of every little thing." In a complex operation like Compact Cable there were a thousand little things that could go wrong, and enough of them did every day to keep Marty hopping from one crisis to another.

This morning's run-in was a perfect example of why he hated David's guts and loved him like a brother at the same time. Marty knew beyond any shadow of a doubt that David was the best chief engineer in the country. He was so overqualified for the job, so good at handling all the hypertechnical stuff, that Marty knew he'd never be able to replace him in a million years. David was his secret weapon, the ace-in-the-hole that kept him in front of the competition. Now that he had finally shown up, Marty knew it was only a matter of time before he could phone corporate headquarters with the good news that they were the first ones to restore service to their customers. But it drove him bonkers how flamboyantly casual David was about everything. If he didn't return phone calls or answer his pager, Marty could huff and puff all he wanted, but there wasn't much else he could do about it. The quirky technical wizard made his own hours and operated independently of Marty's control.

"So what's the big emergency?"

"Nobody can figure it out." Marty calmed himself with a long gulp of soda. "Started this morning around four A.M. Every channel is making like it's 1950.

Picture's all messed up. We're getting static and this weird vertical roll problem. We've been down in the feed room all morning trying everything."

David stashed his bike next to the vending machines in the employee kitchen and was about to head off for the feed room when Marty, expressing his frustration, slammed his empty soda can into the trash.

"Damn it, Marty, there's a reason we have bins labeled 'Recycle,'" David said loudly, turning back. The company's recycling program had been instituted largely due to David's insistence. He was a one man posse for the eco-police. More disturbing still, when he bent down to fish the can out, he found six more identical cans at the bottom of the bin. Appalled, he asked, "Who's been throwing their aluminum cans in the garbage?"

"So sue me," Marty hissed back. Then, before David could launch off into one of his save the earth speeches, his boss took him by the arm and forcibly helped him down a short hallway and through a door marked TRANSMISSION FEED.

Inside were the mechanical guts of Compact Cable. Hundreds of flat steel boxes, signal modulators, were stacked in tall steel racks along the back wall. A long console with mixing and switching panels stretched the length of the room below several television monitors. Taped to the walls were technical charts showing satellite positions, vertical and horizontal transponder polarizations, the different commercial licenses within the megahertz bandwidth and an ancient poster of four hippies in San Francisco with the words "Better Living Through Chemicals" above their heads. And cable. Miles of coaxial cable, the backbone of the industry, snaked off the overhead shelves and ran everywhere underfoot. Like a thousand black asps writhing around an Egyptian tomb, the flexible cord connected every piece of machinery to all the others.

"Okay you guys, make room," Marty squawked as they came in. "The Amazing Dr. Levinson has agreed to grace us with a demonstration of his skills." Paying no attention, David walked over to the mixing board where a technician was fiddling with some knobs. The monitor above his head showed a transmission of the *Today Show*. Like Marty said, the picture was disintegrating into rolling vertical bars every few seconds.

"Looks like somebody's scrambling our satellite feed," David mumbled, thinking for a moment of King Solomon marching around outside.

"Definitely," one of the two technicians told him. "We're pretty sure it's a satellite problem."

"Have you already tried switching transponder channels?"

"Oh, puleeeeze!" Marty howled. He was up on tiptoes looking over their shoulders. "Of course we tried that. What do we look like—idiots? Don't answer that."

David pulled a chair up to the control board and sat down. Almost immediately, his long limbs began to coil around one another. "Bring up the Weather Channel." The technician plinked a command into the keyboard. A text display popped up on the television monitor. "Experiencing Technical Difficulties. Please Stand By."

"May I?" David asked, moving the technician out of the way, "I wanna try something real quick here." His fingers whizzed across the keyboard, switching the monitor over to broadcast reception—regular antenna-on-the-roof reception. Suddenly, the *Today Show* looked fine, then fuzzy, then fine again.

"Oh my God, you're a genius," Marty gushed, "how did you do that?"

"Not so fast, Marty." With his legs woven into a lotus position, David hunched over the board working in trance-like concentration. The *Today Show* was replaced by a computer bar graph. After entering a last few commands, David came up for air. "You're right, it's definitely the satellite. That good picture was a local broadcast. I pointed our rooftop dish over toward Rockefeller Plaza. They're putting out good signal."

"And what's this computer caca on the screen? We're not sending this out to the customers, are we?"

"Will you relax already? No, it's not going out. I'm running a signal diagnostic." David studied the test results on the screen, then sat back, perplexed. "According to this, the satellite signal is fine. It's coming through at full power. Maybe the satellite itself is fritzing out."

Turning to Marty, he came up with a plan of action. "I'll get up to the roof and retrofit the dish to another satellite. You get on the phone and rent some channel space. SatCom Five has plenty of space available."

A self-satisfied grin spread across the heavy man's face. He didn't understand all the technical stuff, but for the time being, he had the jump on David. "Already thought of that," he announced proudly. "I called Sat-Com, I called Galaxy, and I called TeleStar. Everybody in town is having the same problem."

"Everybody in town?" David asked, incredulous. "If those guys are having this same problem, it means the whole country—no, the whole hemisphere—is getting bad pictures." David thought it over for a moment then added, "That's impossible!"

"Exactly," Marty shot back. "Now fix it."

CRASH! Miguel sat bolt upright out of a deep sleep and tried to focus his eyes. He had been dreaming a flying dream. A beautiful girl with pale skin and luminous dark eyes had taken him by the hand and showed him how to lift himself into the air. At first he was afraid of falling out of the sky, but once he got the hang of it and the two of them began looping and diving like a pair of dolphins, his only fear was that the girl would disappear.

CRASH!

He pulled back the plastic windowshade. A squad of fearless soldiers, the seven- and nine-year-olds from next door, were shooting it out with squirt guns. They looked like the Ninja Turtles at the OK Corral. Once they were shot, they died in ostentatious flailing body slams against the back of the Casse's Winnebago.

"*Vayanse!* Quit hitting our damn trailer!" he yelled. The warriors looked up at him then squealed away as a group, fanning out across the Segal Estates, which is what the owner had the nerve to call this place. An RV campground that had gone downhill, it was now a sort of flophouse on gravel and asphalt. Half of the tenants were Mexican migrant laborers, *campesinos,* who pooled their money to buy a mobile home so they could bring their families north. The other half were white folks who had "retired" out to the desert. It was half a mile from the highway, and cyclone fencing on three sides separated it from the surrounding alfalfa fields. Miguel, along with his sister, his half-brother, and his stepfather had been renting space at the Estates for about three months. They'd been living in the Winnebago for almost a year.

Two weeks before, Miguel had graduated from Taft-Morton Consolidated High School, but refused to go through the ceremony. He hardly knew any of the other kids and was afraid Russell, his stepfather, would show up and embarrass him. That evening, Alicia organized a cake and soda party for just the four of them. Halfway through it, Russell, who was drinking something stronger than soda, went off on a drunken, teary-eyed speech about how proud he was and how he wished Miguel's mama was still alive so she could see this. It ended the way so many of their conversations did, in an ugly shouting match with Miguel slamming the door on his way out.

At the front of the trailer, eleven-year-old Troy sat in the "kitchen" slapping the side of the television set. They were about forty miles north of Los Angeles, and the broadcast was being relayed through satellites to improve its signal strength, but it obviously wasn't doing much good.

"What are you doing?" Miguel hollered from beneath his pillow.

"The TV's all blurry and messed up."

"Hitting it isn't going to help. It's probably a problem at the station. Just leave it alone." But Troy didn't have much patience. When the picture failed to improve after ten seconds, he smacked the set again. Miguel threw back the sheets and came to see what was going on. It was already eight A.M. and he should have been gone out looking for a job by now.

"See?" Troy gestured toward the rolling picture. "Should I whack it again?"

"No, Mr. Kung Fu television repairman, I told you. It's not the set, it's the . . . whatevers, the airwaves." His younger brother was unconvinced, so Miguel changed the subject. "Have you taken your medicine?"

"I'll take it later." Troy was born with adrenal cortex problems, the same condition that killed their mother. He was supposed to take a small dose of hydrocortisone every morning, but because of the expense of the medicine, his family allowed him to skip a couple days a week. As long as he ate right and wasn't under a lot of stress, missing the medicine wasn't any big deal.

"Have you eaten anything yet?"

"Nope."

"Alicia, what are these dishes doing?" Obviously, they were sitting in the sink waiting for someone to wash them. She'd made herself breakfast, leaving the boys to fend for themselves. She was up front, stretched out in the Winnebago's passenger seat clipping photos out of a fashion magazine. When she heard Miguel yelling at her, she raised the volume on her Walkman. She was fourteen, bored, and developing a gigantic attitude problem. Since her hormones had started to kick in that spring, she'd taken to wearing makeup, skimpy cut-offs and tight white T-shirts, which had become the unofficial uniform among the ninth-graders at her new school.

Miguel came over and was about to give her hell for being so selfish when a red Chevy truck skidded to a halt in the gravel at the end of their driveway. The driver sat inside for a moment angrily talking into a cellular phone. His name was Lucas Foster, a local farmer who had hired Russell Casse to do some emergency crop dusting this morning. Plant-munching moths had invaded the desert croplands north of LA, just in time for the Casses, who were dangerously low on cash.

The farmer stomped up the driveway with a head of lettuce in one hand. Miguel knew his morning was about to get off to an ugly start. He went to the side door and opened the screen. "Good morning, Lucas. What's going on?"

"Your dad in there?" Lucas Foster, a muscular young man, was steaming mad.

Alicia slipped past her brother out into the sunlight. "He went to spray your fields," she said. "He left a long time ago."

"Well, where the hell is he, then?"

Miguel created a story about how Russell's plane had a mechanical problem the day before, but the other man didn't let him finish. "It's one damn thing after another with that jackass. He's sitting around somewhere with eight hundred dollars of insecticide while these damn moths are eating my crops!" Lucas heard himself shouting and quickly regained control. He was only a couple years older than Miguel and felt sorry for him. Now he was cursing himself for making a business decision based on sympathy for these kids and their crackpot dad.

"Maybe he had to refuel and he's there now," Miguel said hopefully.

"Naw, I just called my dad and he's not in the air," Lucas replied. "He'll probably get there about the same time the wind kicks up. Then we'll have to wait until tomorrow, while these moths eat our entire crop."

Humiliated, Miguel wanted to crawl into a hole and die. His stepfather, a notorious drunk around town, had put him through some embarrassing moments, but nothing like this. Miguel didn't blame Lucas for being mad. Behind him, Troy was still slapping the side of the TV. "Troy, stop it!" Miguel warned.

"If he's not in the air by the time I get back there, I'm going to call Antelope Valley Airport and get somebody else. I can't wait another day."

"Yeah, okay, that's fair. I'll go out and look for him right now." He grabbed the keys to his motorcycle and headed out the door. As he walked with Lucas down to the end of the driveway, Alicia called after them, asking Lucas for a ride down to the Circle K Market. *"No!"* Miguel exploded, wheeling around to face her. "You get in there and make Troy some breakfast before you go anywhere."

Miguel kick-started his bike, an old Kawasaki, and sat in the driveway wondering where to look first.

COLONEL CASTILLO and his crew at the Pentagon had determined that the giant object had taken up a fixed position and parked itself less than 500 kilometers behind the moon. As the moon moved through space, the object moved with it, hiding behind the white orb like a shield. After repositioning three of their satellites, U.S. Space Command was able to get a pretty decent look at the object. They had three live cameras beaming infrared pictures of the object back down to earth, where they were keeping it under constant surveillance.

"Colonel!" one of the soldiers called loudly. "You better take a look at this!" Castillo sprinted across the floor and looked over the man's shoulder at the composite infrared picture. The area under the massive object was undergoing some kind of disturbance.

"Looks like it's exploding," Castillo observed.

"More like a mushroom dropping its spores," the man at the monitor said.

Large segments of the thing were detaching themselves and twirling away into nearby space. After watching the process for a few more minutes, and seeing the way the pieces arranged themselves in a circle, Castillo and the others realized what they were watching. It was time to call General Grey, who'd gone across the Potomac to the White House.

CONNIE TRIED SNEAKING out the side door of her office, but it didn't work. Members of her own staff, along with a dozen White House pages, were milling around in the hallway, and they pounced on her the moment she came through the door. Each one of them had a notepad full of urgent questions. All morning the phones had been as hot as teakettles, ringing off their hooks with one heavy hitter after another: senators, foreign ambassadors, queens and kings, Whitmore's family, network anchors, prominent businessmen that would normally be put straight through to the president. Nobody knew what to tell these people, each one calling with some crisis on their hands.

Connie knew her people needed answers, but didn't have the time to talk to them. She was already five minutes late for the presidential briefing, something that had never happened before. She'd been on the job long enough to know the best way to handle a stressful situation: wear a charming smile, ignore everyone, and bull your way through the crowd. Fran Jeffries, her chief lieutenant, saw what she was going to do. She stepped right in front of her boss and spoke fast.

"CNN says they're going to run a piece that the United States may have conducted an open-atmosphere nuclear test at the top of the hour unless you call to deny."

Connie shrugged, "Tell them to run with it if they want to embarrass themselves."

Everyone started shouting their questions at her. "NASA's been up my butt all morning," a harried aide complained. "Can you read their position statement? It's short and they need approval."

"Our official position," she told him, "is that we don't have an official position."

Constance, still smiling, pushed through, focusing on the portrait of Thomas Jefferson at the end of the hallway. When she got there, she surprised them by turning left, away from the stairs, where more people with more questions were waiting. She pushed the button for the old elevator, the clunky antique installed for Franklin Roosevelt.

When Gil Roeder, a top operative, saw she was about to escape, he yelled over the others. "Connie, what the hell is going on?"

Perfect timing. Just as the doors were sliding closed, she tried to look as if her feelings were hurt by the question. "Come on, people. If I knew anything, would I keep you out of the loop?"

Outside the doors, she could hear them answering in unison, "Definitely!"

IN THE OVAL OFFICE, the president had already called the meeting to order. He sat with his chief of staff, Glen Parness, the head of the Joint Chiefs, General Grey, and Secretary of Defense Albert Nimziki. For very different reasons, Whitmore trusted each of them.

"But I want to remind everyone," Grey was in the middle of saying, "that our satellites are unreliable at the moment. It's not clear whether this thing wants to or will be able to enter the earth's atmosphere. It's still possible it won't come any closer. It might not want to deal with the force of our gravity, for example."

"That's true, Mr. President," Nimziki allowed, "this object might, as the commander suggests, pass us by. But our responsibility is to prepare for the worst-case scenario. Having no information, we must assume the object is hostile. My strong recommendation is that you retarget several of our ICBMs and launch a preemptive strike."

Nimziki was a tall, gaunt man of sixty who had earned the nickname, "the Iron Sphincter." He was a rarity in Washington, a cabinet-level appointee who kept his job through changes of administration. Whitmore was his fourth president, his second Democrat. He was not a likable man, but when he spoke, everyone felt obliged to listen. Some years back *The Post* had written about him: "Not since J. Edgar Hoover has a government official amassed so much power without ever having stood for election." An intensely political animal, Nimziki always managed the appearance of staying above politics. He never let them see him pull the strings. He was, in a word, Machiavellian. His suggestion was precisely the kind of shoot-first-ask-questions-later style of thinking everyone else in the room was trying to avoid.

"Forgive me," Grey broke in, "but with the little information we do have, firing on them might be a grave error. If we're unsuccessful, we could provoke them, or it. If we are successful, we turn one dangerous falling object into many. I agree with Secretary Nimziki about retargeting the missiles, getting them set, but—"

Constance came in the door, but stopped short when she saw all the brass.

"What's the damage?" Whitmore asked her, beckoning her to join the discussion. "How are people reacting?"

"Hello, gentlemen." She nodded around the table as she took the seat next to Nimziki. "The press is making up their own stories at this point. CNN's threatening to plug in a segment suggesting we're covering up a nuclear test. I've scheduled myself a question-and-answer session for six o'clock, which should keep them on ice until then. The good news is nobody's panicking, not seriously."

Nimziki, impatient with the interruption, spoke across the table to Grey. "Will, I think it's time for you to contact the Atlantic Command and upgrade the situation to DEFCON Three."

The others jumped on him at once, telling him that was premature. The majority opinion was that sounding an alarm and causing panic before they even knew what they were up against would be a mistake. Nimziki defended his position, but was eventually talked down. At the end of the flare up, the chief of staff, Parness, was still talking.

"Furthermore, we're two days out from the Fourth of July and fifty percent of our forces are on weekend leave. Not to mention all the commanders in Washington for the parade on Sunday. The only quick way to call our personnel back to their bases would be to use television and radio."

"Exactly," Constance seconded. "We'd be sending up a major red flag to the world."

The door opened again. One of General Grey's men, his liaison to the Pentagon, came in carrying a bombshell. "Our latest intelligence tells us that the object has settled into a stationary orbit which keeps it out of direct sight behind the moon."

"Sounds like it's trying to hide," Grey remarked.

"That sounds like good news for the time being," Parness said, hopefully. "Maybe it just wants to observe us."

Grey's liaison wasn't finished. "Excuse me, but there's more. The object established its orbit at 10:53 A.M. local time. At 11:01 A.M. local time, pieces of the object began to separate off from the main body."

"Pieces?" Whitmore asked, not liking the sound of it.

"Yes, sir, pieces," the man continued. "We estimate there are thirty-six of them, roughly saucer-shaped, and small compared to the primary object. Still, each craft is approximately fifteen miles in diameter."

"Are they headed toward earth?" Whitmore asked, already knowing what the answer would be.

"Looks like it, sir. If they continue along their current trajectories, Space Command estimates they'll begin entering our atmosphere within the next twenty-five minutes."

The president stared back at the young man in the Air Force uniform, dumbfounded and more than a little frightened. For a moment, he thought this must be some kind of joke everyone else was in on, an elaborate piece of theater staged to get a reaction from him this very moment. Then the grim reality of the situation began to sink in. What had seemed so laughable, so far-fetched a few hours before, was coming horribly true. One of the primal fears of mankind, a fear buried under mountains of denial, was coming to pass. The earth was being visited, and perhaps invaded, by something from another world.

Nimziki broke the stunned silence. "Thirty-six ships, possible enemies, are headed this way, Mr. President. Whether we like it or not, we must go to DEF-CON Three. Even if it causes a panic, we must recall our troops and put them on yellow alert immediately."

No one in the room could disagree.

AN ALARM WENT OFF, a red light flashing in time with a piercing beep. A door opened and the alarm died. David's arm reached through the door and pulled out his Cup-O-Noodles. It was lunch hour at Compact Cable. David had hardly left the feed room. As if there wasn't enough equipment in there already, he had gone and retrieved two additional suitcase-sized machines and his laptop computer. They were set upright in the middle of the floor. David was sloppy when he was concentrating. He sat with his feet under him in the chair, elbows between his knees, coiled in concentration. He stared intently at the screen of his laptop computer, watching a visual display that repeated itself about every twenty seconds.

"Hello, you handsome genius." Marty peeked around the corner, all smiles. "I'm not here to pressure you. I'm just checking to see if there's anything you need." Which was, of course, a bald-faced lie. Whenever there was a problem, a mother hen like Marty *had* to be there.

"Marty! Old pal! Have a seat, relax."

Marty tiptoed in like a leper trying not to scratch. David had already kicked him out once for looking over his shoulder and asking too many questions. He had promised himself that he wasn't going to bug David, and for the first ten seconds he didn't. Then his willpower broke down. "David, tell me you're getting somewhere. I'm begging. Say you've got it figured out."

"Well," David said, very leisurely, "I've got good news and bad news. Which would you like to hear first?"

"What's the bad news?"

"The bad news is you're in meal penalty for disturbing my lunch."

Marty put a hand on his hip and got sarcastic. "Don't tell me. The good news is: you're not going to charge me."

"Actually," David took a last spoonful of soup, "the good news is I found the problem."

Marty clutched his heart and took a few deep breaths, hamming it up. "Thank God. Okay, so what exactly is the problem?"

"There's a weird signal embedded in the satellite feed. A signal within a signal. I have absolutely no idea where it's coming from. Never seen anything like it. Somehow, this signal is being cycled through every satellite in the sky.

Marty stared back at him, mouth agape. "And exactly *why* is that supposed to be good news?"

"Because the signal is following an exact sequence, a pattern. So the rest is simple! We just generate a digital map of the signal frequency, then translate it into a binary strand and apply a phase-reversed signal with the calculated spectrometer I built you for your birthday, and bingo, we should be able to block out the overlay completely."

"Block out the overlay?" Marty looked confused. "Does that mean we get our picture back?"

"You're quick."

"Does that also mean," Marty asked slyly, "that we'll be the only guys in town who are putting out a clean program?"

"Unless we share what we have learned," David suggested, angelically. He knew Marty was hypercompetitive with his fellow station managers and would luxuriate, wallow, and bask in this moment of triumph over them.

"Ha-ha, I love it!" Marty erupted with savage glee. "Our secret weapon! The phase-reversed spectrometer calculation analyzer thingee! This is turning out to be a wonderful day."

WHEN MIGUEL FINALLY found him, Russell had sprayed about a quarter of a 1000-square-yard tomato field. A group of field hands was gathered around their cars, unable to work while the spraying was going on. The field was about a mile long and bordered on one side by a row of giant eucalyptus trees that ran right up to the road. Instead of spraying parallel to the trees, Russell was flying straight down the rows and pulling up at the last possible moment, straining the old Liberty engine to clear the tops of the trees. Miguel couldn't tell if he was drunk or crazy, but if this was like most mornings, Russell was both.

The plane was a gorgeous old de Haviland biwing, a bright red two-seater built the same year Lindbergh crossed the Atlantic. The retractable wings were made of cloth stretched tight over wooden frames. The U.S. Post Office had used de Havilands to open transcontinental airmail service in the twenties. The machine belonged in a Saturday air show, not out dusting crops. It was too heavy and hard to maneuver to begin with, but to make matters worse, Russell had an extra 200 pounds of spray equipment strapped to the back with twine and bungee cords.

As Russell dove over the tops of the trees to begin another pass at the tomatoes, Miguel yelled and waved, calling for him to land. The farm workers understood what the boy was doing and a few of them joined in. The plane's pilot waved back stupidly.

"Come on, Russell, wake up," Miguel pleaded. Over the last two years, Russell had been going downhill fast. He was drinking himself to death and losing all sense of responsibility for his kids. He'd straightened up for a while when the neighbors had reported him to the police, who in turn had called in the social workers. He'd always been crazy, but when Miguel's mother got sick and finally died, Russell had plunged totally over the edge. He'd developed a death wish. Every few days, he'd snap out of it and promise to make a new start. Which meant that Miguel was usually the one left to take care of things like paying the rent, getting Troy's medicine, and buying the groceries. That was one thing nobody could take away from Miguel: he was responsible. Russell was less like a parent to him than a burdensome roommate.

As the plane circled around for another pass, Miguel suddenly started up his motorcycle and tore straight across the field, uprooting plants and splattering tomatoes as he bounced over the irrigation ridges. He stopped right in the path of the plane, which raced toward him, a white cloud of liquid poison misting out the back. Luckily, Russell saw him in time and shut off the feeder. As he passed, he focused his eyes and saw that the boy was waving him down. He turned around in his seat and smiled to Miguel, raising his thumb to show he understood. He could see the boy was pointing, trying to tell him something, but he didn't understand until he turned back around in his chair and found himself face-to-face with a picket fence-lined row of hundred-foot-tall eucalyptus trees, and it was way too late to pull up.

"Whoa, Lordy!" he screamed over the sound of the motor. Luckily, for Russell, there was no time to think. Acting purely on reflex, he rolled the plane ninety degrees onto its side and sliced through a narrow gap between trees. He had less than a foot clearance on either side. Rather than kicking himself for being so stupid, or thanking heaven for being so lucky, Russell let out a long, blood-curdling victory whoop, delighted with his own skills.

A few minutes later, the plane coasted to a stop on the remote highway. When Miguel raced up and skidded to a halt, Russell was just climbing awkwardly out of the cockpit. "Did you see that?" he yelled. "That was a damn trip!" He pulled off his leather aviator's cap and lowered himself carefully onto the lower wing. At fifty-one, Russell Casse looked like a big little boy. He had full, round cheeks and a bush of curly blondish hair. He was large, over six feet tall and broad across the shoulders. Over the last couple of years, his drinking had turned his complexion from rosy to ruddy, and he'd started to develop a gut.

"What the hell are you doing over here?" Although there was a sharp tone to Miguel's voice, it didn't penetrate his stepfather's thick skin.

"I'm bringin' home the bacon," Russell sang proudly, "Earnin' my keep. And, if I do say so myself, doing a pretty fine job of it."

"This isn't Foster's place. It's the wrong field," Miguel told him. "You're supposed to be on the other side of town."

Russell, still perched on the plane's wing, took a long look at the field and the farmhouse down the road. "Are you sure?"

"Damn it, Russell. He was doing you a favor. He was just at the trailer asking where the hell you were. And he's gonna make you pay for the spray you wasted."

Russell climbed down to the pavement and stood there, a little wobbly, shaking his head. *No use in getting upset about it now*, he told himself. But this was the first work he'd had all season, and Lucas was about the only farmer in town who was on his side. He looked at his son, but couldn't think of anything to say.

"Do you know how hard it is to find someone who doesn't think you're totally crazy?" the boy hissed. "Now what are we supposed to do? Where are we supposed to go now?"

Russell didn't have any answers. He badly wanted to promise Miguel things were going to start changing right then and there. But he knew the boy wouldn't believe him and he wouldn't have believed himself. So he stood mutely in the center of the road until Miguel kick-started the bike and drove away in disgust.

Russell brought a flask of Jack Daniel's out of his jacket. He was pretty sure something had just ended. Maybe it was just the end of him pretending to put up a fight. The last few years had broken him. His wife's degenerative illness and eventual death, the night he was abducted, the news that Troy had inherited his mother's adrenal cortex deficiency. Screw it. If life was going to be that painful, he didn't want any piece of it. If it weren't for his kids, he would have climbed back into the old plane, flown it to its top altitude, then cut the engine and let her freefall back to earth. Instead, he uncapped the flask and took a long swig of whiskey.

DEEP IN THE DESERT of Northern Iraq, Ibn Assad Jamal squatted before a small campfire, preparing his morning coffee. A Bedouin, he'd been forced off the land his tribe had claimed as their own for countless generations and had been herded into a squalid, crowded tent city along with several other Bedouin clans. It was still an hour before the first light of dawn, but by force of habit, the whole makeshift village was stirring to life.

He reached into the fire and retrieved his grandfather's coffee jar, boiling a thick brew of Arabian coffee. As he was waiting for the grounds to settle to the bottom, he heard a single scream pierce the night air. A second later, many people were screaming and calling out in a panic.

Jamal stood paralyzed from the sounds. At the top of the dunes, he saw the outlines of a dozen figures rushing toward him. His first thought was that the camp was being attacked by the army, but as the people came sprinting past him, shouting and whimpering, he saw what they were running from.

"*Ensha'allah,*" he muttered to himself. He saw something that knocked his knees out from under him. A giant piece of the sky was on fire. A mountain-sized fireball, flaring orange, white, and gray, was plunging through the sky like a flat rock splashing into a river. The fire cast a dark reddish glow on the sand as it sank deeper in the sky. Jamal stared up at the phenomenon for several moments as a pounding terror grew in his heart. Finally, he got back to his feet, stammered something unintelligible then turned to run, screaming just like the others.

A FEW HUNDRED MILES away, in the approximate center of the Persian Gulf, the nuclear-powered submarine USS *Georgia* was plowing along the surface of the dark water, its antenna array rotating atop the conning tower. Inside the sub's radar room, all hell had broken loose. A loud klaxon alarm was blaring, triggered by unusual readings on the radar scopes. Jittery crewmen, who'd been sleeping only moments before, poured through the bulkheads to their combat stations. The sub's commander, Admiral J. C. Kern, stepped through the forward hatch and yelled over the noise for a report. "Ensign, status?"

A sailor wearing a headset wheeled around in his chair. "Sir, we have a total radar blackout over a seventeen-kilometer area." The admiral moved to the main radar map and studied the incoming signal. A large portion of the upper screen was blank, but it was obviously not an equipment failure, because the blank ellipse on the screen was *moving*.

"Admiral." One of his officers stepped closer. "I've ordered a complete diagnostic run. The auxiliary radar units—"

"Sir, excuse me, sir," shouted another sailor from the opposite side of the cramped room. "Radar may be malfunctioning, but infrared is completely off the map. No reading at all." He pushed away from his monitor to give Kern a view of the infrared tracking system. The entire screen was a bright pool of red light.

"Lieutenant," Kern barked, almost amused at the chaos.

"Yes, sir?"

"Get Atlantic Command on the line."

THE OVAL OFFICE WAS crowded with military leaders and the president's advisers. Thirty phone calls were taking place at once, but the noise level stayed at a hushed murmur. Extra tables had been carried in and there was a constant stream of foot traffic in and out of the room. The joint chiefs had arrived an hour earlier having recalled the nation's armed forces. The fleet of nuclear submarines was maintaining launch readiness, and battleships were deployed along both coasts. Civilian advisers had taken over the sofas, and the president sat under the north windows behind Resolute, the impressive desk given to Teddy Roosevelt by the Queen of England. There were also representatives from the Atlantic Command, NATO, and military attachés from the British, Russian, and German consulates.

This impressive collection of decision-makers, one of the most powerful groups ever to assemble at the White House, had adopted a wait-and-see attitude. Many of them had advocated a preemptive strike against the object lurking behind the moon. NASA engineers had been consulted as to the feasibility of sending the space shuttle to attack with nuclear weapons, but, for many reasons, they had eventually arrived at an uneasy consensus not to do so. They waited tensely for the thirty-six segments to enter the earth's atmosphere. When the line from the Pentagon rang, all the major players in the room fell silent.

General Grey, as commander of the joint chiefs, stepped forward to answer the call. "This is Grey," he growled into the receiver, his face as expressive as chiseled stone. "Where in the Pacific?" he asked. After listening for a moment, he turned to the president. "They've spotted two coming in over the west coast, both over California."

"Send the plane from Moffet Field," Whitmore ordered. The plan had already been set in motion. An AWACS aircraft from the facility near San Jose was already in the air, waiting for the order to begin a close-up inspection of the incoming craft.

The door flew open and Connie marched toward the president's desk. "CNN is doing a live shot from Russia. They've got a picture of this thing."

"Put it on," Whitmore said, glancing at Lermontov, the worried Russian ambassador. One of the staffers pulled open the armoire doors and switched on the television.

The broadcast was coming live from Novomoskovsk, an industrial town two hundred miles south of the Russian capital. A local reporter stood at the edge of a wide boulevard which ran through the city's most fashionable neighborhood, shouting over the mayhem that surrounded him. Although it was just past six in the morning, the street was choked with panicked residents, running headlong in every direction. Cars sped past the camera, swerving to avoid pedestrians. The reporters words were being translated by someone in CNN's Atlanta studio.

". . . sightings of this atmospheric phenomenon have been reported here in Novomoskovsk and other parts of Russia. Again, this phenomenon is moving too slowly to be a comet or meteor. Astronomers can't explain this baffling occurrence."

The camera then panned away from the reporter and upward. In the distance, it showed the grainy image of a fireball hanging in the early morning sky. As the camera zoomed in, the flame-spitting giant filled the screen, towers of fire erupting in all directions as the surface of the speeding object moved against the sky, its friction burning up huge amounts of oxygen.

Everyone in the Oval Office stared at the television, grimly transfixed by the strange spectacle. The boiling cloud of fire looked like God announcing himself in an old Charlton Heston movie.

"As you can see from our live picture," one of the CNN anchors broke in, "a sense of panic has gripped the people of Novomoskovsk. We have learned this same type of reaction is happening in all parts of the city. The Russian equivalent of the Red Cross reports there have already been scores of injuries, most of them traffic-related as citizens scramble to get as far away from this strange phenomenon as possible. The situation is even worse in Moscow, where the craft is thought to be headed."

"Mr. President," General Grey interrupted, "our AWACS from Moffet Field has an ETA of three minutes with the contact point. We can put a line from the cockpit through this phone."

"Put it on the speaker phone." Whitmore saw no reason for the others not to hear the report.

Worried faces gathered in a rough circle around the president's desk, looking at the phone and one another as the sounds of the AWACS's cockpit were radioed to the Oval Office, three thousand miles away.

THE PLANE WAS flying south, several miles off the California coastline. The AWACS, Airborne Warning and Control System, was capable of scanning a four-hundred-mile area and tracking five hundred enemy planes simultaneously. But the state-of-the-art radar system, like so many of the earth's communications systems, was malfunctioning.

The calm, professional voices of the aircraft's crew came murmuring over the phone line. "Radar Two, I'm drawing a blank. Forward radar doesn't see a thing and side radar is impaired—what's your status? Over."

"Absolutely correct, sir. Forward radar is totally gone. We're flying IMC blind. Over."

Inside, the aircraft was packed with wall-to-wall computers, instrument banks, radar scopes, and other intelligence-gathering equipment. Technicians in headsets and orange jumpsuits were talking frantically to one another, trying one experiment after another, racing to adjust the navigation systems.

"Little Pitcher," a voice came over the radio, "we're tracking you down here at Ford Ord and you're looking all clear. Are you out of those clouds yet? Over."

"Negative," replied the pilot, squinting out the front window, "we still have zero visibility." A tropical storm had blown unusually far north from Mexico, leaving a thick mass of clouds hanging over the California Coast. "Fort Ord, what's your best estimate on our ETA? Over."

"Sorry, Little Pitcher, we just lost our angle. We can't see you any longer. You're into the blackout zone on our screens. Maybe San Diego can still see you."

After a tense moment of silence, a new voice came onto the line. "This is San Diego. Negative on that. We've got the same problem. Little Pitcher is inside the disturbance field. Sorry, Pitcher. We'll stand by."

Blasts of sunlight came through gaps in the clouds and into the cockpit, only to vanish a split second later. "Ground Control, this is Pitcher. We're starting to experience general instrument malfunction. Our altimeter and environment controls are gone. We're still moving through zero visibility and can't get any kind of reading on what's in front of us. I'm going to climb a little higher and see if we can't get clear over the top of this cloud cover."

"Roger, Pitcher," came the reply from Moffet Field. "It's your call at this point. You are totally manual."

"Don't climb," the president whispered. A former fighter pilot himself, he was imagining himself at the helm of the plane, "just keep it level." But the phone hookup was a one-way transmission.

"That's looking a little better," the AWACS reported with relief. "I think we've found a clearing."

Growing louder, a sonic disturbance, the cracking hiss of static interference, growled over the speakerphone. Then, just as the AWACS broke free of the clouds, the pilot's voice screamed over the noise, "Jesus God! The sky's on fire!"

In front of him was a solid wall of flame five miles high and twenty miles long, a majestic and fearsome sight. Roughly disk-shaped, it was shedding altitude, dropping down right on top of him. The pilot jerked back on the controls, forcing the plane into a steep climb. But when they came too close to the fireball, the plane suddenly shattered like a lightbulb crashing against an anvil.

There was a sharp crack on the speakerphone before the line in the Oval Office went dead. "Get them back," General Grey snarled to one of his men, even though he, like everyone in the room, suspected the plane was lost.

The commander in chief of the Atlantic Air Command stepped closer to a stunned President Whitmore. "Two more have been spotted over the Atlantic. One is moving toward New York; the other is headed in this direction."

"How much time do we have?"

"Less than ten minutes, sir."

With this news, Whitmore's civilian advisers began pushing their way through the ring of military men that circled his desk. The first one through was Nimziki. He spoke very precisely in a voice loud enough for the entire room to hear.

"Generals, we must move the president to a safe location at once. Organize a military escort to Crystal Mountain." General Grey agreed completely. He leaned close to the president's chair and urged him to move immediately to a secure location.

As orders began to fly around the room, the president reached across his desk and put a hand on Nimziki's shoulder. The gesture took the secretary quite by surprise. He froze in place, staring at the hand as if at a tarantula. President Whitmore used the moment to confer with his most trusted adviser.

"Connie, what's your take? Can we expect the same kind of panic here as in Russia?"

"Probably worse than what we just saw," she said.

"I agree," Whitmore said. "They'll start to run before they know which way to go. We'll lose a lot of lives."

Nimziki could see where the president was heading. He stepped backward, out of the president's grip. "Mr. President, you can discuss these secondary matters on the way. But the situation demands that you, as the commander in chief—"

"I'm not leaving," the president announced.

Nimziki was stunned, as were most of the people in the room. Several top-ranking officers stepped closer to the president, urging him to come to his senses and evacuate to a protected location.

"We must maintain a working government in a time of crisis," one of them reminded him loudly, making no attempt to disguise his frustration. A dozen men were all shouting at once, concerned for the president's safety. A pair of Secret Service agents pushed their way close and stood at his side.

With a long, glaring look, the president silenced the room. Slowly, he issued a set of commands. "I want the vice president, the cabinet, and the joint chiefs taken to a secured location. Let's get you men to NORAD. For the time being, I'm going to remain here in the White House."

Nimziki bristled, "Mr. President, we all—"

"I understand your position," Whitmore cut him off, "but I'm not going to add to a public hysteria that could cost us thousands of lives. Before we take off running, let's find out whether these things are hostile and exactly where they're headed."

Nimziki stared icily back at the president. He had hoped Whitmore would be different from the other presidents he had served, that his military training would keep him cool in an emergency. Even though this was a totally new situation, there was still a protocol to be followed. But Whitmore was trying to write his own script. Nimziki still had a few aces up his sleeve, but knew it was too early to play them.

"Connie," Whitmore continued, "initiate the emergency broadcasting system. I'll do an announcement as soon as you can set it up. Write a brief speech advising people not to panic, to stay home if possible. Can you do that in twenty minutes?"

"Give me ten," she said, already on her way out the door.

The joint chiefs were still standing in the office, confused, not quite willing to leave their posts here in what had become the command center.

"All right, people, let's move," Whitmore commanded, "I want you to get to NORAD as quickly as possible." The six generals exchanged glances with their staffers, then began moving reluctantly toward the exits. General Grey broke away from the pack and stood in front of Whitmore.

"With your permission, Mr. President, I'd like to remain by your side." As chairman of the joint chiefs, it was an unusual request, but given the long friendship between the two men, it came as no surprise.

"I had a feeling you would." Whitmore smiled. "And you, Mr. Nimziki?"

The tall, brooding man replied without hesitation, "NSC directives require that the secretary of defense make himself available to the president at all times." Then, after a beat, he tried changing tones. "It's my job to stay." He tried to make it sound friendly, but it came out like most of the things he said: vaguely menacing.

General Grey turned to Whitmore and asked the grave question that had been gnawing away at all of them for the past hour. "Mr. President, what happens if these things *do* become hostile?"

Whitmore thought for a second. "Then God help us."

LIKE THE COB-WEBBED entrance to a forgotten tomb, the feed room door creaked open very slowly. David, his mind wandering through some parallel universe, his nose buried in a computer printout, shuffled absent-mindedly into the central office of Compact Cable. The single-spaced print out was sixteen pages in length and contained only one thing: a single, incredibly long number, a continuous mind-numbing strand of ones and zeroes, a binary mathematical representation of twenty minutes worth of the mysterious, disruptive signal. His custom-built phase-reversed spectrometer had done its job. The device had compiled a precise numerical "portrait" of the oscillating frequency and specified the mirror-image signal that could be broadcast to cancel out the interference. Marty was going to be very happy. He could start pumping a clear picture out to their subscribers then get on the phone and taunt the competition. But David wasn't finished: as soon as he'd figured out a way to block the signal, he started asking himself where it was coming from and *what it meant*.

He was halfway across the office before he noticed it was empty. David glanced at the wall clock. *Way past lunch time*, he told himself. Jack Feldin, an old-timer who worked in sales, was at his desk sobbing like a baby into a telephone. In a vague way, David realized something was wrong, but he was so focused on solving the puzzle he ignored everything else. He was an obsessive puzzle-solver, had been since he got hooked on the *New York Times* Sunday crossword at age twelve. When the "Genius Puzzles" came out in the Mensa magazine each month, he'd plow through them one by one until, an hour or a few days later, he'd cracked them all. This business about the repeating signal in the satellite feed was a real-life riddle David was uniquely qualified to decipher. After all, how many engineers were there with his practical and theoretical skills who could also put their hands on fifty million dollars worth of high-tech communications equipment any time they liked?

He took the pages to his cubicle, slipped a disk into his desktop computer, and brought a sequence analyzing program up on the screen. With a few flicks of his fingers, he created a representation of the transmission. On a hunch, he asked the program if the repetitions of the signal were precisely equal. Negative. It was getting shorter, slowly reducing itself down to nothing. But *it wasn't losing any strength* and television reception was in the same sad shape it had been in all day. Curious. Assuming the signal was being sent for some intelligent purpose, why would it fade to zero? Very weird.

It took David about sixty seconds to do the algebra. According to his calculations, the signal would cycle down to extinction and disappear at 2:32 A.M. EST. *Okay*, he said to himself, *so what?* Because he'd been locked away in the crypt of the feed room all day, he had no idea where the signal might be coming from. After deciding he probably wouldn't learn anything else until that night, he stood up and left the cubicle. It was time to deliver the good news.

Marty's office was, as usual, a disaster area. Yellowing newspapers, take-out lunch containers, extra copies of the latest shareholder's report, and great heaps of unopened mail were piled on top of overflowing file cabinets. In addition to all the mess, there were five bodies crowded into the room, their attention glued to the television.

David barely noticed them. He did, however, spot the only unoccupied seat and slid into it like someone might beat him to the spot at the last minute. He casually draped a leg over the arm of the chair. It took him a moment to pick up on the mood of frightened anxiety in the room.

"I've got a lock on the signal pattern," he announced, "and we should be able to filter it out."

"Huh?" Marty realized he was being spoken to. Then, absently, "Oh, good, good."

"But here's the strange thing. If my calculations are right, and they usually are, the whole thing's gonna disappear in about seven hours anyway." When he didn't get any reaction, he looked up and said with emphasis, "The signal reduces itself every time it recycles. Eventually, it will disappear. Hey, are you listening?"

"David, my God," Marty realized, "haven't you been watching this? This is horrible, David."

"What are you talking about?"

"Look, it's right there."

David wheeled around in his chair and saw a live picture from Australia. A giant plate of fire, fifteen miles wide, was hanging in the sky over Melbourne. David's first thought was that there had been some sort of ecological disaster, the ozone reaching a critical state of frailty and erupting into spontaneous combustion. But a moment later, he asked the same question everyone had when they'd first seen the thing, "Is there a war going on?"

"They don't know what the hell these things are," somebody said. "*Atmospheric phenomena* is the term they keep repeating."

"It's probably some kind of debris from an asteroid," a coworker suggested. "These things are falling all over the earth."

"Oh, will you please wake up and smell the coffee," Marty snapped at the man. "They've said it about a hundred times: *they're not falling objects!* They're moving too slowly. And some of them have started moving sideways. They're flying. They're fucking flying saucers and this is the fucking invasion of the earth, okay?"

David hesitated for a moment, not knowing whether to laugh or shit his pants. The distressed faces of the others in the room confirmed that Marty was serious.

"Whoa! Wait a second." David stood up unconsciously waving the idea away. A sharp chill ran up his back, lodged itself in his brain, then erupted into a creepy variety of terror. Marty came around the desk and put a concerned hand on David's shoulder, then began filling him in on what little was known about the thirty-six "phenomena."

Suddenly, he pointed at the TV screen. "David, look. Isn't that Connie?"

Following the strictures of the Emergency Broadcast protocol, every channel switched over to a live picture of the White House press room. An attractive woman in a white silk blouse stepped up to the microphone and began taking questions from the press. The sight of her immediately wrenched David out of one drama and hurled him into another, more personal one. The woman was none other than Constance Marianne Spano, his estranged wife.

"... emphasize that so far this phenomenon, while it has disrupted our televisions and radios, hasn't caused any lasting damage and we have no reason to assume that it will."

David watched her lips moving, but hardly heard the words. They had spoken only a few weeks before, but watching her now made him realize they hadn't actually *seen* one another for a year. Even through all the signal disturbance, he knew she looked different: a little older, a little more polished, and much further away.

"The president is in an emergency planning meeting at the moment, but he wanted me to assure each and every American, as well as all of our allies, that we will be prepared for any possible outcome. The important thing now is for people not to panic."

A reporter shouted up at her, "Why did you initiate the EBS?"

Connie, composed, congenial, responded. "We have instituted the Emergency Broadcast System. As anyone who has called long distance or anyone who is watching us now understands, we're getting a lot of interference. The system helps ensure reliable communication links between government and military installations, that's all." David was the only person in the world who knew exactly when Connie was and was not bullshitting. She was telling the truth on this one.

"We have a fix on four different occurrences," she continued, "that will soon appear over American cities. Two are headed toward San Francisco and Los Angeles. The other two are on our Eastern seaboard moving toward New York and Washington, D.C."

Marty smiled at Pat Nolan, an enthusiastic new employee who poked his head into the office. "You guys, we found an old bomb shelter in the basement of this building. If any of you care to join us down there, we've got room for a few more. But I wouldn't wait too long." With that, he turned and walked out. Jeanie, one of Compact's copywriters, bolted out the door after him, trying to beat the others in the room downstairs for a spot.

When she was gone, Marty shook his head. "This is going to get very, very ugly."

BURLIE'S WAS A DEPRESSING, dilapidated beer joint just across the highway from the tiny local airport. The felt on the pool table was frayed, and the thumbtacked posters of busty chicks caressing power tools hung on nicotine-encrusted walls. Russell Casse was perched on a bar stool, staring at his second scotch and water, waiting for a man to walk through the door and hand him ten thousand dollars.

As soon as he'd landed the de Haviland, he'd gone to the office to find Rocky, the owner-manager of the two-bit landing strip. Rocky was a terrible name for this obese, oily man, so obscenely overweight he looked like a prize hog.

"How much'll you gimme for that old plane?" Russell asked.

"Ten thousand bucks," Rocky replied, half joking. Both of them knew an aviable 1927 de Haviland could probably fetch seventy-five grand.

"All right, I'll take it," Russell said softly, "but I need the whole thing in cash. I'll wait for you at Burlie's." With that, he had turned and walked away, knowing Rocky would pour himself in his Lincoln and race to the bank.

But it had been well over an hour since their conversation, and Russell was ready to order another drink, even though he couldn't pay for the first two if Rocky didn't show up with the cash. The television set at Burlie's was switched off and Russell was the first customer of the day. Neither he nor the bartender knew about the catastrophe taking place in the skies around the planet. Nevertheless, the topic of conversation turned to UFOs when a trio of greasy mechanics from the airport walked into the bar.

"Well, well, well, speak of the devil," said the largest and dirtiest of them. "We heard you had a little trouble this morning, Russ. Went up and dusted the wrong field?" The other two guys cracked up. Russell faked a smile and kept his eyes on his whiskey. "Don't laugh, you guys," the big man continued, "it ain't Russ's fault. He's still a little confused from his hostage experience." Once again, his two pals began to cackle like a pair of hyenas in coveralls.

One of them stopped abruptly and asked, "Hostage experience? What happened to him?"

"Let the man drink in peace, fellas," said the bartender without much conviction as he slid their beers across the bar. But the leader of the grease monkeys was just getting started.

"You mean he ain't never told you? Well, a couple years back, our boy here got himself kidnapped by aliens and taken up to their ship. And the little fellers did all kinds of nasty experiments on him. Tell him, Casse."

"Not today, guys. Okay?"

"He's not talkin' now," the guy brayed, "but you just wait till he has a couple more drinks in him. We won't be able to shut him up. Hey, Russ, could you do us a favor?" he asked, glancing at his watch. "Would you get stinkin' drunk *before* we head back to work?" That brought on another round of laughs from his buddies.

When the bartender went into the back room for something, Russell stood up quickly and started for the door. As he passed the mechanics, their leader reached out and clasped him by the shoulder. In a mocking whisper, he said, "Hey, Russ, tell us the truth. When they took you up in their space ship, did they do . . . you know . . . any sexual things to you?"

The blast of laughter that erupted from all three of the airport workers brought the bartender into the front room. Russell, no small man himself, was calmly preparing to knock the mechanic's teeth down his throat when the long neon lights hanging from the ceiling began to shake back and forth. A deep rumbling noise, growing louder, came through the building's walls. Beer bottles began to dance across the bar, and the sound of glasses and bottles tinkling against one another grew louder in the dingy barroom. In California, that could mean only one thing: an earthquake.

Their differences suddenly forgotten, the men ran out of the dark bar into the blinding midday glare of the parking lot. Something was wrong. Something about the *way* the ground was shaking, something about the evenness of the noise. It wasn't like any tremor they'd experienced before. It was too smooth.

Russell glanced up, but the sun immediately stabbed into his eyes, causing him to look down at the dusty asphalt. The dark border of an enormous shadow moved toward him across the parking lot. As it passed in front of the sun, the men were able to see what was coming. All at once, the mechanics screamed and took off running in different directions.

Russell stood his ground, his hands clenching into tight fists. One of the thirty-six phenomena was rumbling through the air only a mile or so off the ground. He studied the enigmatic pattern of the object's lower surface, knowing exactly what was happening and exactly who was inside the monstrous rumbling craft: the same frail-bodied, fast-moving freaks who had ruined his life years before.

When Troy was still a baby, and Russell was still in the business of restoring old planes, he'd stayed late at the hangar one night rebuilding an engine. It was a hot July night, so he'd left the rolling doors wide open. All of a sudden, he felt the strength go out of his body. His arms dropped to his sides and the wrench in his hand clattered to the ground. He couldn't understand what was happening to him, thought he might be suffering a heart attack. His whole body had gone numb, paralyzed, except he was still able to move his eyes.

A noise came from the open doors. Glancing in that direction, Russell saw a strange little figure leaning around the corner. It couldn't have been more than three and a half feet tall. This creature had a large head like a yellow lightbulb and two black eyes as lifeless as coat buttons. Gripped by a sudden animal terror, Russell struggled against his rigid body, trying to make it run, but his limbs wouldn't respond. He looked back at the creature peering in at him, and after a few moments, his panic began to subside. *All of this is quite normal, no reason to be alarmed,* Russell told himself, *you will not be harmed.* This idea repeated itself continuously in his brain until he realized that it was a message, a form of mind control, being communicated to him by mental telepathy.

The next thing he knew, he was sitting on the floor, leaning against something. The creature from the door was sitting directly in front of him, its sinewy arms wrapped around its bent knees while others, perhaps a dozen of them, flitted in and out of his peripheral vision. They were doing some sort of work, moving with astonishing speed. The creature seated before him continued to cloud Russell's mind with reassuring feelings. This succeeded in keeping him calm until he noticed something glinting in a narrow container. It was a needle, about six inches long, which was apparently going to be inserted into his skull. As clearly as if it were spoken aloud, one of the creatures told him, *There will be no pain, no damage.*

At that point, Russell remembered thinking of his family, struggling to form the words that would allow him to beg for his life. Then, blackness. The next thing he remembered was being far out in the desert, lifting off the ground. The landscape corkscrewed away as he lifted higher and higher into the air. Then the floor of a ship closed like an iris beneath him. He was in a small, dingy chamber. The dark walls around him glistened with moisture, creating the sensation of being inside the body cavity of a very large animal. He felt their tiny hands moving everywhere over his body. Only then did he notice he was stripped naked. Again he tried to plead with them, mentally howling to be released.

Then the experiments began. Unable to resist, Russell lay stretched out on his back while they invaded his body with several instruments that resembled medical probes. At some point, he remembered one of them lifting his head and laying it on its side so he could look out a window cut into the bottom of the ship. He recognized the vague outline of hills far below and remembered tears pouring off his face as the experiments continued until the whole side of his head was soaking wet.

He was found the next afternoon wandering through the parking lot of a supermarket ninety miles from the airport, suffering from amnesia. He couldn't remember his name or his address, and it took him almost a week to recognize his own wife, Maria. When asked what had happened to him, he said that he'd been chasing a brace of jackrabbits through the desert and had gotten lost. It didn't take him long to figure out this was only a screen memory planted in his mind to camouflage what had really happened.

He never fully recovered. Over the course of the next several months, irritable and depressed, he developed an obsession about reconstructing the events of that night, spending all his money and energy pursuing those fugitive fragments of memory. He put himself in psychotherapy, underwent hypnosis, and traveled to meet others who claimed to have been taken. It was during these months that Maria began to get sick. Her skin turned blotchy and, at night, she'd get terrible headaches that sometimes developed into trembling seizures. By the time Russell looked up from his own problems long enough to realize how sick she was, and drove her into LA for testing, it was too late. The same day she was diagnosed with Addison's syndrome, an easily treated deficiency of the adrenal cortex, she died in her sleep.

As the vast coal-black ship rumbled past over head, Russell clenched his fists tighter. He wanted nothing more than to murder a few of the shifty little runts he thought were inside the ship. The object was moving north at about two hundred miles per hour. By the time it had moved past, allowing the sun to beat down once more on the parking lot of Burlie's, Russell was gone.

IN WASHINGTON, D.C., the first people to make a visual sighting of the oncoming ship were the tourists crowded into the observation platform at the tip of the Washington Monument. They began a stampede down the stairwell of the 555-foot structure, trampling everyone who didn't get out of their way. The first casualty was an eleven-year-old girl visiting from Lagos, Nigeria. Although her father had to shelter her body under his, someone had stepped on her back while her head was resting on one of the steps. She was limp and unconscious when he finally got her outside, the last two people out of the building. The National Park rangers, not knowing they were still inside, had already gone.

The man looked down the grassy hill and saw people running as fast as they could in every direction. In the sky behind Capitol Hill, one of the huge black disks, still trailing wisps of smoke, was looming over the Maryland state line, rumbling closer. In vain, the man shouted to the people running past him, asking them where he could find a hospital for his daughter. No one stopped, or even slowed down.

Thousands of confused visitors were pouring out of the Smithsonian and the other museums lining the mall. As they came outside and saw the disk-shaped gargantuan crawling along the sky, most of them panicked. Great herds of frightened humans were running in all different directions, crashing blindly into one another. Mothers separated from their children stood amid the chaos screaming over and over again the names of the little ones they'd lost. Some froze in their tracks, uttering profanities or calling out the name of God. Here and there, groups of strangers had clustered around trees at the sides of buildings, staring mutely upward. Many others had collapsed to the ground, some praying, others cowering with their arms thrown over their heads. Thousands more, armies of federal employees, came tearing down the granite steps of their workplaces, sprinting, elbowing their way toward the entrances to the underground Metro system. The thing in the sky inspired an immediate, all-consuming sense of dread, an angel of death grinding inexorably closer.

Less than a mile away, at 1600 Pennsylvania Avenue, Whitmore was on the phone with Yetschenko, the Russian president. "Yes, I understand," he said to the translator on the line with them. "Tell him we'll keep him informed and that Russia and the United States are in this together." While his message was being translated into Russian, he looked up at Connie and rolled his eyes. "Okay, and tell him I said good-bye. *Das vedanya.*"

"What was that all about?" Connie asked.

"I don't know. I think he was drunk."

Suddenly the doors flew open and a frightened staffer bolted into the room. "It's here!" the woman shouted, leading the way to a set of tall windows that opened onto a balcony. Whitmore and Grey shared a look, then stood up and followed the excited woman to the windows.

"Daddy!" Patricia Whitmore came tearing across the carpet toward her father with tears in her eyes.

"You're supposed to be downstairs," her father snapped at her. But the next moment, realizing his mistake, he was down on his knees to catch the girl as she threw herself into his arms. Alarmed by the tense mood that had seized the White House, Patricia had escaped from her baby-sitters. Whitmore picked the girl up and carried her to a quiet corner of the office, consoling her.

When he turned around again, he noticed his entire staff standing frozen in place on the balcony. Still holding his little girl, he walked out to join them.

The black mass of the ship was prowling low over the capitol, almost on top of them. Its front edge came sweeping over the Anacostia River, casting a circular shadow fifteen miles in diameter. Unconsciously, Whitmore tightened his grasp on his sobbing daughter, pulling her closer to his chest to shield her from the awesome, terrifying sight. Without realizing it, Connie and the others had taken hold of one another, hands and arms laced together in order to keep their balance and stave off the deep dread the ship inspired. Only the Secret Service agents patrolling the edge of the roof remained detached, focused on the job of protecting their leader.

"Oh, my God, what do we do now?" Connie whispered.

"I've got to address the nation," Whitmore said. "There are a lot of frightened people out there right now."

"Yeah," she looked at him, "I'm one of them."

HAVING COMMUNICATED nothing to the people of earth except their arrival, the three dozen ships fanned out over the globe's most populated and powerful cities including: Beijing, Mexico City, Berlin, Karachi, Tel Aviv, and San Francisco.

In Japan, the citizens of Yokohama had watched the fireball splashing out of the heavens then level off at six thousand feet, a cauldron of boiling smoke. Out of the dense clouds, the clean front edge of the ship came plowing forward. The audacious scale of it staggered the thousands of people watching from the docks, then turned them into a screaming mob as the endless bulk of the ship continued to emerge. It had moved directly over their heads, plunging the great port into a quaking artificial twilight for several minutes until it moved away to the north. It was still visible from the rooftops, hanging in the air forty miles away over the nation's capital, Tokyo.

In Yokohama's central train station, the mood had calmed considerably once the object was no longer directly overhead. People loaded down with personal belongings jammed onto the platforms, waiting impatiently for the trains they hoped would carry them off to the safety of the countryside. Transit officials in blue uniforms and white gloves stood on crates above the throng, blowing whistles and urging the crowd to cooperate. Visible through the Plexiglas walls, a battalion of American soldiers from the nearby base were trotting down the street in formation toward an unknown destination. For the moment at least, the evacuation was proceeding in an orderly fashion.

The same scene was repeating itself in cities around the world. One of every five people on earth found themselves trying to get out of the cities, great hives of humanity, only to learn what a tiny fraction of them could be accommodated by all of their roads, trains, and subways. As they stood waiting, sardined onto loading platforms, crowded at bus stops, or stacked into the backs of pickup trucks, they were having the same conversation in every conceivable language: Who or what was inside these gigantic ships, and what were their intentions? Their sinister exteriors convinced the vast majority of people that they had not come for an exchange of gifts and ceremonial handshakes. Still, many remained optimistic. The advanced technology of the ships, they argued, suggested a correspondingly high degree of evolution. Perhaps the extraterrestrials inside were representatives of a higher form of civilization. They would certainly be able to teach us many things about the universe. The optimists compared their situation to that of Stone Age humans on some undiscovered island who looked up and saw an airplane circling overhead. Terrified, they might naturally assume the world was ending when the crew of the airplane was there merely to satisfy their curiosity and thirst for discovery.

Arguments such as these usually led to the depressing admission that humans had never gone anywhere new merely for the sake of curiosity. The people who first populated North America had slaughtered the American Indians. The Spaniards wiped the Incas out with prisons and disease. The first whites to visit Africa were slave-catchers. Whenever humans had "discovered" a new territory, they had turned it into a conquest, subjugating or killing those who were already there. Everywhere, the prayer went up that the newcomers would treat humans in a more civilized way than they had treated one another.

ONE OF THE fifteen mile shadows swallowed New York Harbor, dimming the Statue of Liberty. It was moving directly toward Manhattan. Sporadic clusters of New Yorkers littered the banks of the Hudson, hundreds of frightened strangers, most of them poor, who'd come to see with their own eyes the grim spectacle they'd spent the day following on their TVs. The mood of hushed anticipation ruptured into a wave of human screams rushing north along the river when the dark ship came into view. Long before the craft's low rumble could be heard over the growl of traffic, the city's collective anxiety swelled to a crescendo. Given their visual cue, the riverside crowds bolted off in separate directions, running for home, the subways, their cars, or wherever they instinctively felt they would be safe.

Over the Bowery and Wall Street, the sky disappeared and a bone-rattling vibration began pulsing through Lower Manhattan. Taxi fenders crashed like cymbals. Pedestrians walking along the avenues cleared the sidewalks, hiding themselves in doorways and behind corners when they saw the giant swooping above the city. Everywhere, as car horns blared, people ran out of their houses to watch the ship pass overhead, or ducked into offices and restaurants to get away from it. And everywhere, it seemed, people were screaming.

David's legs churned through the pitch blackness, taking the stairs three at a time. He came to the top, rammed the door open with his shoulder, and stepped outside. The rooftop lay beneath a web of thick cables connecting the satellite dishes and transmitters with the offices below. A moment after he stepped into the sunlight, it was obliterated. Midtown Manhattan was plunged into the same semidarkness the earth usually experienced during a total eclipse.

"God help us," David muttered, face-to-face with the low-flying colossus. His first, irrational reaction was to stoop down, physically oppressed by the sheer weight of the thing rolling over him. The underside of the ship was an endless black-and-gray surface stretching away into the distance. Like the computer-designed tread on a knobby tire, it was studded with sharp outcroppings, building-sized projections arranged into complex patterns. Although the thing was well above the city, its overwhelming size was much larger than the island on which David stood. Its western edge protruded well into New Jersey while the other end was still over Long Island. It seemed to be crushing down on top of him, a mosquito facing the front bumper of a semi. Around him, the equipment on the roof began vibrating, adding its rattle to the steady rumble pulsing through the city. He ran to the north side of the building and watched Central Park fall under the blanket of artificial night.

David imagined his father, terrified and alone in his brownstone. He knew Julius would never in a million years abandon his home. He was probably boarding up the windows and barricading the doors, preparing for another Masada. Yet, for some strange reason, the picture in David's mind changed to Julius calmly playing chess at the kitchen table. He flashed back to that morning's match in the park and then, all at once, a horrible realization unfolded in his mind. He made the connection.

"Oh my God, the signal!"

IN THE MIDDLE of the Los Angeles basin, the Baldwin Hills were an awkward mix of derelict oil fields and million dollar homes. Many of the houses commanded views which stretched from downtown all the way out to the ocean at Santa Monica. Magazines called it the "most affluent Afro-American neighborhood in the country." Lots of Jaguars and circular driveways. At the top of Glen Clover Drive, sandwiched between a pair of traditional four-bedroom houses, was a narrow piece of property with a bungalow built on the bluff. This red-and-white cottage with a neatly manicured yard featured a redwood deck hanging over the city. The rent was obscenely reasonable, making it one of the best rental deals in all of LA. The tenant was a young woman named Jasmine Dubrow who had moved west from Alabama only two years before.

A minivan pulled into her driveway. Its driver, an energetic housewife, "Joey" Dunbar, unbuckled her passenger's seat belt and helped him open the door.

"Here's your key, Dylan," she warbled.

"Thank you, Ms. Dunbar." Dylan, Jasmine's six-year-old son, accepted the house key, then slid down the seat until his feet reached the sidewalk. He was dressed in Oshkosh overalls, Nike sneakers, and a You & I backpack, the fashion statement of choice among the neighborhood's younger set.

"Everybody say good-bye to Dylan!" Ms. Dunbar chirped. The three kids strapped into the backseat waved over the top of the seat. Dylan could see nothing but their hands, but he waved back anyway. "Remember, tell your mommy you can sleep over next weekend, okay? Bye-bye, I'll wait for you to get inside."

A Mercedes-Benz convertible came tearing down the street at fifty miles per hour. It flew over a bump, then bottomed out on the pavement. Joey, outraged, turned to see who was driving like that through her quiet neighborhood and noticed the neighbors standing on their roof looking through binoculars. A busybody, she whipped around the other way to see what they were looking at.

"What? What's so interesting?" she asked, scanning the block in exasperation. Then she saw the thing in the sky and fell quiet. She stared westward over the housetops, unconsciously baring her teeth. She remained frozen until the squealing of tires broke her concentration. Another neighbor had jerked his car into reverse down his driveway, leaving behind rubber as he sped away around the corner.

Before Dylan was halfway to the house, his baby-sitter hit the gas and fishtailed away, leaving the confused boy staring skyward.

"Mommy, wake up! Look at this," he cried, coming through the door. Making a bee-line for her room, he jumped on the bed. "Mommy, come outside and see."

Jasmine quickly covered her naked body with the bedsheet, but remained otherwise immobile. "See what, baby? It's too early."

"A spaceship!" Dylan had seen similar situations on cartoons and knew exactly what to do. Wasting no time, he sprinted back to the front windows intending to shoot the thing down.

"What's with your dog?" a man's groggy voice asked.

Boomer, Jasmine's golden retriever, had started barking and whining a few minutes before Dylan came in. After following the boy into the front room, he returned carrying a high-top basketball sneaker in his mouth and deposited the shoe at the head of a large lump under the sheet next to Jasmine. The lump turned over and threw back the cover. "You're just not gonna let me sleep, are you?"

Steven Hiller, a handsome, muscular man in his late twenties, pushed himself reluctantly into a sitting position and stared back at the excited dog. The sour expression on his face showed he needed another hour of sleep. He and Jasmine had been out late last night, closing down Hal's Restaurant after hopping between nightclubs.

"He's trying to impress you," Jasmine said into her pillow.

Groggily, Steven surveyed the scene around him. Large dolphins splashed and smiled on a poster while several smaller ones, statuettes, were arranged on the dresser and nightstands. A trail of hastily removed clothing led from the hallway to the bed. A framed snapshot of Steve in the cockpit of a fighter jet winked back from the top of the dresser. His and hers robes hung on the hook near the bathroom door. He listened to the dog and the kid in the other room and, for a moment, was surprised to find himself in such a domestic situation. *This is the way married people live*, he thought. If that same idea had occurred to him a few months earlier, he would have dressed quickly and hit the road ASAP. But now, slumped against the headboard, he only smiled. *I think I like this.*

He and Jas had been seeing each other exclusively, passionately, exhaustively for half a year, whenever Steve could get into town for the weekend. But he didn't realize he'd fallen in love with her until a pair of experimental F-19 bombers landed at El Toro Marine Air Base, where he was stationed. Normally, the arrival of such planes would have kept a gung ho pilot like Steve hanging around the base for a chance to fly them. When he chose to spend the time with Jasmine instead, he knew his priorities were changing.

Since graduating from the flight academy, he'd learned to fly every kind of aircraft the service had. When a new airship came through the base, whether it was an old World War II bomber or a highly classified spy plane, Steve always managed to win permission to take her up. On dry weekends, he'd jump in his red Mustang convertible and rip north along the 405 Freeway to LA, his hometown. He'd party all weekend, crashing at his parents' house, or at one of his girlfriends' places. He had the reputation of a lady's man, a smooth operator. Then one night, his parents twisted his arm into going with them to one of their stodgy dinner parties, where, much to his surprise, he became smitten with one of the female guests, the drop-dead gorgeous woman now lying beside him. He turned and examined the perfection of her mocha-colored skin and the graceful way her shoulder curved down to her chest.

Boomer continued to whine. He was whimpering and turning in circles with his tail tucked between his legs. Steve knew there was no use in resisting any longer; he was awake for the day. He stood up and padded into the bathroom. While taking his morning leak, his noticed a tall glass jar set on the back of the toilet. Was it his imagination, or was the bath oil inside vibrating slightly? He knew he didn't pee *that hard.* The sound of a low-flying helicopter caught his attention, a Marietta, judging from the sound of the engine. When he was finished doing his business, he looked out the bathroom's narrow window. He couldn't see the helicopter, but he got a darn good view of the neighbors. A man and wife ran to their Range Rover, flung a few things into the backseat, then tore off in reverse down the driveway.

"Kinda weird," he said to his reflection in the mirror. He looked down at the oil in the tall jar. No doubt about it: it was shaking ever so slightly. He stood absolutely still for a moment. Between the gunshots of Dylan's shoot-out in the living room, Steve thought he heard a low rumbling noise. He hurried out to the bedroom and searched for the remote control.

"Whatcha doing, baby?" Jasmine's Alabama accent was stronger when she was tired.

"I think we're having an earthquake and I wanna put on the TV."

"Where's Dylan?" Jasmine sat up, suddenly wide awake. "Dylan, come here, baby," she shouted into the other room. The television snapped to life, showing a local newscaster reading from her notes.

". . . through the Southland, but so far there are no reports of injury or property damage. Eve Flesher, a spokesperson for the mayor's office, issued a statement from the steps of city hall only moments ago urging people not to panic." As tape of the news conference began to roll, Dylan burst into the room, Rambo-style.

"Hey, Steve!"

"Hey, Dylan!" The men hugged good morning. "What've you been shooting at, outlaws?"

Dylan looked at him like he was crazy. "What outlaws? I'm shootin' at the aliens."

"Aliens?" Steve and Jasmine exchanged a knowing glance. Dylan had a vivid imagination and they loved encouraging him to spin out his fantasies.

His mother asked him, "Did you get any of them?"

Dylan only stared back at her, perturbed. He was old enough to know when adults weren't taking him seriously. "You think I'm pretending, but I'll show you."

"I'm going to see the space ship," Jasmine said to Steve as she was being tugged out of the room. "Want some coffee when I'm done?"

"I'm coming, too. This might be a job for the Marines." On his way to the door, he glanced once again at the television. As they did almost monthly, whenever a small tremor rattled the city, the station cut to a shot of the seismometers at Cal Tech in Pasadena. A true Californian, Steve had learned to ignore earthquakes. But when he switched off the set, the rumbling was still there, growing louder.

Plates crashed to the floor in the kitchen and Jasmine shrieked at the top of her lungs. Steve ran out and found her pulling Dylan away from the window. She was scared out of her wits by something outside. Steve threw open the front door and marched on to the porch, prepared to confront whoever or whatever was out there. Or so he thought.

One of the ominous ships was surging toward downtown like a poisonous thundercloud. On this nearly smogless morning, the Santa Monica and San Gabriel Mountains surrounding the city seemed puny, dwarfed by the stupendous size of the object in the air. The entire LA basin resembled a giant stadium with a mechanical roof slowly rolling closed.

"What is it?" Jasmine called from inside. Steve moved his lips, but no explanation came out. He cleared his head and made a careful observation.

The top of the ship was a low curved dome, smooth except for a craterlike depression a mile across at the very front of it. Jutting out of this hollowed area was a gleaming black tower roughly the size and shape of a skyscraper. It was perfectly rectangular, except where its back wall followed the curve of the depression. The tower was as black as wet tar. Irregularities on its surface suggested doors or windows behind concealing black screens.

The bottom was essentially flat and had a distinct pattern to it. It resembled a perfectly symmetrical gray flower with eight petals. These petals carried a blue tint and ran seven full miles out to the upturned edges of the craft. Seen from a distance, they had the same vein-laced shimmering transparency of an insect's wings. Each "petal" appeared to be built of eighteen thick slabs, planks laid down in long rows that overlapped to create a jagged surface. Crowded onto them was an array of industrial-looking structures. They looked to Steve like cargo bays, docking equipment, storage containers, observation windows, and other large-scale mechanisms. These structures were not separate pieces bolted individually to the underbelly, but parts of the body, protruding like innumerable hard-edged tumors just below a glistening skin. Further away from him, the eye of the flower was a smooth steel plate with deep lines etched into a simple geometric pattern. At first, he thought these lines might be some kind of hieroglyphic decoration, but when they passed overhead, they looked more like the seams to a set of complicated doors. There was nothing decorative about the ship. It was a floating barge, obviously designed to do a job, not to look pretty.

Steve's first reaction was revulsion. It was not only the sheer volume of the thing hanging over them, or the instinctual dread of feeling trapped beneath a potential predator. There was also something disturbing about the design of the craft, something built unconsciously into its architecture. There was a sinister, joyless necessity to it that revealed something ugly and starkly utilitarian about the personalities of its builders. As if all the industrial waste ever produced had been mixed together into one vast sludge heap and transformed into this stunning, intricate, terrifying machine. Still, there was a certain dark magnetism about it, like microscopic photographs of fleas or fungus that reveal a certain hideous beauty.

WHEN DAVID RETURNED to the ground floor, the office was completely empty. The wall of television monitors played for no one. Adjusting the volume on one of the sets, David listened for any information that might confirm or deny his new theory. CNN, still distorted, had pasted together a flashy letterbox logo—a bold graphic that twirled toward the viewer until it filled the screen: "Visitors: Contact or Crisis." Wolf Blitzer, looking frazzled, was standing in the false night outside the Pentagon.

"Officials here at the Pentagon have just confirmed what CNN has been reporting. Additional airships, like the one hovering directly above me, have arrived over thirty-six major cities around the globe. No one I've spoken with here is willing to make an official comment, but speaking off the record, several people have expressed their dismay and frustration that our space defense systems failed to provide any warning."

A graphic superimposed on the screen. It was a world map showing the locations of the spaceships. David nodded. It was exactly what he had expected to see. He heard a voice coming from Marty's deserted office and walked closer.

"Yes, I know, Mom. Calm down for a second, will ya?" Marty had crawled under his desk and was yelling into the receiver. When David stuck his head in the doorway and said hello, Marty got such a scare he banged his head hard against the underside of his desk. "Ow! Nothing, I'm fine. Somebody just came in. Well, of course he's human, Mother, he works here."

"Tell her to pack up and leave town," David said.

"Hold on, Mom." Marty covered the phone. "Why? What happened?"

"Just do it!" he yelled.

"Mom, stop talking and listen. Pack up a few things, get in your car, and drive to Aunt Ester's. Don't ask. Go. Call me when you get there." Marty hung up and crawled out from under the desk. "Okay, why did I just send my eighty-two-year-old mother to Atlanta?"

David was pacing around the cluttered office, thinking. "Remember I told you that the signal hidden inside our satellite feed is slowly cycling down to extinction?"

Marty suddenly recalled the television disruption he'd been so worried about a few hours ago. "Not really. *Signal inside a signal*, that's all I remember."

"That's right, the hidden signal. Marty, it's a *countdown*."

"Countdown?" That didn't sound too good. Marty parted the shades and peeked at the dark shape outside. "Countdown to what?"

"Think about it. It's exactly like in chess. First you strategically position your pieces. Then, when the timing's right, you strike hard at the opponent's major pieces. You see what they're doing?" David motioned toward the television picture of a ship parked above Beijing, China. "They're positioning themselves over the world's most important cities and they're using this signal to synchronize their attack. In approximately six hours, it's going to disappear and the countdown will be over."

"What then?"

"Checkmate."

Marty took a minute to digest the information, then he started having trouble breathing. He opened a can of soda and picked up a phone. "I gotta make some calls. My brother Joshua, my poor therapist, my lawyer . . . Oh, fuck my lawyer."

David grabbed a second phone and punched in an eleven digit number he'd rarely called yet knew by heart. While the phone was ringing, every television in the office switched to the same image.

The president of the United States approached the podium in the White House press room, doing his best to project calm and confidence. *Everything is under control, no need to panic.* While a number of people, including Grey and Nimziki, joined him on the small stage, Whitmore smiled tensely around the room.

"My fellow Americans, citizens of the world, a historic and unprecedented event is taking place. The age-old question as to whether or not we humans are alone in the universe has been answered once and for all . . . "

"Communications." The voice on the phone was curt, all business.

"Yeah, this is David Levinson. I'm Connie Spano's husband. This is an emergency call. I need to talk to her right away."

"I'm sorry, she's in a meeting," the man answered, "can I take a message?"

"No. I need to speak with her *right now*. I know she's busy, I'm watching her on the television. This is more important, believe me. Now go get her." David's voice was full of command.

"Hold please."

David turned his attention back to the president's speech. Connie was standing with a group of people near the stage, just inside the doorway that led into the White House offices. A young man, probably the guy he'd spoken to, came to the door and whispered something in her ear. A moment later she slipped discreetly, professionally through the guarded entrance. David felt a wave of relief. He hadn't been sure Connie would take the call.

"What do you want?" she hissed into the phone.

Taken completely aback, David sputtered, "Connie, listen, you have to get out of there. The White House, I mean. You have to leave the White House." Neither of them knew what to say for a second. It sounded like David was rehashing an unpleasant conversation they'd had countless times before. Aware that he wasn't communicating what he had to say, he bulled forward. "Wait, you don't understand. You've got to get out of Washington all together."

Connie, angry with herself for leaving the press conference, tried to get off the line. "Thank you for being concerned, but in case you haven't noticed, we're in a little bit of a crisis here. I've got to go."

Realizing she was about to hang up on him, David yelled into the phone. "I've been working on the satellite disruption all day and I've figured it out. They're going to attack," David blurted.

The line went silent for a moment. David thought she must be thinking over what he'd said but soon realized she was only covering the receiver while talking to one of her assistants. "They're going to attack," she repeated, "go on."

That made him angry. He was calling to try and save her life, and the last thing he needed was for her to speak to him in a condescending tone. "That's right, *attack*," he said with an edge to his voice. "The signal is a countdown. When I say signal, I mean the signal that's causing all the satellite disruption." He could sense her impatience. He knew the information wasn't coming out in order, which only made him more nervous. "I just went up on the roof and it hit me. This morning I . . . Connie?"

She'd hung up. He hit the redial button on the phone, but realized that wouldn't do him any good. She wouldn't take another call. He looked up at the snowy image of President Whitmore.

". . . My staff and I are remaining here at the White House while we attempt to establish communication . . . "

When he heard that, David knew what he had to do. He packed up his laptop and a few diskettes, then grabbed his bike and headed for the door. "Marty," he called across the office, "quit wasting time and get out of town right now."

Marty, still on the phone, listened to the end of Whitmore's address. ". . . so remain calm. If you are compelled to leave these cities, please do so in a safe and orderly fashion. Thank you."

SLAM! A taxicab trying to drive along the sidewalk crashed into a delivery truck doing the same thing. David, pedaling furiously, weaved in and out of the thick traffic. Everywhere around him, the streets were in total gridlock. Even when he got onto the bridge, the people crossing on foot were making much better time than the cars.

Fifteen minutes later, he coasted up to a row of tidy brownstone houses in Brooklyn. He swerved at the last second, narrowly avoiding a mattress being tossed out a second-story window. All up and down the street, residents were packing up whatever they could, preparing to evacuate.

He banged and banged on his father's front door until suddenly it flew open and David found himself nose to nose with a pump-action shotgun. "Whoa! Pops, it's me."

Julius lowered the gun, peering both ways down the street and dragging his son through the doorway. "Vultures. They said on the TV they've already started with the looting. I swear before God, if they try breaking in here, I'll shoot."

"Pop, listen, you still got the Valiant?"

Julius arched an eyebrow, suspicious. "Yeah, I still got it. What do you care? You don't even have a driver's license."

"I don't need a license." He looked the old man in the eyes. "You're driving."

STEVE STOOD BY THE BED, repacking the weekend clothes he hadn't had a chance to wear. Wearing his officer's uniform and a cocky grin, his movements took on a disciplined intensity and athletic grace that showed how anxious he was to get back to El Toro and, if need be, teach the uninvited guests a lesson. Jasmine leaned against a wall chewing on a fingernail, visibly upset.

"You could say you didn't hear the announcement," she told him.

He just chuckled and kept on packing. "Baby, you know how it is. They're calling us in, and I've got to report."

"Just because they call . . . I bet half those guys don't even show up."

"Whoa." He stopped her. "Jazzy, why are you getting like this?" She looked like she was about to start crying, and Steve moved to comfort her. He reached to put his arms around her, but she slapped them away, accidentally knocking one of her dolphin figurines off the nightstand.

"I'll tell you why I'm getting this way," she shouted, tearing the curtains back to show him the sky, "because that thing scares the hell out of me!" She slumped against the closet door and let herself slide to the floor.

"Listen to me." Steve squatted down to face her and picked up the glass dolphin, which was still intact. "I don't think they flew ninety billion light years across the universe just to come down here and start a fight. This is a totally amazing moment in history."

It was a corny thing to say, but Steve meant it. He feared nothing. Not in a tough-guy-with-a-death-wish way; he just didn't understand letting yourself get frightened. He knew lots of people who let themselves be crippled by a thousand small fears, who let fear become a habit. They were so afraid of failure or humiliation or physical pain they stopped taking risks, stopped living large. What he had always admired most about Jasmine was her bravery. Like everyone else, she lived with uncertainty, but never seemed to sweat the little things that kept other people in straight jackets: money, schedules, what other people thought of her.

He reached for her hands again, and this time she let them be held. While they were looking into one another's eyes, the big question suddenly appeared again. The same one they'd been doing their best to ignore for the past couple months: what they meant to one another and whether their relationship had a serious future. Steve gulped. He had a small box in his pocket that he wanted to take out and show her, something he'd had custom made several weeks ago. His lips tried unsuccessfully to form the words that would let him broach the subject. He wanted to ask her a question, *the* question. But the consequences of asking would be devastating to his career. So, unable to choose between the two things he cherished most, he executed an evasive maneuver.

"C'mon, walk me out to the car."

Jasmine was brave, but she wasn't fearless. She'd been abandoned too many times and lost too much to meet this situation with Steve's breezy confidence. She felt like she had finally put her life in order, that for the first time everything was working out for her, and now, with the arrival of the ship, it all threatened to come unraveled at once. Intellectually, she knew Steve was under orders to return to the base, and it didn't mean he was abandoning her. But at the same time, this was a crisis, and Steve's first move was to pack his bags.

"Can I take this?" He held up the little glass dolphin. "I'll bring it back, I promise."

She smiled and nodded. She had no choice but to try and believe him.

HE'D LEFT HIS Mustang's top down all night, and when he came outside, Steve found Dylan behind the steering wheel. After lifting the boy out of the car, he reached into the backseat for a bag he'd left there.

"I've got something for you, kiddo. Remember I promised to bring you some fireworks?" Steve turned over custody of the package, adding, "But you've got to be real careful with them."

Dylan tore back the wrapping to reveal a bundle of brightly colored paper tubes with sticks attached. They looked like overgrown bottle rockets and the name FyreStix was printed on each one.

"Wow, fireworks!" the boy said in awe, holding the sacred objects out for his mother's inspection. "Cool big ones."

Jasmine shot Steve a look: *Oh, thanks a lot!*

"I was gonna set 'em off myself in the park tonight, but . . . You're supposed to plant 'em in the grass, and they shoot off a bunch of pretty colors straight up about twenty feet."

Jasmine was half listening, distracted by the sight of the huge ship, which had parked itself over downtown LA's tallest building. Soon after it had ceased to move forward, it started rotating very slowly and the rumbling disappeared.

Steve reached into his jacket pocket and fingered the small box inside. It was hard for him to see Jasmine feeling scared. "I was thinking," he began thoughtfully, "why don't you and Dylan pack up some things and, you know," he looked up and down the street, "come stay with me on the base tonight?"

The invitation took Jasmine by surprise. He'd never invited her anywhere near the base and she'd never asked to come. She knew he had good reason for not wanting to be seen with her. Suddenly she was concerned for him. "You sure that's okay? You don't mind?"

"Well," he moaned, "I *will* have to call all my other girlfriends and put the freaky-deaky on hold till later, but no, I don't mind."

She punched him in the arm. "There you go again, thinking you're all that. Let me tell you something, Captain, you're not as charming as you think you are."

"Yes, I am." He grinned, hopping into the car.

"Dumbo ears."

"Chicken legs," he shot back, firing up the engine. Then, after a final kiss, he drove off, calling over his shoulder, "I'll see you tonight." Watching them wave good-bye in his rearview mirror, he wondered if he'd done the right thing, inviting Jasmine to El Toro. It was only a compromise solution.

For her part, Jasmine felt elated and terrified at the same time. She and Dylan stood in the street waving until the red convertible disappeared behind the crest of the hill, then looked once more at the slowly twirling cancerous daisy blotting out the sky. She picked up her son and carried him toward the house, snatching the package of FyreStix from his hands. "I'll take those, thank you."

"Mom, come on!"

JULIUS'S '68 Plymouth Valiant was in mint condition. He kept it under a tarp inside his garage and most of the miles he put on the car were his once-weekly drives to the grocery. His top speed on the highway was usually a maddeningly slow forty-five miles per hour, even during out-of-town drives, which helped explain why David had never applied for a driver's license. But, because this was an emergency situation, the old man tore down the highway at the blistering pace of fifty-five. The highbeams of faster cars bore down on them like the eyes of mechanical wolves. Many of these cars were stuffed to the windows with people and suitcases and boxes of food. Some had mattresses lashed nonaerodynamically to their roofs and when they zoomed past, the passengers would all turn and stare at the two men in the midnight blue classic who were tooling along like they were out enjoying a Sunday drive. The faces behind the windows were hardened into masks of fear by the first twelve hours of the invasion.

"Slow down, you ding-a-ling!" Julius waved a fist and shouted as a van whizzed past at double the Valiant's speed.

"Fifty-five, Dad, please," David said, calling the old man's attention once more to the speedometer. "You're dipping."

"I'm dipping?"

"Dipping below fifty-five. Keep your speed up." David would have liked to be passing every car on the road, but he knew his father's limits, and fifty-five was one of them. Any faster, Julius felt, and the car would self-destruct beneath them. David bit his tongue and tried to relax. There was still time. Besides, he couldn't push too hard after the way Julius had accepted the mission.

David had expected him to put up a fight, to rant and rave for at least half an hour about what a ludicrous idea it all was. But as soon as he'd explained why he *had* to get there in one breathless tumble of words, Julius had leaned close and stared into his child's eyes for a long moment as if searching for something in particular. Something he saw convinced him. "Fix me a sandwich," he said, shrugging. "I'll get my coat."

Thirty minutes later, they were out of town, thanks in large part to David's incredible prowess at navigation. Having spent a good deal of his life in the back of a taxicab, he knew every short cut there was. Once they were out on the highway and pointed for D.C., David broke out his laptop to learn more about the signal, still surprised that his plan had met with so little resistance from his usually resistant father.

"It's the White House, for crying out loud," Julius suddenly erupted, as David stared at the numbers on his computer, "you can't just walk up and ring the doorbell. 'Good evening, hey, let me talk to the president for a minute.' You think they don't know what you know? Believe me, they know. They know everything."

"This they don't know, trust me," David said, trying to concentrate.

"If you're so damn smart, explain me something. How come you went ten years to MIT, graduated with honors, and won all those awards just so you could become a cable repairman?" The question, like many Julius asked, hit below the belt.

"Please don't start in on me about that," David muttered in a way he hoped would close the subject. It was one of his sorest spots, what everyone else referred to as his lack of ambition. He was grossly overqualified for his position at Compact and had been headhunted by research labs all over the nation. He still got occasional letters asking if he'd be interested in working for scientific projects as diverse as the super collider in Texas or the Biosphere in Arizona. He could have pretty much written his own ticket in jobs like those, but he preferred to stay where he was. He loved his city, his job, his father and, until she left to work for Senator Whitmore, his wife.

Stung by the question, David pretended to work at the computer. He couldn't have cared less what other people thought of him, but his father's disappointment was a thorn in his side. "Seven years," David grumbled.

"Seven years? What are you saying?"

"I was only at MIT for seven years, and I'm not a cable repairman, I'm the chief consulting systems engineer."

"Excuse me, Mr. Bigshot," Julius said derisively, leaning close to the steering wheel. "All I'm saying is: they've got people to handle this kind of thing. If they want HBO, they'll call you."

Another low blow. David bit his lip and checked the speedometer again. "You're dipping."

THE FIRST LADY had the swank hotel lounge to herself. Her retinue of assistants and Secret Service agents had backed off to give her some privacy while she telephoned her husband. Whenever the door opened, she could see the herd of reporters waiting for her out in the main lobby. A handful of LAPD cops had corralled them behind velvet ropes while they waited for her to emerge and hold the press conference they'd been promised.

"Mare?"

"Tom, hello. How are you holding up?" she asked.

"Considering the circumstances," Whitmore answered, "pretty well." It was 11 P.M. his time, and his voice sounded weary.

"Where are you?"

"In the bedroom. I thought I should try and lay down for a while."

"Good idea. What's the mood like back there?"

"Listen," he changed the subject, "I'm arranging to send a helicopter to the Biltmore. There's a helipad on the top of the building. I want you out of Los Angeles as soon as possible. If these things decide to get ugly on us . . ." He didn't finish the sentence.

Marilyn smiled. "I thought you'd say that, but I just saw Connie's press conference. Tom, I'm proud of you for staying in the White House. I think it's the right thing to do. But the statement you're trying to make isn't going to be very convincing if they watch me hightail it out of here."

"You're directly below that thing, aren't you?" Indeed, her hotel, the historic and luxurious Biltmore, was only two blocks from the old First Interstate Building. The center of the slowly spinning craft was directly overhead. Downtown LA, usually crowded on a Friday night with an incongruous mix of stretch limousines and promenading Centroamericanos, was nearly empty, a ghost town.

"Yes, it's still up there," she allowed, "but I've got a dozen news crews waiting in the lobby. Johanna's out there setting up a news conference and then a few interviews. I'll leave as soon as they're finished. I promise."

"No way. I appreciate what you're trying to do, but we have no idea what these ships have planned. I'm going to —"

"Tom, listen to me." She cut him off sternly. "I know you're worried. But I have a responsibility here, too. People will listen to me."

He couldn't argue with that. In one public opinion poll after another, Marilyn Whitmore had proven to be the single most popular figure in all of Washington. What Jacqueline Kennedy had done with glamour, Mrs. Whitmore had done with her down-to-earth style. She had won the heart of the nation by being the first First Lady to wander the halls of the White House in blue jeans and bare feet. She had the simple, heroic beauty of a pioneer woman and a no-nonsense manner of speaking to the public that inspired trust. The political establishment disliked her, but for ordinary Americans, she was a symbol of hope; their representative-at-large in the corridors of power. As her husband's presidency had floundered over the previous several months, she had become the administration's most potent political weapon. She felt it was her duty to get on the airwaves and try to keep the evacuation of the cities as orderly as possible.

There was a long pause on the phone line. "Oh, all right," her husband relented, his tone making it clear how little he liked the idea. "But I want you on the roof in ninety minutes. I'll have a helicopter waiting to fly you to Peterson Air Force Base in Colorado."

"Make it two hours and you've got yourself a deal." Then, switching gears, she asked about their daughter. "How's the munchkin?"

"Good. She'll be airlifted out of here and meet you at Peterson. We had a little jail break this afternoon. She got away from the nanny and ran into the Oval Office just as the ship was coming in over the city."

"Oh God," the girl's mother moaned, "how did she react?"

"Like the rest of us. It scared her half to death. She's conked out right next to me. Want me to wake her up?"

"No, let her sleep. But I'm worried about her making that trip by herself. Will you make sure there's a phone on board so I can talk to her?"

"Of course. But she won't be alone. In exchange for staying on at the White House, I'm letting the staff evacuate all their kids to Peterson. I think I'd have a mutiny on my hands if I didn't." A soft knock came at the president's bedroom door. "Just a second," he called across the room before returning to his conversation. "I've got to go. I'll probably see you at NORAD in the morning." Neither one of them wanted to get off the phone, but both felt the tug of their responsibilities. "And, honey . . . "

"Yes?"

"I love you."

"I love you, too. Very much. And I'll see you in a few hours."

"Bye."

Whitmore, still wearing his slacks and dress shirt, walked across the room and opened the door. Standing in the dim hallway were General Grey and Chief Nimziki.

"We have the report you asked for, sir," Grey said, handing over a fax. "There are still only thirty-six of the ships. We haven't spotted any more entering our atmosphere for several hours now."

"And these are the affected cities?" Whitmore asked, studying the report.

"Yes, sir."

Whitmore took his time studying the data. He could see that Nimziki was edgy and seething, chomping at the bit to say something. When the president finally handed the sheet back to Grey, the defense secretary could contain himself no longer.

"Excuse me for saying so, but this is insane," he said between clenched teeth, "absolutely suicidal. By sitting on our hands like this, we're giving away our first strike capability. We've come here to urge you to take action, to initiate nuclear attack."

The word "we" took Whitmore by surprise. He looked at Grey and asked for his opinion. "General?"

"As you know, Mr. President, I'll support whatever course of action you choose. This is a tough call, whether to fire first or sit tight. But I'm inclined to agree with Al on this one. Perhaps we should strike first." It was a surprising answer coming from Grey. There was no love lost between him and Nimziki, but they'd joined forces to present this plan to their leader.

Whitmore leaned against the doorway and rubbed his eyes. He thought about it for a few moments. "I don't think so," he finally announced. "You don't punch the biggest kid in school till you're damn sure he's the class bully."

Nimziki was about to press his argument further, but a sharp look from Grey shut him down. *The president has spoken*, the look said, *and that ends the discussion.*

"What about our attempts to communicate with them?" Whitmore asked.

Grey filled him in. "Attempts on all frequencies have led nowhere. Atlantic Command is trying to rig up a kind of visual communication we can put right in their backyard. They'll have to answer us."

"Let's just hope we like what they have to say."

NO ONE NOTICED what a gorgeous night it was, a million evening stars washed by a comfortably warm breeze. The nervous souls in the trailer park were completely absorbed with questions of safety and survival. That afternoon, neighbor after neighbor, people who had lived there for years, had packed up their belongings and driven away, many without any specific destination. At the same time, new arrivals, mostly dilapidated

RVs on the verge of engine failure, were pulling up to the gates, where the manager had erected a flimsy road block. An obese woman in a floral muumuu collected what she considered a fair price before allowing the refugees, their pitiful faces cowering behind the windows, to roll past and claim one of the narrow dirt lots. Field workers stood around their battered Fords listening to Spanish-language radio stations, deciding which way they should run. Anxious women peered through their screen doors every few minutes for signs of danger before locking themselves inside once more. Everybody was on edge, keyed up like high-stakes gamblers hanging around a casino waiting for the rules of a strange new game to be announced.

Barefoot and cross-legged, Miguel surveyed the whole scene from above. He'd climbed onto the roof of his family's trailer bringing their small television with him, hoping to get some decent reception. After several experiments with wire coat hangers and wads of tin foil, he achieved the best picture quality he was going to get. He leaned back on his hands and watched the news, the warm wind playing through his shoulder-length hair.

There had been no word from Russell since their confrontation alongside the tomato field that morning. *Typical*, he thought, *whenever there's any kind of a crisis, he evaporates*. Like he'd done a thousand times that day, Miguel glanced in the direction of Los Angeles. The dark hump of the mysterious ship was visible above the foothills separating the city from the desert. The rising sliver of moon cast a shadowy gloss along the eastern edge of the craft. Just below the ship, miles of headlights snaked through the canyon as thousands of motorists continued to escape from the city. Watching the lights come toward him down the highway then change into glowing red tail lamps speeding away to the safety of Bakersfield, Fresno, Bishop, and points beyond, Miguel thought again about his plan. All afternoon, he'd been turning it over in his mind. He had to get Troy and Alicia out of the area, away from the danger of the ship. The only place he knew to run was a relative's house in Arizona. The Casse family had burned all their other bridges over the last couple of years.

Flipping channels, he thought about how he would propose the idea to Russell, if and when he ever returned. Then he saw something on the screen that stunned him almost as much as his first glimpse of the spaceship. One of the local channels was running a story supposedly showing the lighter side of the invasion. With a smirking, ironic tone, the anchorman read from the TelePrompTer.

". . . a local man who works as a crop duster was arrested today after he flew over parts of the San Fernando Valley in an antique airplane tossing thousands of leaflets over the side." Miguel moaned out loud when he saw the videotape of his stepfather, feral and handcuffed, being escorted into the Lancaster police station.

"You people better do something," Russell snarled at the news crews. "I was abducted by these aliens ten years ago, and nobody believed me. They did all kinds of tests on me—they've been studying us for years! We've got to do something. They're here to kill us all!" One of the deputies dragged Russell away and pushed him through the front doors of the stationhouse.

Back in the news room, the anchorman's eyebrows lifted. "A rather unique reaction. The man, a drifter identified as Russell Casse, is being held at Lancaster police station for further questioning. The handwritten, photocopied leaflets claimed—"

"Whatcha watching?" A voice from behind startled Miguel, who instantly switched the channel. It was Troy, climbing up the ladder to see what his brother was doing.

"Nothing." Miguel's voice was strangled with emotion. He cleared his throat and spoke again. "Hey, Troy, you remember Uncle Hector, from Tucson?"

"Of course. He's got that SEGA Saturn CD, sixty-four bits. Remember?"

"Yeah. What would you think if we went there to stay with him for a while?"

The younger boy nodded his approval. "That'd be pretty cool."

Miguel looked at the highway for a minute, thinking. Then he made a decision. "Start packing up. We're going." On the television, First Lady Marilyn Whitmore was making a speech, another plea to remain calm. Miguel unplugged the set and brought it carefully to the edge of the roof.

"We're leaving now?" Troy asked from the ladder, confused.

"Right now."

"What about Dad?"

Miguel jumped off the side of the trailer, landing softly on his feet in the dirt. He stepped up onto the tire to retrieve the television. Noticing his little brother hadn't moved, he snapped angrily, "You heard me, Troy, get your stuff ready to go." Then he stomped off into the darkness of the trailer park to find his half sister. He had a pretty good idea where he would find her.

"But we can't leave without Dad," the boy complained. Miguel didn't look back.

HE SLIPPED HIS hand under her shirt. "This could be our last night on earth," he whispered. "You don't want to die a virgin, do you?" He tried to make it sound half joking and half serious, rolling the dice to see how far he could get.

The question made Alicia nervous. She bought some time. Her mouth opened onto his for yet another long, hot, grinding, twisting kiss that pushed him backward against the driver's door. On top of him now, she came up for air and stared down at him. The yellow glow of a porch light seeped through the windows of the truck.

"What makes you think I'm still a virgin?"

The question embarrassed and encouraged him at the same time, made him think that tonight, after weeks of making out, he would finally have her. Alicia was no mind reader, and she didn't have to be one to know exactly what he was thinking. She could feel his excitement in the arch of his back, the way his fingers dug into her hips.

Living in a twenty-two-foot-long travel trailer with three other people was like spending an endless weekend in hell. Alicia, almost fifteen, wanted out. And the only way she could see that happening was for a man to take her away. The guy she was kissing wasn't exactly a man, but he was as close as Alicia had come to finding one. Andy was eighteen, and around the trailer park, he felt like a pretty big wheel. He and his mom, the manager, shared the largest permanent trailer in the park. He had a steady job, a new Toyota truck with a killer sound system, and plans for getting his own apartment. Alicia liked him, but at the same time, she wasn't ready for sex. She knew she'd allowed the conversation to go too far and found herself trying to figure a way out of the situation without looking like a big tease.

Andy was still thinking about the virginity question when the door he was leaning on suddenly opened. The young lovers nearly toppled out onto the ground. Alicia's brother stood looking down at them.

"What the hell are you doing, Miguel?" Untangling herself from Andy, she sounded angry and embarrassed, but was secretly relieved.

"Come on, we're going to Tucson."

"Right!" She rolled her eyes. "Like I would go anywhere with you."

Without further discussion, Miguel reached past Andy and put a vise grip around Alicia's wrist. He pulled her out of the truck, bringing Andy with her. She landed outside with a thump and a growling scream.

"Hey, dude, take it easy," Andy demanded.

Miguel prepared to take him out with one skull-crushing punch. The savage look in his eyes paralyzed Andy, making him sit back down muttering, "Whatever, it's cool."

Alicia, fuming, shouted as she stomped across the dusty yard, "Miguel Casse, you are such an ass. You're a psycho who needs help. I'm telling Dad what you just did, and I hope he whips the hell out of you." Then she took off running, disappearing into the shadows.

WHILE ALICIA POUTED INSIDE, the two boys grabbed flashlights and went to work. Twenty minutes later, they'd disconnected the water, electrical and sump lines, strapped the bicycle and the motorcycle to the back frame, brought in the folding chairs and the hibachi. The Casse trailer was ready to roll. Miguel buckled himself into the driver's seat, fired up the engine, and muscled the column shift into Drive. But he did not move.

Standing in the glare of the headlights, wobbling slightly, like an overweight, retarded elk, was his stepfather. Russell was out of jail, just in time to make their lives even more miserable. Miguel's first impulse was to hit the gas and run him over, slam into him and run over his flabby drunken ass. Instead, he shifted into neutral and waited, eyes straight ahead.

As carefree and cheerful as ever, Russell shuffled over to the driver's side window. "All right, kids! You read my mind. Let's get as far away from that thing as we can." He looked toward the dark shape over Los Angeles and shook his head. "Nobody understands, Miguel. Nobody believes me, but that thing is going to turn LA into a slaughterhouse, mark my words."

Miguel only looked back at him, a blank and hostile stare. Ignoring it, or not noticing, Russell told the boy to open up and let him get behind the wheel. Instead, Miguel slipped out the door and closed it behind him.

"They let you out?"

It never occurred to Russell that he ought to feel guilty or embarrassed. "You're damn right they let me out! Since when is it a crime for a man to exercise his right to free speech? What ever happened to first goddamn amendment? Anyway, they've got bigger fish to fry right now, believe me. Come on, let's go." When Russell started toward the trailer, Miguel stepped in front of him, trembling.

"We're leaving without you, don't try and stop us."

Finally, he had his stepfather's full attention. "What are you talking about?"

"We're sick of it," Miguel said as calmly as he could. "We're sick and tired of picking up after you, of carrying your dead weight around." The boy took a breath, keeping his eyes on Russell's hands. "We've got enough money to make it to Tucson and stay with Uncle Hector for a while."

Russell stared at him as if it was the craziest thing anyone had ever said. "The hell you are," he thundered loud enough for the entire park to hear. "I'm still your father, boy, and don't you forget it!"

That was the last straw. Miguel's fuse had burned all the way down and now he exploded, going off like a rocket.

"You are not! You are not my father. You're just some drunken fool that married my mother. And she took care of you like you were a stinkin' baby and when she got sick you did *nothing*! You're a lunatic, Russell, and you are *nothing* to me. Now please," he said more calmly, "move out of the way. I'll take care of us and you take care of you."

Russell took a long, deep breath, thinking it over. He was always half expecting something like this to happen, but now that the moment was here, it felt like being stabbed in the heart. "What about Troy?"

"That's exactly what I'm talking about! You're so damned selfish. Try, for once in your life, to think about what's best for him. Who's the one who actually takes care of him? Who has to go around begging for money and jobs and medicine? Huh? Who? Every time you screw up, *I'm* the one. I'm the one who has to do all the dirty work. I'm the one who has to get out there and scrape together enough to buy that damned medicine." Miguel could have gone on and on, but the sound of shattering glass stopped him.

"Stop it! I'm not a baby!" Troy screamed. He had come outside and was breaking vials of his medicine on the pavement. "I don't need this stupid medicine!" he yelled, hurling another one against the ground. "I don't need anyone to take care of me."

As soon as he realized what was happening, Miguel darted through the headlights and grabbed his brother before he could throw the last vial, but as they struggled, Troy managed to drop the bottle and crush it under his sneaker. Furious, his brother grabbed a handful of the boy's hair and shook him.

"You know how much that stuff costs? Now what happens when you get sick again? Answer me!"

He waited for an answer, but his anger changed suddenly to sadness, and then to crushing despair. He'd tried. He'd taken a stand against his stepfather and tried to engineer an escape. All at once, he realized that he had failed. And failed miserably. Speechless, thoughtless, Miguel turned and disappeared into the trailer.

"Sorry," Troy said softly.

"C'mon, let's get going, Troy-boy." Russell led the way to the idling vehicle.

DAVID KEPT REMINDING himself that the gentleman seated behind the wheel was his father, a man to whom he owed love, patience, and filial gratitude. On the other hand, Julius was driving him absolutely berserk. The Levinson men hadn't spent so much time in a small space together since the summer David turned thirteen and the family had taken that hellish road trip down to Florida to visit Aunt Sophie who was ill and couldn't make it to

David's bar mitzvah. As they drove, Julius, always a kibitzer, seemed less interested in traffic than in his nonstop conversation. He'd been talking since they left New York, jumping from one subject to the next, analyzing, criticizing, posing questions then answering them. Twice a week over a game of chess in the park, it was fine. But confined to the cabin of the antediluvian Plymouth, bobbing along on bad shocks like an ocean liner at fifty-five miles per hour, his constant chatter was pushing David to the brink of insanity. For the last twenty miles Julius had been pouring over the plotlines of some of the most recent movies he had seen, such as 1959's *The Blob* and the earlier *War of the Worlds*. There were too many similarities for Julius, amateur conspiracy theorist, to believe somebody somewhere hadn't known all this would come to pass. The only time he was quiet was when he was listening to some strange new noise coming from the engine compartment.

David bit his tongue and stayed quiet. This was, after all, the only way he had of getting himself to D.C. Every couple of minutes he would glance over at the speedometer, then check his watch.

"Fifty-five!" Julius would boom when he noticed his son checking the speed. "I'm going fifty-five miles per hour. Any faster and the engine will blow up. Trust me."

There was nothing for David to do but sink back in the seat and try to remain patient. Every mile or so they shot past another vehicle pushed to the side of the road, out of gas or radiator hissing hot jets of steam into the night air. Traffic was backed up all the way to Washington, forty miles away. David thought it was only a matter of time before the frustrated motorists knocked down the meridian barriers and took over the southbound lanes as well. That was exactly what was happening, under police supervision, further up the highway. But for now, the boxy chrome-and-steel Valiant had the highway all to itself. David turned and looked out the rear window. There were no headlights behind them, only open empty road. He looked ahead. No taillights either, except for a seemingly abandoned police car parked sideways in the fast lane. The lights were flashing and both doors stood wide open, but as they sped past, there was no sign of the Maryland State trooper who had stopped the car there.

"We must be getting close," David said. "We're the only ones on this road."

"The whole world is fighting each other to get *out* of Washington, and we're the only schmucks trying to get *in*!" The highway led up a hill and around a long bend. As they came to the crest of the hill, they had their first direct line of sight toward the District of Columbia. Both men stared wide-eyed at the sky ahead. The lights of the nation's capital, rising into the night sky, reflected off the underbelly of a giant dark shape hovering over it: a spacecraft identical to the one they'd seen in New York. The city lights were just bright enough to show the massive gray outlines of the ship's dark flower design. Neither man uttered a word as they coasted down the hill. When a stand of pine trees blocked the view, Julius cleared his throat.

"David, I suddenly have a strong desire to visit Philadelphia, where there aren't any flying saucers. What about we turn around and just—"

"Check your speed, please." Without realizing it, the old man had slowed to thirty-five miles per hour.

Now that they were approaching the city, David's manner became more urgent. Quickly, he reached into the backseat, retrieved his laptop computer, and booted it up. From a plastic file sleeve, he extracted a CD-ROM and popped it into the computer's external drive slot.

Julius knew what a CD was, but he'd never seen one in person before. "What the hell is that thing?" he wanted to know.

David held up the companion disk, volume two, waving it around with a fair amount of showmanship. "On these two little disks, Pops, is every single phone book in America."

"On two little records?"

"Incredible, isn't it?" David's fingers darted around the keyboard, punching in commands.

Julius wasn't going to admit it, but he was impressed. He leaned over and watched the names scroll by on the screen. "Let me guess. You're looking up her phone number."

"Precisely, Sherlock."

"One problem. What makes you think an important person like Constance is going to be listed in the phone book for every crackpot to call her?"

"She always keeps her portable phone listed, for emergencies. The problem is figuring out which name she's put it under. Sometimes she uses only her first initial, sometimes her nickname . . ." He began trying various options while Julius looked on trying to keep up. After twenty or so possible names failed to yield a match, David started to show his frustration.

"Not listed, huh?"

"I'll find it." David's voice sounded almost convincing. "I just haven't figured it out yet. It's usually under something like C. Spano, Connie Spano, Spunky Spano . . . "

"Spunky?" Dad was obviously amused. "I like that one. Try Spunky."

"Spunky was her college nickname."

"Have you tried Levinson?"

David frowned. "Please. She didn't take my name when we were married. Now that we're separated she's going to start calling herself Levinson? I'm sorry, but I don't think so."

Julius shrugged and looked away. So what if his ideas weren't worth trying? What did he care? Eventually, David gave in.

"Oh all right, we'll try Levinson." Julius leaned over and watched the names zip past as avidly as if he were watching a roulette wheel. Abruptly, the names stopped and the machine beeped to signal a match.

"So what do I know?" the old man asked sarcastically.

A loud piercing scream made them glance up simultaneously. Headlights flashing and siren wailing, a police car was speeding down the wrong side of the road. Worse, it was leading a highwayful of traffic, hundreds of stressed-out drivers determined to get away from Washington.

"*Oy, mein gott!*" Julius pushed his glasses higher on his nose, bent closer to the wheel, and prepared for the inevitable.

As soon as David realized they were too close and moving too fast to avoid the oncoming traffic, he did the only sensible thing: he let loose a blood-curdling scream. Julius jerked the car to the left, narrowly avoiding the lead car's front bumper, then to the right just before they went head-on with a station wagon. A pair of sedans locked up their brakes, fishtailed into a collision, then bounced apart. Julius split the narrow gap between them, inches to spare on either side.

"*Slow down!*" David yelled, his face as white as the headlights bearing down on them.

Julius, leaning over the steering wheel, chewing on his lip, hardly touched the brakes. As car after car crashed around them, spinning like bowling pins, the Mario Andretti of the over-seventy set swooped between them skillfully and, from the looks of it, fearlessly. Two hundred yards from where the mayhem began, there was an off-ramp. With one long tire-squealing tug on the wheel, Julius pulled the car from the fast lane to the right shoulder and then up the ramp.

Adrenaline pumping, mouths open, knuckles gone bloodless white, the two of them stared straight ahead until Julius rolled the car to a gentle stop. Awed by what his father had just done, David turned and stared at him.

"Dad! Nice driving, man." Without knowing why, he started laughing.

Julius was breathing pretty hard. He took out a handkerchief and wiped his forehead. "Yeah. Not bad, eh? I didn't even scratch the paint job." Then, although there was nothing funny, he too started chuckling. It was the nervous, triumphant laughter of two men who had just lived through what should have killed them.

For a few moments they forgot about getting to Washington and simply sat there in the car laughing their heads off, the vast, dark ship looming in the distance.

JASMINE DIDN'T KNOW why she was about to walk out on stage, she just wanted to get it over with. The whole day had been a slow walk through a brightly lit nightmare. Even now, adjusting the straps on her silk bikini, she felt as if she were floating.

The advent of the giant ships had plunged the entire globe into a deep state of confusion. Some believed they were the black angels of the apocalypse, come to drown God's green earth in flood, famine, and fire. Others anticipated a beatific ceremony announcing intergalactic harmony and cooperation. While many were scrambling desperately to escape the city, others, like the man who owned the shoe store at the base of Jasmine's hill, were keeping to their regular schedules. All the rhythms of the workaday world, the infinite number of small routines which had seemed so real the day before, turned out to be no more solid than reflections on the surface of still water. The arrival of the ships dropped a large stone into the center of the pond, turning daily life into a rippling, distorted dream. Robbed of its rules, the world didn't know how to behave.

The only reason she'd gone in to work was to pick up her paycheck. It was supposed to be a fifteen-minute stop on her way down to El Toro. But then she'd run into Mario. Fifty, expensively tailored, hair slicked straight back, a notorious name-dropper, he was the very picture of a middle-aged Mafioso wannabe. His club, the Seven Veils, was all he had in the world, and his reaction to the crisis was to insist that the show must go on. Many people over the years had accused him of being a vampire, draining the life out of his girls, sucking every nickel from their bodies before tossing them out for dead. When Jasmine came in for her paycheck, he begged, cajoled, and threatened until she agreed to perform that night. If her head had been clearer, she would have laughed in his face, told him where to shove it, and disappeared. But no one's head was clear.

After all, what if the ships turned around and left? What if Steve decided a woman with a checkered past and a six-year-old son were more than he wanted to handle? Where else was she going to find a job that let her choose her hours and paid her so generously? She desperately wanted to believe Steve wasn't going to let her down and was fairly certain he wouldn't. But she and Dylan had had the rug pulled out from under them before, and Jasmine was nothing if not protective of her son.

Mario took full advantage of her history while trying to convince her to stay and work. He'd known Jasmine for a long time, knew all about her life before Dylan in her native Alabama. She'd started dancing in some podunk club in Nowheresville before being "discovered" and brought to Mobile. That's where Mario had found her. One night after a show he bought her a drink and listened sympathetically to her entire life story, then convinced her to head out west, where she could put her past behind her, start over, and make some very serious money.

The good thing about Mario was that he never tried to get her into bed. He maintained a professional relationship with Jasmine and respected her work ethic. She showed up on time, steered clear of the drugs most of the girls took, and never dated the customers. The bad thing about him was that he knew all the right buttons to push when he wanted something out of her. That's exactly what he'd done when she walked in asking for her paycheck. He reminded her of the men she'd trusted, including the one who had left her with a child and no way to support herself. When he figured she was feeling vulnerable, he switched gears and threatened to fire her if she wouldn't help him keep the club open, a pathetic tyrant desperate to keep control over his little fiefdom.

The thumping bass line of her song pulsed over the club's sound system and the announcer's taped voice boomed over the top: "Gentlemen, loosen your collars and get ready for something extremely hot. Put your hands together for the lovely . . . Sabrina!"

She burst through the curtain and into the blinding glare of the spotlight. Twirling gracefully on her high stiletto heels, she circled the stage until she arrived at the polished brass pole. Grasping it a finger at a time, she pressed her entire body against it, then broke away into another set of pirouettes, tossing away her see-through cape.

Suddenly, "Sabrina's" tigress-in-heat expression disappeared. There was no one in the audience. The hundred chairs surrounding the stage were all empty. The only customers were a handful of men clustered around the big-screen TV at the far end of the room. All of them were regulars who had neither homes to defend nor families to rescue, guys who had wandered over to the Seven Veils for the same reason they always did: the company. Four or five of the other dancers sat with them at the bar watching the news.

Without a doubt, it was the worst moment of Jasmine's career as a stripper. She suddenly felt very angry and very stupid. Standing there, nearly naked, in the blazing stage lights, she began to realize why she had really come to the club. She had *wanted* Mario to confirm all her suspicions about Steve, to remind her of all her failures with men, or more exactly, all the men who had failed her. After all, hadn't he taken off, leaving her and Dylan when the spaceship appeared? But what really made her angry was that she had kept Dylan with her, exposing him to danger unnecessarily. It was time to drive like hell down to El Toro and see whether Steve was for real. She slipped out of her high heels and, unnoticed, walked back through the tacky foil curtains.

She came into the dressing room cussing mad. "I can't believe I let that son of a dog talk me into this. I only came here to get my check. What was I thinking?" She collapsed into the chair in front of her dressing table, wiping off her stage makeup in disgust. At the next table, a washed-out girl of nineteen or twenty sat staring at her portable television set.

"Can you even believe this is going on? It is so totally cool." She called herself Tiffany. She had a long, graceful body, enormous boobs, and armfuls of straight black hair pinned haphazardly atop her head. Lighting a fresh cigarette with the butt of another, she spoke in a slow, spacey voice. "I told you they were out there and you thought I was nuts."

On the television screen, between static interruptions, a pair of newscasters with serious expressions were reading the news. "This next story comes from the 'It Could Only Happen in California' file. Hundreds of UFO fanatics have congregated on the rooftops of several skyscrapers in downtown Los Angeles. Soon after the craft parked at ten A.M. yesterday, with its center positioned directly above the old First Interstate Building, sign-toting individuals made their way to the rooftops, apparently to welcome the ship's occupants. Gordie Compton is live and on the scene in the Nose for News CamCopter."

The screen cut to an unsteady helicopter shot, its powerful search beam like a shaft of lightning in the night sky, swooping over the crown of the LA skyline, the First Interstate Building. Crowded onto the helipad atop the building were fifty or sixty people. When the light hit them, they went mad, shouting and waving hand-painted signs. Some held up signs like "TAKE ME!!" and "EXPERIMENT ON ME."

"Oh, signs, I forgot," Tiffany remembered. "Look at the one I made." She reached into a shopping bag and took out the side of a cardboard box. In loopy, girlish letters were the words "WE COME IN PEACE" and a crayon drawing of a space alien.

Jasmine gripped Tiffany's arms. "Don't even dare!" she hissed. "Girl, listen to me. You're not thinking about *joining* those idiots, are you?"

Tiffany rolled her eyes and blew smoke at the ceiling. "I'm going over there as soon as I'm off work," she admitted. "Wanna come?"

"Look at me." Jasmine took hold of Tiffany's chin and lifted it until they were eye to eye. Like most of the dancers who worked there, Tiffany was a

mental and emotional basket case. She had a drug habit plus an addiction to abu-
sive men. As soon as they'd met, Jas had taken the girl under her wing. "Tiffany, I
don't want you going up there," Jasmine continued. "Promise me you won't." A
pair of puppy dog eyes looked back until Jasmine snapped, "Promise me!"

"Oh, all right, I promise." Tiffany pouted, tossing the cardboard sign over
her shoulder and onto the floor.

"Thank you. Look, I'm going out of town for a while, and I need you to stay
out of trouble until I get back."

Jasmine checked her watch. Steve was probably starting to wonder where
she was. She didn't want to leave Tiffany, but she had to get on the road. She
had changed into her street clothes when Mario barged into the dressing room,
heading for his office. He pulled the door open and stared into the room.

"What the hell is this kid doing in my office?" he bellowed. "And why is
there a damn *dog* in here?" Dylan was inside watching a video on Mario's set.
Jasmine pushed past Mario and gathered her son up in her arms.

"How many times I gotta tell you damn broads, *no kids* at the club!"

"You try finding a baby-sitter today," Jasmine shot back, grabbing her bag
with her free hand and heading toward the exit.

"Whoa! Stop right there, young lady. Where do you think you're going? You
promised me you were gonna work today. You leave, you're fired."

Jasmine paused for a moment at the door, glancing back for a last look
around. "Nice working with you, Mario."

THE MOOD IN THE PILOTS' locker room at El Toro was seri-
ous, pensive. Captain Steven Hiller strolled in and noticed most of the men
were sitting by themselves, or huddled in quiet, brooding conversations. Turning a corner, he found his squad in a very different mood. The men of the
Twenty-Third Tactical Air Wing were relaxing in groups, talking, flipping
through magazines, kidding around. "The Black Knights," the squad's official
nickname, was emblazoned on lockers, T-shirts, and jackets. There were even a
couple of tattoos.

Steve's flight partner and best friend, Jimmy Franklin, was kicked back
with his feet up on a locker door, arms behind his head, listening to a portable
radio. Without turning around, he knew Steve had come in. The two of them
had spent so much time training and watching each others' backs, both in the
air and on the ground, they automatically knew where the other one was.

"Where the hell you been, Captain?," Jimmy called out. "Wait, don't tell
me. Traffic was a bitch, right?"

Steve dropped his bag in front of his locker and moved into the group of leathernecks. "I bet you guys have been sitting on your butts all day waiting for me to get here, right?" Steve asked facetiously, knowing the group would have spent the day running through one emergency drill after another. The marines responded by pelting Steve with half a dozen towels. Grinning, Steve strolled back to his own locker. Jimmy got up and followed him.

"This is some real serious shit, Stevie. Mucho serious. They've recalled everybody on the base, and we spent the whole day on yellow alert."

Steve opened his locker and saw the mail had been delivered, stuffed through the vent. He flipped through the stack until he came to a legal-sized envelope with the blue NASA insignia printed on one corner. He picked it out of the pile like a negative out of developing fluid and tossed the others aside. He stared at it for a moment before handing it to Jimmy.

"You open it for me. I can't."

"You're turning into a real wuss, you know that?"

If Steven Hiller was the most talented and hardworking pilot on the base, Jimmy Franklin was the most fearless. Nothing scared him, and he'd prove it to you any time you liked. He tore the letter open and read it aloud so only Steve could hear.

"It says here, 'Dear Captain Hiller, Marine Corps blah blah blah. We regret to inform you that despite your excellent record of service . . . '" Jimmy's voice trailed off. He knew the news would knock the wind out of his pal. "Listen, buddy boy, I've told you this before. It don't matter that you've learned to fly everything from an Apache to a Harrier to a dang hang glider. If you want to fly the space shuttle, you're gonna have to learn to kiss a little ass."

That was the third time they'd turned him down. Disgusted, Steve reached into his locker and ripped down a glossy photo of the space shuttle *Columbia* landing at Edwards AFB. Hanging right beside it was a snapshot he'd taken of Jasmine.

Jimmy made it his job to cheer Steve up. "Let me explain my personal technique. The first thing is to get the right ass-kissing height. When I see a general coming, I get down on one knee, see? This puts me at a perfect level with the ass that needs kissing."

Steve felt like he'd just swallowed a dagger, but he tried to look amused. As he stuffed his jacket into his locker, something fell out of the pocket and on to the floor. Before Steve could grab it, Jimmy snatched it up. It was a small jewelry box, which Jimmy immediately opened. Inside there was a beautiful diamond engagement ring. The sparkling white stone was set in a gold band shaped like a dolphin jumping out of the water.

For the first time in many weeks, Jimmy was rendered speechless.

"Jasmine has this thing for dolphins," Steve told him, a little embarrassed.

"This is a . . . is this a wedding ring?" Jimmy asked, still on his knees.

"Engagement." Steve heard an edge of accusation in his friend's voice. They'd talked many times about Steve's goal of flying the shuttle into space, and every time they did, Jimmy gave him the same advice: dump the stripper.

"I thought you were going to break it off, man," Jimmy growled.

Just then, some guys from another flight team walked by. They saw Jimmy down on one knee, holding out an engagement ring to Captain Hiller. A couple of them did a double take. Realizing how queer it must look, Jimmy and Steve jumped away from one another in a panic. Steve snatched the box back and put it away.

"Steve, listen to me. Them boys at NASA are real careful about their public image. They want everything to be wholesome, all-American apple pie. You've already made one mistake: being born black. If you go ahead and marry a stripper, you will never ever in a million years get to fly that shuttle. And you know I'm right."

Steve knew it was all true. As soon as Jasmine signed in at the guardhouse as his overnight guest, his hopes of flying the shuttle would probably die forever. He pressed his head against the row of lockers, the metal cool against his forehead.

THE POWERFUL KLIEG lights that would normally have been shining on the White House were blacked out for security reasons. A pair of tanks and a platoon of rifle-bearing Marines were posted at the front gates on brightly lit Pennsylvania Avenue. Hundreds of Washingtonians were there with them. Along with the reporters, and those who were simply too nervous to sleep, were small groups holding candlelit prayer vigils. A bunch of militant pacifists paraded back and forth holding signs with slogans such as "DON'T PROVOKE!" and "VIOLENCE BEGETS VIOLENCE." The police, uniformed and plainclothes, were everywhere.

When a pair of cops pulled a road block aside to allow a line of news vehicles on to the street, Julius cut into the line and drove past the road block like he was Walter Cronkite. Even after years of studying him, David couldn't tell when his father was being sneaky and when he was simply blundering along. When the Valiant lurched to a stop, Julius turned and dryly addressed his son.

"Okay, we're here. You want to ring the doorbell or should I?"

David shot his father a Clint Eastwood stare as he flipped open his cellular phone and dialed Connie's number from his computer screen. He got a busy signal. "Perfect, she's on the phone right now."

Sometimes David made no sense. "How," his father wanted to know, "can it be perfect if you need to talk to a person and her line is busy?"

"Because," David explained, his fingers issuing commands across the keypad, "I have a service that allows me to triangulate her signal and establish her exact position. Even inside the White House."

Julius started to say something else, then stopped short, realizing what David had said. "You can do that?" he asked, honestly curious.

David answered with a diabolical grin, "All cable repairmen can."

INSIDE THE WHITE HOUSE, Connie was in one of the hallways taking care of some personal business. She had called her friend and neighbor, Pilar, who was just about to leave for her parents' place in New Jersey. The woman promised to take Connie's cat, Thumper, with her. As soon as the two of them said good-bye, the phone rang again.

"Yes?"

"Connie, don't hang up."

Her eyes rolled toward the ceiling when she heard David's voice. She leaned against the wall. "How did you get this number?"

"Walk to the window. There should be a window right in front of you."

Reluctantly, she looked around. Sure enough, there was a window only a few feet away. She walked over to the tall windows and pulled back the white lace curtains to peer outside.

"All right, I'm at the window. Now, what am I looking for?"

There was no need for more explanation. As soon as Connie looked up at the street, she saw a tall, awkward figure climb up onto the hood of an old blue car and start waving wildly in the air.

Secret Service men quickly surrounded the car and "helped" David down. Filtered through the phone, Connie could hear him telling the men he was talking to someone *inside* the White House.

A moment later, an all-business voice came on the line. "Who is this?"

Connie identified herself and, despite her own doubts, assured the agent that the man on the hood of the car wasn't a lunatic. She checked her watch and decided she could come down and talk to him for a minute or two.

A SHOWER OF SPARKS from a welder's torch bounced off the helicopter and onto the tarmac at Andrews Air Force Base, then fizzled away. The hooded man was putting the final touches on something called "Operation Welcome Wagon," a hastily organized attempt to communicate with the visitors. Portable work lights, designed for nighttime road construction, had been trucked onto the runway along with a fleet of loudly chugging generators needed to power them. Scores of news crews from around the world moved as close to the scene as the soldiers would let them.

The center of all this attention was a sixty foot long, thirty foot high, eighteen-ton piece of machinery, the most advanced instrument of its kind: an Apache attack helicopter. A special steel frame was fitted into the copter, designed to hold a giant light board.

Searching for some way to communicate with the mute Goliaths hovering over the world's capitals, the army engineers had finally seized on a plan. They'd descended on RFK Memorial Stadium, home of the Washington Redskins, and dismantled a large section of the ballpark's message board. The aluminum box, forty feet tall, had 360 lights that could be programmed by computer to display just about any kind of pattern or message. Once the box was delivered to Andrews AFB, it was mounted to the floor of the Apache, extending like a pair of bulky wings from the doors on either side.

A thousand cameras began to flash when the long rotor blades started to turn. Reporters shouted questions at the soldiers and press officers assigned to keep them at a distance, rushing to their positions to do stand-up remotes. Within seconds, they were patched in to live network broadcasts and millions of people around the world were watching the beginning of Operation Welcome Wagon.

"What you see behind me," a CNN reporter shouted over the din, "is an Apache attack helicopter refitted with synchronized light boards. Pentagon officials hope these lights will be our first step in communicating with the alien craft. But what message will we be sending? And in what language? We spoke with one of the men responsible for designing earth's first message to these inscrutable visitors just a few moments ago. He told us that it would be a message of peace sent in the language of mathematics. . . ."

As soon as the blades were at full speed, the ground crew moved away and the pilot lifted off, careful to keep his craft level so that the light board wouldn't slip out. It rose straight up, then began moving toward the dark metallic menace slowly turning in the night sky. A swarm of smaller helicopters, equipped with cameras, followed it away from the base.

People everywhere followed the scene on their television screens. Even in the White House, a large contingent of military personnel and civilian advisers watched as the tense drama unfolded.

"Where are we?"

Suddenly half the room jumped up and saluted as the president strode into the room.

"We're in the air," General Grey reported, "ETA approximately six minutes." As he said these words, the pounding *thwack* of the Apache was audible over the city. Several officers went to the windows and watched it lifting higher and higher as it flew to the rendezvous point at the tall tower which seemed to mark the front of the ship. President Whitmore stood shoulder to shoulder with the rest of the room, watching in grim silence.

Just down the hall, the doors of the old executive elevator rolled open and out stepped an unshaven Julius Levinson, his trousers wrinkled from the long drive. He made no secret about being impressed with his surroundings. As Connie and David headed down the hallway speaking in urgent whispers, Julius stopped to inspect his appearance in a mirror.

"Oy! If I had known I was going to meet the president," he said loudly, "I'd a worn a tie. Will ya look at me, I look like a schlemiel."

Without a word, Connie hurried back, hooked her father-in-law's arm in hers, and tugged him along until the three of them were standing in the Oval Office. The room was empty, but to Julius it felt as if all the great names of American history were in there with him. He couldn't believe where this strange day had taken him. As a reflex, he combed his fingers through his hair, trying to make himself look presentable.

"You two wait right here. I'll be right back," Connie told them. Before she left the room, she warned David, "I don't know how happy he's going to be to see you."

"Connie, we're wasting time," David urged. "I'm about the last person he's going to listen to."

"Of course he'll listen," Julius erupted, suddenly ready to defend his son, "why shouldn't he listen?"

"Because the last time I saw him I punched him in the face."

Julius gasped and clutched his heart with his hands. He looked at Connie, then at David. "You actually *punched* the president? My son punched the president?"

Connie paused at the door. "He wasn't the president then," she explained. "David was convinced I was having an affair with him, which I *wasn't!*"

With that, she closed the door and walked down the hall to the briefing room. A smile crossed her lips as she heard Julius raising his voice, incredulous, in the room behind her.

Connie stopped outside the door to the briefing room. She was taking an enormous personal and professional risk, pulling the president out of a high-level meeting for a conference with her erratic ex-husband. But David had managed to convince her that he was on to something real, something she thought the president ought to know about. She took a deep breath and plunged in, walking straight up to Whitmore and whispering something into his ear.

"Right now?" he asked, incredulous.

His communications director nodded. Everyone in the room had turned to watch this conversation. The timing couldn't have been worse. The welcome wagon would reach its destination in just over three minutes. But Whitmore was accustomed to relying on Connie's good judgment. Without another word, he turned away from the window and walked to the door.

"You aren't going to leave *now*, are you?" Nimziki made sure everyone in the room was aware of the president's curious decision as Whitmore ignored him and left the room.

"Ugh! How in the world do you put up with that cretin?" Connie asked once they were out in the hall.

"He ran the CIA for years. He knows where all the bones are buried. It comes in handy," Whitmore told her. "Now, exactly who is this I'm going to talk to?"

Rather than answering him, Connie ushered him into the Oval Office. The moment Whitmore saw David, he froze in place. "Damn it, Connie, I don't have time for this!"

Anticipating exactly that reaction, she had shut the double doors and stood in front of them. There was an icy silence.

Julius, understanding the situation better than he let on, broke the tension by marching up to Whitmore, hand extended. "Julius Levinson, Mr. President. An honor to meet you."

"I told you he wouldn't listen," David said, pouting at Connie.

"This will just take a moment of your time," Julius assured him.

President Whitmore shot a dumbfounded look at Connie, amazed that she had dragged these two weirdos into the White House at a moment like this. As he moved to leave the room, David finally spoke up.

"I know why we have satellite disruption," he said calmly.

Whitmore turned and looked back at him. "Go on."

"These ships are positioned all around the globe," he began, coming around to the front of the president's desk and drawing a circle on a notepad. "If you wanted to coordinate the actions of ships all over the world, you couldn't send one signal to every place at the same time." He drew lines between the ships showing how the curve of the earth would block their signals.

"You're talking about line of sight?"

"Exactly. The curve of the earth prevents it, so you'd need to relay your signal using satellites—" David added a pair of orbiting communications satellites to his sketch "—in order to reach the various ships. I have found a signal embedded in our own satellite network, and this signal is actually—"

Before he could finish, the door was forced open behind Connie. An aide poked his head in the door with an urgent message. "Excuse me, Mr. President. They're starting right now."

So far, David hadn't told Whitmore anything he didn't already know from intelligence reports coming out of Space Command earlier that day. The president picked up a remote control and switched on the television. The Apache had just reached the front of the huge spaceship and turned on its light boards. The powerful lights began to flash on and off, creating a repeating sequential pattern. The staff at SETI, after several hours of furious on-line discussion and a blizzard of faxes, had come up with a simple mathematical progression, a message written in what they hoped would be a universally comprehensible language. The entire sequence would repeat every three minutes, followed by a display of the word "peace," written in ten different earthly languages. It wasn't much, but it was a beginning. The message spelled out by these flashing lights was utterly incomprehensible to most humans, including the president.

He turned back to David. "So, they're broadcasting to one another using our satellites?"

David had turned on his computer. He showed Whitmore the graphic he had created to express the signal. "This wave is a measurement of the signal. When I first found it, it was recycling itself every twenty minutes. Now it's down to three. It seems to be fading out, losing power, but the broadcast power remains stable. It's like they're slowly turning down the volume, shortening it down to zero. It has to be some sort of a countdown."

The president stared back at the television, lost in thought.

"Tom, these things are—" David caught himself and started over with greater composure. "Mr. President, these things are using our own satellites against us, sending out a countdown. And the clock is ticking."

"When will the signal disappear?"

David opened a window on his computer screen. "Thirty-one minutes."

Whitmore stared at the television. The giant helicopter looked like a mosquito beside the endless gray bulk of the intruder ship. What David had told him made sense, confirmed his worst suspicions. Until then, he'd taken a wait-and-see attitude, but if David was right about the countdown, it was time to spring into action. He nodded his head and walked out of the room, down the hall, and came into the briefing room with a whole new battle plan.

"General Grey, I want you to coordinate with Atlantic and Southwest Commands. Tell them they have twenty-five minutes to get as many people out of the cities as possible."

"But Mr. President—"

"And get that chopper away from that damned ship. Call them back immediately."

Grey picked up the direct line to Andrews AFB and relayed the commander in chief's orders. Nimziki, on the other hand, used the moment as an opportunity to advance his career and accumulate personal power. With a series of glances around the room, he tried to cement the impression that Whitmore was cracking under the pressure, reversing himself for no apparent reason.

"Mr. President," his tone was full of false civility, "why are we pulling back now? What changed your mind?"

Whitmore ignored him. "We're evacuating the White House, effective immediately. Let me have the two choppers on the lawn in five minutes. Somebody go downstairs and get my daughter." Advisers and staff broke into thirty separate conversations, scrambling to execute their new marching orders.

"Sir," Grey held a hand over the phone, "I've got General Harding of Atlantic Command on the line. Just how orderly should this evacuation be?" Grey was as confused as anyone by Whitmore's sudden change of direction. But there was no time to answer the question.

"They're responding!"

All the movement and chatter stopped abruptly as everyone turned toward the bank of television screens. A thin shaft of green light, two inches around, sprouted from the base of the tall tower on the alien ship. Almost like a long finger extending through the darkness, it grew in length until it reached out and poked against the helicopter, a mile away. The Apache, moving sideways through the air to keep itself in front of the tower as the giant ship spun slowly through the air, reacted visibly, jolting backward several feet when the light nudged against it. The beam, bright enough to be visible from the ground, was the pale color of milky jade. The millions watching on television could see that the helicopter was struggling to maintain its position relative to the vast, menacing ship.

The pilot's cool voice came over the radio. "This ray of light seems to have some type of mass or energy to it. We're experiencing some turbulence, getting knocked around pretty good up here."

As he spoke, a huge screeching noise drowned out his words. A pair of huge armored plates concealing the source of the mysterious pole of green light had begun to grind open with an earsplitting squeal.

"Sounds like God's fingernails on a big chalkboard," the pilot purred in a southern accent.

As the panels pulled open, the light from inside the big ship overpowered the 1500-watt bulbs of the light board. The men inside the helicopter shielded their eyes, still struggling to maintain position. Then the president's order reached them. The lead pilot flipped the switch on his radio, his voice broadcast to millions worldwide.

"We have received orders to return Operation Welcome—"

He never finished. A spike of green light suddenly streaked across the night sky and smashed against the helicopter, shredding it in a single burst. It looked like a dragonfly being taken out by a .22-caliber shell. After the brief explosion lit up the sky, everything was suddenly dark once more. The bright light coming from the spaceship was gone. All that remained were a few pieces of smoking debris drifting earthward like fiery snowflakes. The doors at the base of the tower rolled closed and the huge saucer covering the sky went back to sleep.

A PHONE RANG in the Los Angeles hotel room. Then rang again. Marilyn Whitmore was too stunned by what she had just seen to answer it. She had been packing a few last things into her briefcase when the helicopter exploded. The television was showing it again in slow motion. Grainy enlargements of the pilot showed him covering his head in the last frame of videotape before the blast hit him. Marilyn sat down on the bed feeling sick for the man and his family, but even worse for what the extraterrestrials' response meant to the human race as a whole. When the phone rang again, one of her Secret Service escort picked the cellular up and identified himself. He listened carefully, saying, "Yes sir, I understand," and "Yes sir, immediately. She's right here, do you wish to speak with her, sir? . . . Yes, sir, I understand."

He clicked the phone off and turned to Mrs. Whitmore. "That was the president, ma'am. He said he loves you very much and gave me orders to evacuate you from Los Angeles at once. We have the southern stairwell secured. We'll take it up to the roof."

"Okay, let's rumble," she said, pulling herself together and heading out the door.

As they came out on the roof, an army transport helicopter was fifty feet above them, coming in for a landing on the rooftop helipad. Mrs. Whitmore wondered aloud whether getting into a helicopter was such a good idea. The city-sized spaceship overhead might have developed an appetite for them. As the whirring blades stirred up the warm night air, Marilyn scanned the city's skyscrapers and noted something curious happening on one rooftop after another: helicopters buzzing around, shining search beams down on the tops of the brightly lit buildings.

JASMINE OPENED the door and stepped onto the asphalt. She was in the fast lane on the old Pasadena Freeway. Traffic on her side of the road was jammed solid, crawling along at one mile per hour. Just over the guard rail, things were moving much faster. Drivers pushing to get north out of the city had taken over the empty southbound lanes. Just ahead was the mouth of a tunnel cut into the side of a steep hill. The idea of being inside a tunnel while the ship was overhead gave Jas the creeps.

Frustrated, she got back into the car. As soon as she was beyond the tunnel, she told herself, she'd find some way to get across the center divider and make some time, even if she had to ram her way through the guard rail. At the rate she was going, she wouldn't make it to El Toro until next month. Dylan and Boomer were both starting to get bored and restless. Jasmine switched on the radio for another traffic report.

"... authorities have called for a complete evacuation of Los Angeles County. Motorists are being urged to avoid the freeways wherever possible and take surface streets instead. You'll make much better time that way."

"Now he tells us," Jasmine looked over at Dylan and shook her head in exasperation. The boy just shrugged his shoulders. Traffic advanced another thirty feet.

THE PRESIDENT AND his entourage were moving fast. At the bottom of the stairs, they met an aide who had brought Patricia out to meet them. From there it was out onto the lawn and into the waiting helicopters. The twenty men and women, all looking sharp and polished despite being in their twenty-first consecutive hour of work, jogged across the lawn, up the stairs, and into the big blue-and-white choppers with the presidential seal emblazoned upon the door.

General Grey had already boarded and was on a telephone when the president entered. "Is my wife in the air?" The edge in the chief executive's voice told Grey the answer had better be yes.

"She'll be in the air at any moment. They're loading right now."

Connie was the last one in the door. She looked confused and she was. The Marine guards controlling access to the helicopter had stopped David and Julius behind the cordon. They couldn't come along. There were a couple of unoccupied seats on the chopper, but the president had his nose buried in a fax from the State Department and Connie couldn't imagine asking him to bring David along with them. Besides, it was too late. The ground crew was closing the door and the Air Force pilot was revving the blades up to liftoff speed. Somehow, David and Julius would have to make it out of the city by themselves. Connie knew if David's theory about the countdown were correct, they only had about ten more minutes to do so.

"Tom . . ." The sound of the voice surprised her, even though it was her own. When President Whitmore wheeled around to face her, Connie found herself at a loss for words. Instead, she pointed out the window to where the Marines had detained David and Julius.

As soon as the president saw them standing out there, he stood up and moved to the door, pushing it open again. Over the roar of the copter blades, he yelled something to the men outside. One of them immediately turned and ran across the lawn, bringing the Levinsons back with him. As the two of them came up the stairs and into the cabin, the expression on Whitmore's face let them know they were expected to sit down and shut up. That's exactly what they did. Finding seats next to Connie, David had his laptop up and running before the copter lifted off. Looking over his shoulder, Connie could see the display on the computer screen ticking down.

11:07 11:06 11:05 . . .

As the helicopter lifted quickly away, Connie looked out the window, watching the people below on the White House lawn. None of them looked like people about to die. They were all so busy, so focused on properly executing their individual responsibilities. Somehow, Connie felt, their concentration made them seem safe, protected. They still had so much work to do. For a moment, she thought she was watching a scene like the one she had imagined taking place at the gates of heaven: some were allowed to pass toward salvation while others were left outside to perish. She shook it off. Certainly, these people, these hard-working background players she had worked side by side with for the last three years would be there as always when the chopper returned.

11:01 11:00 10:59 . . .

SHE WAS LIFTED up the last several flights as if by magic, drawn upwards toward the sounds of the party raging above. At last, she pushed open the fire door and stepped into the open air. Hundreds of laughing, shouting, drinking people were dancing to the blaring cacophony produced by three competing stereo systems. Some were waving signs, others lighting fireworks. A group of women who looked like secretaries had dressed themselves up in "alien suits," white body stockings with tall cone head caps strapped under their chins. One couple, taking themselves a little too seriously, came as the king and queen of a distant galaxy, complete with velvet robes, elaborate crowns, and jeweled scepters. They sat stoically amid the mayhem as if waiting for a messenger to arrive from the ship. The birthday suit was another popular costume. In the big dance circle at the center of the roof, a bunch of young hippies, Deadhead types, had stripped off their clothes and were entranced in a writhing naked group dance. A rumba line was snaking its way through the crowd, and as they passed, one of the dancers shoved a bottle of tequila into Tiffany's hands. She felt as if she'd come home. As if she'd finally found the wildest, coolest, craziest spot on earth. The one she could never find or get invited to. And the ironic thing was that most of the people atop the old First Interstate Building shared one important characteristic in common: they were nerds. Tiffany laughed out loud then gulped down a long slug of tequila.

More amazing than the party was the view of the ship. The dead center of it was directly overhead. *I'm at ground zero,* she thought. She took a long look at the lustrous surface of the craft. The long silver streaks, the ones people said looked like insect wings, were actually a whole network of lumpy projections, warehouse-sized tubs, tanks, and docks that made the thing look like a city hanging upside-down. It was certainly large enough to be a city. Gaping up in awe, she pictured what the inside of the ship must look like, imagined herself whisking around inside doing some important business. A tug at her arm brought her back to earth. An older guy with a beard was working on a joint. Pointing toward the naked snake dancers not far off, he told her a little story over the noise.

"In the last days of the Third Reich, as the allies advanced on Berlin and everybody knew it was all over, that their world was about to end, they started having wild orgies. It's how they dealt with the stress of the situation." He reached out and stroked her arm. It was the lamest come-on line she'd ever heard.

"Whatever!" Tiffany laughed in the guy's face, handed him the tequila, then waded deeper into the thick of the party, pulling her WE COME IN PEACE sign out and waving it to the spaceship. It was crowded, far too many people for the small rooftop. Some of the "alien lovers" were only a few feet from the edge, sixty-five stories straight down without a guard rail.

All of a sudden, a police helicopter lifted over the side of the building, its bullhorn turned to full volume. "You are commanded to leave the roof at once. The president of the United States has ordered the evacuation of Los Angeles. Make your way to the stairs immediately in a safe and orderly fashion."

The crowd reacted predictably, booing and throwing whatever they had in hand. Most of them had already defied the police to get up here, pushing through the cordon they'd set up at ground level. The chopper circled the building once, repeated the order, then peeled away toward the next rooftop.

A tremendous noise erupted overhead, a low, steady rumble like the sound of a hundred thousand timpani drums. Everyone stopped and craned their necks back to witness the amazing spectacle unfolding overhead. The center of the ship was opening. The aliens were preparing to communicate. Huge interlocking doors began to tilt downward. The entire mile-wide center of the ship, the dark circle at the center of the flower, slowly broke open to reveal the dimly lit interior. At the absolute center, one small area didn't move. This was the tip of a long needle-like structure. As the doors around it continued to drop away and apart, the needle began to lower itself over the city. It was long and thin, except near the bottom, where it flared out into a diamond shape, like a snake swallowing an apple. This shaft had a quality to it which made it look both biologically natural and utterly repulsive at the same time. The long neck of it poked below the bottom of the ship, dangling into the night sky like a newly budding flower while the doors continued to lower themselves, spreading apart like the bloom of a black steel rose. When the doors were perpendicular to the ground, the rumbling noise ceased, but the shaft of the needle continued forcing its way deeper into the sky until the tip of it was only two hundred feet above Tiffany and her new friends.

THE FIRST LADY'S helicopter darted between the skyscrapers, moving at its top speed. The pilot had seen what happened to Operation Welcome Wagon and was anxious to get his passengers out of harm's way. Although their destination lay to the northeast, the pilot took off south, the fastest way out of downtown.

"Maybe it's some kind of observation tower," one of her aides said of the hanging needle.

Then the green light began. From the tip of the needle, a wide glimmering ray lit up downtown, the light the same milky jade that had annihilated Operation Welcome Wagon. From the ocean to the foothills, everything human stopped to gasp at the light's eerie beauty. The soft beam was so lovely, so peaceful and magical, it seemed to be a sign of friendship. For a few minutes it seemed everything was going to be all right. There wouldn't be a confrontation after all. The light made it seem obvious earth was about to experience a harmonious close encounter. The parties on the several rooftops fell quiet. The history of the planet was about to change forever, and they knew they were right at the heart of the action. Holding their signs skyward, they waited for the communication to begin.

OUTSIDE WASHINGTON, at Andrews Air Force Base, the door of the helicopter was kicked open before the runners touched down on the tarmac. David's theory about the countdown was being taken very seriously now and there wasn't a moment to lose. Secret Service agents hustled President Whitmore and his entourage out the door, across the open runway, then up the boarding ramp into Air Force One. The 747's turbine jet engines were already revved up to full power, ready to launch the plane down the runway. Like clockwork, the boarding ramp was disengaged, and the pilot released the brakes, sending the airplane lurching forward into its take-off run. As they gained speed down the runway, the flight crew was buckling Julius, the last person up the stairs, into his seat. David, flipped open his laptop and watched the last few seconds tick off on the screen.

00:25 00:24 00:23 . . .

A WHITE TRACER beam shot straight down through the center of the green light onto the old First Interstate Building. Every alien lover within fifty feet wanted to claim the spot where the beam touched the roof, believing perhaps that one of them was about to be selected and lifted into the ship. They fought each other like wild dogs for the privilege of being earth's ambassador.

While they pushed and wrestled, Tiffany retreated to the mellower energy of the area near the stairs. Lots of portable televisions were plugged in, all showing the same sharp white ray was coming from the other ships around the world. In Paris, the beam was on top of Notre Dame cathedral; in Berlin it fell on the old Reichstag building; in Tokyo, the Emperor's Palace; the convention

"THIRTY-SIX SHIPS, POSSIBLE ENEMIES, ARE HEADED THIS WAY, MR. PRESIDENT. WHETHER WE LIKE IT OR NOT, WE MUST GO TO DEFCON THREE."

"MARTY, QUIT WASTING TIME AND GET OUT OF TOWN RIGHT NOW."

"MY GOD! MY GOD! IT'S DESTROYING EVERYTHING. WIDENING—"

"ALL SATELLITES, MICROWAVE, AND GROUND COMMUNICATIONS
WITH THE TARGET CITIES ARE GONE. WE BELIEVE WE'RE LOOKING
AT A TOTAL LOSS."

"MOMMY, WHAT HAPPENED?"

"I DON'T KNOW, DYLAN. MOMMY DOESN'T KNOW."

"HA! NEVER ANY SPACESHIPS RECOVERED BY THE GOVERNMENT?"

"THIS, LADIES AND GENTLEMEN, IS WHAT WE AFFECTIONATELY
REFER TO DOWN HERE AS THE FREAK SHOW."

"LISTEN, DOCTOR, MY BOY IS VERY SICK. HE NEEDS IMMEDIATE ATTENTION."

"IT'S FROM THE AMERICANS. THEY WANT TO ORGANIZE A COUNTEROFFENSIVE."

"WE'VE DONE WHAT WE COULD TO DIS-
GUISE IT. THE MISSILE'S NOSE CONE
IS GOING TO PROTRUDE SOMEWHAT."

"I'M A PILOT, WILL. I BELONG
IN THE AIR."

"NO, NO, NO. WE CAN'T GO YET. CIGARS, MAN. I GOTTA FIND SOME CIGARS."

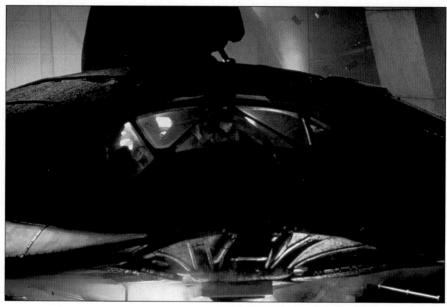

"I HAVE A CONFESSION TO MAKE. I'M NOT REAL BIG ON FLYING."

center in San Francisco; Central Park in New York; the Forbidden City in Beijing; the enormous dome of Tel Aviv's Great Synagogue; the statue of Nelson in London's Trafalgar Square, and, in Washington, D.C., the beam was fixed at the very tip of the Washington Monument.

Then the waiting was over. The white beam amplified noticeably. It turned brighter, much too bright to look at. Everyone within two miles turned away, burying their faces in their arms. Those who didn't felt their retinas begin to burn and warp. A whirring hum like a dentist's drill grew louder and louder until it was a piercing thunder. Terrified people on the rooftops fell to their knees clutching their overburdened ears and eyes, screaming silently into the sea of noise. Then, for a brief moment, everything stopped.

For the space of two heartbeats, the light disappeared and everything was quiet once more. The stunned believers had just enough time to uncover their eyes and look upwards for an answer.

WHAM!! A streak of blinding white light slammed down out of the needle. All at once, the old First Interstate exploded from the inside out, shattering into a billion fragments, none larger than a playing card. Tiffany never had time to scream. The thundering light poured down with unbelievable force, and within two seconds, the civic center was gone. A tidal wave blast of fire flared up, then began rolling outward, spreading in all directions at once. A wall of destruction, an awesome sea of fire, crashed through the city, taking everything in its path. Every wall of every building, every tree, every street sign, even the asphalt of the streets was burned up and blown away. A hurricane, a flood, and an atomic bomb blast all rolled into one, the wall of destruction hurled cars high into the air, shattered buildings like scarecrows in a tornado, and smothered the city under a thick layer of fire. The wall of destruction rolled outward from the epicenter, scouring the City of Angels off the planet.

Perhaps the most horrible aspect was how slowly it moved. An atomic blast would have incinerated its victims instantly, before they realized what was happening. But this fireball rolled through the city like a flash flood, allowing its victims plenty of time to see it coming. Everyone turned and ran, but there was nowhere to hide. The few people who managed to make it belowground, into cellars and bomb shelters, were suffocated. The firestorm sucked the oxygen right out of their lungs and cooked them where they hid.

In Washington, the White House and all the buildings flanking the mall area—the Lincoln and Jefferson Memorials, the Smithsonian museum complex—were instantly torn to shreds, decimated. From there, the blast materialized into a tidal wave of fire rushing outward. In the blink of an eye, it blew apart and instantly consumed the Capitol Building, taking most of the hill with it. In the other direction, the Pentagon was flattened, blown to smithereens.

The same grisly scene was repeating in cities around the world, everywhere the giant ships were stationed. Thirty-six of humanity's proudest creations, home to millions upon millions of people, were swiftly and systematically obliterated.

THE DIGITAL DISPLAY on David's laptop had ticked to zero six seconds before the rear wheels lifted off the runway. The savage burst of light which signaled the obliteration of Washington, D.C., had already flashed through the windows. David dug his fingers into the cushioned armrests of his chair and looked at the ceiling, waiting.

Julius was the only one who wasn't sweating. He understood there was nothing left to do except hope it wasn't his time. As the plane began to climb, everyone in the cabin took a relieved breath and allowed themselves to believe they'd survived. A second later, the wall of destruction reached Andrews AFB, still a hundred feet high. It tore through the base, ripping it to shreds as it chased the plane down the runway. The 747, slowly lumbering upward, was five hundred feet off the ground when the wall of fire caught up and shot past below. Although they were above the brunt of the blast, the air pressure at the front of the wall swelled up under the tail of the big plane and gave it a violent shove. Bottles shattered in the service area and luggage toppled into the aisle, but Air Force One narrowly escaped.

THE TUNNEL WAS a long gloomy concrete tube built back in the twenties. Narrow walkways on both sides gave way to alcoves with grime-caked wooden doors every few hundred feet. Along with her fellow drivers, Jasmine was listening to live news reports on the radio. The announcer's descriptions of the enchanting green light lured many drivers out of their cars. They took their keys and ran to the end of the tunnel, where they could stand on the cliff and witness the phenomenon for themselves. Jasmine leaned on her horn. She was only ten car lengths from the end of the tunnel and didn't care about any damned green light. Eventually, realizing she was pinned in, she cut the engine to save gas.

She listened with concern as the man on the radio described the blinding white ray cutting through the soft green light. Then, as the blast pounded down on the city, turning it to an inferno, the newsman began shouting hysterically.

"My God! My God! It's destroying everything. Widening—" Abruptly, the voice was gone.

Jasmine's instincts took over. She reached across and picked up Dylan, hoisting him out of the car. He had just enough time to grab his backpack with the precious fireworks Steve had given him. With her child in her arms, Jasmine broke into a sprint for the mouth of the tunnel, glancing over her shoulder as she went. Already, the sky behind her was burning orange and white. Needing somewhere to hide, she ducked into one of the maintenance alcoves cut into the rock wall. She tried the handle of the flimsy wooden door, but found it was locked. She turned around and checked the tunnel. The wall of destruction was speeding straight toward her. Terrified people bolted out of their cars and ran; others rolled up their windows and cringed.

All the lights in the tunnel suddenly went dark. She was out of time. She turned once more and kicked blindly at the door. The howling firestorm reached the mouth of the tunnel, gushing into the narrow opening with a deafening boom. Anguished screaming and the thunderous noise of cars being swept up and torn apart blasted toward her. Jas put Dylan on her hip, lowered the other shoulder, and rushed the door. The flimsy wood splintered and she crashed through to the other side, landing in a heap.

"*Boomer!*" she called, quickly scanning the inside of the workroom, lit by the approaching fire. She had landed on top of a wire mesh grating that opened onto an engineer's tunnel and the city's vast network of drainage canals. Boomer leaped off the hood of a car into the room, just as the fire tossed the vehicle away.

She rolled on top of Dylan, shielding the boy's body with hers. As the firestorm raged through the tunnel, a stiff wind came shooting upward through the wire grating. The stone walls of the alcove protected them from the brunt of the blast, but the fire had instantly consumed all the available oxygen. Now fresh air was sucked through the grating, creating a wind tunnel strong enough to blow Jasmine and Dylan into the fire. With Dylan locked under one arm, Jasmine put her fingers through the grating and held on for dear life as the fire fed itself. Without the steady rush of cool air moving over their bodies, the three of them would have been incinerated by the heat.

Then, suddenly, it was over. Thousands of tons of boulders and loose earth clogged the tunnel at both ends. The hillside had collapsed. Jasmine, still trembling, rolled over on to her back. She knew she was lucky to be alive. What she didn't know was that the three of them, the only ones still alive inside the tunnel, were buried under millions of pounds of dirt.

TOKYO SUSTAINED the highest number of casualties. More than anywhere else, the Japanese had tried to go about their business as usual without panicking. Once the intricate train scheduling system had gotten knocked out of synch, the stations turned into madhouses. Half of those who did manage to get out of the city in time did so on foot or on bicycles. The destruction of the high-rise city, until then the world's most expensive real estate, was utter and complete. The area leveled by the blast was four times as wide as the H-bombs exploded over Hiroshima and Nagasaki decades earlier. The wall of destruction ended every human life within a twenty-mile radius. As far away as Yokohama and Omiya, half the population had been killed.

Manhattan was gone. The island was transformed into a barren shelf of land, swept clean of buildings all the way up to Yonkers. Amid the choking swirl of dust and smoke, natural gas lines shot towers of flame into the sky. Twisted brick and concrete foundations showed where the buildings had been torn away. Only a few hundred people, mainly those in deep sections of the subway system, had survived. On the south side of Staten Island and deep into New Jersey, those who had not been killed outright by the wall of destruction lay trapped beneath their collapsed homes, their bodies blistered with severe burns.

There was not a single human survivor anywhere on earth close enough to watch the long, needle-shaped firing cones retract into the ships. The petal doors raised slowly to form an impenetrable, airtight seal. The huge ships, the city destroyers, were ready to move on to the next set of targets.

"GOD DAMN. I KNEW IT. I knew it. I knew it! I've been trying to warn everybody about these suckers for ten years." Russell lowered the volume on the radio without taking his eyes off the road. "Kids," he yelled over his shoulder, "haven't I been trying to warn people?"

Liquored up, he had no inkling of how distressed and traumatized his children were by what they'd heard on the radio. Alicia was sobbing, her face resting on the linoleum tabletop. Miguel, his arm around her, stared blankly out the window at the Joshua trees passing through the headlights.

"Where's Troy?" Russell asked into the rearview mirror.

The youngest member of the Casse clan called from his bed at the back. "You guys," he said in a weak voice, "I don't feel so good."

Russell looked over his shoulder. "When's the last time you had any medicine?"

"I can't remember," the boy moaned. "I think about three or four days ago."

"That's not true," Miguel said, "I gave you some this morning."

"I know, but I didn't take it. I thought I didn't need it anymore."

"What did you do with it, Troy? Where's the medicine?"

Instead of answering, the boy stood up and moved to the door, gesturing that he needed to go outside. Russell pulled to the side of the road and Troy ran outside. A moment later, he was vomiting into the weeds while Alicia helped him keep his balance.

Russell wandered away down the road a bit, far enough to sneak a swig of whiskey without hearing it from the kids. They were in the middle of Death Valley, somewhere near the Nevada border, and it was a spectacular night. A billion stars burned in the sky. Russell strolled along with his head rolled back on his shoulders. At the crest of a small hill, he noticed something odd, a different sort of constellation.

"Miguel!" he called quietly. "Come take a look at this!"

Spread across the floor of a shallow desert valley, a thousand campers, trailers, RVs, and passenger vehicles had congregated at a rest stop in the middle of nowhere. The shimmering lights coming from this makeshift refugee city echoed the stars above. In a way, it was a beautiful scene.

"Ain't that somethin'?"

"Maybe somebody down there's got some medicine," Miguel said. "Let's go ask."

AT THE BEGINNING of the end of the world, Steve was in the empty cafeteria building trying to make a call. Over and over, he dropped the quarter into the slot and carefully pecked out Jasmine's telephone number. And every time, a mechanical voice answered: "All circuits are presently busy. Please hang up and try your call again later."

Fishing the coin out of the cradle, he dumped it right back in. He knew the base commanders were itching to order a counterstrike, but until they got the go-ahead from Washington, there was nothing for Steve to do but imagine all the horrible things that might have happened to Jas and Dylan.

"All circuits are presently busy. Please hang up and—"

"*Damn it!*" Steve slammed the phone down on the hook just as Jimmy turned the corner and came sprinting down the hallway.

"Let's roll, daddy-o," he shouted. "Orders just came in." Jimmy, already in his flight suit, was pumped full of adrenaline, but he calmed himself when he noticed Steve was torn up about something. "Wassup?"

Steve didn't try to hide his feelings. "I can't get through to my parents' house or to Jasmine. She was supposed to be here *hours* ago, man."

Jimmy moved approached his friend carefully, as he would a spooked thoroughbred race horse. "Hey brother," he said laying a hand on Steve's shoulder, "didn't you hear what happened? These freakazoid spacemen took Los Angeles out. Blew it up. Did the same thing to Washington, San Francisco, and New York. They're packing some very serious firepower, bro."

When he heard the news, he pressed his hands to his head. "No," he moaned, "don't tell me that, man. Oh, I fucked up, Jimmy. I fucked everything up. Why didn't I just put her in the car and bring her with me?" Steve kicked a nearby vending machine a couple of times, then punched himself in the forehead. "What the hell was I thinking?"

Jimmy grabbed him by the shoulders and slammed him up against the wall, shocking him temporarily out of his anger. "Listen. She might still show up. If she was on her way here, maybe she got out in time. But either way, don't you go ballistic on me. We still have a job to do." He let go of his friend's uniform and backed away. Steve was looking straight at him, but his mind was obviously elsewhere. Jimmy didn't know what else to say, so he decided to give him some space. "There's a meeting in J201 in five minutes. Be there."

Fifteen minutes later, Steve stood outside the briefing room. After a deep breath, he threw the door open and sauntered in, his old cocky self. In all, there were thirty-five pilots sitting at school desks listening to Lieutenant Colonel Watson feed them intelligence about the enemy. Watson, muscular and fifty, was one of those spit and polish marines who expected everything to be by the book and wasn't real bashful about criticizing you if you did it differently. He never knew exactly what to think of the Hiller/Franklin team. They were his best pilots, his aces. But they were also a pair of jokers who were constantly bending the rules.

When Steve walked in, one look at Watson stopped him dead in his tracks. The colonel wasn't in uniform. He was wearing Levi's and black crew shirt, the clothes he'd rushed back to the base in. Caught up in the crisis, none of the other men had commented on the boss being in civvies. But when Steve walked in, the whole atmosphere of the room changed. He gave Watson a long, dead pan stare, then let his jaw drop wide open as he turned to the roomful of pilots. They had to laugh.

"Captain Hiller, you found time to join us!"

Steve knew what that meant and quickly found the seat his boys had saved him. Watson described how the mother ship was lurking behind the moon, well out of missile range, and how the city destroyer ships had detached themselves for the flight down to earth. He showed them the piss-poor satellite photo faxed to him by Space Command, but there was little he could tell them about it.

It didn't take long for Steve to figure out that Jimmy had said something to the other guys. He felt them looking at him, searching his face for signs of distraction. But Steve was too good, too smart, too much of a pro to show the slightest hint of doubt to the men he expected to follow him into battle. While Watson lectured, he leaned over real slowly and, with a sideways glance at Jimmy, asked, "You scared, man?"

"No," he whispered. "You?"

"Naw." Steve dismissed the idea, but then twisted his face up as if he were about to cry. "Actually, I am. Hold me!" That was it. The Black Knights burst out laughing in the back of the room.

Watson was just about finished when the laughter erupted. Normally he'd be angry, but he knew why Steve was acting the way he was. Besides, he didn't know if any of these boys were going to live past lunchtime.

"Captain Hiller," he asked sarcastically, "did you want to add something to the briefing?"

"Sorry, sir. It's just that we're all real anxious to get up there and kick us some alien ass."

Watson smiled. "Then let's do it."

THE BLACK KNIGHTS marched to their planes, clearly in possession of something no amount of equipment or training could give them. They had the supreme confidence that only comes from knowing you are the very best. They came striding across the airfield in a loose cluster around their leader, Captain Steven Hiller. As they approached their fortified hangar, the huge doors rolled open exactly on cue. Inside were thirty-five F/A-18s, the USMC's elite air-fighting equipment, the gleaming planes surrounded by technicians making last-minute adjustments.

"Now remember," Steve shouted to his men before they scattered, "we're the first ones up there, so we're just gonna check 'em out. See what they got. If we run into anything real hairy, we'll break it off and regroup back here. All right, let's fly." The men broke ranks and headed for their individual planes. As their boots squeaked across the polished concrete, Steve asked over his shoulder, "Jimmy, you bring the victory dance?"

"That's a big affirmative, Captain." He pulled a long Cuban cigar out of his breast pocket, popped it in his mouth, and sparked up his lighter. It had become a ritual with them to light up these expensive, smuggled cigars after every successful mission.

"Don't get premature on me, Flash Gordon," Steve called out, climbing into the cockpit. "Remember, we don't light up till the Fat Lady sings."

"Gotcha, cap," Jimmy answered, feeling good that Steve had bounced back from the loss of his girlfriend.

As soon as Steve was alone in his plane, he doubled over in pain. He couldn't stop thinking about Jasmine and Dylan. The pilots strapped themselves in, ran through their equipment check, then fired up their engines and taxied out to the runway.

THE PRESIDENT SAT by himself in one of the conference areas, lost in thought. Connie slipped into one of the big leather chairs next to her boss. For a few moments, the two of them sat there listening to the muted roar of the engines. Everyone on the plane was suffering through their own personal state of shock, but it troubled her to see the president sitting motionless, staring blankly at the palms of his hands. She didn't need to ask what he was thinking. She already knew his conscience was torturing him. Millions of Americans had died within the last hour and he took personal responsibility.

"You played it as well as anybody could, Tom. You saved a lot of lives. There's no use in second-guessing yourself."

Whitmore didn't look up at her, didn't move a muscle. "I could have evacuated the cities hours ago. I should have." He sighed deeply. "Everything was so simple when I flew in the Gulf War. We knew what we had to do, and we did it. Nothing's simple anymore. A lot of people died today, Connie." He looked up at her for the first time. "How many of them didn't have to?"

Connie realized he was in no mood to be comforted. Instead, she showed her support by staying with him, sitting quietly until General Grey came down the walkway. Before he could deliver his news, the president looked up and asked eagerly, "Is there any news on my wife?"

Grey's face lost all its strength. He hesitated for a moment before delivering the blow. "The helicopter still hasn't arrived at Nellis and there's been no radio contact. I'm very sorry." The general looked down at the tops of his shoes and added, "I've instructed the tower at Nellis to send out a search plane to look for the beacon signal." Each of the presidential helicopters was equipped with an isotope-powered signal beacon allowing the authorities to trace it in the event of a highjacking, but so far nothing had shown up on the radar screens. Either the cloud of debris and smoke in the air around Los Angeles was blocking the signal, or, as Grey suspected, the machine had been hit so hard that everything, including the titanium casing around the transmitter, was blown to shreds.

All three of them were positive now that the First Lady had been killed in the blast. The president's face lost all its color. He felt like he'd just been kicked in the gut. But he was still the leader of his nation and he responded by quickly refocusing on his duty. "What other news have you got?"

"The fighters are in the air."

Whitmore took a deep breath, got to his feet, and followed the general to the rear of the plane. Everything had just gotten a lot simpler. It was time to make war.

The two men stepped into the military command center set up aboard Air Force One. In sharp contrast to the muted colors and executive comforts on the rest of the aircraft, the command center was a tight space crammed to the gills with sophisticated equipment that hissed, blinked, oscillated, and scanned. From floor to ceiling, the narrow room was buzzing with radar screens and multichannel radio consoles, technicians in headphones working at computers, maps, and a small glass war table along one wall on which they could keep track of enemy positions.

Nimziki was already inside, staring down into the lights of the war table, studying the movements of the city destroyers. The expression on his face was somewhere between sorrow and disgust. Without being able to pinpoint what it was in Nimziki's attitude, Whitmore knew at a glance that the man was acting a role, trying to convince the others in the flying fortress their president was incompetent. Right from the start, he'd been using the crisis to chip away at Whitmore's self-confidence.

And it was working. Although he despised the secretary of defense on a personal level, he began to wonder whether this kind of situation would be better handled by a stone-hearted tactician like Nimziki. Whitmore felt like perhaps his instincts were beginning to fail him. His political instincts, he knew, were already in sad shape, but he was also starting to lose confidence in his combat instincts. He knew beyond question that he was a warrior, but the business of commanding whole armies was another matter. He strode over the war table and looked into it, assessing the depth of the catastrophe.

"All satellites, microwave, and ground communications with the target cities are gone. We believe we're looking at a total loss," Grey explained in hushed, somber tones. Another slug in the president's gut.

Maintaining his composure, Whitmore looked up at one of the several tracking screens.

"Where are the fighters?"

Grey checked with a technician quickly before calling out, "ETA with target is four minutes."

Nimziki crossed the room and sat down at one of the radio consoles, putting on a set of headphones for a phone call to NORAD and the joint chiefs.

FLYING THROUGH POCKETS of mild turbulence over the Midwest, the 747 experienced some slight shuddering. The unsteadiness went completely unnoticed by the men inside the command center, but out in the passenger area, David suffered through each lift and fall as if it was the Coney Island Roller coaster. His face was covered with sweat and he had a barf bag, emblazoned with the presidential seal, lying ready on his lap. Connie sat nearby, making a string of phone numbers on her cellular. Julius kept a watch out the window, trying to enjoy the view, but David's behavior was becoming an embarrassment.

"It's Air Force One, for crying out loud," he said in disgust, "and still you get airsick?"

"Dad, please. Don't talk."

Either Julius didn't hear him, or he didn't care. "Look at me," he stood up in the aisle and pounded his fist against his stomach, "solid as a rock. Good weather, bad weather, doesn't matter." Then, with David looking weakly up at him, he used his hands to illustrate his story. "We can go up and down, up and down and it doesn't get to me. Back and forth, side to side . . . "

David's eyes went wide and watery as he watched his father show all the ways a plane ride could make you sick to your stomach. Suddenly, he and his barf bag hightailed it toward the restrooms at the rear of the plane. Julius looked at Connie. "What did I say?"

Connie slid into the seat beside her father-in-law. "He still gets airsick, huh?"

"Hodophobia. Fear of travel, that's what he calls it."

"Listen," Connie reached across the seat and took the old man's hand, "in all the excitement, I haven't had a chance to thank you two. You saved a lot of lives. Mine included."

Julius leaned closer and smiled mischievously. "Think nothing of it, *Spanky*."

"You mean *Spunky*." She laughed. "Haven't heard that in a long time. He told you about that?"

He checked to see who might be listening, then confided a secret to her. "As soon as he figured out this thing with the signal, all he could think about was getting to you. There's still love there, I think."

Connie sighed. "Love was never our problem."

"'All you need is love,'" Julius quoted. "That's John Lennon, a smart man. Shot in the back. Very sad."

Connie nodded in agreement, trying to conceal a smile.

FOUR HOURS AFTER the blast came ripping through the tunnel, sealing them inside a vast tomb, Jasmine thought she had finally found an exit.

She had lifted the wire grating and climbed down into the labyrinth of storm drainage pipes that crisscrossed the city. The concrete passageways had flat floors, twelve-foot ceilings, and absolutely no light. There was the sound of trickling water and the faint smell of oil. At first, Jasmine tried to convince Boomer to lead the way through the pitch darkness, but the dog was a coward, leaving it to her to feel their way along. The moist walls were full of damp, slimy surprises. They had moved slowly along for a few hundred feet, when Jasmine heard something that sounded like footsteps. Her heart turned to stone as the idea occurred to her that the invaders might already be in the sewer with her.

She knelt down and put her hand over Dylan's mouth, whispering very low, "Listen."

The smell of the gunpowder in Dylan's fireworks reminded her there was a book of matches in his backpack. As quietly as she could, she unzipped the pencil pouch, found the matches, and lit one. The chamber was empty in both directions. The match burned low and was extinguished by an imperceptible breeze. Realizing a breeze must mean an opening to the outside, she led her family forward as quietly as possible, listening for more footsteps. She picked her son up and could feel how scared he was becoming.

"You're doing a great job, baby, keep quiet." Any other six-year-old kid would be bawling his eyes out by now, Jasmine thought.

Creeping steadily along the wall, Jasmine's senses were on full alert. Several times, she thought she heard the footsteps again. Each time, she lit another match and saw nothing. Then she sensed a faint flow of air brushing across her face. She set Dylan down and searched the walls with her hands until she found an opening. It was a small square gap about four feet off the ground. Cautiously, she reached an arm through the hole and explored what lay beyond. She was half expecting her fingers to find something from another, unfriendly galaxy. Suddenly she gasped and pulled her hands back. She had seen something moving through the darkness. It took her a few moments to realize it had been the faint outline of her own hands. There was light seeping through the opening which connected to another tunnel above, a way out of this watery indoor grave.

"Baby, I think there's a way out of here. I'm gonna lift you up and you tell me if you can see anything, okay?"

As soon as Dylan's head was through the opening, he yelled, "I see a light! It's outside light!"

A few minutes later, Jas was walking toward the sunlight at the open mouth of the upper tunnel. An overturned car was smoldering just outside. With Boomer in the lead, they picked their way between dangling electrical cables and hunks of mangled automobiles, crumpled like wads of used tin foil.

When they came to the mouth of the tunnel and looked out into the blinding morning light, they saw a new world: postapocalypse LA. Eighteen miles from the epicenter, the neighborhood into which the Dubrows emerged looked like Nagasaki after the bomb. Most buildings, especially those along the east-west streets where the firestorm had moved fastest, were gone, kneecapped at their foundations and blown away. The ground was the gray color of ashes and the sky was a sickly off-white color, swirling with a mixture of dust and ash. There was no sign of life, and for a moment Jasmine wondered if she and Dylan might be the last two people on earth.

The boy reached for his mother's hand and without knowing why began to cry. "Mommy, what happened?"

Jasmine picked him up and stepped out of the tunnel. "I don't know, Dylan. Mommy doesn't know."

High above, the roar of engines punished the sky. A squadron of thirty-five jet fighters was flying north, toward the spaceship over Los Angeles.

"Is that Steve in the planes?"

"It might be. I hope so. Why don't you wave, just in case."

HUGGING THE Orange County coastline, the Black Knights thundered toward the battle at an elevation of eleven thousand feet. The missile fields at Seal Beach looked to be operational, but inland the destruction was complete. The wall of fire had cut a large circle of devastation into the area. All around the perimeter, fires continued to burn, lit by the flaming debris the blast had sent flying through the air.

The spaceship was visible on the horizon, hanging like cast-iron doom over the ring of mountains surrounding Los Angeles. Towering columns of black smoke roiled upward from the remains of the oil refinery at Wilmington, causing the Knights to swerve a few miles out over the postcard blue Pacific, its shoreline awash with a million tons of spilled oil and twisted wreckage. Steve studied the destruction, stone-faced. It was now clear to him that Jasmine must be dead. If she had made it beyond the reach of the blast, she would have reported to El Toro long ago. He muttered something in frustration and punched the wall of the cockpit.

"Don't you sweat it, daddy-o," Jimmy's voice came through the earphones in stereo. "I'm sure she got out in time." The line stayed quiet for a long moment until Steve spoke to the entire squad.

"Here we go, boys. Time to lock and load."

Steve reached forward to the computer screen set into the instrument panel and entered a series of commands. Immediately the cantilevered doors along the belly of the fighter dropped open ready to dump their AMRAAMs (Advanced Medium-Range Air-to-Air Missiles). At the same time, a mechanical arm inside the cockpit brought a sighting device to within inches of the pilot's headgear. This was the scope on the plane's FLIR (Forward-Looking InfraRed) targeting system. Looking through the eyepiece, the sky in front of him was transformed into a pulsing gray-and-yellow computer world. He brought the crosshairs down on the image of the spaceship, adjusting them until the tower was in the bull's eye.

The technicians aboard Air Force One took over the air waves. "Los Angeles attack squadron has AMRAAM missiles locked on target."

"New York and Washington squadrons also reporting lock on."

A new voice came over the radio. "Gentlemen, this is Air Force General Grey, Chief Commander of Allied Space Command. On behalf of the president of the United States, who is here aboard Air Force One, and the joint chiefs operating out of NORAD, I want to wish you all a successful mission. Godspeed. You may fire at will."

The Black Knights were still ten miles away, thirty seconds out of firing range, but the sheer enormity of the ship made them feel much closer. As the details of the ship's exterior grew clearer and more defined, so did the lump in each pilot's throat. The normally boisterous radio communication between the Knights was grimly silent.

"Hold tight," Steve told everyone, "fifteen seconds."

"Looks like one of those seventeen-year ticks we get down in Charlotte," drawled one of the pilots, trying to lighten the mood.

"We'll let's do a little exterminating," Steve held them steady, "five more seconds . . . and . . . *fire!*"

The AMRAAMs dropped away and went sprinting out ahead. Radar targeted, they banked slightly toward the target area like a school of minnows swooping to attack a giant gray whale. With their payloads away, the F-18's began to pull up. Few of the pilots seriously expected a ship of this size to go down all at once. The mission called for them to hit the ship in several different areas, reconnoiter to see which type of strike had done the most damage, then provide intelligence to the next wave of attack planes, already sitting on the runway at El Toro. As the F-18s banked away, they kept a careful watch on their missiles. Suddenly, a quarter mile from their target, they all exploded at the same time.

"Damn it!"

"I didn't even see them fire," Jimmy said, obviously impressed. When the smoke began to clear, it was obvious that the alien ship had sustained no damage.

Steve radioed back to Air Force One. "Command, this is Knight One. The target appears to have shot our AMRAAMs down. Zero damage to target. Repeat: zero damage. We're going to switch over to Sidewinders and take it in a little closer."

"Good call, Knight One," Grey replied. "Spread formation."

"Six times five, fellas. Six times five."

The smaller Sidewinder missiles were short-range munitions that would give the spacecraft a tougher test of its air-to-air defense capabilities. This time, instead of thirty bombs, the Knights would give them one hundred and eighty to shoot at. The squadron broke into six separate groups, roaring off in different directions to surround the fifteen-mile-wide disk. It made sense that if the aliens had air-to-air defenses, they'd be located in the tower at the nose of the craft. When everyone was in position, Steve gave the order to charge.

"Everybody check your radar, we're starting from seven miles out. Let's bring it in closer this time. Launch at one mile."

One mile? That's a comfortable distance when you're standing still, but when you're streaking along at four hundred miles per hour on a collision course with something a hundred times larger than the Superdome, it doesn't leave much margin for error. Steve knew that was shaving it pretty close, but he was hungry to inflict some damage on the craft before they headed back to the base.

"Attack!"

At the signal, all thirty jet fighters wheeled in unison and rocketed toward the spaceship, moving in from all sides. Looking through the scopes on their FLIR systems, the pilots nervously watched the numbers count down on their "Distance to Target" displays, the yellow sky disappearing into a growing blot of gray. When it felt like they were right on top of the craft, the one mile marker clicked in, triggering the Sidewinders to fire automatically. Six missiles blasted forward from each ship, their solid rocket fuel leaving a thin contrail in their wake. Almost at once, they reached the same quarter-mile perimeter and, like the AMRAAMs, exploded as a group.

"Pull up! Pull up!!" Steve screamed. "They got a shield!!" From his front row seat, he suddenly realized why the missiles weren't hitting. Yanking back on the controls, Hiller threw the plane into a right angle turn straight up, the kind of turn that holds you against a seat as if an elephant was sitting on your lap. Twenty-nine Knights made the turn in time. The last man, Zolfeghari, came in too fast. Trying to duck under a slower plane ahead, the hull of his jet did a belly flop against an invisible force field, splattering his plane into explosion of jet fuel that spilled down the side of the invisible shield.

Steve's group streaked vertically up the face of the tower. "They must have some kind of protective shield surrounding their hull. Let's head home."

But it wasn't going to be that easy. As the squad continued up the face of the tower, a set of massive doors were opening. They pulled back fast, as if yanked open by the strong hands of a giant, and from the opening came a storm of small attacker planes. Forty or fifty pearl gray ships came darting out of the port, single file. They were exiting the city destroyer through the exact airspace Steve and his men had already committed to using.

As he headed into the cross-fire intersection, Steve looked toward the open door and saw the next attacker speeding toward him, the face of the plane almost at his canopy window, bearing down like a huge, hungry insect. By the time, he braced himself for the impact he was already one hundred yards beyond the danger point. The next three pilots made it through, but the fourth, a man called "Big Island" Tubman didn't. His jet collided head-on with one of the disk-shaped ships, causing a thunderous explosion right at the city destroyer's front door. While Tubman's plane fragmented on impact, the enemy fighter remained intact. It wobbled forward, as if momentarily stunned, before regaining its balance and flying off as if nothing had happened.

On his way through the cross-traffic, Steve had glimpsed a massive staging area inside the city destroyer. The ship's attack bay looked like an indoor airport, with hundreds of the small attackers parked in clusters along the walls. The monumental architecture of the room reminded him of some sort of hive or nest. Adjusting the yaw to flip his F-18 upside-down, Steve watched the gray planes pour into the sky. Instead of moving in a stable formation, the pack, now perhaps one hundred strong, bobbed up and down, weaving from side to side. Seen from a distance, they seemed to flutter like a swarm of bats.

Without warning, they broke off in different directions to answer the attack on their ship.

"Mayday! Mayday! Enemy planes in the sky. Coming out of the tower." A shriek of light whizzed past Steve's plane, then another. "What the fudge?" He craned his neck around and saw one of the hungry-looking gray ships had come out of nowhere and slipped in behind him.

"Check six," Jimmy warned him. "Check your six, Stevie."

"I see him." Steve knew he had to think fast. The whole group of American planes was still moving toward a rendezvous over the top of the city destroyer and the faster enemy ships were surrounding them. Should he have the squad meet at the top where they could defend one another, or would that make them sitting ducks in a shooting gallery? He'd never seen a situation like this and didn't know which tactic to order. Multiplying his confusion was the fact that he had been made by the alien pilot in no time flat. Steve considered himself the craftiest pilot he knew, and to be outfoxed at the very beginning of a dog-fight was another new experience for him.

"Evasive maneuvers!" he yelled, jamming his own plane into a sudden sideways loop only milliseconds before a barrage of laser shots sailed by. "Stay in your groups! Keep your spacing."

The gray enemy planes, gliding like metallic stingrays, were firing pulses of super-condensed energy, deadly balls of light that screamed as they sizzled through the sky, leaving a bright white trail. Trying to lose his pursuer, Steve bobbed and weaved his way toward the edge of the black city destroyer. In the commotion, he saw a pair of abrupt explosions as two of his team were blown away. At flight school, they'd emphasized over and over how quickly air battles were won or lost, how drastically they could change in only a few seconds. Here was the proof. The proud Knights, champions of the sky a moment before, were now having their asses handed to them, hunted down and killed. Disorganized and on the run, they broke into pairs, covering one another as they ran for cover.

Steve plunged into a nose dive, accelerating straight toward the ground. His attacker followed. As the blackened earth that had been Los Angeles rushed closer, Steve fought the impulse to slow down. He remembered what happened to the Apache helicopter during Operation Welcome Wagon and increased his speed. In the next ten seconds he would be either very lucky or very dead.

"Where you at, Jimmy?"

"Right where you need me, Stevie, on this motherfucker's tail. If you can straighten him out for me, I'll waste him."

Steve ceased evasive maneuvers and flew in a straight line for as long as he dared—a total of about 1.5 seconds. Fortunately, that was all Jimmy needed.

"Away!" he yelled. As Steve peeled away into a starboard bank, Jimmy's Sidewinder shot forward and overtook the alien attacker. Five yards before the missile reached the surface of the ship, it exploded. The ship flipped over in midair, staggered forward for a moment, then zipped back into action as if nothing had happened.

"Shit! These little guys got shields, too!"

Steve came out of his dive and looped upward, ready to take a shot at the disoriented attacker plane. In the distance, he watched two more of the American fighters shredded by tracer fire. By the time he was in position again, Jimmy had an enemy on his tail.

"Jimmy, roll right. I'll cover."

Jimmy barrel rolled away just in time to avoid a new burst of tracer fire. Steve brought the crosshairs down on one of the gray stingray planes and fired another sidewinder. The alien pilot banked away, but the tracking system inside the missile chased him down and detonated against his rear protective shield. Radar-guidance was about the only hardware advantage the humans had in this dogfight, and it wasn't buying them much time. For a few seconds, Hiller and Franklin flew unmolested along the crest of the Hollywood Hills. Above them, they watched the fluttering gray ships hunting in packs, tearing the F-18s, and their brother pilots, to ribbons. The sky was littered with tracer fire and the fiery wreckage of America's elite air strike force. A new pair of attackers came racing toward them from above the ship, unleashing a hailstorm of firepower.

"Maybe we can outrun them. Follow my lead."

"Let's run, then. Here they come at two o'clock, Stevie."

The powerful jet engines of the F/A-18s surged into a higher gear when the Americans hit the SuperCruise control. They shot forward, speeding east over the mountains and leaving the enemy aircraft far behind. Or so they thought. As the planes accelerated, both pilots experienced the phenomenon of "pulling a few gees." One gee is equal to the force of gravity at sea level. Moving from below Mach speed all the way up to Mach 2 in a matter of a few seconds was something like being strapped to the nose cone of a moon rocket. It was the extreme physical discomfort of feeling your organs crash backwards against the seat as the plane rocketed forward. Ears, lips, cheeks—everything tried to slide backwards off their faces. The landscape below them rushed past in a blur. When they were up to speed, both men felt dizzy and slightly nauseated. Steve struggled to get a look behind them. The stingray ships were close behind and gaining.

"Jimmy, kick it, man. They're gaining on us."

"We're already over Mach Two." Jimmy sounded woozy.

"So push it!" Once again, the two pilots were flattened against the backs of their cockpit chairs. The instrument panels showed that they were pushing their planes way beyond the intended limits, zooming out across the California desert at twice the speed of sound.

"Gotta get off the ground, partner. I'm . . . uh, I'm feeling . . . I don't know." Jimmy was losing consciousness. He knew increasing his altitude would make the landscape, now flashing by at a dizzying pace, appear to move slower.

Steve thought the attackers showed some reluctance about getting too close to the ground, but Jimmy was already building altitude, so he followed.

"Keep it straight, Jimmy, you're veering right."

"You get out, Stevie."

"Don't start that crap on me. We're together all the way, you hear? But you gotta keep your speed up, man."

Steve slowed to keep him in sight, watching his jet continue to drift right. The attackers began to close in. "We gotta go, Jimmy! Gotta push it!"

It was no use. The attackers were tucked in tight behind them, tracer fire whizzing past. Steve screamed into his microphone, begging Jimmy to wake up, but it was no use. He took a quick glance backward and saw his partner's silver jet flying itself, already miles away. Just as he was about to turn and follow, he saw the flash of light. The enemy planes had split up and the one following Jimmy had shot him down.

Steve screamed with his whole body and began shaking the controls, making the plane convulse with his anger. He rammed the engine thrusters forward so hard he bent the shaft against the stop, and still screaming, he pushed the plane to the very limit of its speed. At Mach 2-plus, the desert was a fast blur of brown scrub hills crossed by flashes of highways and small towns. It felt like being in the flight simulator with the pursuit speed setting stuck on "Impossible." For a couple of minutes, anger and pain still clouding his mind, Steve flew in a straight line without checking behind. Given the opportunity, he would have flown kamikaze, head-on into any attacker in his way. His rage subsiding, he finally checked behind and found he had a single attacker at five o'clock, trailing him patiently. He knew there was no way he could win a firefight. Escape was his only hope. But, as he flew through a cloudless sky over the vast empty stretches of Death Valley, there weren't too many places to hide. Something glinted far out on the white horizon of the desert, a city rising out of nowhere. He banked north and flew that direction. Within seconds, the distant city was beneath his plane. Steve could see enough, just enough, to tell him the city was Las Vegas.

The engines were feeling the strain. Their whining told Steve they wouldn't take this kind of punishment much longer. Still running north, he flew past what looked like a small airbase with a pair of crisscrossed runways built on a dry lake bed. A pair of radar dishes were pivoting on their towers, and it looked like there were camouflage trucks parked next to a couple of hangars. His eyes searched for any sign that they knew what was happening to him and were sending help. He didn't recognize the place at all, didn't know of any base this far north of Vegas.

Then, all at once, he knew exactly what he was going to do. He pulled a hard right over the airbase and lifted over the chain of hills that had created the lake bed ten thousand years before. He checked his compass for due east and turned in that direction. In less than two minutes, he found what he was looking for, his secret weapon: the Grand Canyon.

He cut his engines without warning. The stingray ship, surprised, sailed past as Steve executed a soft dive over the edge of the canyon wall. He drove the plane deep between the red rock walls until he was almost low enough to fish in the Colorado River, the body of water which, over millions of years, had cut this awesome, jagged wonder out of the hard desert floor. The attacker followed him down and caught up in no time.

"Okay, jerk-off. Let's have some fun."

Weaving at high speed through the twisted, eerie rock formations, Steve put on a clinic in advance aerobatics, banking, diving, and swerving like mad. The much larger attack plane followed clumsily behind, the tips of its wings chipping spires of rock into the abyss below. The alien's protective shield allowed him to make mistake after mistake and survive. Not only that, but he seemed to be getting the hang of flying through this obstacle course, managing to get off a few shots at Steve's F-18.

Feeling the pressure, Steve ducked into a much smaller side canyon. Here there was almost no room for error. The serpentine path narrowed in some places to only twice the jet's wing span. Steve knew better than to fly defensively at a time like this. He hit the gas and attacked the turns, climbing and falling with grace. He felt certain that if he kept this ballet going long enough, his clumsy dance partner would eventually plaster himself face-first against the rocks. Then a sensor on the instrument panel began flashing on and off. His fuel tank was almost empty.

"Damn it! You're really starting to burn me up, you damn Darth Vader wannabe."

Not far ahead, a massive wall of stone stood where the canyon came to a dead end. Knowing that once he was out of the canyon he was a dead man,

Steve decided to go for broke. He eased off on the speed and hit a switch labeled "Fuel Drop." Reserve fuel in both tanks spewed into the air behind him, splattering the gray ship. Then he hit the afterburners, igniting the fuel in the air, leaving a trail of superheated fire in his wake. Steve looked back just in time to see the attacker burst through the wall of flame, undaunted.

"Damn you! Okay, if you're the sucker who's gonna take me out, I want to see if you can fly under cover."

Pulling the cord marked "drag chute," a large parachute suddenly shot open behind his fighter. With a lightning reflex, Steve hit the release, detaching the cords from the plane before he was rear-ended. As he hoped, the chute fluttered shapelessly in the air for a second before the attacker ran into it nose first. The alarm buzzer was now ringing in Steve's earphones, the signal that his fuel was completely gone. He felt the engines hesitate as pockets of air came through the fuel lines.

"Now let's see if you're fully equipped."

Steve unplugged his headset, tightened up his seat belt, and pointed his plane right at the dead end wall. Behind him the attacker brushed against the side of the gorge tearing the parachute away. He accelerated hard to catch the F-18.

Two hundred feet from impact, Steve shut his eyes and yanked up hard on a cord running down to the bottom of his seat. A moment later, there was an ear splitting *thwack* as the plane demolished itself against the precipice.

The alien pilot saw what was coming and swerved violently upward. He came within ten feet of cleanly scaling the wall, but instead, the stingray ship went nose to nose with a boulder one hundred times its size and lost. Sending a shower of dust and splintered rock into the air, the craft plowed into the rock, then glanced away, flipping end over end over end, crashing across the rocky desert floor until it finally came to rest, looking like a coin bent almost in half.

Still strapped in his pilot's chair, Captain Hiller laughed as loud as he could at the broken UFO. He was slowly falling through the hot Arizona morning beneath the shade of his open parachute. When he finally hit the ground, it was a quick, hard landing. Rolling over, he popped the buckles on the chair and freed himself. Wasting no time, he marched across the sand and rock toward the nearby attacker, the cicadas chirping a strange high pitched tone in the scrub brush. He was dazed, maniacal, angry.

The closer he came, the more menacing the fallen attacker appeared. It was protected by a dozen plates of armor. One of these had torn partially loose where the tail of the ship had bent upward. Beneath the gray plate, it had the raw look of a freshly skinned animal. The ship's muscles, tendons, and ligaments were actually thousands of tiny interlocking mechanical pieces. A delicate, ghastly white, they lay exposed to the sun, embedded in a thick layer of transparent, sticky gelatin.

Steve took the last few steps toward the ship slowly, hands out in front of him, feeling for the invisible protective shield. It was down. Spotting what looked like a hatch that had been broken open, he hoisted himself up onto the wing, and after seven full strides, he came to the center of the craft. With all his might, he yanked the door fully open.

Immediately, he screamed and jumped backwards. Just inside the door, struggling to pull itself out of the plane, was a living creature, an alien. A large shell-like head emerged unsteadily into the sunlight. Beneath deep empty eye sockets, the creature had a protruding snout, a tangled mask of cartilage jutting forward like the oily white roots of a tree. Moist tentacles ran off the chin and ears, feeling the edge of the escape hatch. Its thick bony neck flared outward before tapering to a point at the top of its head. A deep gash ran right up the center of the face from the chin to the tip of its pointy head, where the two halves of the skull had fused together. It looked like the result of a crossbreeding experiment between a fully armored medieval warrior and a cockroach.

After watching the repulsive animal struggle toward the sunlight for a moment, Steve performed his sworn duty. With one savage punch, he clocked the alien square in the face. With a sickening crack, the monster's bony head bounced off the side of the hatch then collapsed, knocked unconscious.

He stood over the alien's limp body until his anger and fear subsided. Eventually, he sat down and reached into his breast pocket, withdrawing a slightly damaged Victory Dance cigar. He bit off one end and spit it into the face of his unconscious enemy. Then he lit it up and took a long, angry puff.

"Now that's what I call a close encounter."

IN DEATH VALLEY, the refugees spent the night milling about under the stars, locked in a thousand grim strategy sessions. They were gathered in a bone-dry valley, their RVs and trailer homes parked at odd angles to one another. All night long, groups of people congregated in the dusty glare of headlights, silhouettes holding coffee cups and shotguns, ready to defend their campground against unwanted visitors, terrestrial or otherwise. Dead Joshua trees were collected to fuel a central of bonfire around which one plan after another was proposed, hashed out, and agreed to, until some new motorist arrived with a fresh supply of rumors. Then, all their arrangements fell apart and had to be renegotiated from scratch.

Russell, for once, had done well. Not once did he mention his famous abduction, and he helped keep the others in his group focused and steady. He held fast to the very first plan they had made: drive into Las Vegas for gasoline and supplies, then get into the open space of Arizona.

By midmorning, the fifty or so trailers the Casses planned to travel with were in the final stages of preparing to leave the campground. Some were already parked alongside the road, their motors idling while the drivers stood around in weekend T-shirts and baseball caps waiting impatiently for the others. The Casse family, however, was distracted by Troy's condition. He was getting worse, the way he did when he'd had his first seizures. Blotches were coming out on his skin and although he wasn't in convulsions yet, he was starting to get awful shaky.

Miguel decided to try once more. For the third time since they arrived, he went through the camp, going door to door asking for medicine. He knew he was unlikely to find any hydrocortisone, but hoped someone might be a diabetic who could spare some insulin. Lots of people offered hydrocortisone cream, an anti-itch medicine, and were a little put off when Miguel didn't stay to explain the difference.

The morning was turning hot outside, but Troy lay in the bed shivering under a thick pile of blankets. Russell sat next to him, wiping down his forehead with a cold compress while Alicia made him some more sweet tea.

"You know, you're just like your mother used to be. She was stubborn too. She was a sweet, sweet woman—rest her soul—but when it came time to take her medicine, she'd get ornerier than a mule."

Troy was scared. "I'm sorry, Dad. I shouldn't have wasted the medicine. I'm sorry."

"Hey, that's past history, Troy-boy. We'll find some more, you'll see."

"I'm not going to die like Mom, am I?"

The question caught Russell by surprise and hit him hard. Before he could dismiss the idea and reassure his weakening son, he remembered sitting at Maria's bedside telling her the same thing.

"You're going to be fine," Alicia was adamant. "Of course you're going to get better. Don't even say that."

Miguel returned to the trailer, empty-handed. "I tried everyone. I couldn't find anything. And now everybody's packing up to leave. Some guy drove by yelling that a spaceship is heading this way."

The family looked at one another, startled by this news. "Then we'd better make ourselves scarce. We need to leave anyhow," Russell said with a nod toward the boy.

"Don't let the spaceship get us, Dad. Let's go. I'll get better."

"Our group's headed south. We're going to take back roads the whole way, but we'll pass a hospital near Las Vegas. It's only a couple hours away, so I think we should leave now."

Russell agreed. Then a knock came on the door. Alicia edged past Miguel and stood in the doorway. On the other side of the screen was someone she recognized, a handsome boy of sixteen, with a mop of reddish hair. He had something in his hand.

"Penicillin," he announced, holding up a bottle of pills.

"Hello, Penicillin. My name's Alicia."

When he realized he was being teased, he broke out in a warm grin. "Oh. I'm Philip. Philip Oster. You remember me from last night?"

A sudden rustling noise behind her in the trailer made the boy realize his question could be taken the wrong way. He raised his voice a notch and hastily added, "You told me your little brother was sick."

That was true. After noticing each other several times during the long evening and engaging in several bouts of significant eye contact, they'd finally found the nerve to approach one another. They had a brief conversation about Troy's condition, and Philip had promised to try to help. And now there he was with a vial of penicillin.

"Anyway, I know this isn't exactly what he needs but it should keep his fever down."

Alicia glanced down at the ground, blushing. "It's really nice of you to help," she said softly, opening the screen to accept the medicine. Behind her she could feel her father looking over her shoulder. Philip took a full step backward when he saw the large, unshaven Russell staring down at him.

"I wish I—I mean, my family wishes we could do more," he stammered, "I mean, like, if—well, anyway, we're leaving in a few minutes."

Alicia's face brightened when she heard that. A little too eagerly, she told him, "Us, too. We're going with you!" Then, hearing her father groan behind her, she added, "I mean, we're leaving, too."

"Cool." Philip smiled warmly. "That's a great old plane you guys are towing. Does it work?"

Russell had had his fill of this tender little balcony scene. "That's enough," he grumbled. "Thanks for the medicine. Now quit sniffing around and get back to your own trailer."

"Dad, please!" Alicia said through her false grin.

But Philip didn't seem to mind very much. With a charming smile, he backed away from the doorstep. "So, talk to you at the next stop?"

Smitten by this gallant young man, Alicia watched him jog back to his parents' fancy RV. When he was gone, she turned around and found the Casse men, even ailing Troy, staring at her expectantly. "What?" she demanded. "I was just being nice to him because he brought us some medicine."

"Yeah, right."

NORAD, THE NORTH AMERICAN Aerospace Defense system, was the safest spot in the world. Built deep within Cheyenne Mountain near Colorado Springs, it was an impregnable underground military command post, a high-tech sanctuary for the nation's leaders—the president in particular—in the event of nuclear attack. The walls of the bunker were designed to withstand the force of a nearby nuclear blast by themselves. Buried, as they were, deep below the surface of the earth, they offered even greater protection. Everything could be controlled from the giant war room, which was at the heart of the facility. Even if every city in the U.S. were to be wiped out, the technicians in Colorado would be able to track enemy movement, coordinate troops stationed overseas, and launch several different kinds of missile attacks. The vice president, the joint chiefs of staff, their advisers and families were already safely sheltered in the mountain, waiting for the president to arrive. NORAD computers were linked to those aboard Air Force One.

Approximately twelve minutes into the bloody, one-sided dogfights in the skies over New York, Los Angeles, San Francisco, and Washington, the technicians crowded into Air Force One's command center began losing the ability to coordinate the nation's military response. First, they lost radio contact with the surviving F-18s. Next, global radar capability was interrupted. Finally, they lost their links with NORAD and had to switch over to microwave telephone.

"They must be targeting our satellites. We're losing all satellite communication, tracking, and mapping."

They switched over to Air Force One's ULR (UpLooking Radar) then, and watched a sweep screen showing the positions of the most important Comsats. One by one, they were vanishing. The only explanation was that the invaders were up there, 33,000 miles into the heavens, the altitude where a satellite could stay in geosynchronous orbit over a fixed spot on earth. As the awkward multimillion dollar transmitters floated past, they were being blasted out of the sky.

The military had satellites stationed in different orbital paths at other altitudes, but switching over required ground crews in several locations to retarget receptor dishes. Before that work could even be ordered, the bases them-selves came under massive, virulent bombardment. The last thing Air Force One heard from El Toro was the flight tower screaming, "Incoming! Hostile incoming!" Before a single plane could get off the ground, the base was trans-formed to a smoldering ruin. Slowly, the president's flying fortress was being cut off from the rest of the world.

Moving to the circle of chairs just outside the command center, Whitmore and his advisers discussed their dwindling list of response options. Connie and Julius sat within earshot, listening carefully to the tense conversation.

General Grey spoke to one of his aides. "I don't care how you do it, but I want the line to NORAD reestablished as quickly as possible. Get it done!"

"Yes, sir," the soldier said crisply before returning to the squawking may-hem of the control room.

"What's the report from Peterson?" the president asked, referring to Peter-son Air Force Base near Colorado Springs, where they were scheduled to land in less than thirty minutes, the base closest to NORAD.

The demoralized expression on Grey's face told more than his words. "We're continuing to evacuate as many of our forces from the bases as possi-ble, but we've already sustained deep loses."

"Damn it." The president slammed his fist down on the arm of the chair. "Not only do they know *where* to hit us, they've got the order of priorities down. They're moving right down a damned checklist."

"Yes, sir," Grey allowed, "it's an extremely well-planned attack. They seem to understand our defense system."

David came stumbling out of the bathroom with a sickly look on his face. He overheard the conversation and stopped in the passageway, hoping for more. What he heard next made him forget about his queasy stomach. Nimziki stood up and walked to the center of the conference room, speaking in his imperial tone.

"As you know, I've been speaking directly with Commander Foley and the other joint chiefs since they arrived at NORAD." His every sentence was apparently calculated to make the president look bad. "We agree that there is only one sane and prudent course of action. We must launch a large-scale counteroffensive with a full nuclear strike. Hit them with everything we've got."

It was another Nimzikian moment of badly executed theater. He was trying to force the president's hand by presenting the plan as if it were a foregone conclusion. Whitmore resented the attempted manipulation, but was too inter-ested in the idea to criticize the man.

"Above American soil? You understand the implications of that move? We'd be killing tens of thousands, maybe hundreds of thousands, of innocent American civilians."

Utterly calm, almost amused, Nimziki had already planned his answer. "To be perfectly honest with you, Mr. President, I expected you'd balk at the idea. But if we don't strike back soon, there won't be much of an America left to defend. In my conversations with the joint—"

"Sir," General Grey's aide interrupted, returning from the tank.

"It can wait, soldier," Nimziki shot back, although technically he had no authority to do so.

"It's NORAD, sir," the man continued, his face white with fear. "It's gone, sir. They've taken it out." It took a moment for the idea to sink in. The group went from confused to stunned to mortified.

"That's not possible . . ."

"My God, the vice president, the joint chiefs."

"Perhaps their communication systems are out, but all of NORAD can't be *gone*."

The aide explained more fully. "I have it from pilots out of Peterson. They were in the sky when alien attack planes massed over NORAD and began firing continuously for several minutes. Eventually, the entire complex was exposed and destroyed. Shortly thereafter, Peterson itself came under attack and they lost radio contact."

"Isn't Peterson where we're heading? We need a new destination!"

"Mr. President, we must launch a nuclear attack," Nimziki insisted, highly agitated. To make sure his message got through, he hit below the belt, adding, "A delay now would be even more costly than when you waited to evacuate the cities."

The president shot out of his chair and stood nose to nose with Nimziki. "That is *not* the issue here." He was on the verge of punching the taller man when they were interrupted.

"You're not serious!" David came around the corner, outraged. "Tell me you're not considering firing a bunch of damn nuclear weapons at our own people."

Connie reacted immediately. She bolted toward her estranged husband and tried to move him backwards, "David, don't . . ." she warned, remembering the time he'd slugged Whitmore. If he did that again, it would be a federal crime. She knew it took a lot to get David riled up, but once his fuse was lit, he almost always exploded.

"If you start detonating nukes," he went on, shouting, "so will the rest of the world. Do you have any idea what that amount of fallout will do to the planet?

Think! Do you know what the long-term consequences will be? Why don't we just blow our brains out right here?"

David, slim but deceptively powerful at six feet four inches, easily brushed Connie to one side and advanced across the floor. General Grey quickly put himself between the hysterical computer genius and his president. Although he was the much smaller man, he was fully prepared to knock David to the carpet if necessary.

"Mr. Levinson," his voice was controlled, stern, "let me remind you that you are a guest here."

Ignoring him, David raged on. "This is insanity! We don't even know if nuclear explosions will dent their armor, but we know for certain it's going to kill *us*. There won't be anything left!"

Nimziki had suffered this idiot long enough. Accustomed to being obeyed, he pointed at David and boomed, "Shut your damn mouth and sit your ass down this instant!"

His insulting tone of voice backfired on him. It brought Julius into the fray. "Don't you tell him to shut up! You'd all be dead right now, blown to high heaven, if not for my David."

The old man shook a finger in the face of the secretary of defense. Connie, sensing all hell was about to break loose, ran back across the room and grabbed her father-in-law. The septuagenarian stood his ground, giving the Washington hotshots a piece of his mind.

"I blame all of you for what's happening. You did nothing to prevent this! You knew! You knew it was coming and yet you did nothing! Now you attack my son."

Julius's strange outburst probably prevented an all-out fist fight aboard the presidential aircraft. Like so many things he did, it was impossible to know how much was accident and how much was by design. The image of him shaking a bony finger in Nimziki's face while being dragged backwards by Connie temporarily distracted everyone from their anger. The president knew it was time to get back to business. He took a breath, regained his composure, and answered the old man's charges.

"Sir, there wasn't much more we could have done. We can be blamed for a lot of things, but in this instance, we were taken totally by surprise."

"Don't give me that taken-by-surprise crapola. Since nineteen-fifty-whatever you've had that flying saucer, the one that crashed in New Mexico."

"Oh, Dad, please!" David was trying to make an impassioned plea to save the planet, and his father was starting in with the UFO hogwash he got from watching too much TV.

"What was it," Julius kept right on talking, "Roswell? That's right, Roswell, New Mexico. You found the spaceship, the three alien bodies, the whole schmeer. Then everything got locked up in a bunker, the . . . oh, what was it? . . . fifty-one. Area Fifty-One! That was the name. Area Fifty-One. For years you knew and you didn't do nothing!"

For the first time in a long while, President Whitmore smiled. Every month or so, he'd be shaking hands with some citizen who'd ask him about the notorious Area 51. He'd looked into it, and learned that it was all mythology, an elaborate conspiracy theory concocted by UFO nuts.

"Regardless of what you've read in the tabloids, Mr. Levinson, there were never any spaceships recovered by the government. You can take my word for it: there is an Area Fifty-One but there are no secret flying saucers." The president looked around the room, sharing his amusement with the others. It didn't last long.

"Uh, excuse me Mr. President," Nimziki said, swallowing hard, "but that's not entirely accurate." Shocked, everyone looked at the former head of the CIA, the man who knew where all the skeletons were buried, waiting for him to explain.

AS SOON AS Jasmine Dubrow came out into the bright dusty air of the ruined city, she told Dylan to wait with Boomer, then climbed an earthen embankment up to what remained of the freeway. From this vantage point she surveyed the damage, and what she saw sent a long chill down her spine. Everything was gone, pulverized down to a smoking gray rubble. The massive black ship still hung in the air, a tranquil death angel cloaking the city with its wings. Downtown Los Angeles had been scoured completely away by the blast. The ring of skyscrapers and historic buildings where a multitude had worked each day was now a blackened depression in the earth. She looked away and felt the delicate ocean breeze on her face. In the distance, buildings still stood, their windows blown out and dwindling fires trailing rags of smoke into the morning air.

Studying the pattern of destruction, she suddenly understood how very lucky she had been. For miles in every direction, the devastation was nearly absolute. Houses built along the freeway had been torn in half, and everything inside, furniture, water heaters, photographs, half-read books, the dishes in the sink, and sleeping children had been vacuumed out into the firestorm and incinerated. A refrigerator, one of the old-fashioned kind with rounded corners, had landed upright in the middle of the freeway, badly warped by the heat. Absently, Jas looked inside and found a jar of mustard still in its place on the door shelf. *Strange*, she thought, *what survives.*

She hurried back down the slope and found Dylan examining something on the ground. When she came closer, she saw it was some sort of animal, probably a dog, its body torn apart and still smoking. Dylan wanted to know what it was, but Jasmine picked him up and carried him away without a word. With Boomer leading the way, they scouted around for a few minutes, until they found a parking garage full of utility vehicles. The garage was built into the sheltered side of the freeway, and the dump trucks, bulldozers, and mobile cranes were still where they'd been parked for the three-day holiday weekend. The vehicles closest to the outside had been charred in the firestorm, tires and wires melted away. But deeper inside the cavernous structure, Jasmine found an old eight-wheeler, a flatbed truck with the emergency red paint job still in mint condition. She climbed up into the cab and searched around until she hit the jackpot. The keys fell into her lap when she lowered the sun visor. She yelled for Dylan and Boomer to get in, then she fired up the engine and barreled toward the barrier of equipment and a collapsed tin roof. She slammed through the debris and into the sunlight.

Within a few minutes, she had found what remained of a wide boulevard and was bumping along in a southerly direction, swerving around collapsed storefronts and driving over half-incinerated telephone poles. Every few minutes she came to a road block the old truck couldn't clear. She would stop and climb up onto the hood, searching for a clear path through the debris. It was like trying to get out of a labyrinth.

After three or four miles, she found her first survivor, a man about fifty years old dressed in what was left of a three-piece suit. She found him sitting quietly by the side of the road. He had been cut up pretty badly, probably by flying glass. She couldn't tell for sure because the man wouldn't say a word. She helped him into the back of the truck, where he sat down quietly. They drove on. Over the next half an hour, she found six more survivors. Three of them accepted her offer of a ride, glad to be with someone who knew somewhere else to go. She put the passengers in the back, while Dylan and Boomer rode up front in the cab.

In time, they found their first street sign. A steel traffic light, knocked flat against the earth by the blast, had a blue shingle still attached. Jas jumped down and used her boot to wipe away the dust and ash: SEPULVEDA BLVD. That gave her a better idea of where she was. She looked up at the sun, then out toward where she guessed the ocean would be, trying to get her bearings.

"Repent, sinners!"

Jasmine spun around, heart pounding. Not far off, a derelict-looking man was standing on a giant pile of bricks, the collapsed side wall of an aging movie theater. Somehow, he'd found a piece of unburned cardboard and scrawled a biblical quotation onto it. In the other hand he held a tire iron, the kind with four prongs, brandishing it like a crucifix. From Jasmine's point of view, the crumbling interior wall of the movie house was directly behind him. Painted with a lavish mural of cowboys in old Western scenes, it made an eerie, incongruous backdrop.

"The end hast come! Almighty God speaketh his word and the end hast come!"

"I'm headed down to El Toro. Hop in the back, if you want to come."

"He has spoken in tongues of fire," he screamed toward the sky. "Yours is the torment of the Scorpion, it is the end!" The tortured creature, still shouting into the void, turned his back on the people in the red truck.

Reluctantly, Jasmine left him there. She decided it wasn't her business to try and save any more of these people. But she hadn't driven a city block when she spotted another possible survivor. An olive drab army helicopter, belly up, lay smoldering in what was once the parking lot of a minimall.

Jas and the silent man got out of the truck and approached the wrecked chopper. Dangling in their shoulder harnesses, the pilot and copilot were both dead, crushed to death. But laying on the ceiling of the smashed machine was a woman in an expensive blue dress. Jasmine crawled inside and dragged the woman out. Dried blood was streaked all around her nose, mouth, and ears, sure signs of internal hemorrhaging. Laying her gently on the ground, Jas and the silent man looked at each other. They both recognized the woman as First Lady Marilyn Whitmore.

As they were preparing to lift and carry her back to the truck, Dylan came jogging toward them.

"Hey," Jasmine shouted, "I thought I told you to stay in the truck."

Then the unmistakable sound of a pump-action shotgun being cocked sliced through the silence. Jasmine wheeled around to see a beer-bellied white man in a hunting jacket approaching. Two more men, dressed in filthy camou-flage gear, trailed along behind him, one of them pushing a battered shopping cart piled high with treasures they'd scavenged from the rubble. They looked like a trio of greasy vultures who had come in after the blast to pick through what little was left.

"Looks like we've solved our transportation problems. That's a damn nice truck you got there. Are the keys in it?" the armed man demanded, speaking with a mountain accent.

An angry white redneck threatening her with a gun was the last thing Jasmine needed right now. Somehow, she forced herself to smile warmly. "Hey, you're welcome to come with us. We're leaving here anyway, headed south down to—"

"Keep your damn mouth shut, you black bitch," he screamed, training the gun at her head. His partners ran over to the truck like overgrown children. While the larger one began dragging the injured out of the flatbed, the other one checked the ignition switch. Boomer, still in the cab, nuzzled up to the intruder, hoping to get petted.

"Keys aren't in the truck," he yelled to the man with the gun.

"All right," he turned to Jasmine and the silent man, "I'm gonna ask nicely once more, and then I'm gonna blow your brains out. Which one of you has the goddamn keys to the goddamn truck?"

"Repent, sinners! The end has come!" The crazed preacher had followed the truck down the street. "Almighty God's judgment is upon you!"

"Back off, mister. This ain't none of your business," warned the lead vulture.

As the preacher stalked forward, Jasmine pulled her son close to her, easing one of the FyreStix out of his backpack.

"You cannot go against the will of God," the ragged evangelist frothed, "you cannot resist His word!"

"Sure I can." The hunter laughed, pulling the trigger.

A load of buckshot knocked the preacher backward with a hole in the middle of his chest. The explosion echoed across the empty, ruined landscape. Jasmine had sparked one of the matches, but when the rocket wouldn't light, she quickly pinched the match out between her fingers. The man with the gun looked as surprised as anyone by what he'd done. He'd obviously never shot anyone before. His buddies looked on nervously.

"Now you'd better hand over those keys, bitch."

Boomer, the world's worst guard dog, had been making nice-nice with the rednecks until the gunshot sounded. Suddenly he came charging from the direction of the truck, snarling and barking at the man with the gun. Perhaps the guy was a dog lover, or maybe he felt guilty about having killed an innocent man. For whatever reason, he hesitated to shoot the dog.

"Call off the dog," he shouted, the barrel of the shotgun inches from the retriever's bared teeth. "Call him off, or I'll shoot him, I swear to God."

Jasmine reached down and lit the FyreStix. The blast of brightly colored gunpowder shot out the end with more force than she expected. She pointed the ten feet of sparkling fire right at the gunman, moving in on him at the same time. The burning sulfur stuck to his face and hands. Involuntarily, he dropped the gun as his arms went up to protect his face. Jasmine picked up the gun, broke open the breech to check the cartridges, and snapped it back closed before the redneck had quit screaming. When he looked up again, the tables had turned.

"This *bitch* was born down in Alabama with a daddy who loved to hunt." She worked the pump action on the gun. "So don't you think for a minute I don't know how to use this thing." She squeezed the trigger, sending a shot sailing past the fat man's ear. She pumped the gun again, the spent shells twirling to the ground, new ones moving into the chambers. "Now why don't you take a nice long walk back the same way you came."

The three vultures were only too happy to oblige. They jogged away over a short hill, turning to curse Jasmine before disappearing for good.

As she and the silent man carried the unconscious Mrs. Whitmore back to the truck, the First Lady's mouth opened. Quietly, almost choking, she said with a smile, "That was brave."

STEVE LOWERED HIS shoulder and strained against the weight of the straps. He'd wrapped the unconscious alien in his ejection seat parachute and was towing him across the scorching sand, muttering the whole way.

"Ya know, this is supposed to be my weekend off. But nooooo! You had to come down here with an attitude, and now you got me out here pullin' your potato-chip munchin', slime-drippin' ass across the burning desert with your dreadlocks hanging out the back." The creature's long tentacle arms had worked their way free and were dragging limply behind. "Think you can just come down here, acting all big and bad, and mess with me and my guys?" He turned around like he was expecting an answer. His anger rising, he screamed, "I coulda been at a barbecue, you freak!" He staggered toward the orange nylon chute and delivered one vicious kick after another to the lump of comatose biomass wrapped inside until he had to stop for breath. Panting, he added, "but I'm not mad."

Drenched in sweat, Steve knew he was going to need water pretty soon. Leaving his package behind, he grunted up a short hill and surveyed the desert. Empty brown hills stretched away to infinity beneath powder blue sky. Heat lifting off the desert floor shimmered like silver ocean waves. Just before he trudged back down to gather his prisoner of war, a glinting light caught his eye. It came from the top of a hill several miles away. Soon he realized what it was: traffic. There was a road less than a thousand yards in front of him. He dashed back for his cargo and began a furious charge toward the road. He arrived a few minutes later, sat down at the edge of the old two-lane highway, and watched in amazement as an armada of a hundred trailers, campers, vans, and trucks rolled steadily closer.

"Hey, mucous-head, our ride's here." Steve put a big fat grin on his face and stood in the center of the road, waving his arms. "Gonna have to run me over if you won't stop."

Fortunately, the mile-long caravan rolled to a gradual halt. Steve walked up to one of the lead vehicles, the one towing an old biwing airplane behind it.

"Captain Steven Hiller, United States Marine Corps."

The driver, a big curly headed guy with a sarcastic sense of humor, leaned out his window and asked, "Need a lift?"

Two minutes later, Steve was surrounded by two dozen curious members of the caravan. He took a long slug of water before explaining what he had in the parachute. That got their attention. He told them he needed to get into Las Vegas, to Nellis Air Force Base, that it was a matter of urgent national interest.

"Sorry, soldier," an old guy with a rifle on his hip said, "they told on the radio that Nellis got all shot up. It's wiped out."

Steve walked over to the parachute and gave it two more swift kicks. "All right, then, when I was flying past here, I spotted an airbase next to an old lake bed. I need somebody to take me over there."

Several people produced maps of the region. Although some were quite detailed, none of them showed an airbase. According to the maps, the whole area was nothing more than a missile testing area, off-limits to civilians. To make matters worse, there was not one, but *four* dry lake beds.

"Trust me, it's there," Steve told them.

The whole thing was too spooky for most of them. They wanted to *get away* from the aliens, not chauffeur them around. The leaders of the group were willing to take Steve and his package with them, but they weren't going to waste precious fuel on a wild goose chase through a restricted military area.

That's when the guy with the sarcastic attitude came to Steve's defense. He pushed a couple of the map readers aside and stepped to the center of the blacktop conference.

"Groom Lake," he said to Steve. "Groom Lake Weapons Testing Facility is the base you saw. Pair of runways crossing in an X, four or five real large hangars up against a mountain, right?"

"That's right." Steve and the others listened as the big man explained exactly how to get there, drawing in roads the map-makers had left off. When the man was done, Steve asked, "How come you're such an expert on this place?"

The man's son, a long-haired kid about seventeen years old put in, a little too quickly, "Because we live around here."

"My name's Russell Casse," the man said in a low, almost conspiratorial voice. He shook Steve's hand and continued, "About ten years ago I had a run in with these little blood suckers, and I'd do anything to help you kick their nasty little asses. You mind if I take a look?"

Steve didn't care if the man was crazy, as long as he was willing to help. "Not at all," Steve said, "but it's not a real pretty sight."

"I've seen 'em before," Russell assured him. "Big black eyes, puckered little mouth, white skin." His son, Miguel, followed close behind and seemed to be less than enthusiastic about cooperating with the Marine pilot. Even from twenty feet away, Russell knew something was wrong. The long tentacles hanging out of the parachute had nothing to do with the aliens he "remembered" taking him from the airfield almost a decade ago.

Steve tore back the nylon material. The motorists who had followed them to the parachute jumped back in visceral disgust. Russell stared down at the creature, horrified for a completely different reason. The creature was too large, too bony, and too fearsome to be one of the delicate little monsters who had kidnapped him a decade earlier. *Could this be a completely different species of alien?* he wondered. *Or did I imagine the whole thing, make it up?* Suddenly, the most real thing in Russell's past, the moment that ruined the rest of his life, didn't seem very real at all. He felt himself getting a little bit dizzy and put a hand on Miguel's shoulder to steady himself.

"Dad, don't forget about Troy. We need to get to that hospital."

Russell stared at the boy for a moment, trying to focus his mind. Then he nodded and turned toward the trailer.

"So, sir," Steve called to his ally, "are we headed to Groom Lake or what?"

Russell had already forgotten about his promise to Steve. "Look, friend, I'd like to help you, but I've got a sick boy in the back of my rig over there. He's going to die in a few hours if we can't find the medicine he needs. You just follow those directions I gave you. Take you about two hours from here."

"We'll get you over there," a tall, sunburnt man said. "Philip, clear everything out of the pickup, put it in the RV." The redheaded boy shot a sad look at Alicia before running off to follow his father's command.

"Hey, Mr. Casse, wait up." Steve jogged up to Russell, who appeared to be in pain. "Your boy needs medicine, I understand that. Look, a base that size will have a complete clinic with everything you need. You said it's two hours from here."

Russell looked at his son, "Your call."

Miguel thought about it for a moment. "Let's try to make it in an hour and a half."

SOARING OVER THE endless Nevada desert, Air Force One's pilot, Captain Birnham, announced that the Nellis Range could be seen off to the left. Peeping out the little opera windows, the passengers were disappointed by the sight of a small- to medium-sized air base in fairly shabby condition. On the surface, Area 51 consisted of one very large airplane hangar surrounded by several smaller ones, a pair of crossed landing strips, plus a smattering of radar dishes and bunkhouses. Here and there, scattered around the wide open desert, they spotted other buildings, but the unspoken consensus among the passengers was that there was nothing especially interesting about this secret facility tucked against a set of steep brown hills.

By agreement, there was no ceremony to welcome the president. As soon as the big bird touched down, Captain Birnham was directed toward the largest hangar, the doors of which rolled open as they taxied up. As a small contingent of soldiers pushed mobile stairs toward the blue-and-white Boeing, Whitmore and his entourage crowded the doorway, waiting impatiently to be let out. Sheepishly, Nimziki came forward from the command center, where he'd been contemplating his next move. Everyone did their best to politely ignore him until the doors were thrown open.

At the bottom of the gangway, they were met by the base's top administrator, Major Mitchell. He had fifty or so of his soldiers lined up for the president's inspection.

"Welcome to Area Fifty-One, sir," he said with a crisp salute.

Whitmore returned the salute, explaining, "We're in a hurry."

"Right this way." Mitchell didn't need to be told why the president of the United States had decided to visit his backwater base in the middle of a global catastrophe. He had come for the ship. And, although technically speaking, it was a violation of federal law for him to show it to anyone, even the president, he led the way without the slightest hesitation.

Mitchell was a large, intimidating presence, handsome in the way square-jawed prize fighters are handsome. Although he was young, just shy of thirty, he was a climber, moving quickly up the ranks. His superiors at Fort Cayuga, impressed with his work, had steered him into his current position of supervising operations at Area 51. He was responsible for everything that happened on the base except research. If something was happening, Mitchell always knew about it and was most often standing right there to watch it happen. He was well aware that the job was only a stepping stone to something higher up, something in Washington. But he also knew that any breach of security, whether it was an infiltration from the outside, or information leaks coming from within, anything at all that put Area 51 into the newspapers, would get him swiftly busted back to a desk job in rural Idaho. He took his job seriously.

He ushered the group into a drab dead-end hallway with locked office doors on either side. At the end of the room there was a water cooler and a few wilted plants. Mitchell stepped inside and closed the door behind him.

"Stand clear of the walls," he warned, unlocking a cover plate and flipping a switch.

Suddenly there was a loud hydraulic hum and the whole room began to sink into the ground. The office doors appeared to climb the walls, as the floor lowered down a concrete shaft. The entire room was an enormous elevator.

While the others gaped around them, impressed, the president's anger slowly boiled over.

"Why the hell wasn't I told about this place?" he demanded, staring at Nimziki for an answer.

"Two words, Mr. President." For once Nimziki appeared humble and earnest. "*Plausible deniability*. The decision was made way, *way* before my time to keep this thing under wraps. Hoover knew it would be turned into a political football, so it was classified 'need to know,' and until today—"

"Enough!" Whitmore snapped. Nothing Nimziki said could erase the harm he had already done. "Plausible deniability, my ass," he muttered.

What Nimziki failed to mention was that one of the reasons the army, CIA, and the FBI had conspired to keep the crash secret was to gain advantage over the Russians in the Cold War. They slapped a twenty-five-year gag order on the project at Area 51. Both the Cold War and the secrecy order had expired under Nimziki's tenure, but he hadn't made the discovery public. He had ambitions of running for national office, maybe even the presidency, and the way he saw it, he had everything to lose by admitting he'd kept the thing secret and everything to gain by keeping control of the whole project to himself.

Metal doors slid open onto what looked like a scrub-down area in a research hospital. Dozens of masks and white coveralls hung on hooks near a series of sinks. Proceeding through this area, the group came to a set of Plexiglas doors. Beyond them was a partial scene of a busy workspace, several workers dressed from head to toe in sterile white overalls, masks and hair caps were moving in and out of view.

"This is our static-free clean room," Mitchell announced proudly, giving them a moment to gawk before showing them the way to the next exhibit on his tour.

"Well, let's see," the president said.

Mitchell didn't know exactly what to say. There wasn't much of interest in there and he was sure if Whitmore knew how many hundreds of thousands of dollars it would cost the American tax payers to decontaminate the facility, he wouldn't insist. "Actually, sir, entrance to this room requires—"

Whitmore heard the wrong answer coming out of the soldier's mouth. He explained what he wanted in a way that left no room for interpretation. "Open this goddamn door right now."

Suddenly Mitchell couldn't get the door open fast enough. He slid his magnetized ID badge through the scanner lock and the glass doors whisked apart with a smart hum. The group, eleven strong, marched into the state-of-the-art, dust-free research facility. Once they were inside and turned the corner, they realized they had only been able to see a tiny slice of it from the scrub room. The chamber was at least a hundred yards long with a raised walkway, two and a half feet higher, running straight down the center. On either side, like astronauts in their white suits, bonnets, and shoe bags, the staff was busy with a number of projects on either side of the aisle.

They moved around their workstations tweaking robotic arms, conducting laser experiments, studying graphs and charts, or sitting around doing nothing. But all of them stopped what they were doing when President Thomas Whitmore unexpectedly walked past. Mitchell stayed a step ahead of the others, explaining in a word or two the work being done at each station. The quality and sophistication of the equipment was astounding, and in many cases it was *beyond* state-of-the-art. In every detail, the lab was well staffed, well supplied, and well organized.

"Where the hell did all this come from?" the president whispered to Grey without breaking stride. "How did this get funded?"

Doddering along at the back of the pack, seemingly out of earshot, Julius overheard the president's question. "You didn't think they actually spent ten thousand dollars for a hammer and thirty thousand for a toilet seat, did you?"

The old guy gave a little laugh, not realizing he was partly correct. Military procurement officers had been funneling money to Area 51 for decades by padding other expenses, but the bulk of the funds came straight from the American congress. Part of the national budget was always listed as "the Dark Fund," money for projects deemed too sensitive for the lawmakers to know about, usually R&D on new weapons systems for the military.

A steel ramp at the far end of the room led up to a thick titanium and steel door. An electric motor shook the door to life, lifting it straight up. Ducking underneath and starting down the elevated walkway to meet the president came a pair of scientists dressed in white lab coats.

Dr. Brackish Okun was the director of research at Area 51. About forty-five years old, Okun had a full head of wild gray hair falling to his shoulders. He had an unmistakable hippie bounce in the way he walked, hands thrust deeply into the pockets of his lab coat. He was smiling one of those uncontrollable, ear-to-ear smiles the president often saw on the faces of kids when they walked up to meet him.

"Oh God, what now?" the president muttered under his breath. He'd already had so many strange encounters over the last thirty-six hours, and here came another one.

Mitchell did the honors. "Mr. President, I'd like to introduce you to Dr. Okun. He's been heading up our research here for the past fifteen years."

Okun was an odd, hyperenergetic man who had obviously spent too much time in underground isolation. He stood nodding and grinning for an awkward moment, his wrinkled gray and yellow tie blending with his pale skin, before suddenly reaching out and shaking the president's hand with too much enthusiasm.

"Wow, Mr. President, it is truly an honor to meet you, sir. Oh, and this is my colleague Dr. Issacs." Issacs, a handsome man with close-cropped hair and a goatee, appeared to be the normal half of the team.

As Issacs leaned forward to shake hands, Okun turned to one of the researchers and whispered, "This is so cool." Whitmore shot him a disapproving look, which Okun seemed to recognize. "If any of us seem a little odd down here, it's because they don't let us out much," Okun said in apology.

"Yes, I can understand that," the president said, barely disguising his irony.

"So! I guess you'd like to see the Big Tamale," Okun surmised. "Follow me."

Every member of the group glanced around in befuddlement. They did, however, follow the odd scientist toward the next room. Leaving the long research hall, they walked up a ramp into a tight space between concrete walls. Inside, there was a small, level area and then another steel door. Issacs swiped an access card through the magnet lock, took a quick breath, then slapped a large button on the wall. A small red siren light began twirling to the sound of a buzzer as the wall in front of them lowered like a drawbridge, revealing a spectacular sight.

On the other side was a huge, dimly lit concrete chamber, five stories deep and just as wide. Armed guards patrolled a series of steel catwalks high above, automatic weapons at the ready. But the centerpiece of the room, perched on a custom-built platform and dominating the rest of the space, was an alien attack plane, its armored exterior a lustrous midnight blue beneath the work-lights. It was a replica of the ships that had laid waste to the Black Knights. The members of the president's entourage were suitably impressed. Mouths agape, they came down the ramp.

It was unlike anything they'd seen before and not at all what they had expected. The basic shape was familiar, like two saucer plates stacked rim to rim. That explained the thousands of descriptions of UFOs people had registered over the years, but it was the details of the sixty-foot craft that made it compelling and fascinating. Along the spine of the ship, starting at the crown, then tapering to a sharp point at the tail, was a tall, bony, six-foot-tall projection that the scientists called "the fin." The surface seemed to be made of large, armored plates connected at the seams by countless pieces of intricate machine tooling, tiny metallic gadgets set in place with the same precision as the muscles in a human hand.

The group moved onto an observation platform, face-to-face with the darkly fascinating bird, displayed like a sleeping stegosaurus in a hushed museum. At the front of the machine was a sort of cockpit with broad, flat windows. Below these, at the very nose of the plane, curved projections came forward to form sharp tips, almost like the mandibles on a huge insect. More than one of the amazed visitors imagined being squeezed between those powerful claws before being consumed.

A score of scientists and technicians moved around the ship, taking readings, making minor adjustments, scanning the surface with curious blue lamps, their equipment on portable tool carts, making them look like high-tech auto mechanics. In several places, long gray scars zigzagged across the surface, showing where the scientists had patched the craft up after it cracked apart in the New Mexican desert.

"She's a beaut, ain't she?" Okun wiggled his bushy eyebrows.

Julius whispered loud enough for everyone to hear, "Ha! Never any space-ships recovered by the government?"

Whitmore brushed past Okun to get a better look. He walked directly under the spacecraft and reached up to touch the surface. Etched into the surface of the plate armor were thinly cut grooves arranged in patterns.

"These designs," the president asked, "what do they mean?"

"We have no idea," Okun replied, as if he'd never thought about it. In fact, he'd thought about the markings obsessively. He'd even managed to arrange a security clearance for one of the world's leading cryptographers, Dr. D. Jackson, who had once spent three frustrating weeks trying to figure the markings out before being called away to another government project.

"Are you telling me we've had one of their ships for forty years and we don't know anything about them?" Whitmore asked testily.

"No, no, no, no, no," Okun assured the president, "we know *tons* about them. But the supercool stuff has just started happening in the last couple days. See, we can't duplicate their type of power, their energy. But since these guys started showing up, all the little gizmos inside have turned themselves on. The last twenty-four hours have been wild—really, really exciting."

The president exploded. "Millions of people are dying out there! I don't think *exciting* is the word I'd choose to describe it!"

The cavernous room echoed the words as everyone fell silent, letting the president blow off some steam. Whitmore walked to the far edge of the ship, trying to gather his thoughts, but a single image had plastered itself like a billboard to the inside of his forehead: his wife Marilyn being overwhelmed by a sea of fire. Staring blankly into the dim recesses of the room, his eyes began to fill with tears. He wasn't going to cry, wouldn't allow himself that kind of personal indulgence. He sucked in a long stiff breath, then wiped his eyes, trying to make it look like he was massaging a headache.

General Grey took over, filling the silence. "Doctor, I'm sure you understand we're in the middle of a very severe emergency. Now, what can you tell us about the enemy we're facing?"

Beginning to appreciate the urgency of the situation, the long-haired scientist answered more soberly than before. "Well, let's see. They're not all that dissimilar to us. They breathe oxygen and have similar tolerances to heat and cold. . . . That's probably why they're interested in our planet."

"Whoa! Why do you assume—" David started to blurt out a question, then stopped to check if that was okay. Grey and Whitmore both signaled it was. "What makes you think they're interested in our planet?"

"Just a hunch," Okun said, cleaning his glasses with his tie. "They're animals like us and they have a survival instinct. Perhaps some catastrophe drove them from their home planet and now they're wandering around. Also, I'm guessing they need space because they're ranchers or farmers; they do some sort of animal husbandry."

"How do you know that?"

"You're standing under the answer. Those large plates, the ship's armor. If you examine them under a microscope, you'll find hairline striations and even pores!" Okun saw that none of the visitors understood the implication. "That means, of course, that the plates are *grown* rather than forged. Each one is as individual as a human fingerprint. We don't know how they do it. I think it's done through bioengineering, manipulating the DNA so that the shells grow to precisely the same size. But Dr. Issacs believes they grow the animals in molds, the way the Chinese used to bind women's feet to keep them under a certain size. As to their age, we can't be entirely sure. We've developed a variation of the carbon fourteen test which indicates the plates take about eighty years to grow. And, if our methods are reliable, the plates on this ship are between three and nine thousand years old." Okun, still a geeky college boy at heart, looked around at the visitors mischievously. "Hey, you guys wanna see them?"

REPORTS OF UFOS hovering in midair for several moments then darting off at unbelievable speeds were not uncommon over the southwestern desert of the United States. Nearly all of these sightings were made by unreliable witnesses who say they were alone at the time. Inevitably, reports filed by highly credible sources, such as the one made by former President Jimmy Carter while governor of Georgia, inspired dozens of copycat observances.

But on the night of July, 4, 1947, something happened that no one could explain away. Hundreds of citizens in and around the town of Roswell, New Mexico, claimed to have seen a glowing, disk-shaped object, about sixty feet across, streaking northwest across the sky. Immediately, they flooded the local sheriff's office, radio station, and newspaper with a deluge of phone calls. Certain the thing they had seen was not of this earth, the entire town spent the night gathered in restaurants and the parking lots of supermarkets trading accounts of what they had seen and nervously watching the sky for signs of unusual movement. Public reaction bordered on near-hysteria at times. It was still the main topic of conversation when, a few days later, the United States military issued a press release: they had recovered the wreckage of a crashed flying saucer which they believed to be of extraterrestrial origin. This startling announcement was made by Colonel William Blanchard of the 509th Bomb Group at Roswell Field, who later went on to become a four-star general and vice chief of staff of the United States Air Force.

The afternoon after the mass sighting, a local rancher, W. W. "Mac" Brazel, had found the wreckage of an unusual aircraft on his property. The pieces were made of a material he'd never seen before and some of them had markings on them, something like hieroglyphics. Mac followed the trail of debris out to where he found the ship—and the body he would never admit to seeing later.

Figuring it was one of the experimental aircraft from the nearby army air-field, he drove into town and called the base at Roswell, seventy-five miles away. A squad of intelligence officers hurried to the scene to examine the wreckage. That night they broke the story to the press.

Then, just as surprisingly, they denied their own story. Following visits to the site by one high-ranking military delegation after another, a second news conference was called. They said it was a weather balloon. A strange new type of weather balloon, possibly put up by our dreaded enemies, the Soviets. No one believed a word of it, but the army stuck to its story. The reporters who had descended on the scene were not allowed to examine the evidence. It had already been airlifted out of Roswell to an undisclosed location, where it would undergo "further testing."

The glowing object observed that night over Roswell was a scout plane that had broken off its much larger parent ship, which was hovering at the edge of earth's atmosphere. Like hundreds of flights before and after it, the ship had conducted several hours of research and observation. It was only moments away from completing its mission when the parent ship was suddenly threat-ened with discovery and bolted away. The scout ship had wandered further than it should have and now lay behind the curve of the earth, preventing the energy flowing from the parent craft from reaching its engines. The occupants of the craft, realizing they only had a few minutes of reserve power, panicked. Rather than raise their ship higher into the air, they darted northwest, back to the area they were assigned to explore. As they tore along, their sensors screaming of imminent engine failure, a shield of negative ions covered the ship and, reacting with the ship's own strange form of energy, created the soft moon-bright glow seen from the ground. Too late. The left engine exploded into a thousand fragments, and a moment later, the ship bottomed out on the desert.

Two of the aliens inside had survived the crash; the third was dead. The stronger of the two survivors struggled for over an hour before finally opening the hatch and pulling himself outside. He dragged himself off the edge of the ship and 120 feet across the sand before he was attacked by a pack of coyotes. As they nipped and gnawed him to death, his comrade inside the ruined ship felt every hideous bite and heard every soundless scream. He sat paralyzed inside the vessel until, the next morning, the earthlings began arriving. The surviving alien was airlifted by helicopter to Roswell Field, then flown by an army medical plane to a new super-secret facility, Area 51.

OKUN LED THE WAY to a door as thick as a bank vault. Using a distinctive triangular key, he opened it. Issacs slipped into the pitch-black room and fumbled around until he found the light switch. Once a high-security lecture hall with theater chairs facing a podium, the room had become, over the years, a graveyard for Okun's obsolete scientific equipment. The president and his entourage stepped over and between the piles of expensive junk, moving to the front of the room. The focal point of the space was a trio of metal cylinders, five feet wide, running from floor to ceiling.

"Is everybody ready?" Okun asked like a barker outside a circus tent. "This, ladies and gentlemen, is what we affectionately refer to down here as the Freak Show."

He was on the verge of saying more—he had a whole routine he usually went through—but a frown on the president's face made him cut it short. He entered a sequence of numbers into an old-fashioned security keypad and the three cylinders began to lift upward into the ceiling.

Behind the cylinders were three glass tanks, each one containing the body of a dead alien floating as peacefully as mermaids in a murky solution of formaldehyde. Their long frail bodies, orange and yellow under the lights, were in various states of decay. Their spindly bodies hung like kite tails from large bulbous heads. Gentle black eyes the size of eight balls on either side of a tiny beaklike nose gave the faces a startled expression, as if they were just as surprised as the earthlings on the other side of the glass.

Okun studied the faces of the visitors and noted all the usual reactions. Some looked frightened, some lit up with curiosity, and others turned away in revulsion.

"When my predecessor, Dr. Welles, found these three, they looked a whole lot different. They were wearing biomechanical suits, horrible looking things with long tentacles coming off the back and shorter ones on the face. The two on the sides died in the crash, and it was only during the autopsies that Welles discovered the creatures inside. Once the suits were off, we were able to learn a great deal about their anatomy. Their senses are many times more sensitive than ours. The eyes, as you can see, are much larger than ours and have no irises to limit the amount of light they can receive. The auditory nerves and olfactory organs are coterminous, ending here in the nose. Our theory is that they can not only hear sounds, but also smell them. The same goes for odors; they must be able to 'hear' the scent and smell it at the same time. Cool, huh?"

Oops, he'd done it again. Okun held up his hands, apologetically, but the president was too involved with learning about the aliens to pay much attention.

"Continue."

"Okay, let's see. Circulatory system. They don't have a central organ, a heart, like we do. The blood is kept moving through their bodies by the peristaltic motion of the muscles. They have no vocal cords, so we're assuming they communicate with each other through other means."

"What kind of other means?" David broke in. "Obviously you're not talking about hand gestures or body language."

"No. They seem to use some kind of extrasensory perception."

"Telepathy," Issacs put in bluntly. "They read each others' minds."

"Well, now, Dr. Issacs," Okun looked up at the ceiling, a sarcastic tight grin smeared across his face, "as we have discussed many times, there is still no trustworthy scientific evidence to support that claim. I don't want to start engaging in speculation and give our visitors the impression that we're a bunch of crackpots." He shot a dagger glance at Issacs, who stared back just as icily.

"What the hell are you two talking about?" demanded the no-nonsense Grey.

Issacs came forward out of the shadows and explained. "The one in the middle survived for eighteen days after the crash. Dr. Welles did everything he could to save the creature's life. On the tenth day, he reported having the sensation that the thing was reading his mind. On the eleventh day, he claims that he and the creature 'spoke,' not with words, but in images and feelings. These conversations continued until the creature became too weak and eventually died. The sense he took from these 'conversations' was that these beings meant us no harm, that their intentions were peaceful. That's why we didn't warn anyone. We had no idea anything like this was going to happen."

When the bearded doctor finished speaking, everyone looked at Whitmore for his reaction. If they were expecting him to forgive the scientists for not alerting the world to the danger of invasion by these powerful predators, they were wrong. Instead, he turned again to Okun.

"I'm still thinking about something you said out there by the ship. You said 'that's probably why they're interested in our planet,' and then you said they raise other animals. Do you know what these things eat?"

The image of humans being herded together in pens, fattened outside the doors of the slaughterhouse, naked and crowded, occurred suddenly to everyone.

Julius couldn't bear the thought of it. "That's revolting. Are you saying these things are going to make us into sausage?"

"I don't know. That's what I'm asking the doctor," Whitmore replied.

Okun was visibly disturbed out by the idea. The way his face twitched, he must have been imagining it pretty vividly. For the first time, he started to understand just how serious the situation was.

"They do have mouths, very small ones right there under the beak, but they're nothing more than slits in the skin. The autopsy also found a set of digestive glands that secrete a highly corrosive substance. Nothing was found in any of the stomachs, so we don't know what they eat."

"One more question." The president walked closer to Okun. "How can we kill them?"

"Geez, that's a toughie," he said, lacing his fingers on top of his head to help him think. "Of course, their bodies are even more frail than ours. The real problem is getting past all the technology they've developed to protect themselves. And judging from the little bit of it we've seen, that technology is far more advanced than ours."

David had wandered around to the other side of the glass tubes and was making a close inspection of the sinewy corpses when his nation's leader called on him.

"David, you've already unlocked one part of that technology. You cracked their code, translated their signals in a relatively short time."

David hadn't realized that he and the president were on a first name basis. With the curve of the tube distorting his face, he answered, "Oh, I don't know about that, *Tom*. All I did was stumble onto the signal because it was disrupting the . . . I don't know how helpful I can be."

"Show them what you've discovered. I want the two of you," he meant Okun and David, "to put your heads together and, hopefully, come up with some answers." Then he leaned close enough for David to know it was a challenge. "Let's see if you're really as smart as you think you are."

UNAUTHORIZED VISITORS SUBJECT TO IMMEDIATE ARREST.
TRESPASSING ON THESE GROUNDS IS A FEDERAL OFFENSE PUNISHABLE
BY UP TO THREE YEARS IN FEDERAL PRISON.

The signs were posted every five hundred feet beside the single lane of asphalt leading toward Groom Lake. Other signs warned of hidden cameras and radar observation. All the warnings were real. They were put in place to discourage the intrepid UFO fanatics who were always trying to infiltrate the area for a look at the flying saucers the government had either developed or captured, depending on whose story you believed. If this were like any other day, two teams of military police would have been lurking in the sagebrush, waiting to make arrests. But it was like no day the earth had ever known.

Steve was riding in the back of a pickup truck with his prisoner and four men carrying shotguns. They kept a close watch on the thing beneath the orange parachute. If it woke up, they were ready to open fire. It seemed to take forever before they reached the tall chain-link fence with the barbed wire looped around the top, and the guardhouse that stood at the main entrance.

Two enlisted men, unfortunate enough to draw gate duty on the day the world was ending, shut off the news and came outside holding some serious-looking assault rifles. When Steve stood up in the back of the pickup, one of them hollered to him.

"Sorry, Captain. We can't let you through without clearance."

"You wanna see my clearance. Come over here, Private, I'll show you my goddamn clearance."

The soldier reluctantly came toward the bed of the pick up truck. Steve grabbed a fistful of the guard's collar and tore back the parachute, holding his face inches away from the ghastly exoskeleton.

The guy jumped back, shitting in his pants.

"JesusMaryJoseph! Let 'em through," he yelled to the other guard. "Let 'em through."

WHEN DAVID'S HEAD popped up through the floor, he experienced the sensation of entering a strange, darkly exotic galaxy. The interior of the attacker was a dim, oppressive chamber. Its rounded walls, dripping with creepy, semiorganic technology, felt more like the inside of a crypt than a flying machine. His first impulse was to call the whole thing off and climb back down the ladder. Okun, already inside, made matters worse by grinning maniacally through the gloom and saying, "I think you'll find this supremely cool. I do."

David squeezed his tall frame into the honeycomb cabin, then made his way to the front of the craft, where at least he could look out the dark windows at the "normal" environment of the concrete bunker. As Okun had promised, the cockpit was alive with a mad assortment of gizmos and flashing lights. There was a main control panel, but David hardly recognized it as such. Swollen irregular lines that resembled veins ran through the dashboard, and the lights of the instrument panel didn't flash on and off; they throbbed brighter then relaxed, like a beating heart. The whole place made him feel like he'd crawled inside some prehistoric insect.

"We've had people in here working around the clock trying to get a fix on what all this crap does. Some of it, we figured out immediately. Like this whole clump of stuff." He picked up a tube that looked like a piece of dried intestine. "This is part of the life-support system for the cabin. It runs back to a set of filters. This do-hickey over here," he pointed, "is a governor for the engines, either a manual override or the accelerator pedal."

"Did these seats come standard?" David asked planting himself in one of the leather chairs bolted to the floor.

While Okun told him the whole story of how the chairs got there, replacing a set of slimy "body-pods," David took an interest in one of the instruments. It was some type of screen that seemed to be composed of a translucent membrane, possibly the thin amber shell of some animal, with green patterns of light dancing through it. He stared at the strobing green light for several moments, then started tapping his foot to keep time. Okun was asking him something, but getting no response.

"Hello! Earth to Levinson!"

"Sorry. What did you say?"

"I asked if you'd found something interesting?"

"Maybe. Excuse me," David said absently, still transfixed by the pattern emerging on the screen. "Connie," he called out, "are you still out there?"

"Yes, I am." Her voice came in through the open hatch.

"Are you still holding my laptop?"

"Yes, I am."

"I need it."

Before she could answer, David realized how he sounded. Just like he used to when they lived together, like a spoiled genius who thought the world had to revolve around him. He jumped out of his chair and came to the hatch. Connie had already kicked off her heels and was climbing the steel rungs of the ladder. David's face at the hatch so suddenly surprised her.

"Ms. Spano, have I told you recently that you're a hell of a good sport?"

Connie handed the computer up to him at a loss for words. "No, you haven't."

"Thank you." David smiled down at her before disappearing again. There was something vaguely familiar about the green light on the screen, something similar to the broadcast signal he'd found. He flipped open the computer and booted up, explaining to Okun as he worked, "These patterns here on the, er . . . I think you called it the do-hickey."

"No, this is the thingamabob," Okun said wryly. "Please keep it straight. We're trying to be scientific."

"A thousand pardons, doctor. The patterns here on this instrument, they're repeating sequentially, just like—" he spun the machine around so Okun could see the screen "—just like their countdown signal. I think they're using this frequency for some kind of computer communications. It might be how they coordinate their ships."

Okun nodded, but still had questions. "Let's say you're right. Two problems: what's being said over the computer, and second, so what? What do we *do* about it? Where'd you go to school, anyway?"

"What I did with the countdown signal was apply a phase-reverse transmission to cancel out the signal."

"Did it work?"

David frowned. "Well, it didn't stop them from firing on the cities, but it cleared up the satellite reception problem I was working on. I went to MIT. Why? Where'd you go?"

"Cal Tech. No reason, I was just wondering."

Just when David was starting to doubt that Okun knew anything at all, the oddball doctor showed that he understood the situation.

"Okay, we still have two problems. First, we don't know what's being sent on this frequency. Could be attack plans, or it could be classical music. Maybe it's their version of an FM radio. Second problem: with the satellite disruption, you had a way of transmitting the countervailing signal, but this instrument here looks like a receiver. How are we going to send a canceling signal?"

David collapsed into the chair, all the steam taken out of him. "Another slight problem is that I ran out the door and left my phase-reverse spectrometer behind."

Okun, impishly comforted him. "Luckily, you've come to the right place. Not only do I have a spectrometer, but I also have another piece of technology which I think we're going to need. Feast your eyes on this." From his pocket, he withdrew a $1.98 screwdriver. "Let's take this screen apart and see if we can jerry-rig it to act as a transmitter."

"Cal Tech, huh?" David was learning to like this guy, up to a point.

It only took the pair of brainiacs a few minutes to solve their first problem. They tore the green screen loose and delicately attached a pair of alligator clamps to the sinewy wiring on the back. Although the machine had been built thousands of years before in another part of the universe, the data feeding into it was arranged in a binary system, a continuous string of ones and zeros, or whatever the alien equivalent was. Neither Okun nor David cared at that point, just as long as the little laptop could read the sequence.

A crew of technicians hauled Okun's spectrometer out of storage and brought it into the cockpit. As they were leaving the ship, planning to sneak back into the "freak show" room for another look at the dead aliens, David hit the enter key and applied the reversed sequence. For a moment, nothing happened and the two technical wizards felt the sinking feeling of disappointment. Then, cursing and shouting erupted outside the ship. Through the cockpit windows David and Okun could see the group of technicians laying flat on their asses. The men stood up and tried to walk away, but bounced off some unseen force field.

"Hey," Okun said, "we got the force field to work! I guess we must have put something in backwards when we repaired it the first time."

David sank back, depressed and deflated. He had been sure the amber screen was the way in to some kind of central command structure, but now he realized that he'd just spent a couple of hours making an insignificant repair. Disgusted with himself, he looked around the instrument panel. There were at least forty more gizmos to work on and no assurance that any of them would lead anywhere.

He shut off the force field signal when he saw Major Mitchell come racing across the concrete hangar toward the ship. The major spotted Okun behind the windows of the attacker and yelled up at him.

"They've got one! And it's still alive!"

AS SOON AS the elevator doors slid open, Mitchell took off at a dead run, leaving Doctors Okun and Issacs to jog along by themselves. Issacs, who had once run an emergency room in Boston, had the presence of mind to grab his black bag. As they ran toward the crowd gathered just inside the giant hangar doors, Okun's lab coat gave up a steady stream of pens, electrical caps, hand tools, including the slide rule he'd been using since high school, and several stray pieces of the attacker's instrument panel. By the time they crossed the hangar, someone had handed Mitchell a bullhorn.

"All nonmilitary personnel step away from the stretcher," he yelled at the hundred or so civilians who were helping deliver the creature. "Clear out of this hangar immediately. Step behind the doors and wait outside."

Okun shoved his way through the dispersing crowd and found a large body wrapped in a parachute strapped tight to a medical gurney. He pulled enough of the nylon material free to recognize the surface of the biomechanical suit.

"Who found this thing?" he yelled.

"I did, sir. Captain Steven Hiller, U.S. Marines. His ship went down in the desert."

"Alone? Weren't there others?"

The question took Steve off guard. "As a matter of fact, there were two more. Both killed in the crash," he reported. He looked the long-haired doctor over carefully and couldn't help asking, "How'd you know that?"

"How long has this one been unconscious?" Issacs asked.

"Since I kicked the—" Steve decided not to tell them how the creature got to be unconscious. Instead, he finished, "About three hours."

The gurney was on the move, soldiers wheeling it fast across the smooth hangar floor. All the civilians had obeyed the command to return to their vehicles outside, all except two.

"Doctor, excuse me," Russell said for the tenth time, his arm around Miguel's shoulder. Steve remembered that the big red-headed man needed to find some medical help for his son and, from his position on the far side of the stretcher, tried to get Okun's attention. It was no use; everyone was completely focused on the alien specimen.

"Let's get him down to containment, stat," Okun yelled. Then, to his colleague, "Is it still alive?"

Amidst the turmoil of the speeding gurney and people shouting in every direction, cool-headed Issacs had put a stethoscope to the monster's chest. "Still respiring," he reported.

"Listen, doctor, my boy is very sick. He needs immediate attention."

Okun seemed to look up at Russell as they entered the elevator hallway, but he was only searching for the button that would take them down to the operating room. "He's drying out. Let's have some saline solution ready by the time we get down there."

Okun pushed past Russell and moved to the switch. He touched the button and the room began its hydraulic, humming descent. But before the elevator had moved a foot, it suddenly lurched to a halt.

Russell slammed his fist against the emergency stop button, then grabbed a fistful of the first thing that looked like medical help. He came up with Dr. Issacs's white lab coat. He pinned the man so tightly against the elevator wall that the doctor's toes were off the ground and stared at him with furious bloodshot eyes.

"My boy has a problem with his adrenal cortex. He's going into adrenal shock and collapse. If he doesn't get some medicine right now, he is going to die." Issacs could smell the stale liquor on the man's breath.

Miguel, for once, felt proud of his father. "He needs an injection of cortecosteroid, or at least some insulin."

Issacs, unflappable, spoke calmly to his burly attacker. "Sounds like Addison's syndrome. I've got some cortecosteroid right there."

Russell followed the doctor's eyes down to where his black bag rested beside the gurney. Issacs didn't like the idea of missing any part of this history-making medical procedure, but he knew Okun could handle the OR until he got there.

"O'Haver, Miller, come with me." Then to Russell, "Take us to him."

NEAR ANAHEIM, Jasmine found the freeway and headed south. Because she had the First Lady bumping around in the back of the truck, she couldn't go any faster than thirty miles per hour. As the sun began to set, turning the sky a thousand hues of orange and purple through the smoke on the horizon, it was almost possible to forget the destruction behind them. The electricity was out, but otherwise the neighborhoods surrounding the freeway seemed fine, normal. There was light traffic headed in both directions, and the heat of the day was relaxing to a warm evening.

She followed the signs and took the El Toro exit. Miles before, still driving over and around the rubble, she met several people who told her that the base had been hit. They advised her not to waste her time, but the news only increased Jasmine's anxiety to hurry up and get there. No matter how much damage the base had incurred, she assumed she'd be able to find medical attention for Mrs. Whitmore and, if she were lucky, find Steve. She imagined herself driving up to his broken plane out on a runway where he was working on it, determined to patch it up so he could join the fight.

As soon as she was off the freeway, the signs of destruction were all around her. Soon she found herself driving through low, rolling hills along a road that disappeared into giant potholes every few yards. She spotted a group of kids poking through the smoking remains of a building further up the road. She drove up the hill onto a level plain and yelled to them.

"Hey, you guys, you know where El Toro is? The Marine base?"

"This is it, lady," one of them yelled back.

Jasmine drove another hundred yards through the wreckage before coasting to a stop and suddenly turning off the engine. She stepped down out of the truck and walked a few feet to the collapsed facade of a building.

WELCOME TO EL TORO

MARINE CORPS AIR STATION

HOME OF THE BLACK KNIGHTS

Nothing was left standing. The whole area had been pulverized under a hailstorm of laser blasts until not a single building was left standing. Instead of a thriving military base, the area looked as flat as freshly plowed farmland interrupted by a few piles of charred rubble. Jasmine sat down and cried until the last light of evening faded from the sky.

THE NATION'S OFFICIAL military headquarters had trans-
ferred from the Pentagon to a noisy, makeshift office 150 feet below the floor of
the Nevada desert. The experiment control room at Area 51 was designed to
monitor test flights by prototype jets and other experimental aircraft. It was
well stocked with electronic gadgetry, everything from old rotary dial phones
on up to worldwide radar tracking screens, but almost none of it was working.
The earth's great communications networks had all been torn apart, and the
damage was getting worse by the hour.

Major Mitchell's men were joined by the crack squad of communications
specialists from Air Force One. They'd requisitioned three CB radios from the
horde of RVs parked outside and were busy gathering information from guys
that said such things as, "10–4, good buddy." The second wave of cities had
already been destroyed and the big ships were moving on, apparently firing at
will. Even deep in the earth, hundreds of miles from the nearest city destroyer,
people were scared. They were starting to realize that even if the destruction
were to stop immediately, the country and the world they had known would
never be the same. Not even close. They knew they were totally at the mercy of
the creatures in the huge ships.

Nimziki was scared, too. He wasn't afraid of dying physically, but the idea of
political death terrified him. He'd spent his whole life working harder than anyone else to grab and keep control, never leaving tracks, never leaving his back
exposed, making himself indispensable to others in power. He'd risen to the top,
being appointed the chief of the CIA, then becoming Whitmore's secretary of
defense, and even that didn't give him enough control. "The Iron Sphincter" was
losing his grip. He knew that beating these invaders was a real long shot, but by
force of habit his mind planned on being back in Washington, picking up the
pieces, reestablishing his network of allies and, most of all, trying to beat the rap
he knew he was going to take for withholding the Area 51 secret too long. He
came into the war room, as they were calling it, and picked up one of the phones.

"Got any other secrets up your sleeve that might help us win this fight?"

"That's a cheap shot, General, and you know it." Nimziki knew Grey,
doggedly loyal to Whitmore, would come after him sooner or later.

"I seem to remember a staff meeting yesterday in Washington. You sat there
on that damn couch while we presented options to the president on a code yellow emergency and you didn't say anything about this place."

"I gave President Whitmore my best advice: hit them with nuclear
weapons. That is still my recommendation, and if he had followed it, we
wouldn't even be here right now. Besides, all I knew was that there was some
old spaceship down here."

"Don't feed me that line of crap. You keep your fingers up more asses than a proctologist, so don't claim you didn't know everything about this place. When were you planning on informing the rest of us?"

"Look, The whole project was deemed classified, black shelf."

Grey didn't pretend to hide his disgust. "Christ, why didn't you say something when they first arrived? You could have saved the lives of over a hundred American pilots." Grey stared at him, trying to fathom the man's banal form of evil. He knew full well that Nimziki had sat on the information as long as he did to save his own political hide.

"Look, don't lay the lives of those pilots at my doorstep. Knowing—"

Everything changed when President Whitmore came through the door. Nimziki and Grey turned away from each other and the dozen technicians manning the communications equipment went back to work. Connie led the way over to a paper map of the United States that was taped to the wall, the destroyed cities circled in black.

"Oh my God." She gasped when she saw the update.

"Are these confirmed?" Whitmore asked, staring at the bad news on the map. "Atlanta, Sacramento, and Philadelphia?"

"Yes, sir. Those sites are confirmed hits. We're also hearing of several raids on isolated targets, mainly military air bases."

"Which way are they heading?"

Grey answered. He walked over and used the map to illustrate. "It looks like their plan is to send the Washington ship down the Atlantic coast, then possibly head in over the Gulf states. The Los Angeles craft looks like it's going to continue up the West Coast, while the New York ship is moving toward Chicago right now."

The president moved to the conference table, took a seat, and poured himself a glass of water while Grey went on.

"They're actually attacking corridors, sending out those little attack fighters as they pass through an area to hit specific targets. They aren't moving around blindly, that's for sure. We heard from Europe that the ship over Paris moved immediately to Brussels and hit NATO headquarters while the smaller planes picked apart Western Alliance installations." Then, with an accusatory glare in Nimziki's direction, he added, "They've obviously scouted us, planning this attack for some time. The shits know exactly where and how to hit us."

Seething with anger, the president turned toward his secretary of defense ready to unload on him. Then, just as quickly, he turned away. There was no time to dwell on his treasonous behavior now. He would deal with Nimziki in the future, if there was one.

"What about our forces? What kind of capability have we got left?"

"We're down to approximately fifteen percent, sir." Grey gave him a moment to soak that in before spelling out the dreadful consequences. "Calculating the time it's taking them to destroy a city and move on, we're looking at worldwide destruction of every major city within the next thirty-six hours."

Whitmore took a long, calm drink of water. "We're being exterminated." That was an ugly way to describe the situation, one that made the players in the room bristle uncomfortably, but no one could think of a more accurate term. A knock came at the door.

"Mr. President." Major Mitchell entered. "I have that pilot you wanted to meet."

"Show him in."

Whitmore stood up and straightened his tie as Mitchell waved Steve in the door. Still wearing the same sweat-soaked undershirt and combat pants he'd marched across the desert in, Steve didn't feel ready to meet a roomful of powerful white people, especially the president.

"Captain Steven Hiller, sir," he announced with a ramrod salute.

"At ease." The president smiled without returning the salute. His enthusiasm immediately put Steve more at ease. "It's an honor to meet you, Captain. You did one hell of a job out there today."

"Thank you, sir. Just trying to do my job."

"You're out of El Toro, aren't you?"

"Yes, sir. Black Knights, first squadron."

"Have you ever heard of the Hellcats out of Fort Bragg?"

Steve couldn't repress a quick smile. He knew Whitmore had been a fighter pilot, of course. During the Gulf War, the Hellcats had become a household word. But he hadn't expected any pilot talk during a meeting with the commander in chief. "I've heard of them," he said.

"What have you heard?" Whitmore pressed him.

"Second best unit in the whole damned armed services, sir. Right behind the Knights."

Now both of them were grinning in mutual admiration. "Where's that prisoner you brought in?"

Mitchell saw his opening and jumped in. He wanted to get over to the operating theater and observe. "He's in a medical containment area, sir. The doctors are optimistic that he'll survive."

"I don't know if that's cause for optimism," the president said, "but I'd like to have a look at this thing."

That was the cue for the president's staff to snatch their papers off the table and prepare to move. General Grey stepped forward and expressed his misgivings about the plan, but Whitmore was determined. "See to it this man gets whatever he needs," he said, pointing to Steve before leaving the room at the head of his entourage.

"Excuse me, General." Steve caught Grey's attention as he was about to leave for the medical area. "I'm real anxious to get back to El Toro."

Now that he'd turned the alien over, there wasn't much reason for him to stick around. And he kept hearing Jimmy's voice in his head telling him Jasmine might have survived the blast. If she had, there was only one place he knew to look for her. He asked the General if he could have some time on one of the radios or if a message could be sent.

Grey stopped dead in his tracks and put a hand on Steve's shoulder. "I'm sorry, son. I guess you haven't heard. El Toro was destroyed this morning in the attack."

Shattered, Steve stood still, trying to breathe as the general hurried off to join the others.

A BLOOD ORANGE moon lit the path through the ruins. An hour after they'd left to search for supplies, Jasmine and Dylan came picking their way through the dark toward a roaring campfire. Each of them carried a box loaded with cans of food salvaged from the remains of the base's cafeteria. Dylan's box held an industrial-sized can of baked beans that weighed half as much as he did and a bunch of bent spoons they'd found in the dirt. Before they left the pantry, they'd thrown boards over the opening and covered them with dirt.

"Okay, folks, dinner is served." Jas set the box down and then took a set of steak knives from her pocket. "We'll use these for can openers."

The quiet man had taken charge in Jasmine's absence and done quite a job. The First Lady was laying on a bed of cardboard and folded clothes, his jacket neatly folded under her head as a pillow. Jas had started a small fire before she left, but he'd improved it considerably, building a neatly stacked bonfire straight off the cover of a scouting magazine.

"Hey, you did a nice job. I hardly recognize the old place."

She went to check on the president's wife, who tried to sit up when she saw Jasmine coming. The effort cost her a great deal of pain. She went into a coughing fit, her lungs filling with fluid.

When Jas got her settled down again, she scolded, "Don't move like that.

I'm serious. You keep as still as you can tonight, and in the morning we'll get you some help."

She helped the injured woman sip some pineapple juice. Then the two of them stared into the fire for a long time without saying anything.

The quiet man had opened a can of frankfurters for Dylan who was doing the Dance of Happiness while he ate. The dance consisted of staring at the sky and wiggling his butt back and forth to express how good the food was. The motion was repeated with each mouthful. Jasmine watched him gyrate, stone-faced. Tonight they would feast, but in the days to come she knew there would be famine. Where would tomorrow's meal come from?

"Your son," Mrs. Whitmore said weakly, "he's beautiful."

Jasmine was about to scold her again for not resting, but instead, she allowed, "He's my angel."

"Was his father stationed here?"

Jasmine let out a deep, resigned sigh. "Well, he wasn't his father. I was sort of hoping he'd want the job, though." She threw a pebble into the flames. She was about to start bawling her eyes out again, but forced herself not to.

The other woman could sense it was time to change the subject. "So, what do you do for a living?"

"I'm a dancer."

"How wonderful. Modern? Ballet?"

Jasmine smiled at the flames. "No, *exotic*," she announced, glancing at the president's wife, wondering how many strippers she'd ever met and whether that wouldn't be a bee in her high-class bonnet.

"Oh . . . sorry."

"Don't be," Jas told her, "I'm not. It's not where I thought I'd end up, but the money's real good, and besides," she lifted her chin toward Dylan, "he's worth taking good care of."

Jas didn't usually go around telling people what she did for a living. She wasn't ashamed of it, but she wasn't proud, either. When the subject came up, she'd sometimes lie, sometimes tell the truth, and sometimes give no answer at all. This is one of those times she wished she hadn't told the truth, because she was pretty sure a respectable gal like the president's wife wasn't going to have a whole lot to say to her afterward. She wanted to say something else, something like "Don't worry, just cause I'm a stripper. I'm still going to find you a doctor in the morning." But that would have sounded stupid.

"And what are you going to do when the dancing's over?" Marilyn asked. "What about your future?"

Jasmine smiled again, this time because the First Lady's question was one she'd asked herself a million times. It had been a monkey on her back from which she suddenly felt herself released. "You know, I used to ask myself that question every day, but you know what? I don't think it matters anymore."

"Mommy, can I have some more weenies?"

"Sugar, come over here to mama for a minute. I want you to meet the First Lady." Dylan, hoping it might lead to more weenies, came over to be introduced.

"That's funny. I was sure you didn't recognize me."

"Well, I didn't want to say anything. I voted for the other guy."

DR. OKUN PUT his face close to the lens of the video camera. "This recording is being made on July Fourth at six forty-five P.M. The alien sustained a violent plane crash this morning at approximately nine o'clock. As you can see—" he stepped away revealing the eight-foot-long creature strapped down to an operating table "—the thing appears to be very weak." Indeed, the only signs of life came from the short tentacles on the face which twitched and twisted sporadically. The four longer dorsal tentacles, measuring between six and twelve feet, had been tucked haphazardly under the thick retaining straps and remained motionless.

The operating theater, as this tiled room with stainless steel trimmings was known, had several tall windows of reinforced glass looking out onto the storage/lecture room Okun had called the Freak Show. The great tubes holding the bodies of the three dead aliens were visible in the darkened chamber beyond. Three assistants moved efficiently about the room: a woman anesthesiologist and two male orderlies. One of the men made adjustments to a complicated piece of machinery connected by a series of flexible hoses to a large vat of formaldehyde. The other orderly handed Okun a set of tools, a mallet and a chisel as thick as a railroad tie. Okun, ever the showman, held them in the air, pretending to be Dr. Frankenstein in an old movie.

"All the life-support monitors are recording?" The anesthesiologist nodded her head then the doctor continued speaking to the camera. "We're going to split the skull open and peel it back in order to reach the living creature inside. This," he said, rapping on the yellowish exoskeleton, "is only a suit of armor. The animal you are seeing now is actually a completely separate species which the aliens raise to maturity, slaughter, then gut. The internal organs are scooped out, but the musculature is preserved. The skull and chest have a seam down the middle allowing the aliens to slip in and out. So they wear the body of this other creature, sort of like crawling inside a zombie.

Then, by a process we may never understand, the physical impulses of the frail creature inside are carried out by the corpse of this much larger, much stronger animal. Notice how the tentacles seem to flop around with little control. As you will see in a moment, the animal inside has no tentacles, so it may be that they are not able to manipulate these extra arms. Alas, until we find a healthy specimen to study, this bio-armor will remain a mystery. Gentlemen, are you ready?"

His assistants were more than ready; they wanted to get this business done and get out of there. While Okun hammed it up for the video camera, the others were keeping tense eyes on the bony leviathan strapped to the table, half expecting it to roar to life at any moment.

Working the chisel into the seam of the skull, Okun delivered a few sharp whacks, each one causing the gruesome sound of cracking bones. The men, Colin and Patrick, tugged in opposite directions until the skull gave way. They peeled the meat and ligament back until it lay flat on the table.

"Oh, Jesus!" The smell coming from the inside of the suit backed the four humans away. "Stinks like ammonia," said Patrick, his eyes watering up. "We gotta open the door." He was already at the security keypad when Okun realized what he was doing.

"No!" the doctor shouted. "We can't risk releasing an airborne virus. Turn up the ventilation system. Jenny, stand by with one hundred cc's of sodium Pentothal just in case our little friend here decides to get rowdy."

While the others gagged on the fumes and tried to clear their eyes, Okun returned to examining the creature. The crown of the alien's head was visible tucked into the chest cavity of its host animal. He ripped open the throat and upper chest of the armor until the fleshy, bulbous head of the alien lay exposed. The huge lidless black eyes stared back up at him. Okun bent close to examine the creature's face, slathered in a thick coat of gelatinous slime, the material that passed the alien's impulses out to the armor-body. The eyes showed no response, but the beaklike nose began to twitch as Okun hovered over it. One of the facial tentacles curled towards the eyes, moving weakly back and forth. Okun poked at it once before letting it curl around the finger of his gloved hand with the strength of a newborn baby. It seemed to be the same kind of friendly gesture he had read about in the extensive notes left by his predecessor, Dr. Welles.

"Damn!" Colin returned to the table as the ventilation system began filtering out the worst of the powerful, pungent odor. "They've conquered space travel but not BO."

"Release me," Okun said softly to no one in particular.

"Pardon?" Everyone looked up at the doctor for an explanation, but he seemed not to realize he'd said anything.

"Okay, let's pull him out of there. I'll—" He broke off in midsentence, staring out into space.

"Doctor? Doctor Okun, you all right?"

He stared back at them for a moment as if he were having trouble remembering who they were and where he was. Then, just as quickly, he snapped out of it. "Yeah, I'm fine. I think the fumes are starting to get to me a little."

"The tentacles are showing increased activity, doctor. Shall I go ahead and inject the Pentothal?" Jenny asked.

Sodium Pentothal, most famous as a supposed "truth serum," was a common barbiturate used to tranquilize patients during medical procedures.

"No. Bad idea. No injections." Okun was staring straight ahead once more, talking in a calm, almost slurred voice. "Remove the restraints."

His assistants were accustomed to Okun acting strangely, but they'd never seen him do anything downright spooky. Seemingly disoriented, his head slowly swiveled around on his shoulders while his eyes darted from one thing to the next, investigating the room around him. Then he reached up and grabbed his head with his free hand, obviously in agony. He shouted once, gripped by a vicious pain coursing through his head. Jenny nudged the orderly standing next to her, using her eyes to call attention to the doctor's wrist. One of the tentacles from the creature's back had slipped free and wrapped itself around Okun's wrist just above the rubber glove.

"Let's stick him," she ordered.

Patrick pulled back the thick flesh of the armor-body and wiped at the alien's neck with an alcohol swab. Jenny stabbed the hypodermic needle into the translucent flesh and began to squeeze the plunger. Before anyone had time to flinch, the tentacle holding Okun's wrist flashed over the table and whipped Jenny across the face, knocking her across the room in a spatter of blood. Lightning fast, the same powerful arm tore the restraining belts away, breaking them off where they were bolted to the steel frame, then cracked down savagely on Colin's head as he turned to run for the door. Patrick picked up a surgeon's scalpel, waving the small weapon threateningly, as if that would be enough to protect him from this ferocious, overpowering beast. It stood up, its sharp claw-like feet clacking on the clean linoleum floor, and charged across the room. Two of the tentacles pinned his arms while a third impaled him, stabbing into his heart and coming out the other side. Patrick's body smashed into the formaldehyde tank, shattering it. As the contents of the tank flooded onto the floor of the operating theater, one of the vacuum tubes was torn loose, gushing great quantities of steam into the air.

The vaultlike door pushed open and Mitchell showed the president, his advisers, and bodyguards into the storage vault. The operating theater was completely hidden by a thick cloud of steam. When Mitchell saw this, he reached down and unsnapped the flap on his pistol. Before he could withdraw it, one Secret Service man had pulled the president away and the other had a revolver pointed directly at the major's head. The big soldier never noticed. Realizing something had gone wrong, he rushed to the window and activated the intercom system.

"Dr. Okun, can you hear me?" he called. "If you can hear me, sir, say something so we know you're all right." There was no response. The clouds of steam rolled silently behind the glass. Mitchell turned to the president. "Sir, there's a—"

Slam! Okun's blood-smeared body smashed violently against the glass, a thick tangle of quivering tentacle wrapped around his throat. It was impossible to know if he was dead or alive. Camouflaged by the thick fog, the alien forced the scientist's face tightly against the glass, pushing it out of shape. Okun's mouth opened and words came out, but the voice was not his. The words were barely intelligible, like a dead man's last breath passing over his vocal chords.

"Lelethe meh. lelethe meh," the voice croaked.

"We've got to get him out of there," Mitchell yelled. "I'll go around and open the door."

"Stay where you are," General Grey ordered. He stepped closer to the window. "Doctor Okun, can you hear me?"

Slowly, Okun's lips opened again, and this time the words were more intelligible. ". . . will kill . . . release me. Now!"

Grey and the others began to understand what was happening. The alien was speaking through Okun, controlling his body like a ventriloquist controls a wooden dummy. The formaldehyde tank had shut itself off and the ventilation system was slowly clearing the atmosphere inside the room. Slowly, they were able to see where the tentacle holding Okun to the glass came from. It led up to where the creature hung from the ceiling, frantically clawing at an air duct in an attempt to escape. Frustrated, the animal dropped to the floor, then advanced toward the windows through the swirling steam.

Its indistinct outline stood writhing at the center of the clearing room. Okun had been half right about the tentacles. The creature inside had no corresponding limbs to control those on the suit. They danced and jangled without direction until the alien, by force of concentration, made them do its bidding.

They were, in fact, the alien's weapon of choice, having trained with them from birth.

Whitmore and the others could see how the torn skull and chest of the suit flopped lifelessly from the rigid backbone. The larger animal had been gutted, sliced from navel to forehead, providing a sort of open hood for the creature within.

Once more, it punched at the window with Okun's limp body. It was quickly learning how to work the speech organs of the man's not-quite-dead body. This time the words were clear and loud. "Release me!"

Whitmore came halfway to the windows. "Why have you come here?" he demanded. "What do your people want?"

The pulsing, livid crown of the alien's skull appeared from between the hip sockets of the suit. Black eyes peered over the wall of flesh. Then with an audible slurp, the creature raised up out of the suit's lower abdomen to face his captors. Its yellow skin glistened in the dim light under a thick slather of clear jelly. Its huge, startled eyes gave it the look of a naturally meek animal surrounded by predators.

Okun, under the creature's control, gasped suddenly for breath. "Air. Water. Food. Sun."

"Yes, we have all of these," Whitmore replied through the intercom. "Tell me where you have come from. Where is your home?"

"Here," it said slowly, "our new home."

"And before here, where did you come from?"

"Many worlds."

"We have enough air and water and sun. We could share them. Can we negotiate a truce? Can your people coexist with us?" There was no answer, but the president persisted. "Can there be peace between us?" A voice behind him suggested that the thing might not understand the world peace, so he tried a different angle. "What is it that you want? What do you want our people to do?"

The alien answered the question. This time it did not use the humans' clumsy grunting form of communication. It "spoke" in its natural language, free of sound, gesture, and emotion. Perhaps the sodium Pentothal was taking effect, or perhaps the alien had read their minds and learned he could not escape. It began a high-speed telepathic communication with Whitmore. It was a language of images and physical sensations, a lightning fast download of a virtual reality rocket ride through the alien's entire memory. The exchange of information was happening faster than the synapses of Whitmore's brain could fire. The result was that the president fell over backward clutching at the left side of his brain, screaming in pain.

In a few seconds, he moved through battles on other worlds, learning how the aliens had conquered planet after planet, flying from place to place like a swarm of locusts, feeding on an environment, expanding their population, until its resources were ruined, exhausted. Provisions would be made for the journey to the next feeding ground, and they would all board the mother ship, the temporary hive. All the creatures would sleep during the long journey and awaken famished, warriors ready to do battle for new food. He understood there would be no mercy, that the concept of it was nowhere in the alien's mind, as foreign to him as it would be for us to spare the lives of roaches. To him, we were vermin, filthy little things that needed to be exterminated. And that was their plan, to wipe humanity off the face of this small planet. The objective of the initial wave of attack would be to exterminate the largest nests of humans, disable their weapons, and establish beach heads, room for the aliens to establish their colonies. Then, for many years, they would live and breed here, developing new tools, until it was time to travel, stronger and more numerous, to the next home.

"Kill it!" Grey shouted.

Mitchell and both of the president's bodyguards spun around and started blasting, shattering the window, squeezing off every round of ammunition they had. The bullets tore into the alien's delicate white body, smearing him against the shell of his armor like thick glops of paint. The armor-body collapsed backward with a crash onto the wet tiles, both creatures dead. Okun slid down the window and collapsed in a pile.

"Stand back," Grey yelled, returning to the president, "give the man some air."

Woozy and disoriented, Whitmore lay on the floor breathing hard. When he sat up, he was still holding the side of his throbbing head. "Wanted me to understand . . . communicated with me. They're like locusts," he said. "They travel from planet to planet. The whole civilization moves. After they've consumed everything, the natural resources, they move on."

As if slowly untangling himself from a strong dream, Whitmore sat on the floor piecing the images together. He wanted to explain it all to the others, but there was only one conclusion to draw from the experience. He stood up the best he could and turned to Grey. "General, coordinate a missile strike. I want a nuclear warhead sent to every one of their ships. And I want it done immediately."

Grey looked the president in the eyes to make sure he realized what he was saying. The poisonous fallout from that number of simultaneous explosions would cripple the planet and every creature on it. Satisfied that Whitmore was lucid, he nodded.

"It'll take some time, maybe an hour." Under the weight of this order, Grey started off toward the war room. On the way, he passed Nimziki, who had remained silent until then.

As Grey passed him, Nimziki smirked. *I told you so.*

STEVEN HILLER WAS a hero to the horde of people parked outside the hangar. He was also someone they could talk to, a member of their group. The guards outside the hangar were tight-lipped and unfriendly; as far as they were concerned, these campers weren't welcome. Their orders were to keep the people supplied with fresh water and let them use the bathrooms two at a time, which meant the bushes off in the distance were getting most of the business. It was night when Steve walked out, telling the guards at the gate that he was sent by Dr. Issacs to check on the sick boy. Steve never made it to the Casse trailer. A bunch of people waiting in line to use the restrooms recognized him and walked with him as he disappeared into the thicket of vehicles.

Steve moved through the trailers shaking hands and answering the same questions over and over again. Was the ET still alive? What were they doing with it? Were there any spaceships coming this way and why couldn't they come inside? Why were they being made to sit out there like sitting ducks? They made him promise to ask whoever was in charge if they could come inside.

Steve moved among them, listening and smiling, but he hadn't come out there to fraternize. His concentration was on a pair of Hueys, fat gray transport helicopters standing outside another hangar three hundred yards from the perimeter of the trailer camp. Steve watched for a few minutes, until he decided they were unguarded. Excusing himself from the conversation, he strode across the tarmac trying to look like he was on official business. He kept expecting someone with a bullhorn to stop him, but to his surprise he made it all the way unchallenged, climbed into the pilot's chair, and switched the systems on. There was plenty of gas, so he reached for the switch that fired the motor. A split second after the twin rotors, front and back propellers, came groaning to life, Steve had an M-16 rifle pointed at his chest.

"What are you doing? Get out of there, this minute."

The soldier on the other end of the rifle looked to be no older that eighteen. Dressed in camouflage fatigues, his desert helmet fit him like an old wash pail bouncing loosely around his head. Although he was the one holding the weapon, it was clear from the start who was afraid of whom. Steve decided to brazen it out. He reached back and pulled the seat belt forward, locking himself in.

"Captain Hiller, Marine Corps. I'm going to borrow your chopper for a couple of hours."

"You can't just—" The kid looked around for help, but they were alone. "The hell you are . . . sir."

Steve figured there was a fifty-fifty chance the kid would shoot. He decided to gamble. Reaching up, he switched on the lights and prepared the craft for liftoff.

"Soldier," he shouted over the blades, the air knocking the kid's desert helmet around, "I know you don't want to shoot me, but if you're gonna do it, do it right now, because otherwise I'm leaving."

The kid stared unblinking at him for a minute. Without lowering his gun, he yelled, "You're gonna get me into a world of trouble, Marine."

"We're both in one already." A jeep was barreling toward them on its way across the tarmac from the main hangar. "I'll be back in a couple hours and explain everything." Then the big bird thumped into the air and twisted away to the west.

NEWS OF WHITMORE'S decision to launch a nuclear attack spread through the underground scientific complex, plunging the place into a deep silence. Work came to a standstill as people huddled into groups, most of them sitting silently, resigned to their doom. No one was happy with the decision, but neither could they suggest a workable alternative. There was nothing to do now but wait.

Connie, on the verge of tears, slipped away from the oppressive gloom of the war room, where Whitmore sat drumming his fingernails on the tabletop, while the strike was prepared. She came into the echoing concrete hangar, keeping one eye on the stingray attacker. Through a set of windows, she could see David pacing back and forth in an office lounge, talking to himself. She came up the stairs and into the room to discover he wasn't talking to himself. He was speaking to a bottle of scotch he'd found in one of the closets.

"I take it you've heard," she said, closing the door behind her.

"Ah, Ms. Spano, you're just in time!" His voice was too loud. He was already drunk. Hoisting the bottle into the air, he declared, "A toast! I would like to propose a toast to the end of the world." He threw back his head and took a long slug of whiskey before handing her the bottle.

"He didn't come to this decision lightly, David." She felt guilty, complicitous in his eyes.

"Connie, honey, come on! Don't tell me you still believe in this guy."

"He's a good man."

"He must be." David laughed, flopping into a swivel chair and pushing himself in a circle. "After all, you left a gem like me for him. No. Excuse me, not for him. For your *career*." David knew how to be nasty, but Connie wanted to explain herself.

"It wasn't just a career move, David. It was a once in a lifetime opportunity. It was a chance to make a real difference, to make my life mean something."

"And I just wasn't ambitious enough for you," David said casually. It was an idea that had crippled him with pain for the last few years, but now it all seemed rather humorous. "I couldn't get the lead out of my ass and start climbing up the ladder."

"You could have done anything you wanted," she yelled, "research, teaching, industry. You've got so much talent."

David broke out into a vicious imitation of the familiar voices: "Oh, that David Levinson, so much potential and all he does is work for that silly old cable company. All that brain power going down the drain. What a shame." That attitude disgusted him. "What's the matter with being happy right where you are?"

"But didn't you ever want to do something more? Didn't you ever want to be part of something really meaningful, really special?"

Those last few words mixed with the scotch to punch David square in the solar plexus. He leveled a wounded stare at Connie and told her the plain simple truth. "I felt like I *was* part of something special."

She immediately realized that the whole time she'd been talking about their careers, he'd been thinking about their marriage. She could see that she'd hurt him. He came across the room and took back the bottle.

"If it makes any difference," she said softly, "I never stopped loving you."

"But that wasn't enough, right?" he spit back. He returned to his chair and took a good long swig of whiskey.

Connie suddenly realized why she'd come to find him. She wanted to make peace with a man she still loved. Somewhere in the back of her head she thought they might forgive each other, renounce their anger, and try to find some comfort in one another now that the end of their lives was clearly within sight. But instead, she'd encountered a venomously angry boy. As he did so often with her, David's way of coping with pressure was to retreat into himself, or his work, or whatever was close at hand and offered escape. Tonight it was a bottle of Johnny Walker .

She left him there, spinning around in the swivel chair, singing to himself. With tears in her eyes, she slipped out the door, closing it quietly behind her.

GREY WAS ABLE to orchestrate the nuclear strike in less than a quarter of the time he'd anticipated. Returning to the war room, he got the good news that military radio and radar capabilities had been partially restored thanks to some quick thinking in San Antonio. The cluster of Air Force bases surrounding the city had scrambled two dozen AWACS into the skies over the United States. The large spy planes, with their trademark radar dishes whirling on top and sophisticated eavesdropping equipment within, took over the job orbiting Comsats had done so reliably for decades. Their multichannel switching relays allowed military personnel to begin communicating once again. One of the first messages they broadcast came from Area 51. There was to be a simultaneous nuclear strike against all the ships over American airspace.

Within minutes, a quartet of B-2 Stealth bombers was in the air, streaking toward their targets. They flew "dark," meaning their radar-deflecting systems were up and their radios were switched off, hoping to avoid detection by the city destroyers until they came within striking distance. The president was in the infirmary being examined by Dr. Issacs when word came that the B-2s were airborne. Without hesitation, Whitmore pushed the doctor aside and hurried to the war room.

"Which target are we going to reach first?" he demanded, barging through the door.

A soldier turned from one of the monitor consoles. "The ship approaching Houston. Approximate intercept time is six minutes. We can't say for sure because the B-2s are flying dark."

Whitmore thought for a minute before issuing a change. "Wake the B-2s up. I want to make sure we all stay on the same page."

The soldier spun back to his console and typed in the code word that switched the B-2s' radios on automatically. Instantly, the radar scans spotted them and the four planes blipped up on the screens. The Houston plane was easily the closest to its target.

"All right, here's what I want," Whitmore explained to the room, "one plane, one bomb. Let's see what happens in Houston. Maybe we can hit that one before it arrives over the city. If we're successful, we'll go ahead and fire on the others right away." He looked at Grey, who was scowling over a computer printout.

"General, has there been any word from our friends?" At the same time he was authorizing the use of an atomic weapon, he was trying to restrain their use by the rest of the world. ICBMs in many locations were programmed to respond automatically to radar-perceived attacks. The last thing the earth needed was a chain-reaction nuclear launch initiated by computers.

"We have commitments from most of our friends. They'll wait to see our results," Grey said. "But I think we're too late to save Houston."

"That's affirmative, sir," a voice rang out from the consoles. "The enemy ship is already over the city."

The president didn't flinch. He knew Houston would be lost one way or the other. He sent orders to the other B-2s that they were to hold their fire until the Houston bomb's impact on the invaders' ship could be assessed.

Grey had arranged for observers in armored tanks to position themselves around the perimeter of the expected blast area. One of the San Antonio AWACS spy planes also positioned itself over the Gulf of Mexico at high altitude.

The people of Houston had wasted no time. With only a few hours of warning, the city was almost ninety percent vacant by the time the ground began to tremble under the approaching ship. The evacuation had turned ugly, causing almost two thousand casualties and countless injuries as escapees were trampled under foot or hit by speeding vehicles. Similar frenzied exoduses were underway in Kobe, Brussels, Portland, Chicago, and all the other major cities standing in the paths of the great black ships.

Whitmore called for a moment of silence. After whispering a brief prayer, he ordered the strike with a simple nod. "May our children forgive us."

The B-2's bay doors dropped open, depositing its twelve-foot-long missile into the air. It flew parallel with the batlike plane while the tracking system in its nose cone scanned the horizon and configured its telemetry. A second later, it blasted forward to its rendezvous with the gigantic ship's protective screen.

"Payload is deployed," the pilot reported. He pulled a long U-turn and put distance between himself and the coming explosion.

Everyone in the war room held their breath, following the bomb's approach on their radar screens. As planned, the cruise missile approached the shield on the ship's top side in an attempt to minimize damage to the city below.

From the AWACS plane, there was a violent shock of ultrabright light followed immediately by the sight of suburban Houston vaporizing, folding and collapsing like tall grass in a sudden wind. The destruction traveled outward in concentric circles at an awesome rate of speed. In a few seconds, the racing explosion was over and the entire area was covered with dense smoke. An immense mushroom cloud gathered and floated higher into the sky. In the war room, the destruction showed up as nothing more than a small patch of fuzziness, an atmospheric disturbance bleeding across lower Texas, but no one felt the loss of innocent lives more than the men and women in that small room. With pained expressions, Whitmore and his staff watched and waited.

Minutes later, the AWACS pilot broke radio silence. "Unfortunately, it looks like our target is still in the air."

The team at Area 51 let out a collective groan. After twenty-four hours of shocking disappointments, this one was possibly the worst. This had been humanity's last line of defense, its last chance.

"Yes, that's confirmed," the pilot went on, "we've got a good look now. Target looks to be in good shape. In fact, it's still moving in over Houston. Jesus Christ, we didn't even put a scratch on her."

"Call the other planes back," Whitmore said softly.

Nimziki couldn't believe it. "The other bombers might have better luck," he argued. "One of their destroyers is en route to Chicago. We still have time to intercept it and deliver multiple warheads. We can't just give up!"

"I said call them back."

The president sank into a chair and stared up at the ceiling. The failure to inflict any damage on the aliens' ship convinced him there was no way to prevent them from landing. Suddenly, he felt like there was plenty of time. Somehow, he knew from his mind-meld experience with the captured alien, it would take them a couple of years to move the entire population down to earth from the mother ship.

In light of what happened in Houston, it seemed to be time now to rethink the strategy of fighting the aliens and time to begin organizing ways to resist them once they began their invasion. The only logical course of action Whitmore could see was to wait for them to establish their cities, then blow the world to smithereens. Mankind was going to be exterminated, he knew, without mercy. *If we're lucky,* he told himself, *we might be able to take them down with us.*

JASMINE, FIGHTING SLEEP, watched the embers of the dying fire. Although she was exhausted, too many dangers, real and imagined, lurked in the darkness for her to close her eyes. Marilyn Whitmore, near by, seemed to be resting easily. The quiet man wasn't as quiet as before: he was snoring, really sawing some logs.

In the distance, Jas could hear the sound of helicopter blades and wondered if removing the First Lady from the crash site had been the right thing to do. For all she knew, the helicopter in the distance was out there searching for Marilyn. Coming to El Toro, especially after all the warnings she'd heard along the way, felt like a horrible mistake. She would have left immediately to get

Marilyn to a hospital, but in her haste to find Steve, she had smashed out the headlights on the truck by crashing through barricades of rubble. Traveling in the dark could be too dangerous.

The helicopter would come closer, scanning the ground with a searchlight. Not until it was half a mile off did Jas think it might actually find their tiny camp. She grabbed a branch and stirred the fire, sending a shower of sparks into the air. The others awoke to see the chopper heading toward them, the blinding searchlight in their eyes. Jas waved her arms and pointed at Mrs. Whitmore. To everyone's surprise, the helicopter began to set down not far off. Jas ran toward the spot, eager to get some help. When she saw who was piloting the big olive green bird she burst out weeping and laughing at the same time. Overwhelmed, she ran to the helicopter and jumped through the door into Steve's arms. She smothered him with kisses, then yelled over the noise of the blades, "You're late!"

He grinned and yelled back, "I know how much you like big dramatic entrances."

Steve brought a stretcher from the helicopter and, together with the quiet man, loaded Marilyn in the back for the ride back to Area 51. It didn't look like she would live to see her husband again. She was coughing badly again, hacking up blood.

Steve pulled the quiet man close and shouted, "We got room for one more, buddy. You wanna take a trip to Nevada?" When the man shook his head no, Steve shrugged, "Suit yourself. Jas, let's go!"

As Jasmine passed the quiet man, she asked, "You're not coming?"

The man just looked at her, droopy-eyed, then gestured toward the band of wounded people they'd collected during the afternoon. He didn't want to leave them. She handed over the keys to the truck and told him where the supply of food was hidden. Before she turned to go, she looked into the man's eyes. "Hey, my name's Jasmine Dubrow. What's yours?"

The man looked at her sadly, as if he hadn't understood.

Steve bellowed, "Jas, let's go. We've got to go now."

Tearing herself away, she trotted to the copter and strapped herself in, then watched the quiet man grow smaller and smaller as she flew away.

DR. ISSACS FELT like a marathon runner hitting the wall. Thirty hours of nonstop work were taking their toll. Bleary-eyed and sallow, he looked in on Mrs. Whitmore, a fake smile smeared across his face. When he saw her sleeping, his face dropped back into a mask. A moment later, he saw the president trotting down the corridor carrying a child in his arms. Behind him, Connie and a Secret Service agent jogged along on either side.

"How is she?" he demanded.

Issacs gave the president a look that told the whole story. Turning to the little girl riding in her father's arms, he said, "I'll bet you're Patricia Whitmore."

"Hey, how'd you know that?" The six-year-old was always amazed when strangers knew her name.

"Because your mommy is right inside there and I know she wants to see you. But you have to promise to be gentle, okay? She's very sick." The moment she was turned loose, Patricia tore around the corner like she hadn't heard a word.

"I'm sorry, Mr. President," Issacs said. "Perhaps if we'd gotten to her sooner. She's bleeding internally. Even if we had gotten to her immediately, I'm not sure . . ." His voice trailed off. "There's nothing else we can do for her, sir."

The president put a hand on Doctor Issacs's shoulder before straightening himself up and pushing through the double doors.

"Oh, my munchkin!" Marilyn was doing her best to wrap an arm around her daughter. She looked weak, but not on the verge of death.

Remembering to be very gentle, Patricia reached up and patted her mother's stomach. "Mommy, we were so worried. We didn't know where you were."

"I know. I'm so sorry, but I'm right here now, baby."

Issacs waved the medical staff out of the room. When the last of them were gone, Whitmore walked over to the bed and knelt down next to Patricia. "Honey, why don't you wait outside so Mommy can get some rest."

Reluctantly, the little girl kissed her mother and went outside to wait with Connie. As soon as she was gone, Marilyn's brave smile shattered into tears and whimpers of pain. She reached for her husband's hand.

"I'm so scared, Tom," she whispered, tears pouring freely down both cheeks.

"Hey, none of that," he said bravely, "the doctor said he's optimistic, said you're going to pull through this."

She smiled and rolled her eyes. "Liar," she said, squeezing his hand with fading strength. Then the two of them put their heads together and cried. They cried and kissed and looked into one another's eyes until she fell asleep for the last time.

WHEN THE PRESIDENT finally stepped out of the room, his face was drained of color, his eyes bloodshot. A number of people waited at a respectful distance down the hallway, most of them with questions for their leader. They needed his approval on communiqués and authorizations for troop movements, the thousand decisions presidents made every day. But the man who stepped into the hallway didn't feel at all presidential. Overwhelmed with grief, he didn't feel capable of acting as the leader of anything. Without a word, he moved through the people in the hall until he came to Jasmine. Before he could find his voice, she reached out and took his hand.

"I'm sorry," she told him. "I'm so sorry." She still felt a lingering guilt about not being able to get Marilyn to a doctor sooner.

Whitmore shook his head. "I just want to say thank you for looking after her. She told me. You sound like a very brave woman." He turned to Steve and managed a weak smile. "And you again! Thank you for letting me say good-bye to her."

Patricia had followed her father down the hall. "Is Mommy sleeping now?"

He reached down and picked the girl up, realizing he didn't have the strength to explain it all just yet. "Yes, baby," he said, squeezing her in his arms, "Mommy's sleeping."

BY THE TIME Connie found Julius and asked him to speak to his son, David had turned the small office space into a disaster area. Acting much drunker than he actually was, he had thrown the chairs against the room and overturned the refrigerator. He was storming around kicking the furniture when Julius saw him through the plate-glass windows and hurried into the room.

"David! David! What in the hell are you doing? Stop already!"

David was just about out of gas anyway. He stopped flailing long enough to explain, "What's it look like I'm doing? I'm making a mess."

"This I can see," Julius assured him. "And why? Why are you messing?"

"We've gotta burn the rain forest, pops. We've got to dump all our toxic waste!" To illustrate his point, he emptied out a waste paper can, then threw it against the far wall. "We've got to pollute the air! Rip us the ozone! Maybe if we screw this planet up badly enough they won't want it anymore." Taking careful aim at a coffee cup someone had left at the edge of the counter, David did his best to kick it. He missed by a mile and ended up sprawled on his ass in the middle of his own litter.

"Well," Julius looked around the room, admiring the work his son had accomplished, "you've gotten us off to a good start. This room is officially polluted. Now it doesn't matter if the Martians kill me, because when the bill comes for this office I'll die of a heart attack."

He walked over to David, who laid back and put his arms over his head, moaning. Clearing a spot, Julius sat down next to his son. He suspected David's tantrum had more to do with Connie than he was willing to admit. He searched for the right thing to say. "Listen," he began, "everyone loses faith at some point. Take me, for example. I haven't spoken to God since your mother died."

David opened one eye, surprised by his father's revelation.

"But sometimes," the old man went on thoughtfully, "you have to stop and remember all the things you do have. You've got to be *thankful*."

David snorted and covered his head again. "What have we got to be thankful about anymore?"

"For instance . . ." Julius looked around, searching for an idea. At a temporary loss, he said the only thing he could think of. "Your health! At least you've still got your health." He knew that was a pretty lame argument and didn't blame David for moaning again. Nevertheless, he took hold of an arm and began tugging his son to his feet. "Come on, let's go look for a jacket and a cup of coffee. Drinking weakens your system. I don't want you catching a cold."

Reluctantly, David let himself be pulled to his feet. Then suddenly he stiffened, caught in the grip of a startling idea. Something like a smile twitched across his lips.

"What did you just say?"

"About faith? Sometimes a man can live his entire life . . . "

"No, the second part. Right after that." David turned and looked through the glass at the alien attacker resting just outside.

"What? That you might catch a cold?"

"Pop, that's it. That's the answer. Sick. Cold. The defenses come down! It's so simple. Pops, you're a genius!!"

Julius gave him a long, suspicious look, wondering if his son had finally gone off the deep end.

WHEN JULIUS FINALLY persuaded her that David was sober enough to be on to something worthwhile, Connie had gone to the president and asked him to come into the storage hangar where David wanted to demonstrate something about the alien attacker. He claimed to have a plan.

The group had gathered on the observation platform, standing around waiting. "All right, Ms. Spano, what's this all about?" Nimziki demanded, impatient from the second he'd walked in.

"I really have no idea," she said, talking to the whole group. "He wanted everyone here to show us something about the spacecraft."

Nimziki bristled at the idea of being summoned by a civilian and not even being able to get a straight answer. "Well, let's get on with this," he said testily. "We've all got more important things to do."

Connie was fed up with this pompous ass. She put her hands on her hips and was about to lay into him when the president came striding down the steel ramp into the hangar. He called a group of advisers to one side of the ramp and had a quick word with them.

Dylan standing beside Steve, asked loudly, "Does that plane fly in outer space?"

"It certainly does," Steve told him.

David came through the cabin hatch and climbed down the ladder to the large pedestal holding the attacker. He gave a technician inside the ship a few last-minute instructions, then jogged toward the observation platform.

"What have you got for us, David?" This time Whitmore's use of David's first name implied no challenge. He'd been hit in the gut so hard, so many times over the last two days, he was way too weary to try to pull a power trip on anyone. He spoke as one frightened man to another.

"Ladies and gentlemen, boys and girls," David began, sounding a lot like the late Dr. Okun, "I've worked up a little demonstration. It'll just take a moment of your time."

David reached into a trash receptacle and fished out a soda can. "We'll just recycle this guy," he said to himself, trotting back to the attacker and reaching up to set the can on the tip of the wing. When he returned to the observation platform, he waved a signal to the technician sitting behind the windows of the attacker. The man hit a switch, then gave David a thumbs up. Looking at the crowd on the platform, David could see he'd captured their interest. "Major Mitchell, from where you're standing, do you think you could shoot that can off the ship?"

Mitchell looked at the president, who returned a "why not?" shrug. Unsnapping the flap on his holster, he withdrew his pistol. After a last quizzical look around, Mitchell, a pretty fair marksman, raised his firearm and sighted on the can, slowly squeezing the trigger. With a crack, the bullet blasted out of the gun and crashed against the protective shield. A loud clink sounded when the ricochet struck one of the iron catwalks above. Suddenly everyone lost enthusiasm for the experiment.

"Oops, I didn't think about that," David apologized. "You see, the can is protected by the ship's invisible shield. We can't penetrate their defenses."

"We know that already," Nimziki said. "Is there a point to all of this?"

"My point," David said, getting to the good part of his show, "is that since we can't break through their shields, we've got to work our way around them."

David walked over to a rolling tool shelf where he'd set up his laptop computer. It was connected to a cable that ran through the shield, into the cockpit of the alien craft, and plugged into the shield receiving unit he'd repaired earlier that day.

"This will just take a second." David typed instructions into the machine, then stared down at his wrist watch, silently counting down.

"Now, Major Mitchell, as far as my assistant sitting in the cockpit is concerned, the ship's shield is still protecting the can. He hasn't made any adjustments. Would you mind trying to shoot the can again?"

Reluctant to send another bullet ricocheting through the concrete bunker, Mitchell looked testily at David. Not until Grey gave him the go-ahead did he unholster his gun.

"Hold on now!" Steve wasn't taking any chances. He carried Dylan to the top of the ramp and got behind the concrete corner. Most of the observers followed him up there. Mitchell took careful aim and shot again. This time, the can flipped over backwards and the bullet clanged off the wall at the far end of the big hangar.

"How did you do that?" General Grey asked, suitably impressed.

"I gave it a cold."

Julius, beaming with pride, nodded to the others in the group. The president, intrigued, moved closer to where David continued working with his computer.

"More accurately," he went on without looking up, "I gave it a virus. A computer virus. Nasty little things, very hard to shake once you've caught one." With a final, artistic tap, he hit the ENTER key, then turned the machine around to show Whitmore and Grey the graphic he'd brought up. The president studied the screen for a moment, nodding in agreement with what he saw.

Grey, who knew computers but hated them at the same time, kept his eyes on David. "Are you telling us you can send some kind of a signal that will disable *all* their shields?"

David touched his fingertip to his nose. "Exactly. Just as they used our satellites against us, we can use their own shield signal against them . . . if."

"If what?"

"If we can plant the virus in the mother ship, it would then be sent down into the city destroyers and the attack ships like this one. Okun told us that this ship's power was coming directly from the mother ship, so that must be true of the large ships, as well."

"I hate to poop on your party," Nimziki had snuck to the edge of the observation platform and was leaning over the railing for a look at the computer screen, "but just how are you proposing to 'infect' the mother ship with this virus? They don't have a Web page on the Internet." He looked around for others to share his joke.

David responded without hesitation. "We'll have to fly this attack craft out of our atmosphere and dock with the mother ship." He said it as if it were the most natural, obvious idea in the world.

Steve's ears perked up the way they always did when space flight was mentioned. He set Dylan down and walked down the ramp to hear more. David unrolled one of the satellite photos of the mother ship, the 415-mile-long titan which was waiting patiently behind the moon for the destroyers to pave her way. All concentration, David handed the president one corner of the blurry poster-sized satellite photo.

"Here—" David indicated what looked like a docking bay "—we can enter right here. They seem to follow a certain logic in the design of their ships. If this one is like the city destroyers, this is the front door."

David could sense that the politicians and military bigwigs around him were more than skeptical.

"You know what? He's probably right." Steve surprised everyone, including himself by interrupting the intense discussion. Everyone turned to look at him, so he continued. "When I flew past that door on the LA ship—city destroyer, I guess you're calling them—I could see this big-ass—I mean, this giant docking bay inside. The ships park in clusters around a central towerlike thingie.

"Dr. Okun showed me that the long finlike structure on top of the attacker is full of terminal wiring. He hypothesized that whatever type of computer link they run, the fin is the connector. When one of these attackers docks inside the larger ships, some type of connection is established through the fin."

"Oh, spare me the bad science fiction," Nimziki moaned from his rail. "This plan is so full of what ifs, it's ridiculous."

Ignoring him, Grey asked, "How long would their shields be down?"

"That's anyone's guess," David told him. "Once they discover the virus, it could be only a matter of minutes until they figure a way past it. It's not very complicated, because I don't know enough about their system."

"So you're suggesting that we coordinate a worldwide counterstrike with a window of only a few minutes?" Nimziki shook his head; it was ludicrous.

Grey turned around to face the intelligence chief. "We've got our radio link to Asia reestablished. The signal is weak, but we should be able to send some sort of instructions. If we could get past those damn shields, it might be possible."

Nimziki's mocking grin disappeared. He was angry that this lame brain idea was getting so much attention when the perfectly plausible option of a nuclear strike, *his plan*, had been dumped after a single failure. If he could have, he would have locked the whole group up in the spaceship and ordered the strike himself.

Thinly masking his criticism of Whitmore by seeming to address everyone in the room, he boomed, "I don't believe you're buying into any of this nonsense. We don't have the resources or the manpower to launch that kind of a campaign. If we had two months to plan it, maybe. Not to mention *that* piece of rubbish," he shouted, pointing at the alien ship. "The whole cockamamie plan depends on this untested flying saucer that no one in the world is qualified to operate."

Once again, Steve interrupted. He stepped forward and cleared his throat. "Er . . . I believe I might be qualified for that job, sir." Nimziki shot him a murderous look, but Steve went on. "I've seen them in action. I know how they maneuver." He looked the president in the eyes. "With your permission, sir, I'd like a shot at it."

"That thing's a wreck. It crash-landed in the forties, for chrissakes. We don't even know if it's capable of flying."

"Aha!" David took center stage once more. He had a group of Okun's staff waiting in the wings. "Release the clamps!" he called out like the ringmaster at a circus. He looked up at Connie standing on the observation platform. She rolled her eyes to show him how crazy she thought he was, and how proud she was. "C'mon, c'mon, remove the clamps."

It took longer than David expected, but once the technicians opened the last of the steel locks, there was a loud clank as it lifted up and flipped over onto the ground.

In a moment, the mass of the sixty-foot ship had lifted into the air, wobbling unevenly above them. At a height of fifteen feet, it stabilized and sat as perfectly still as it had for the last fifty years. Their mouths open in amazement, the gallery of spectators looked at David.

"Any other questions?"

Everyone looked at everyone else. Not even Nimziki knew what to say at that point. Finally, Whitmore broke the silence. He shook his head, showing what he thought of the plan before announcing, "It's a long shot, but let's give it a shot."

Suddenly everyone was talking, asking questions, or, like Nimziki, offering their opinion of why the idea was doomed from the outset. David came to the side of the observation platform, reached up and tugged on the leg of Steve's fatigues. The young pilot quit staring at the alien plane and leaned closer to hear David better.

"You really think you can fly this thing?" he asked, showing a clear lack of confidence in Steve's ability.

Steve returned the favor. "You really think you can do all that bullshit you said you could?"

WITHIN MINUTES, Connie was escorting General Grey and the president back to Area 51's makeshift war room, all of them talking at once, fleshing out the details of the plan, figuring out some of the tough communications hurdles that a simultaneous worldwide strike would entail. They felt a spark of hope for the first time in what seemed like a long while.

"Hold on!" It was a command, not a request. The three looked back to see Nimziki storming down the hallway after them.

"What now?" Connie mumbled under her breath.

The secretary of defense stepped close to the president, ignoring the two others. There was an iciness in his voice. As usual, his words were calculated to cut as deeply as possible.

"I understand that you're still upset about the death of your wife," he said, leaning over Whitmore, "but that's no excuse for making yet another fatal mistake. An objective analysis of the situation from a military standpoint—"

Nimziki never finished the sentence. Before he knew what was happening to him, Whitmore took him by the lapels of his suit and slammed him against a wall, pinning him. The president put his face close to Nimziki's, an inch away.

"The only mistake I made was appointing a sniveling weasel like you to run a government agency. But that's one mistake, I am thankful to say, I don't have to live with anymore. Mr. Nimziki, you're fired!" With a final shove, he released his grip on the man and took a step backward. Impaling Nimziki with a threatening glare, he added a final warning. "Stay as far away from me as you can get, or I'll have you arrested as a threat to national security."

Nimziki looked for support from Connie, then from Grey, but received none.

Starting once more down the hallway, Whitmore picked up where he left off. "I want Major Mitchell to organize every single airplane he can get his hands on and find us some goddamned pilots who can fly them."

Behind them, they heard Nimziki talking to the walls. "He can't do that!"

Connie couldn't help it. She looked over her shoulder and said, with uncon-cealed pleasure, "He just did!"

FOUR BRITISH PILOTS, sweat-stained and unshaven, were doing their best to avoid the oppressive heat of the Saudi summer. They'd pitched a large canvas tent that one of them, a pilot named Thomson, had had in his personal cargo pod, and were sitting around talking to pass the time as they waited for something to happen. One of the men, Reginald Cummins, seemed to be in charge. By no means the senior officer, Reg was nevertheless put in the position of group leader because he was the only one who knew the first bloody thing about the Middle East. The other three men had simply been delivering new planes to the base at Khamis Moushait when all hell had bro-ken loose. Reg was on permanent assignment there. He spoke Arabic passably well and, more important, he knew how to talk to groups of pilots without offending anyone, a tricky bit of business in the Middle East, but even more important given their present situation.

"We listened in to the Americans as we were coming over Malta," Thomson was saying. "They weren't encrypted, scrambled, nothing, and one of them was saying the Syrians still had a squadron intact near the Golan Straights."

"Heights," Reg corrected him. "The Golan Heights," and he showed Thom-son where it was on the map. "If we could get them to cooperate, they'd be in excellent position to reinforce us if it comes to a dogfight. Unfortunately, they're a difficult bunch, not exactly team players."

Suddenly the tent flap tore open in a barrage of shouting. Thomson fell over backwards in his flimsy folding chair, drawing his pistol by the time he crashed to the ground. A tall dark man, with a full beard and mustache, was yelling something unintelligible into the tent. His green jumpsuit identified him as one of the boys from Jordan, probably the only one of them who didn't speak English. Reg never flinched. He looked back at the man calmly until he dropped the tent flap and hurried away.

"What in bloody hell was that all about?" The three tourist-pilots were still riding a shock-wave of adrenaline.

"Seems they're getting a signal. Old Morse code, but they can't read it. He wants us to come and see if it's English."

"Morse code? What have they got out here, old telegraph cables?" Sutton, one of the others asked. With a serious look at Reg, he asked, "Couldn't be some sort of trap, could it?"

Reg shrugged and led the way out into the blinding hot afternoon. Halfway around the world from Groom Lake's Area 51, on the smooth surface of another ancient lake bed, a hundred or so fighter planes had set down out in the middle of nowhere. The jets were parked at odd angles to one another, ready to take off in a hundred directions as soon as the alert came. It was a truly international scene, with pilots from eleven different nations, many of whom would be shooting at one another under any other circumstances, hiding together out in the middle of nowhere. They had become reluctant allies.

"I still can't believe this," Reg said with a smile, enjoying the irony of the situation. "Seventy-five years of frantic diplomacy gets us essentially nowhere, then twenty-four hours after these bastards show up, we're all one happy family."

"That's not exactly how I'd describe it," Thomson said, sticking close to Reg, offering a nervous little salute and smile to a band of Iraqi pilots smoking cigarettes in the shade of their planes. They stared blankly at the Brits as they marched past. "I don't think those chaps have caught the family spirit of the thing."

"How do you think the Israelis feel?" Second only to the Saudi contingent in size, the Israeli planes, the impressive F-15s, sat a short distance away, their planes fanned out at precise angles, prepared for a simultaneous take-off.

"What's up?" one of them called out, an Uzi propped lazily against his shoulder.

"They're getting a signal. Morse code," Reg called back.

The man tossed away his cigarette and came jogging over to join the Brits. "Am I invited?"

Reg smiled without breaking stride. "I don't see why not."

The inside of the elaborate Saudi tent looked like an electronics swap meet. They'd imported a good deal of radio equipment from a nearby air base and had it spread out on an odd assortment of carpets, parachutes, and tarps. Saudi pilots from a handful of different nations were engaged in a dozen conversations. Everything ground to a halt as the visitors came into the tent. There was a tense moment as the pilots from enemy nations stared each other down. The Arabs seemed particularly nervous about an armed Israeli coming into their space. For a tense moment, no one took a breath, let alone said anything. Finally, Reg broke the ice.

"*Latuklaka ya awlad enho nel mohamey betana*," which translated roughly to "Don't worry, boys, he's our lawyer."

Suddenly the whole tent broke into hysterical laughter, everyone except the three visiting English pilots. They smiled along, though, anxious to help alleviate the tension.

"*Ana shaif ho gab mae kommelhaber betae,*" (I see he brought along his fountain pen,) one of the Arabs cracked, causing another laugh.

The Israeli surprised everyone by playing right along. In Palestinian slang, he joked that it was a "*Wakeh el-police Israeli ala estama rat el-ehtafalat elmausda ra,*" a ceremonial document-signer issued by the Israeli secret police. They were laughing so hard, other pilots poked their heads in to see what was going on.

"So where's this Morse code?" Reg asked in English.

One of the Saudis handed over the headphones. Instead of the dots and dashes he'd expected, he heard a voice that seemed to be making an urgent announcement. But there was too much static coming over the line. Reg signaled for quiet and the men in the tent complied. The broadcast was originating from the war room at Area 51. By the time it reached Ar-Rub Al-Khali, it had been relayed so many times Reg couldn't make heads or tails of it.

"Wait, you will hear," one of the Saudi Royal Air Force pilots told him. Sure enough, as soon as the muffled, inaudible voice finished the announcement, it was repeated in Morse code, loud and clear. It took a few minutes for Reg to get the whole thing written down, then a few more for him to decipher his own writing.

"It's from the Americans," he announced. "They want to organize a counteroffensive."

"It's about bloody time. What's their plan?" Thomson asked.

"It's . . . well, it's damn creative." He grinned before going on to explain the particulars.

A SQUADRON OF twenty-four Russian MiGs were parked in pairs on a vast sheet of ice. They'd been ordered into the air for an attack on the city destroyer that had already blown Moscow away and was at that time en route to St. Petersburg. When other planes began splattering themselves across the ship's protective force field, the mission was aborted. On their way back to their base at Murmansk, they listened in horror as the base was overrun and destroyed by a swarm of stingray attackers. Murmansk lay above the Arctic Circle, and the squadron flew even further north to hide among the glaciers they knew so well. They crossed the eighty-fifth parallel and set down between the rocky islands of Franz Joseph Land, where the ice hadn't thawed yet.

They arrived in the morning and had been sitting tight waiting for orders ever since. During the daylight, the sun coming through their glass canopies had warmed the cockpits, but the temperature at night was numbing cold. Miserable and starving, they sat in their planes waiting hour after hour.

Around nine o'clock, one of them was fiddling with his radio and found something at the low end of the dial. At first he thought it was the ETs talking to each other in clicking voices, but eventually he realized it was Morse code and called it to the attention of the other pilots. Fortunately, the message repeated itself several times. Almost two hours after they'd run across it, the squadron's leader, Captain Tchenko, talked to the others by radio.

"The Americans say they can bring down the shields for at least five minutes."

"Da, da! Maladietz!" The others endorsed the plan enthusiastically. Any plan sounded better than spending the rest of the night in the ice fields.

"When do they want to attack?"

IN SAPPORO, on Japan's northernmost island of Hokkaido, some of the world's most powerful civilian signal receivers and transmitters dotted the mountainsides. A thousand miles from the television and radio headquarters in Tokyo, the sensitive machines were the information link between the provinces and the capital. The engineers had come to work as usual and stayed late when they realized they might be able to help. Along with them, several members of the volunteer army were crowded around radio and television transmitters. Although Japan had no more than a symbolic air force, mainly cargo and munitions transport planes, they were determined to participate. They broadcast the message in several different languages to most of Asia.

"The attack will begin in thirteen hours," their message said, "at nine P.M. GMT."

As confirmation was received from various governments or scattered battle forces around Asia, the Hokkaido station relayed the information to Hawaii via short wave radio. From there it was sent to the USS *Steiner*, 200 miles off the Oregon coast, which bounced the signal up to the 747s out of San Antonio. As confirmations trickled back to Area 51, the data was recorded on the foldout map of the world taped to the wall of the war room.

"How are we doing?" the president asked.

"Better than we thought." Grey nodded, showing him the map. Hundreds of tiny stickers, each one representing a combat-ready air squadron, littered the map. "We're still taking inventory, but it looks promising. Europe is being hit almost as hard as we are, but the Middle East and Asia seem to have fifty percent of their capabilities intact. Plus, we still have our aircraft carriers."

"What about our troops here?"

"Unfortunately, we're the weak link. The bastards have taken out almost every air base west of the Mississippi. A handful of pilots escaped from Lackland and they're headed this way. Plus, we've got a shipment of munitions flying down from Oregon, but . . ." The general shook his head.

"But what?"

"Mitchell's got plenty of planes stashed around the base, but we haven't got the pilots to put them in the air."

"Then find them," Whitmore ordered, as if it were only a matter of Grey trying a little harder.

THIRTY MINUTES LATER, Miguel stepped into the Casse trailer as quietly as he could. All the lights were out and he didn't want to wake up Troy. He pulled the door closed and began to kick off his shoes.

"Where the hell have you been?" Russell's voice boomed out of the darkness. "And where's that sister of yours?" The voice startled Miguel, who switched on a light. Russell was sitting on the bed at the rear of the narrow space, next to a sleeping Troy.

"Yow, you scared me!"

"Answer me!"

Miguel thought they'd gotten past all the bullshit this afternoon when they'd teamed up to save Troy. He didn't know why Russell was acting like this all of a sudden. "Alicia's talking to that kid, Philip. That's where I was. He's a pretty cool guy." Before Russell could comment on that, Miguel took him in another direction. "How's Troy?"

It worked. Russell looked down at the sleeping kid, his mouth pushed into a strange shape by the pillow, and smiled. "He's out solid. Watch this." He tapped the boy's cheek hard with his finger. "See that? He's a log. I think he's gonna be fine. What a relief, huh?"

"Yeah," Miguel agreed, even though he was starting to sense that something was wrong. Not with Troy, but with their father. "Can I ask you something and you won't have a cow about it?"

"Shoot."

"Have you been drinking?"

Russell smiled his guilty little boy smile. He'd taken a solemn oath just a few hours before that he wouldn't take another drink until this whole mess was over, since he was out of booze anyhow. "I couldn't help it, man, I forgot about the little stash I had in the plane." The cockpit of the old biwing had more Jack Daniel's bottles rattling around than a liquor store in an earthquake.

"Hey, why don't you join me in a little celebration." He waved the bottle in the air as if it might tempt the boy.

Crestfallen, Miguel grabbed his shoes and headed out, slamming the door behind him.

"Miguel, get back in here," Russell called, stumbling to the door. "Don't be mad. Come on, Miguel!" He watched the boy storm away into the refugee camp. Determined to explain himself, Russell took off after him. The hard-packed sand was still hot under his bare feet. Turning a corner, he arrived at the center of the temporary village.

A Jeep with speakers attached to the back was parked near a large camp-fire. One of Mitchell's soldiers was standing in the back compartment of the vehicle talking into a microphone.

". . . which is when we plan to launch the counteroffensive. Because we're in a situation of depleted manpower, we're asking for anyone with flight experience, anyone at all who can pilot a plane, to volunteer. Military training is preferable, but anyone who thinks they can handle a plane would be useful."

"Hey! Me!" Russell yelled to the officer, pushing people out of his way in a hurry. "I fly. I mean, I'm a pilot. I got a plane, too!" In his enthusiasm, Russell pointed back toward his old de Haviland biwing, the bottle of J.D. still in his hand. Some of those in the crowd laughed.

"I'm sorry, sir, I don't think so," the soldier said, trying to be polite.

When Russell heard that, he got mad. Sloppy drunk and smelling like it, he moved in on the officer, vaguely threatening. He didn't notice the MPs sliding their clubs free from their holsters. "You don't understand, mister. I gotta be part of this. They ruined my whole life, and this is my chance to get revenge on those shitty little . . . things, guys, whatever they are."

"Get rid of this joker," the officer said quietly. A pair of military police grabbed Russell under his arms and escorted him roughly back the way he'd come, ignoring his blubberings about being abducted years before.

"You're unfit to pilot a plane," one of them said, turning him loose with a shove. "Go sleep it off somewhere. Maybe when you're sober they'll still need pilots."

Russell watched them walk away, then lifted the bottle to his lips for another drink. Realizing what he was doing, he spit the booze out and threw the bottle hard against the ground, spraying shards of glass around his bare feet.

THE BIG CIRCULAR door to the storage lab was left ajar. Connie pushed it all the way open and found Julius sitting inside. The old guy faked a big smile.

"There you are, I've been looking for you," she said, but her father-in-law only nodded and smiled back at her. She sniffed at the air and asked him, "Are you *smoking* in here?" Busted, Julius exhaled a big puff of smoke and brought the cigar out from behind his back.

"A little," he admitted. "Don't mention it to David. He's such a health nut, he always gives me grief about my cigars."

David's health was precisely what she'd come to discuss. "I hope you're not planning on letting him go through with this idiotic scheme of his, are you?"

"Letting? You see me *letting* him do anything? He's a big boy."

"A big baby is what he's acting like. He's going to get himself killed."

Julius shrugged and glanced toward heaven. He knew there was no fighting David on this one. He was already committed.

Not finding the kind of support she was hoping for, Connie stomped away, frustrated, to the door. She turned back to say, "I don't think you're supposed to smoke in there."

STEPPING OUT of the Freak Show, Connie found David standing under the wing of the attack plane. Along with Steve Hiller and General Grey, he was listening to one of the staff scientists explain a last-minute addition to the ship. He was showing them the work his team had done to one of the gun turrets that hung like jet engines from the bottom of the spaceship, the one that had been torn away during the crash. They'd emptied out the six-foot-long structure and inserted a cylindrical frame. While that was going on, a crew of mechanics was very gingerly wheeling a two-ton bomb across the floor, a big baby in a steel cradle. Connie noted that these mechanics, in blue jumpsuits, were new faces, not part of the Area 51 staff. They were ground crew specialists who'd flown the bomb in from Arizona.

"We've done what we could to disguise it," the scientist was saying of the hollowed-out turret, "but it's not going to pass a real close inspection. The missile's nose cone is going to protrude somewhat."

The mechanics worked the crane dolly, keeping the bomb perpendicular to the floor as they lifted it up to the underside of the attacker. When the tail fins of the bomb were even with the cylindrical frame, the mechanics began the delicate process of loading it into the chute.

"Don't anybody sneeze," the chief mechanic told David and the others. "We had to put the warhead on there before we loaded it. If my boys drop that thing, it'll be all she wrote."

"Pretty powerful bomb, huh?" David asked, clueless.

All the military men turned and looked at him, surprised he hadn't been informed.

The chief mechanic filled him in. "This, my friend, is a laser-guided cruise missile with a thermonuclear warhead slapped on the front end. If we drop that sucker, we all go boom, big time. And that's why our man, Captain Hiller here, is going to be extra careful getting this ship out the door."

David looked over at Steve, too surprised to actually form words.

Steve flashed him his trademark grin. "Piece of cake, Dave." The young pilot's audacity went a long way toward calming David's nerves.

Before he had a chance to think twice about what he was getting himself into, the staff scientist went on with his lecture. "We found some room in the ship's manifold and that's where we hid the launcher. As you can see, we didn't have any way to disguise the wiring, so we just welded it down to the surface. If you stand way back, you can't even see it."

General Grey stepped to a nearby table and picked up a small black box. "This will be attached to the ship's main console."

"It's just like an AMRAAM launch pad on the B-2 Stealth," Steve noted.

"That's exactly right. Use it the same way. There'll be one difference. We've programmed the nuke so it won't detonate on impact. You'll have another thirty seconds to get as far away as you can."

David felt himself getting lightheaded. All the talk about nuclear explosions was going to make him pass out if he didn't get his mind on something else. "I think I'll go see how they're doing with the radio transmitter." As he started to stagger away, Steve checked his watch.

"Holy smokes, David, we're late!"

David and Connie were the only two who knew what he was talking about. They told him not to worry, that they'd be there in time, as Steve jogged out of the hangar. David started toward the attacker to check on the progress his assistants were making inside when Connie stopped him.

"Thirty seconds? Maybe I'm a little dim or something, but isn't thirty lousy seconds cutting it a little close when you're trying to run from a nuclear explosion?"

"Not really. We're not going to fire the bomb until we're on our way out the door. Beside, that Hiller is supposed to be an amazing pilot." A shower of sparks rained onto the platform as one of the technicians began welding a device to the bottom of the ship. When David looked his way, the man pulled off his welding mask.

"This is the strongest UHF transmitter we could get our hands on. It'll tell us when you've uploaded the virus."

"Right. Then we all cross our fingers and pray the shields go down."

"Why you?" Connie wasn't finished. "Why does it have to be *you*? I mean, isn't it just a matter of pushing a button once you're connected? Can't you just show someone else how to plant the virus, somebody trained for this kind of mission?

David wondered what she meant by trained for *this kind of mission*. "I don't think there's ever been a mission like this. And if anybody's trained for it, it's me, because I designed the virus. What if something goes wrong, or doesn't match the way I think it will? I'll have to think fast, adjust the signal, or . . . who knows?" He walked over and picked up a soda can Mitchell had knocked to the floor. "Con, you know how I'm always trying to save the planet? This is my chance."

He tossed the can into a government-mandated RECYCLE container, planted a kiss on Connie's forehead, then rushed toward the attacker's cockpit.

Connie watched him go with mixed emotions. Speaking out loud to no one in particular, she said, "*Now* he gets ambitious."

WHEN JASMINE ASKED where she could borrow a dress, everyone in the labs gave her the same hesitant response. "Try Dr. Rosenast," they suggested, making it clear this was a last resort, something to be done only in the case of severe emergency.

After knocking repeatedly at the indicated door, Jas could hear someone muttering and cursing on the other side. Just as she was about to give up, the door was yanked open and she was confronted by a huge pair of bifocals with the face of a sixty-year-old woman behind them. She looked like a sweet old thing, round rosy cheeks and big blue eyes magnified even larger by her glasses. Her gray hair was carefully coifed into a towering hairdo, and beneath her lab coat, she was dressed to the nines in a forest green blazer and matching skirt made of high-quality silk. The crowded room behind her was a combination office/laboratory/living quarters, every inch of space crammed with scientific equipment and the woman's personal effects. To Jasmine, she looked more like Santa Claus's wife than one of the world's leading electrical engineers.

"Dr. Rosenast, I hate to bother you but—"

"I already told that other son-of-a-bitch, *it's not ready*," she snapped.

The rebuilt alien attacker was scheduled to lift off in less than half an hour and she still hadn't finished a crucial piece of technology: a combination wattage booster/power transformer that would run off the ship's energy. Without it, David wouldn't be able to use his computer to upload the virus and infect the mother ship's signal.

"I'd be done already if it weren't for all the fuckin' interruptions!"

"I need to borrow a dress," Jasmine interjected, "something to get married in."

The old woman looked both ways down the hall as if to make sure she wasn't on *Candid Camera*. When she was satisfied that Jasmine was serious, she pulled her inside and brought her to a closet overflowing with the outfits she'd collected during the dozen years she'd been living underground. "I live for mail order," the woman admitted guiltily. "I think your tits are too big for what I've got here, but go ahead and borrow anything you like. I've got to get back to work."

Jasmine rifled through the closet as the doctor went back to work on the transformer. The doctor was a real clothes horse, with a penchant for Chinese dresses with slits running dramatically up the sides. *When does she wear these things?* Jasmine wondered. Then her search came to an end with the discovery of a simple red sun dress with a pattern of white and yellow flowers. On her way to the door, Jas planted a kiss on the surprised woman's cheek, then dashed off to the women's locker room. Eight minutes later, she was showered, powdered, rouged, and wriggling into the dress. It fit the curvaceous Jasmine snugly.

"Dylan, zip me up."

After struggling for a minute to bring the zipper to the top, the boy gave up. "It's too tight."

"Okay, I guess that's good enough. Let's go, kid, we're late!"

It had been a long time since the men she passed in those hallways had seen anything like Ms. Dubrow. They were accustomed to seeing their female coworkers covered from head to toe in sterile white cotton. From the looks she was getting, Jasmine knew the dress was too tight, especially in the chest. Beginning to feel self-conscious, she asked Dylan, "How do I look, kiddo?" The boy put his hand out and wobbled it back and forth: *so-so*. "Oh, thanks," she said, "you're a lot of help." They turned a corner and arrived at the chapel.

The space was a combination house of worship and recreation room. Stained glass windows with fluorescent lights behind them shone down on felt-covered poker tables. Area 51's multidenominational minister, Chaplain Duryea, an elderly gentleman with an Einstein hairdo, had come in and pushed a Ping-Pong table out of the way. He shook hands with Jasmine and they stood talking for a few minutes until the others arrived.

"Somebody call the fire department before I burn to the ground!" Steve stood in the doorway, palms pressed to his cheeks. Admiring the way Jasmine looked in the dress, he came down the aisle and planted a kiss on her cheek. "You look . . . Jas-alicious."

"You're three minutes late," she chided, showing him her wristwatch.

"You know me. I like—"

"I know, I know," she finished the sentence for him, "you like to make a dramatic entrance."

The chaplain put himself behind a lectern and made sure everything was ready. "Steve, do you have the ring?"

"You bet." From the pocket of an Air Force jacket he'd borrowed, he produced the same leaping dolphin ring Jimmy had caught him with the day before.

"Witnesses?"

Just as he asked the question, David and Connie came through the door, both of them working feverishly on the necktie David had borrowed seconds before. They never did get it right and finally just let it dangle in a sloppy knot. They came forward and took their places on either side of the happy couple. When he could see that everything was set, Chaplain Duryea smiled and said, "Then let's get this show on the road."

The short ceremony proved to be as meaningful and as moving for the two witnesses as it was for the bride and groom. During the vows, Connie reached for David's hand and toyed with the wedding ring she had given him years before.

THE TEAM OF mechanics making repairs to a line of ten F-15s were putting on quite a show. Shouting instructions to one another, calling for tools to be handed up, they moved with the frantic grace of an Indy 500 pit crew. They were racing against the clock to make the sleek jet fighters air worthy. The sounds of rivet guns and pneumatic wrenches echoed off the walls. Similar work was going on in every corner of the gigantic hangar, which now stood packed to the gills with aircraft of every description.

As soon as the orders came upstairs around midnight, Major Mitchell's crew had worked feverishly, scouring not just their own hangars, but the entire Nellis Weapons Testing Range, an area of approximately six hundred square miles, to gather up every working and half-working plane. Since Area 51's ostensible purpose was R&D of experimental aircraft, they had accumulated quite a collection of planes over the years. Most of them were early models of standard American transport and attack planes, but there was also quite a number of specially-built prototypes, exotic ships that never went into production. Planes like the wedge shaped Martin X-29 and the awkward MSU Marvel Stol, with its turboprop engine set into a wind cone above the tail. These planes had been "liberated" from America's enemy or "accidentally misdirected" from her allies.

The most exciting find had been the fleet of F-15s, stored in one of the half-underground storage hangars surrounding the "minibase" at Papoose Lake, nine miles to the north. Like many of the planes they found, the F-15s had missing parts, having been cannibalized over the years for the sake of other projects. A radar system was missing from one, while the tail fins had disappeared from another. Still, these planes were legitimate, state-of-the-art fighting machines that had one great advantage over almost all the others: there were missiles for them to fire. The five that could move under their own power taxied back to the main hangar; the other five were towed. The lead mechanic figured eight of them would be ready by the time the counteroffensive was scheduled to begin.

The base had received much-needed reinforcements, and quite a scare, when a score of F-111s arrived without warning at approximately two A.M. They were a group of foreign pilots-in-training and their army instructors who had been stranded at a proving grounds in the California desert when the invaders began to arrive. They had no way of responding to the message being broadcast from Area 51, so they decided to come and join the crowd. Only three of the pilots were experienced instructors. The other seventeen were trainees from allied countries: Czechs, Hondurans, and a group from Nigeria. Like most pilots around the world, they spoke English, the international language of aviation. There were no lights on the runways and they were fortunate not to have lost anyone during the landing.

Everyone in the hangar knew both the plan of attack and their odds of surviving it. Mitchell had made no bones about it, bluntly explaining that even if the shields came down, the aliens would still have them outnumbered and outgunned. At *best*, they could expect an aerial dogfight with the faster, tighter-turning attackers, the swarming flock which had downed thousands of jets worldwide while suffering only a single casualty. When Mitchell was done, he looked around and asked if anybody wanted out, told them it was better to quit now than once they were up in the air. No one said a word. "Good," he told them, "because we're going to need all the help we can get."

The Jeep with loudspeakers was parked between the huge rolling doors. Mitchell got up on the back of it to assign the pilots to their planes. While the men were crowded together in a group, they were noisy, macho, and fearless, bragging to each other about all the ways they would crush their foes. But an hour later, the only noise in the room was the buzz and thump of mechanics' tools. A few of the warriors spoke quietly to one another in groups, but the majority of them had wandered away to private corners, isolating themselves with their thoughts.

This was the scene the president found when the elevator doors slid open an hour before the makeshift air force was to head north and engage the West Coast city destroyer. Instead of his usual entourage, Whitmore brought only General Grey and one of his Secret Service agents along.

"Where'd they dig up some of these contraptions? It looks like the Smithsonian's Air and Space Museum in here."

"Beggars can't be choosers," Grey reminded him. "I think Mitchell might have gone a little overboard, but the order was to bring in everything that could fly."

"How many planes can we put in the air?" Whitmore asked.

"If you're asking me how many combat-ready pilots we can put into planes in decent working order, the answer is thirty. But we're going to lower our standards and stretch it to one hundred and fifteen."

Whitmore had come up top to review the troops before they left for battle. He hadn't expected to find so quiet, so desolate a scene. These people, unexpectedly pressed into service, weren't exactly fired up. The worried, defeated expressions on their faces made them seem like a football team down 211–0 at halftime. Whitmore wished there were something he could say, some ringing motivational speech he could deliver, but he knew he wasn't a talented improviser. He always knew the ideas he wished to convey, but relied heavily on Connie and his staff to script the actual words for him.

He began to walk down the long aisles of planes, stopping here and there to offer a word of encouragement or inspect an airplane. Many of the men hardly glanced up at him as he passed, so deep were they in their personal reflections. Whitmore imagined George Washington moving among the freezing, starved, troops at Valley Forge, quietly measuring their morale and their will to fight. He came upon a man sitting cross-legged on the floor who seemed to be talking to himself. Closer inspection revealed he was praying, whispering hurried incomprehensible words to heaven, aware there wasn't much time left. Around the next corner, he came upon a muscular young man wearing nothing but a pair of jeans. He was sobbing uncontrollably. All the photos were out of his wallet arranged in a neat row on the concrete. Wiping away his tears, he was taping them one by one to the side of his plane, an old P-51 Mustang. Whitmore realized they were snapshots of his dead, loved ones he'd lost to the blasts. The young man's grief was hypnotic, and as Whitmore watched, he couldn't help thinking about the way Marilyn's hand had gone limp in his. Suddenly, Grey's hand took hold of his arm and pulled him away from the scene. Without realizing it, Whitmore too had begun to tear.

From a military standpoint, the new recruits were a pitiful sight. A frowning man of sixty sat in the cockpit of a Russian MiG studying an impossibly thick operating manual, badly translated from the original Russian. Whitmore exchanged a few words with him and discovered he hadn't flown any kind of plane since the Korean War. Still, he was the most experienced pilot in his flight group. Most of the others had never flown at all. A group of them was standing on the wings and fuselage of a plane while one of the California flight instructors sat in the cockpit giving them a "crash course" on how to keep a plane in the air. This group had volunteered for the last, and the ugliest, assignment Mitchell had handed out. Their task during the battle would be to fly the planes for which the base had no ammunition. They would act as distractions and decoys, something for the aliens to shoot at while the more experienced pilots attacked the larger ship. Whitmore interrupted the training session for a moment to greet these doomed young men and women, then moved on.

Eventually, he came to the front of the hangar and the row of F-15s. Whitmore knew the vessel well. He had logged many an hour in the sleek jet before being promoted to flying Stealths. Among the men assigned to pilot this elite weapon, he was surprised to find the captain of Air Force One, Captain Birnham. Even more surprising was the fact that Birnham was listening intently to a stick-thin man with a bushy beard named Pig explain certain features of the plane. Pig had a hog, a motorcycle he rode with his gang, an off-shoot of the Hell's Angels, every weekend. He wore black leather pants, a denim jacket with his name in gothic letters over an obscene cartoon logo, and a bandanna tied around his wild red hair. Whitmore joined their conversation and learned that the biker had been a navy master chief mechanic stationed for years in San Diego. Whitmore refrained from asking how Pig had learned to fly an F-15, positive he didn't want to know the answer.

Many of the nervous pilots had followed Whitmore and Grey toward the front doors, and news of his presence had already leaked outside into the campground beyond the hangar doors. Lights inside the tents and vehicles switched on as the displaced civilians began coming out into the night air. The president stepped up into the back of the Jeep with the loud speakers, tapped the microphone a couple of times then spoke into it.

"Good morning," he said uncertainly. Everyone inside the hangar quickly came out from behind their planes to assemble in the open space near the line of F-15s. Turning around to check the night sky for signs of the approaching dawn, Whitmore watched the bedraggled refugees marching toward the hangar doors. For several moments, he stood quietly at the microphone, staring awkwardly into the expectant faces of his audience, not knowing what he would say to them. Then, without knowing where to begin, he began.

"In less than an hour from now, over one hundred of you will fly north to confront an enemy more powerful than any the world has ever known. As you do so, you will be joined by pilots from around the world as they launch similar attacks against the other thirty-five ships attacking the earth. The battle you will join will be the single largest aerial conflict in the history of mankind." He paused to consider that idea.

"Mankind," he repeated, allowing the word to hang in the air. "The word takes on a new meaning for all of us today. If any good has come from this savage and unprovoked attack on our planet, it is the recognition of how much we humans share in common. It has given us a new perspective on what it means to live on this earth together. It has shown us the insignificance of our thousand petty differences from one another and reminded us of our deep and abiding common interests. The attack has changed the course of history and redefined what it means to be human. From this day forward, it will be impossible to forget how interdependent the races and nations of the world truly are." As he spoke, Whitmore began to feel less self-conscious. He knew what needed to be said and began to trust his instincts. The words felt like they were being drawn out of him.

"I think there's a certain irony that today is July the Fourth, America's anniversary of independence. Perhaps it is fate that once again, this date will mark the beginning of a great struggle for freedom. But this time, we will fight for something even more basic than the right to be free of tyranny, persecution, or oppression. We will fight against an enemy who will be satisfied with nothing less than our total annihilation. This time we will be fighting for our right to live, for our very existence."

His voice grew stronger as the words took on a life and momentum of their own. "An hour from now, we will confront a strange and deadly adversary, an army more powerful than humanity has ever faced. I'm not going to make any false promises to you. I cannot offer any guarantee that we will prevail, but if ever there were a battle worth fighting, this is it. And as I look around me this morning, I realize how extraordinarily lucky I am to be here, at this critical moment, surrounded by people like you. You are patriots in the original and truest sense of the word: people who love their home and are willing to lend their talents, skills and, in some cases, even their lives to the task of defending it. I consider it an honor to be allowed to fight alongside you, to raise my voice in chorus with yours and declare, whether we win or lose, *we will not go quietly into the night!* We will not vanish without a fight, but struggle fiercely for what is rightfully ours, our heads held high until the very last moment.

"And if we succeed," he said, smiling into the mic, "if we somehow accomplish this thing that seems so impossible, it will be the most glorious victory imaginable. The Fourth of July will no longer be known only as an American holiday, but as the day when all the nations of the earth stood shoulder to shoulder and shouted: 'We will not lay down and die. We will live on! We will survive!' Today," he thundered, "we celebrate our Independence Day!'"

Whitmore stepped back from the microphone as a tremendous roar of approval swelled through the crowd. Deeply moved by his words, the men and women surrounding him forgot their fear and pumped their fists into the air and cheered, ready to fight. They would have followed their leader anywhere.

As the applause and the shouting continued, Whitmore hopped down from the Jeep and made his way to the line of F-15s. Grey watched as he exchanged a few quick words with Major Mitchell and the pilot of Air Force One, Birnham. The general had noted with disapproval the shift from *you* to *we* midway through the speech. When he saw Birnham hand over his flight jacket and helmet to the commander in chief, Grey began pushing his way through the crowd.

"Tom Whitmore," Grey rasped, playing the incensed mentor, "what in hell do you think you're doing?"

Whitmore was already suiting up and inspecting one of the jets. He smiled at his old friend and explained. "I'm a pilot, Will. I belong in the air." He pulled his helmet on, adding, "I'm not going to ask these people to take any risks I'm not willing to take myself."

"Think about what it would mean for people to learn the American president was killed."

"Will, I believe this is probably our last chance. If I don't come back, it won't matter tomorrow if there's a president or not."

Grey wanted to argue, but saw the man was determined. He appealed to the Secret Service agent, but the man only shrugged and wagged his head. He didn't officially support what the president was doing, but he sure had to admire him for doing it. When Grey looked back, Whitmore was already climbing into the cockpit locked in conversation with the man wearing a jacket that said PIG. Spitting mad, Grey marched away to take his position in the war room.

IN THE FRANTIC few minutes before takeoff, the technical staff checked and rechecked the equipment. They had festooned the cockpit with a dozen scraps of paper, each hanging from a different place on the instrument panel, with operating diagrams printed on them in marker. Not exactly professional, but it got the job done.

Just outside the ship, people were trying to figure out how to say good-bye. No one said it out loud, but they were all thinking the same thing: Steve and David had a million chances to fail and only one to succeed. They were probably going to die and that made saying good-bye more difficult, more final.

"When I'm back we'll light the rest of those fireworks," Steve told Dylan.

Jasmine rolled her eyes a little and tried to smile. She draped her arms over Steve's shoulders and put her lips to his ear, whispering something that put a dopey grin on his face. When she was done, she kissed him on the cheek, picked up Dylan, and went up the stairs of the observation platform.

A voice came booming over the loudspeakers. "One minute to scheduled liftoff. Clear the area."

"Pssst. David, over here."

It was Julius, hiding something under his sportscoat he didn't want the rest of them to see. He pulled his son off to one side, and with a glance to make sure no one was looking, he pulled back the coat.

"Here, take these. Just in case." Tucked into his belt were a couple of pilfered "barf bags," souvenirs of his ride aboard Air Force One. Each of the starch white receptacles was emblazoned with the presidential seal. David smiled when he saw the gift.

"You're the greatest, Dad. I've got something for you, too." He dug around in his computer case for a second before pulling out a yarmulke and a small leather-bound Bible. Julius made a long face, amazed. A Bible was about the last thing he would have expected David to be carrying. Leaning in close, David whispered, "Just in case."

Julius looked him up and down, then said, "I want you should know, I'm very proud of you, son." Those words meant more to David than his father knew. Julius stepped aside to let his son say farewell to one last person.

Connie's smile wobbled like a house of cards, threatening to crash into tears at any second. She and David had so much unfinished business between them, so much still to say. Now it appeared they would lose one another again, this time for good. With a thousand things left to say, they both felt incapable of words. Nevertheless, the look between them, a look of mutual acceptance and love, seemed to sweep all the residual pain away in a single moment.

"Be careful," was all Connie could say. David turned to follow Steve up the ladder.

"No, no, no. We can't go yet." Steve suddenly started frantically searching the pockets of his uniform. He'd lost something. "Cigars, man. I gotta find some cigars."

Steve was ready to bolt out of the room. He wasn't superstitious about too many things, but without a victory dance waiting for him at the end of the ride, he knew something bad would happen.

Julius grabbed him by the arm and retrieved two cigars from his coat pocket. "Here you are. With my blessings."

"You're a lifesaver," Steve told him, and Julius hoped he was right.

A few seconds later, Steve was scampering up the ladder and into the rebuilt alien attacker. With a last nervous smile, David awkwardly followed him inside.

CONNIE JOINED JASMINE and the others behind the glass windows of the observation booth. It was a small room designed long ago to control security and other functions inside the enormous concrete box that contained the attacker. The equipment inside, most of which had sat idle since it was installed in the late fifties, didn't inspire much confidence. Much of it was custom built, and the embossed strips of plastic that labeled the control panels were peeling off. A couple of them fell to the floor as the vinyl dust covers were lifted away.

Fortunately, the lead technician, Mitch, was able to figure it all out. After punching a couple of buttons, the entire room felt a rumbling tremor. High above, an ancient electric motor chugged to life and a large section of the concrete roof began to open, then another, opening an escape route for the attacker. The hole in the roof gave way to a large, slanted shaft which in turn led up to the open air. The shaft was approximately one hundred feet across, giving Steve a few feet of leeway on either side to get the sixty-foot-wide spaceship into the open air. Of course, the designers of the shaft never expected the ship to have to make it through with a nuclear explosive strapped to its hull.

When confirmation came by radio that the ground-level doors had also opened, Mitch gave the all-clear to Steve. The pilot nodded back and gave the sign to release the clamps.

"Now this is important," Steve announced, waiting to get David's undivided attention. He held one of the cigars out across the aisle. "Hang on to this. This is how we're going to celebrate on the way home. It's gonna be our victory dance. But we don't light up till we hear the fat lady sing." As he handed the stogie across the aisle, he noticed the barf bags sitting on David's lap.

"I have a confession to make," David said, strapping himself in. "I'm not real big on flying."

As he spoke, the clamps released the sides of the ship, crashing against the floor loudly enough to be heard inside the spaceship. The attacker lifted into the air, waffling slightly until it stabilized at twelve feet, steady as a rock. A pair of white handles, like the legs of a spider, unfolded themselves from the instrument console, extending until they were within easy reach of the pilot's chair.

"I'm in love with this plane. This is so damn cool, isn't it?"

David forced a smile. "I'll think it's a lot cooler if we leave the building in one piece." He was thinking about the warhead, which was almost directly under his chair.

Following the instructions printed on the duct tape, Steve made the craft float upward higher and higher, until they were even with the escape shaft. David's fingers were leaving permanent grip marks on the arms of his chair. Steve, on the other hand, was elated.

"Are you ready? Okay, then, let's rock 'n' roll!"

Steve pointed the nose of the ship at the escape tunnel and pulled back on the control stick. The machine responded, but not the way he'd anticipated. It shot backwards across the big room, picking up speed until its rear end smashed into a wall. Fortunately, a mass of fiberglass air-conditioning ducts were there to damped the collision.

"Oops."

David, who had just suffered an imaginary heart attack, gasped, then growled. "Oops? You call that an oops?"

Steve reached forward, peeled a piece of tape off the console, and turned it over before reattaching it.

"Let's try that one again." This time he nudged the steering control gently forward, jerking the attacker forward and into the mouth of the escape tunnel. The shaft sloped upward at an angle. Steve knew he'd gotten away lucky with that first crash. He made sure to go real slow through the shaft, scraping the roof as he went to make enough room for the warhead below. As soon as they nosed out of the tunnel, Steve jacked the controls forward. With a whooshing noise, they zoomed out of the underground shaft and soared into the night sky, dawn just beginning to break on the horizon.

Almost as soon as they were out of the gate, the attacker corkscrewed through the air in a wild set of barrel rolls. They straightened out momentarily, then began twisting and looping once more through the sky.

"Uuuuuugh." David invented a new sound, gurgling and moaning at once. "Steve, what's happening, what's going wrong?"

"Nothing's wrong," the pilot assured him, straightening the ship out, "just getting a feel for this little honey. I have *got* to get me one of these."

"Look, please don't do that. I've got this inner ear thing. Pretty serious."

Steve answered by throwing the rocket-fast ship into yet another series of stunt maneuvers.

THE PRESIDENT WATCHED the attacker take off from the cockpit of his F-15. A group of forty planes had taxied onto the runway, where the eastern skies were slowly changing from purple to pink. The pilots had their canopies open and were listening to their radios. As Steve and David's attacker shot through the sky, it appeared to them as a dark streak, an unidentified flying object disappearing at a terrific rate of speed into the darkness overhead. It was something of an anticlimax, a shadow only briefly visible against the thin line of pink breaking to the east.

Once the show was over, Whitmore settled into his cockpit. Strapping on his helmet as the canopy lowered over him, he got on the radio and spoke with the war room.

"Grey, do you read me?"

"Roger, Eagle One, loud and clear. Stand by, sir." The edge in Grey's voice told the pilots listening in that something was wrong. A minute later, the general returned with the ugly news. "Eagle One, our primary target has shifted course. We're watching the radar right now."

"Which way is it heading?" The president assumed it was moving out of range and all the preparations he had ordered were about to be proved futile.

"I think our little secret is out. The ship is moving east by southeast and traveling at a pretty fair clip. They're headed right for us, sir. Estimated time of arrival is thirty-two minutes."

Whitmore's plan had been to take his thrown-together squadron into the air and put them through their paces, giving them some desperately needed practice time. Now that part of the plan would have to be scrubbed. Aware that the other pilots were listening in, he tried to put a positive spin on this development. "That means we'll have the home court advantage. Let's get up in the air and stake out our territory."

Then he switched over to the private channel Grey had opened for him. "Will, do you read?"

"Go ahead, Eagle One."

"Put the word out for reinforcements. Get us any help you can. We're going to need it."

DAVID WAS COLLAPSED against the back of his seat, his eyes a pair of loose marbles rolling free in their sockets. Between moans, he appeared to be chanting to himself. Either that, or he was about to woof his cookies.

Steve finally took pity on his passenger and straightened the craft out. It was an amazing machine, lightning fast and superbly maneuverable at the same time. It cornered like a dream and seemed to have some sort of gyroscope built into the system so that it came out of any maneuver, no matter how reckless, as steady as a rock. This was no wobbly goblin.

"You still with me?"

David, green in the face, nodded sheepishly.

As the ship began leaving earth's atmosphere, the blue sky darkened to violet, then faded to black. The pilot's mouth dropped open in awe, then blossomed into an ear-to-ear grin. As the last layers of the outer atmosphere brushed past, the attacker suddenly accelerated, liberated. High above the earth, in the eternal night illuminated by the eternally blinding sun, the attacker plunged upward, deeper into the blanket of stars around them. For Steve, it was a moment of wonder and boyish magic, a promise fulfilled at last.

"I've waited a long time for this."

Quietly now, they continued to plummet upward, the sun on one side, the moon on the other. Ahead of them the vast blank wall of space receded to infinity. Steve, joyriding, forgot for a moment what they'd come for. David fought down the stomach acids churning inside him and kept a careful watch on the life-support monitors installed on the floor. He saw something that made him certain he was losing consciousness. The monitors were strapped to the floor with thick strips of woven nylon, heavy-duty seat belt ribbon. One of them seemed to come to life as David watched it, lifting into the air like a tentacle arm.

"Feel it? Zero gravity, baby. We're here!"

Steve had some experience with weightlessness. He'd once finagled an invitation to ride in the cargo compartment of a B-52 flying parabolas through the sky. The plane came to the top of its climb, then began to dive at a carefully calculated angle, producing a simulation of zero gravity which allowed the passengers to float through the air for two or three minutes at a time. For Steve, it was a welcome recognition of a familiar moment. Not so for David. If he had imagined his breakfast worming its way back toward his esophagus before, now he felt it for real.

"Of course," he burbled, "weightlessness. I should've thought of that."

David turned to look out the window, focusing on the moon. Although on earth the moon was a slim toenail shape at this time of month, from David's angle it looked almost full. They were seeing what only a handful of humans had ever seen with their own eyes, the moon's dark side. But what really caught their attention was something no human had ever seen: a black orb lurking in the distance, one-fourth the size of the moon. The mother ship, its smooth surface illuminated by the sun, glinted back at them malevolently. A pair of monstrous prongs, hanging off what looked to be the bottom of the ship like a pair of saber-tooth fangs, curving hungrily through space.

"Thar she blows," David said, coming out of his queasiness. "Head straight for it."

Steve did exactly that. It had been less than five minutes since they'd torn free of the earth's atmosphere and less time still since they'd escaped her gravity. There was no way for them to know, no reference point or speedometer to tell them, that they'd been accelerating the whole time. But as Steve retargeted the ship with a flick of his finger, they were both impressed by the incredible speed at which they rocketed toward the moon. The size of the lunar satellite grew inside the frame of the windows until it seemed to David that they were getting just a little too close.

"You know how to slow this thing down, right?" he asked nonchalantly, trying not to step on Steve's toes.

"Uh-oh," Steve said, suddenly worried.

"Uh-oh? That doesn't sound good," David said, now able to study the individual craters. "What's wrong?"

"Something's happening. Ship's not responding."

David checked his laptop computer. For the first time since the clamps released the ship, David seemed thrilled to be aboard.

"I knew it!" He looked at Steve. "Well, at least I thought it. The way you described the inside of the city destroyer, I thought there must be a tractor beam organizing the flight, a computer-driven air traffic control mechanism. They're bringing us in." David went back to working on the keyboard.

Slightly miffed, Steve asked him, "So when were you planning on telling me about this?"

David looked across the cabin. "Oops."

"WE HAVE VISUAL."

Long before the city destroyer was within range of Area 51, its hulking fifteen-mile wide frame was seen cruising above the horizon. The president and the thirty F-15s had ascended to a height of 30,000 feet, high above the approaching warship and the tangle of amateur pilots who were having trouble maintaining their formations. He had three civilian pilots with him who had never flown a war plane before. They were doing remarkably well. Whitmore had them practice using their sighting devices. On these older planes, the HUD gave neither a "God's eye view" of the battle nor a "dream world" display, functions which came standard on later models. To locate the enemy, Whitmore's team, called Eagle squadron, would have to rely on the technicians in the war room and plenty of old-fashioned looking around.

"Basically, boys, we're gonna keep our eyes open," Whitmore announced, then asked Grey, "any word yet on that delivery?"

"Negative." Whitmore could just about see his scowl over the radio. "Do not engage until we've confirmed delivery of the package."

At least a dozen voices came over the radio at once. "Roger!" the pilots acknowledged the order.

"And keep this damn frequency clear!" Grey barked. He turned and watched the radar screen.

In order to avoid crashing into one another, they'd organized themselves into four main groups, flying laps around the desert. Grey watched them merry-go-rounding across the radar screen, then said to Connie and Major Mitchell in disgust, "This whole operation is the damnedest harebrained thing I've ever seen."

Pulling the major aside, Connie asked about something that had been troubling her for a while. "What if that thing, the ship, gets here before David can plant the virus?"

Mitchell was concentrating on coordinating his part of the battle. He figured Connie was putting two and two together and beginning to worry about her own life. There wasn't time for that now. "We're pretty deep underground here. It should give us some protection."

Connie read him instantly. "It's not us I'm worried about. It's all those people outside."

Mitchell remembered what had happened to NORAD and knew Area 51's defenses were flimsy in comparison. If the city destroyer moving toward them fired its big gun, it wouldn't matter if the refugees were up top or down in the labs—everyone would die together. Still, he knew moving the people below-ground would offer them a slightly better chance of surviving.

He pulled one of his men off his tracking assignment and appointed him supervisor. Without a word of explanation, he grabbed Connie by the arm and they dashed out of the room.

THE MOTHER SHIP was the size of a small planet sliced cleanly in half along its equator. The shimmering half dome was protected by a smooth exterior shell over most of its surface, except where it seemed to have been cut away to expose long swathes of a ruddy black surface beneath. The flatness of the underside was interrupted by bulging projections fifteen miles in diameter. They were the domes of city destroyers, identical to the ones attacking the earth. There were at least one hundred of them still locked on to the under-belly of the mother ship like leaches. Thirty-six empty rings showed where the giant warships which were attacking the earth had once docked. Hanging dra-matically off the side of the craft was a pair of tusklike projections. Glossy white and at least a hundred miles tall, these enigmatic structures arched through space like a mammoth set of cobra fangs.

The ship was pulled toward one of the dark, rugged strips that lay between sections of the steel blue armor covering ninety percent of the ship's exterior. Drawn closer, the bulk of the mother ship overwhelmed the view from their attacker's windows, until Steve and David could see nothing except the black surface directly in front of them. In contrast to the view from a thousand miles away, a close look at this part of the ship revealed it to be surprisingly primi-tive. Beneath the thin blue shell, the ship's surface was composed of a material as wavy and jagged as recently cooled lava, like mile after mile of barren Neolithic stone.

A huge triangular portal, one of several earth's recon satellite photos had failed to detect, had been cut through the dense walls. A pale blue light leaked from within the craft. As David and Steve approached this gigantic three-sided entrance tunnel, they noticed dozens of attackers like theirs sitting idly in space. Made to look microscopically small by comparison to the megalith behind them, these attackers were washing in and out of the opening as gently as if riding the tide of an invisible ocean.

The inside of the darkened tunnel put them in a dramatically different environment. The walls and ceiling were covered with sheets of ceramiclike tile that had turned a rusty brown. At sporadic intervals, shafts of light shot out of the walls and into the passageway like solid columns. As they flew past one of them, it seemed to be some kind of holographic torch, the artificial image of an artificial light source, which nevertheless provided just enough illumination to let them see where they were going. The steep walls plunging to a V-shape below them were connected by a series of massive structures crisscrossing the tunnel. Like the barnacle-encrusted strut wires of a sunken galleon, these structural supports were overgrown with irregular, organic bulges. Light seeped out of pinhole windows on these massive cables, indication, perhaps, that there was life inside of them. Although their stingray was moving at over 300 miles per hour, the enormous size of the passageway and the cablelike structures gave them the sensation of drifting slowly along, deep underwater.

The tunnel ended and the tiny ship reached the source of the pale blue light. They entered the central chamber of the mother ship. It was like swimming through milky blue water on a densely foggy day. For several moments, neither Steve nor David could see anything at all. It wasn't until the first of the towers came into view that they realized the soupy atmosphere was limiting visibility to twenty miles or so. The towers were knobby, bulging structures rising through the fog like endless sections of rope tied into thick knots. They were built in piles, like dripping candle wax that grows eventually into a spire. Along the outsides of these towers were clearly defined pathways, access roads perhaps, for repairs. The dizzying height of these towers, disappearing out of sight both above and beyond, made the humans feel like guppies who had wandered into a shark tank.

As they neared the center of the mother ship, they came across something stranger still, what looked like a tip of a screw hanging above a round platform. This circular platform was a level field approximately fifty miles across and fell away steeply on all sides. As the men were drawn closer, they were treated to a horrifying image of several thousand aliens marching in phalanxes towards the edges of the platform. The area was some sort of parade ground and the creatures appeared to be loading themselves into the long boxy ships that were docked around the platform's edges. An invisible energy shield protected them from the vacuum of space.

"What the hell is that?" David wondered, physically repulsed.

"Looks like they're preparing the invasion," Steve answered with a lump in his throat. For the first time in a long while, he felt himself getting scared.

Their attacker was lifted higher, up toward the massive structure hanging directly above the alien parade ground, what had looked like a screw tip from a distance. Like an inverted mountain peak, this structure spread from a sharp point up to a massive base. It was built in thousands of layers or stories, each one containing numerous large windows that showed a brighter source of light behind them. Near each window, stiff beams extending a short distance into the inner space of the central chamber held two or three of the stingray attackers. This was their central docking point, and the nerve center of the entire alien civilization.

David carefully noted that, just as Okun had predicted, the attackers were moored to their host ship by a set of clamps that closed over the rigid fin running along the top of each stingray. The circuit terminals ended in a fingerlike flange, allowing the small ships to connect directly to the computer-compatible command system of the mother. Dangling off the wall beside each of the million windows on the conical tower was a limp tube. As the humans drew closer, they could see that the tubes were made of a transparent material that resembled nothing so much as a very large intestine. Apparently they could be controlled to reach out from the wall and attach themselves to the bottom of the ships, sealing over the hatch to allow the pilots to enter the tower, providing a passageway into the main ship, shielding those who used them from the vacuum of space.

"This isn't gonna work," Steve said, drawing David's attention to the large window they were approaching. "They'll be able to see us before we can do anything." Indeed, through the large plate windows, several aliens were visible inside a well-lit space that appeared to be a control booth. The distance between them was shrinking rapidly.

"Not to worry," David assured him, "this ship comes fully equipped. Reclining bucket seats, AM/FM oscilloscope and," he pressed a button on the console, "power windows!"

Instantly, a set of heavy blast shields began rising along the windows, blocking the aliens' view, but also sealing Steve and David inside. Flying blind the last few hundred feet, they felt the ship lurch violently to a stop, then heard the powerful clamps locking themselves onto the fin overhead. The only lights in the claustrophobic cabin came from the ever-blinking instrument panel and the sickly greenish glow rising from the screen of David's laptop.

"This is getting a little too spooky," Steve whispered.

David didn't hear. He was too deep in concentration, watching the changes flash across his computer screen. The moment the clamps locked them in place, the movements on the screen, which showed the status of the protective shield, reversed their direction. That told David that they were connected to the source. He switched over to another screen, which flashed the words

"Negotiating with Host." He held his breath as the signal analyzer program sorted through the billions of possibilities. Then, much sooner than he expected, the machine beeped and displayed a new message, "Connecting to Host."

"We're in! I can't believe it, but we're in!"

"Great, now what?" Steve was less than thrilled about sitting in the creepy box surrounded by a hive of aliens. When David returned to working on his computer without answering his question, the pilot unbuckled his seat belt and moved to the entry hatch, ready to plant his boot into the mouth of the first alien who stuck his head inside.

"Okay," David said more to himself than to his companion, "I'm uploading the virus."

Outside the ship, the lights on a small black box welded to the bottom of their attacker blinked on and off, distinguishing it from the thousands of other ships parked around them.

A TECHNICIAN PULLED his headphones off and turned away from his console to face General Grey. "He's uploading the virus."

Grey's scowl suddenly disappeared, temporarily replaced by a look of astonishment. He wasn't expecting any part of this lamebrain plan to work. Then, just as quickly, the furrowed brows and downturned corners of his mouth returned as he picked up a handheld microphone and sent his voice into the sky. "Eagle One, do you read?"

"Affirmative," Whitmore answered, "loud and clear."

"The package is being delivered. Stand by to engage."

Although Grey's furious reprimands had taught the rookie pilots to stay off the airwaves, he imagined their shouts of joy when they heard the news. Even the president could not hide how he felt when he acknowledged the message.

"Roger," he said excitedly, "we are standing by to attack!"

THERE WAS NO such excitement aboveground at Area 51. The effort to evacuate the refugees had begun in an organized fashion. A dozen or so people at a time were ushered inside and took the elevator down to the underground scientific complex, where they were being housed in the long clean room. But as soon as the sinister shape of the city destroyer became visible on the horizon, the camp broke into a panic. People ran into their trailers, searching for one or two last possessions to take with them, the last handfuls of their former lives. The soldiers organizing the elevator shipments were over-whelmed and, in the confusion, precious moments were lost.

Alicia, rampaging through the Casse motor home, couldn't decide what to save. She'd already sent Troy running inside, promising to meet him soon. The door of the trailer swung open. Philip poked his head inside.

"Alicia, let's go! They're coming!"

"I know!" she yelled, picking up the first thing she saw, a large duffel bag filled with dirty clothes. She slammed against the walls trying to drag the heavy bundle toward the door. Philip jumped inside and took hold of the bag, giving her a moment to calm down.

"I'll take the bag," he said soothingly. "This is kind of a crazy first date, isn't it?"

Alicia smiled and took a breath. He'd successfully brought her back to her senses. "Okay, Romeo, where are you taking me?"

Philip hoisted the bag onto one shoulder as they stepped out into the sun-light. Without letting Alicia see him do it, he glanced up to check the position of the approaching warship. All around them, panicked people scrambled in every direction, shouting for family members, sprinting for the open doors of the hangar. Alicia came outside and calmly put her hand in Philip's. She liked this game, pretending this was a normal Sunday afternoon and that this delightful gentleman caller had invited her out for a stroll. While the confu-sion continued around them, they created a small island of serenity, walking across the sand toward the hangar as if they were strolling along the banks of a springtime river.

Their fantasy was abruptly ended when a hand landed on Alicia's shoulder and spun her around. It was Miguel, covered with sweat from running all over the area. With a wild look in her eyes, he demanded to know, "Have you seen Russell? I can't find him anywhere."

UNSEEN BY ANY of the people heading toward the shelter, some-thing moved through the sky. Completely invisible, moving at the speed of light, it was picked up by the base's radar dishes. It was a radio signal, instantly decoded by the machines in the war room. Flashing on the screen dedicated to monitoring radio contact with David and Steve's ship were the words UPLOAD COMPLETE.

"Well, I'll be goddamned," Grey said, admiring David and Steve's work. He got on the radio. "Eagle One, this is Base. The delivery is complete. Engage."

"With pleasure, Base."

Whitmore was flying the lead position in a formation of the thirty fighters. When the clearance came, he gave the pilots on either side of him a visual signal, then accelerated. The others followed his example, increasing their speed for a bombing run on the city destroyer and buzzing over the top of many slower planes in the process. The bay doors at the bottom of Whitmore's jet split open, allowing the first of his three AMRAAM missiles to drop down. Still in its launch harness, the laser guided nose cone computed its flight and locked on to the spot Whitmore had selected on his HUD. He punched one of the buttons and the missile blasted away.

Grey's voice came over the radio. He was tracking the flight of the missile on radar. "Keep your fingers crossed," he rasped.

"Come on, baby," Whitmore said, watching the missile speeding away.

A quarter mile from the surface of the megaship, the AMRAAM exploded harmlessly, seeming to detonate in midair. The shields were still in place.

"Nothing," one of the rookie pilots said, breaking onto the airwaves. "It blew up on the shield, didn't make a scratch."

"That's it." Grey had seen enough. "Eagle One, disengage immediately. I want you out of there ASAP."

"Negative!" Whitmore shouted into his radio. "Maintain your formation."

Although they were now less than two miles away, the president continued to hold his squadron on a collision course with the side of the vast invader ship. Without announcing what he was doing, he allowed the second of his AMRAAMs to dip into the air. He locked a target area not far from the tall black tower at the front edge of the ship, then launched it. The missile shot away and, within seconds, arrived at the same spot where all the others had met an invisible dead end. Nothing happened. The pilots lost visual contact with the AMRAAM. It seemed to disappear, but there was no time to wonder where it might have gone because the jets themselves were quickly approaching the deadly quarter-mile perimeter. Then something took them all by surprise.

A huge explosion flared up, biting deep into the side of the destroyer. A large section of the ship, the size of a city block, ruptured like brittle clay, then exploded in flaming pieces toward the ground.

The war room erupted into wild cheers. Even General Grey, the model of vigilant self-constraint, swung his fist through the air, delivering an imaginary roundhouse punch to an alien jawbone. For the next thirty seconds, the excited pilots, whooping and hollering, made the airwaves unusable, prematurely celebrating a victory they had not yet achieved.

As order began to restore itself, Whitmore led his squad of fighters in a long downward loop that eventually carried them back to their original attack position, several miles from the front of the still advancing ship.

"We're going back in," he announced. "Squad leaders, take point." As they'd planned, the top pilots spread themselves out in a long line. Then, slowly but surely, the others tucked themselves in behind their group leaders, who led them away to their attack positions.

When the massive ship was encircled, the attack coordinators in the war room sounded the battle cry. From every direction at once, the squad leaders led the charge toward the enemy. Not understanding how to attack, the inexperienced pilots began breaking ranks to "improve" their positions rather than diving or climbing. Bombing an airborne target, even one as large and slow as the destroyer, was trickier than it looked, and three-quarters of the missiles flew wide of their mark. Only about thirty or so of the missiles, mostly AMRAAMs fired by the seasoned airdogs, found their target.

Some of the rookies lifted their planes high above the destroyer while others dipped below it. All of them moving toward the center at once, their main concern became not running headfirst into one another. In their confusion, they spit an orgy of Sidewinders, Silkworms, and Tomahawks into the air. Those with heat-seeking guidance systems locked themselves onto friendly planes weaving through the line of fire, then chased them down and killed them. The aerial battle was quickly degenerating into mayhem. But the true battle hadn't yet begun in earnest.

Then, the moment they all feared arrived. The portal door on the gleaming black tower pulled open and a swarm of the nimble gray attackers belched into the sky. After rising high into the air as a group, they flashed off in different directions to begin hunting down the earthlings.

"RUSSELL!"

The scream traveled as far out into the scrub desert as the distant roar of circling jet engines would allow. Miguel had come to the far end of the parking lot cum refugee camp searching for his stepfather when he heard what sounded like a sonic boom. He spun around to face the approaching city destroyer. Although he didn't know the first thing about air warfare, he was positive the last-chance air force which had recently lifted off the very runway where he now stood wasn't doing it by the book. Looping around aimlessly, swerving at the last moment to avoid midair collisions, flying too slow and too close to the ground, he had little confidence in their ability to repel the city destroyer. But the second he heard the boom, he knew one of the missiles had connected. Within seconds, other missiles began to fly. He would have stayed to watch this awesome and unlikely spectacle, but he had to find Russell before the huge ship was overhead.

Miguel was guessing that his stepfather had found a patch of shade where he could feel sorry for himself without being interrupted. And chances were, he'd brought a bottle to keep him company. He was probably somewhere nearby and probably badly wasted. He might even have passed out. The boy knew he should be angry. Once again, Russell's irresponsibility was forcing the boy to protect a family he was reluctant to call his own, but instead of anger, he felt sure Russell would be killed unless he reached the safety of the underground labs.

His search came to a sudden end once the pearl gray attackers swarmed into the sky. Every instinct told the boy to run for cover, and to run as fast as he possibly could. Throwing a glance over his shoulder, he saw a large detachment of the alien planes break off from the main group and head straight for Area 51. They were right behind him and coming in fast. He sprinted through the camp as laser pulses began tearing it up. RVs exploded and flipped off the ground. At least a hundred people hadn't made it into the hangar. They hid themselves behind their vehicles, or went running in zigzags across the open space separating the last trailers from the hangar doors.

Miguel heard a series of blasts strafing the ground behind him and dodged to one side at the last minute, jumping behind a pickup truck. The doors to the hangar were forty yards away, across a wide open stretch of pavement. Bodies littered the territory he had to cross. Inside, he could see soldiers and a woman in a white blouse, waving people inside. The woman spotted Miguel cowering behind the truck and waved to him frantically, beckoning him inside. She had dark hair and dark eyes, and for a moment, Miguel thought he recognized her. Too frightened to think, Miguel darted out into the open in a mad dash. Weapons fire tearing into the earth around him, he put his head down and ran for all he was worth. Leaping over bodies, he focused on reaching the woman in the white blouse. He made it. He raced through the big steel doors just as the soldiers were rolling them closed. The last one to make it inside, he followed the woman to the elevator, which was crowded with injured people waiting for the ride downstairs. A loud blast rocked the huge steel structure. The front doors had been blown out of existence, taking the soldiers along with them.

Connie, the woman in the white blouse, pounded hard on the button inside the elevator and waited through the eternity it took for the doors to close. Laser blasts were raining down on the hangar, and just as the last bit of light disappeared between the closing doors, the entire structure gave way and began to collapse.

STEVE SLAMMED THE engines to their highest rev and shook the steering apparatus so hard David was sure he would snap the delicate steering handles out of their sockets.

"Try something else!" David yelled. "Just get us out of here!"

"Can't you see I'm trying? I can't shake her free. These clamps are too strong!"

Steve let go of the handles, stood up, and paced to the back of the cabin, trying to clear his head. By the time he came back moments later, David was putzing around on his laptop, looking for some way to help free them from the docking mechanism. Desperate, Steve began randomly flipping switches on the instruments the scientists had been unable to identify. When he had exhausted all the options, he returned to his pilot's chair and flopped into it, defeated.

"This is not the way I thought it was going to end. I pictured a balls-out dog-fight, taking nine or ten of these little weevils down with me, you know?" He glanced over at David, who was obviously disturbed by that vision. "Well," the pilot continued, "at least we got the virus into mama's system." Both men jumped halfway out of their skin when the blast shield growled to life, lowering itself from the windows. "What are you doing? Don't let 'em see us!"

David put his hands in the air. "It's not me. They're overriding the system." Steve hit the deck, hiding himself behind the instrument panel. David, who had developed an instinct for protecting his computer at all times, slid gently down the front of the chair until he too was on the floor. When the shield was all the way down, the two men stared at one another, wondering what to do next.

"Take a look." David pointed up toward the windows.

"Be my guest," Steve countered. "You take a look. You're the curious scientist."

"I'm a civilian," David declared proudly "I believe it's your duty as a marine to . . ." he fumbled for the word, ". . . to reconnoiter the enemy position!"

Steve gave him a look as sour as month-old milk. With deep reluctance, he turned his head sideways and inched slowly higher, determined to poke nothing more than an eyeball over the top of the dashboard. Like the view from a periscope, it took Steve a moment to realize what he was looking at. Standing behind what appeared to him to be a thick sheet of crystal, because of the way it refracted the light, was a group of large-headed, big-eyed aliens staring straight back at him.

"Ahhhh!" He landed on the floor, trying to stay as low as possible. "Damn! There's a whole bunch of them standing around out there."

"Did they see you?"

"Yeah."

"I mean did they really see you, get a good look at you?"

"Yes! There are twenty or thirty of 'em looking this way!"

"Then, Steve," David asked calmly, "why are we hiding?"

Setting his computer carefully to one side and taking a deep breath, David peeked outside. Sure enough, the ghostly creatures were staring back at him with giant black eyes. After peering nervously around for a minute, he uncoiled himself and stood straight up, strangely relaxed. More and more of the aliens were crowding into the control room behind the glass. Soon, he knew, they would come through the tubes to reclaim possession of their long lost ship. He looked down at Steve with a defeated grin.

"Check and mate."

THE LIGHTS DIED, then flickered back to life as the energy of another blast shot through the electrical circuits and shook the underground labs at Area 51 like a sharp, two-second earthquake. The muted rumble of more distant explosions pulsed through the earth with a constant roar, terrifying the thousand people crowded shoulder to shoulder in the clean room.

"Julius!" Connie spotted her father-in-law standing to one side of the elevated walkway running the length of the room. She jostled her way toward him through the crowd. "Julius, are you all right?"

"Me? I'm fine." He had appointed himself temporary guardian of a group of children separated from their parents. Connie recognized two of them: the president's daughter, Patricia, and Jasmine's son, Dylan. "Of course, we're all a little scared by the noise," Julius announced loudly, "but we're not too worried because we know we're going to be okay. Right?" he asked the kids.

"Right!" the children agreed in one voice.

Connie couldn't believe it. In the middle of this frantic madhouse, which might have been a scene from London during the worst of the Blitz, doddering old Julius had managed to calm these children who should have been screaming bloody murder. She was more convinced than ever that the man possessed some kind of magic. Another blast plunged the room into a moment of darkness, reminding Connie that she had to keep moving.

"Stay safe," she said when the lights returned. "I've got to . . ." She pointed off in the direction of her business.

Julius only nodded and gave her the slightest wave of the hand, his concentration on the children. He had work to do also. As Connie left, he unfolded a yarmulke and set it on top of his head. He had the children join hands and asked if they'd like to hear a song one hundred percent guaranteed to keep them safe. They said they would, and he began to recite from memory a prayer from the Torah, singing in fluent Hebrew that would have astonished David had he been there. Opening one eye, he spied Nimziki watching him from nearby. Julius didn't much care for the man, but could sense he was lost.

"Join us," he called to the secretary of defense.

Nimziki, terrified, wanted someone to sit with, but he only shrugged and called back, "I'm not Jewish."

"So what?" Julius chuckled. "Nobody's perfect!"

"MIGUEL, DID YOU FIND HIM?"

Connie, standing on the walkway, looked into the dual pits of wall-to-wall refugees and saw a girl of about fourteen shouting over the top of the noise in her direction.

"I'm still looking!" a male voice yelled directly behind her. Connie spun around and found that the boy with the long hair, the last one to make it inside, was following her through the clean room. "Stay where you are," he shouted to his sister. "I'll come back and find you."

Alicia nodded then sat down again, taking her place under Philip's comforting arm. She lifted her head to look him in the eyes. "If I die today after finally finding you, I'm going to be really really pissed off."

He smiled broadly, leaning down to kiss her.

Connie muscled her way through the room, Miguel shadowing her every step of the way.

ALTHOUGH ITS EXTERIOR armor had been battered and torn, the giant ship had sustained no significant damage. Scarred and smoking, rocked by the initial round of bombing, it had nevertheless continued inexorably forward, single-mindedly pushing toward Area 51. It was intent on crippling this last remaining pocket of resistance in the western United States. For a brief moment, it had seemed as if the humans might triumph, that their minuscule explosives might peck away patiently at the fifteen-mile wide ship until it came down. But since the stingray-shaped attackers had swarmed out into the electric blue morning, the ship had sustained almost no further damage.

Their hands already full with controlling their planes, many of the inexperienced pilots went hysterical when the alien attackers began systematically removing them from the battle. Despite Grey's pleas for calm, most of them squandered their last rockets with wild shots at the attackers. On the radar screens, the men in the war room watched the last of the missiles sailing away into the desert.

"We're running out of firepower, General," a technician reported, "and we're not causing enough damage to the main ship."

President Whitmore, surveying the chaos from 18,000 feet, concurred with that estimation. His squad of thirty planes was reduced to just eight. A few had been shot down in the first mad moments of the stingray counterattack. The others had been separated from the main group during the retreat. Taking a quick inventory, he learned that the pilots in his group had fewer than ten missiles left between them.

"Let's make 'em all count," he reminded them.

Connie had come into the war room to see if there was anything she could do. Standing behind Grey, she watched one of the radar screens showing a three-dimensional display of the huge city destroyer. Because some of the base's primary radar receptors had already been destroyed, the image on the screen was incomplete, blinking on and off like a ghost. She felt a long shiver run through her legs up to her scalp when someone reported that the thing was directly overhead, then pointed out to General Grey some aspect of the torn, indistinct image.

Once he understood what the man was showing him, Grey snatched up the microphone and spoke to the remaining pilots.

"Attention! They're opening the bottom doors and getting ready to fire the big gun. Somebody get down there and knock that thing out before they can use it!!"

Dazed and sickened by this news, Connie turned and walked out of the room, moving past Miguel, who had snuck in behind her amidst all the confusion. He stood to one side, keeping out of the way, and eavesdropped on Whitmore's radio communication.

"Roger, Base," Whitmore called. "I've got one AMRAAM left and I'm on my way." He broke into a steep dive, pushing the engines into high thrust. "You boys keep 'em off my tail."

His squad leveled off and cruised along the bottom of the ship. The airspace in front of them was crowded with jets and attackers flying in all directions. Weaving in and out of traffic at high speed, Whitmore angled his attack run so that his missile would slice between two of the huge doors which were lowering themselves over the desert. He activated his HUD and sighted on the tip of the giant gun, the huge diamond-shaped bulb from which the powerful beam was about to fire. Something flashed across his peripheral vision just as the AMRAAM launch mechanism lowered from his jet. Attackers arriving too late, he thought. As he reached forward to fire the missile, the F-15 flying a few yards to his right unexpectedly blew up into a thousand pieces. The explosion rocked Whitmore's craft just as the missile blasted out of the harness, sending it badly off course. For a moment, he watched it speed away toward a collision with the hills.

"Damn it! Eagle Two, take point. I'll drop back and try to buy you some time."

"I'm on it," the pilot returned, moving into the lead position.

Behind him, Whitmore and the other pilots were yelling out the positions of incoming attackers. The opening on the bottom of the city destroyer was apparently a vulnerable point, and as the squad moved in for their strike, a dozen of the stingrays swarmed to the aliens' defense. There was so much confusion over the airwaves that the lead pilot never heard Whitmore warning him to take evasive action. One of the stingrays dropped in behind him, firing a steady storm of laser pulses. Another one of the F-15s, Pig's Eagle Twelve, rushed past the rest of the American pilots until the nose of his plane was practically up the stingray's tail. He pumped the alien plane full of .50-caliber shells, but it was too little too late. Eagle Two burst into flames, then exploded before its pilot could even lock down the targeting system. The wounded stingray peeled away toward the safety of the interior of the ship, but Eagle Twelve swerved with him, firing the whole time, until the ship fell to pieces, ripping apart in midair without an explosion.

"Nice work, Twelve," the president said without much enthusiasm. "Now, does anybody up here have any missiles left?"

CONNIE STEPPED THROUGH the doors of the infirmary and felt like she'd left the frying pan for the fire. Uniformed soldiers and a few volunteers were still bringing bloodied civilian victims of the air raid on the camp into a room already jammed with people. They were laid out on the floor and propped up against the walls. Their moans were accompanied by the constant rumblings of the bombardment from above. As horrific as the moment seemed, Connie knew it was only a prelude to the catastrophe that was to come. All the screaming would end a split second after the mammoth ship hovering overhead fired its awesome destructive beam.

"Put me to work!"

She grabbed Dr. Issacs's arm as he hurried past, carefully stepping over the bodies of the dead and wounded. By now, the bearded doctor was past the point of exhaustion. The only color left in his face were a pair of dark rings below his eyes. After a confused moment, he pointed into the next room.

"Help her," he shouted to make himself heard. "She's doing pre-op." Then he continued on his way.

Connie moved through a doorway and found Jasmine cleaning up a patient who'd taken some shrapnel right above his groin. Despite the thick flow of blood and the exposed view of the man's intestines, Jasmine was talking to him in a calm, friendly voice. When Connie approached the table, Jasmine immediately put a towel in her hands and showed her where to apply pressure to staunch the man's bleeding. Normally squeamish at the sight of blood, Connie pressed down with the rag, keeping the patient's internal organs from spilling out all over the table. Jasmine picked the last fragments of debris from the wound, cleaning it as she went.

"You're pretty good at this," Connie noted. "Keep it up and you could turn pro."

"Thanks," Jas smiled without looking up, "I like doing it and it's helping me keep my mind off other things." Connie thought she must be talking about the blast that was going to crush down through the roof any second, until she realized she was talking about her new husband. "This is a hell of a way to spend a honeymoon, don't you think?"

"Huh? Oh, yes. A hell of a way," Connie agreed absently. She looked at the man laying on the table. He kept raising his head to watch what was happening to him, his teeth chattering the whole while.

Dr. Issacs shouted into the room, "Okay, let's get this one into the operating room."

As an orderly took over Connie's job, she smiled weakly at the man on the gurney, telling him without much conviction that he was going to be fine, just fine.

SEVERAL PILOTS ANSWERED in the negative. After a quick conference with his men in the war room, Grey returned to the radio. "Eagle One, proceed to Headly Air Force Base in Manitoba, Canada. We believe you have enough fuel left. We've radioed ahead and they'll send an escort out to meet you. This will be your new headquarters, sir."

Whitmore refused to break off the fight. They were so close. "Doesn't any-one have any damn missiles left?"

The green beam that began the ship's firing cycle spilled out of the huge fir-ing pin, scanning its target. Whitmore knew it would only be a matter of sec-onds until the blast ripped down and chewed a hole in the ground where his daughter was hiding. He felt completely numb except for a wave of queasiness in his stomach. He didn't want to stick around and watch.

"Eagle Squad," he said with great reluctance, "let's head north. Follow my lead, do you copy?"

"Sorry I'm late, Mr. President!" an unfamiliar voice shouted over a back-ground of engine noise on the radio.

"Who is this?"

"I'm just here to help out."

The president turned and saw the damnedest thing: an unsteady old red biwing aircraft that looked like something Baron von Richthofen might have flown during World War I. The ship was sputtering through the air, piloted by a man in a leather helmet. Strapped to the side with bungee cords and twine was something that looked like a missile.

"What are you doing?"

"Don't worry, sir. I'm packin'."

Russell had stolen the heaviest, nastiest missile he could find. It was too heavy for the plane, and every time the wind shifted, it clanked against the flimsy wall of the cockpit with a frightening thud. A red light the size of a but-ton flashed off and on, indicating the weapon was armed.

"What I need from you, sir, is to keep those guys off me for a few more sec-onds."

Whitmore looked around and saw a fleet of the attackers diving in. The American pilots moved to engage them, laying down a barrage of cover fire to protect the wobbly old biwing. The plane continued lifting uncertainly toward the giant firing pin.

In the war room, all eyes were on the radar model of the ship, a small blip slowly climbing toward the origin of the beam, also visible on the screen. Grey grabbed the radio mike. "Pilot, identify yourself!"

"My name's Russell Casse," the pilot answered, "and I want you to do me a favor . . . "

"Who is this guy?" one of the technicians wondered.

"Russell!" Miguel rushed toward the soldiers gathered around the monitors. They caught him by the arms and held him back.

". . . tell my children I love them very much."

As one of the radio technicians spoke to the president and his squad, keeping them alert to enemy craft positions, Miguel yelled over the open microphone: "Dad! No!"

Russell couldn't help smiling at being called "Dad." He didn't know if Miguel could hear him, but he yelled back over the radio, "I've got to, kid. You were always better at taking care of them than I was anyways." Then he added, "This is just something I've got to do."

He snapped off his radio and pulled the de Haviland into as steep a climb as the engine could bear without stalling out. He had the nose of the plane pointed at the side of the firing pin. The tail of the biwing disappeared into the opening as the president and the remaining fighters banked away, clearing the area. The green light suddenly disappeared. In two seconds, a white light would appear and a massive beam of destruction would fire down on Area 51.

"Hello, boys! I'm back!" Russell hollered at the top of his lungs. "And in the words of my generation: UP YOURS!!"

The old plane flew nose-first into the side of the firing pin, causing an insignificant explosion that puffed out the bottom of the city destroyer without appearing to cause any real damage. But just as the deadly white beam erupted from the bottom of the ship, it abruptly cut off again. The huge ship lifted up and away with astonishing speed. In the same instant, every attacker plane turned on a dime to follow it. The entire swarm raced away over the desert.

None of them got very far.

Beginning at the center of the massive city destroyer, a sharp explosion burst a hole through the domed roof, like a skull exploding outward from a suicide bullet. Russell's bomb had set off a chain reaction that ripped through the body of the fifteen-mile-wide ship, melting the entire vessel from within. One after another, the thunderous internal explosions turned the monster in the sky fire red, exposing its internal architecture like an X-ray. Quickly, it was fully engulfed. Still in midair, it began to implode and explode simultaneously, incinerating itself into fragments, falling in huge flaming chunks to earth.

The chain reaction extended down to the war room, which erupted into a roaring victory cheer. They'd found a way to sink the impregnable alien battleships. Everyone went crazy, jumping into one another's arms, pumping fists in the air, laughing wildly. Everyone, that is, except Miguel. As shouts of triumph filled the room, he quietly opened the door and stepped outside into a corridor full of refugees. They were confused by the discrepancy between his sad expression and the cheering going on behind him.

Grey, permanently levelheaded, took one of the celebrants by the scruff of his collar, calming him down instantly.

"Get back on the wire," he snarled, "and explain to every squadron around the world how to shoot these sons of bitches down."

STEVE THOUGHT he could hear the fat lady singing. Still sprawled on the floor, hiding himself below the dashboard, he reached into his breast pocket and removed the pair of cigars Julius had given him. He held one out to David.

"I guess there's nothing left to do," he said, handing over the smoke, "except nuke 'em before they come in here and do something nasty."

David, still locked in a staring contest with the creatures behind the glass, nodded, coming to grips with the fact that he was about to die. Inspecting the cigar, he mused, "It's funny. I always thought things like *these* would kill me. Okay, let's fire away."

Steve lifted himself off the floor and sat down in his pilot's chair, trying to keep his eyes off the repulsive sight of the creatures straight ahead of him. He opened the cover plate on the black box and punched in the launch code. The LCD screen blinked rapidly, presenting him with two options: LAUNCH and CANCEL.

"Nice meeting you, man." He reached across and shook David's hand.

"Likewise," David assured him. "And we almost got away with it."

"Almost," Steve agreed. "Ready?"

"Bye-bye, Fuzzy. Bye-bye, Blinky." David waved to the aliens, giving them individual names. "See you later, Egghead, and you, too, Froggie."

"Think they know what's coming?" Steve asked, the cigar dangling from his mouth as he reached down to execute the firing.

"Not a chance."

As soon as Steve's finger touched the button, the floor of the tiny cabin kicked violently backwards, knocking both men off balance as the eight-foot-long missile shot away in a shower of rocket exhaust. Fire and shards of glass flew everywhere. By the time Steve and David could look up, the missile had penetrated the crystal observation window, crashed through the back of the observation room, and lodged itself into a distant wall, its rocket engine still spewing a jetstream of sparks.

Their artificially generated atmosphere impeached, the aliens behind the glass began to twist and expand horribly as their bodies were sucked in all directions by the vacuum of empty space. Their bulbous heads burst and splattered like kernels of bloody popcorn.

As this gruesome show played itself out beyond the windows of the attacker, the clamps holding the ship unexpectedly released and the ship lifted several feet in the air. An explosion in the observation tower knocked the ship backwards. It skittered off an identical craft parked next to it and wobbled out into the open.

"We're loose!"

"Doesn't matter," David said, "the game's over."

Steve checked the data from the black launch pad. Its digital counter showed the time remaining until the nuclear warhead self-detonated: 22 . . . 21 . . .

"I don't hear no fat lady," he said, jumping into the pilot's chair and spinning the craft around. David had just enough time to jump into his chair before Steve yanked back on the controls, jerking the ship into a full-speed getaway.

"Forget the fat lady. You're obsessed with the fat lady. Just get us out of here!"

Quicker that any human pilot could have reacted, a handful of attackers roared into pursuit. Although Steve hadn't mastered his plane's steering mechanism completely, he had no choice but to push it to breakneck speed. Swerving dizzily, he rocketed through the dimly lit maze of the mother ship's interior. The pursuing attackers held off firing at their prey until it came to the mouth of the exit tunnel. Suddenly, they unleashed a flood of tracer fire, but they didn't have the angle they needed, and Steve shot into the triangular passageway toward the exit.

"It's closing," David shouted, "the doors are closing."

"I can see that!" Steve had enough to worry about without a sideseat driver. The exit at the end of the tunnel was growing smaller by the moment as three thick doors moved closer, sealing off their last hope for escape. Straining the controls to the breaking point, Steve milked every ounce of speed from the craft, roaring toward the closing porthole. He checked the black box: . . . 09 . . . 08 . . .

"It's too late, they're closed." David watched the last few stars disappearing behind the triangular doorway. When he saw Steve meant to try it anyway, he closed his eyes and held his breath.

They shot through the narrow aperture with only inches to spare.

"Elvis has left the building!" he screamed.

"Thank you very much," David chimed in, lamely attempting to imitate The King.

Once they were out in space, Steve located the earth and steered the plane toward it. . . . 01 . . . 00.

The attacker continued to accelerate, streaking through space at several thousand miles per hour as its occupants stared at North America, perfectly clear but so far away. Then there was a flash of light so bright it seemed to come from the rear of their attacker. Steve and David had just enough time to look at each other with concerned expressions before the force of the blast moving through space caught them from behind. Like a loose board caught in the surf, their little ship rode the crest of the explosion, getting knocked ass over teakettle. Steve tried to steer through the wave of turbulence for a moment but then lost control as the explosion engulfed them completely.

THE CANOPY OF the president's jet lifted and a gloved fist rose in the air. Whitmore tore off his mask and lifted himself out of the cockpit onto the wing of his F-15. Seven of the Eagle Squad had returned, and thirty or so of the ragtag air force were coming in for their landings. They'd stayed in the air dogfighting with the last remaining attackers until the gray stingrays had started losing power and falling out of the sky. Apparently, they had only limited reserves of onboard energy.

Once his feet were on the ground, Whitmore pointed a finger at one of the other pilots, the long-haired, bearded Pig, acknowledging the credit he deserved. Pig pointed right back at the president. Cheering soldiers ran out to greet the planes. When the president gave them the order, they led the way to a hole in the earth. A stone's throw from the collapsed main hangar, a set of iron doors embedded in a slab of concrete opened onto a stairway. It was an emergency exit leading down to the research labs. Whitmore and his fellow pilots followed the soldiers into the passage.

The stairs ended in the scrub room. When the president turned the corner and stepped into the long clean room, it took a moment for him to recognize it. In place of the hooded workers he'd seen before, Whitmore came face-to-face with hundreds of ordinary citizens, the refugees who, only minutes earlier, had been preparing themselves to die. They erupted into loud, sustained cheering for the crew of heroes who had shot the alien destroyer out of the sky. Overwhelmed by their reception, Whitmore waded through the crowd, shaking hands and letting himself be hugged until he spotted someone he knew a short distance away. Julius lifted little Patricia onto the walkway and she ran toward her father as fast as her feet would take her. Whitmore scooped the girl up, wrapping her in his arms.

A young man with long hair stood nearby, watching the scene without emotion. He felt a hand on his shoulder.

"Dang, Miguel," Troy was back to his ornery self, "didn't you hear us? We've been yelling at you for ten minutes."

Alicia pushed her way through the cheering mob with Philip's help. The expression on Miguel's face told her instantly that Russell was dead. She burst into tears, leaving Philip and throwing her arms around Miguel.

"Hey, what happened?" Troy demanded. "What's wrong?" Without a word, Miguel reached out and pulled the boy close.

SLAMMING THROUGH the door of the war room, Whitmore was greeted with more applause. Grey, scowling at one of the monitors, turned and saw who it was. Something like a smile lit up his expression as he came forward to embrace his friend.

"Damn it, Tom, you trying to give an old man heart failure?"

"How's the attack coming?"

"Excellent. We've already got eight confirmed knock-downs and several more probables."

"Got another one, General," one of the soldiers yelled. "The Dutch air force just wasted the ship over the Netherlands."

The man's report sent another chorus of cheers through the room, but when Connie came through the door with a sad smile on her face, most of the men in the room quieted down. Jasmine, carrying Dylan on her hip, followed her inside.

"And our delivery boys?" Whitmore asked. "Any word yet from up there?"

Reluctantly, Grey answered, "Unfortunately, we lost contact with Hiller and Levinson about fifty minutes ago, a moment or two after the mother ship exploded."

Whitmore looked over at Connie and Jasmine as they listened to the bad news. Just when he was coming toward them to offer a few words of condolence, one of the men at the monitors shouted.

"Hold on! Something's showing up on radar. Looks like we have another incoming."

Everyone crowded around the monitor, watching the tiny blip move across the radar screen.

AN HOUR LATER, a Humvee crowded with passengers was speeding across the afternoon desert, kicking up a long trail of dust. Behind the wheel, Major Mitchell steered the transport, half sports car and half tank, toward a towering column of black smoke rising in the distance. The war room crew had tracked the craft moving across their radar screens until it landed about nine miles from the base, deep in the middle of nowhere. In the bucket seat next to Mitchell, Jasmine kept watch out the front window while Dylan bounced around on her lap. Standing just behind her, with their faces to the wind, Connie, President Whitmore, and General Grey held on to the roll bar, scanning the horizon for signs of life. In the roomy cargo area, Julius sat with the president's daughter Patricia. Another vehicle, a jeep loaded with armed soldiers, followed a short distance behind.

At a distance of three miles, they could see that the ship had crash-landed against an isolated set of rocky hills. There was no evidence to support their hope it was the same ship Steve and David had taken into space, and even less reason to believe the men might still be alive. The ruined attacker was completely engulfed in flame.

Tiny dark shapes appeared on the flat brown horizon. As the Humvee came closer, it became clear these shapes were actually a pair of creatures. They seemed to be standing upright and moving. Grey yelled for Mitchell to slow the vehicle down, then motioned the soldiers in the jeep forward. With several assault rifles trained on the two figures, the caravan rolled forward at a cautious pace.

At fifty yards away, Mitchell brought the vehicle to a stop, switched off the motor, and draped his arms over the steering wheel. "Well, I'll be damned," he said in disbelief. The mysterious figures were smoking cigars.

Hiller and Levinson had done the impossible and lived to tell about it. They'd infiltrated the alien fortress, disabled her shields with a dime store computer virus, blown the planet-sized orb to smithereens, then flown back to Nevada before their attacker's energy supply was exhausted. Now they came swaggering across the sand, casual and confident, as if it were all in a day's work.

Jasmine threw open the door and went sprinting across the hot sand. She didn't stop running until she was wrapped in her husband's arms. Squeezing him like she'd never let go again, her voice choked with emotion, she said, "You scared the hell out of me. We thought you got trapped inside."

Steve looked down at her with that cocky grin of his. "Yeah, but what an entrance!"

Jasmine stared at him, shocked and amused in the same breath. Didn't *anything* scare this man? "There you go again." She shook her head. "I guess your ego's gonna be out of control now, and you'll be impossible to live with, right?"

"Probably. You still willing to find out, Chicken Legs?"

She let out a joyous laugh. "Yeah, I'm willing to give it a try, Dumbo Ears!"

Connie and David approached one another slowly, then stopped to face one another as if one step closer might set off a buried land mine. She was mightily proud of him. For David, the sweetest part of living through his ordeal was being able to see her again. But neither of them knew what the other wanted, so they remained standing three feet apart.

"So," David asked, looking around the empty sky, "did it work?"

The question brought Connie suddenly back to earth. She'd been imagining what it would be like to move across the last small piece of territory separating them and feel his kiss again. But, naturally, he wanted to know whether his brilliant plan had been successful. Embarrassed by her hidden thoughts, she suddenly felt the eyes of those watching from the vehicles.

"Yes, yes," she told him, "it worked beautifully. A couple of minutes after the upload, all their shields went down and we started hitting them with missiles"

She started to tell him how the city destroyer had come toward Area 51 and how Whitmore himself had led the air battle, how the mysterious pilot in the old biplane had arrived in the nick of time, but David held up a hand to interrupt the story.

"No, what I mean is," he pointed to her and then back to himself, "*did it work?*"

The smile that spread across Connie's face was brighter than the afternoon sun. "You bet it worked," she told him. They stepped across the no-man's land between them and into one another's arms, "you bet it did."

When the couples returned arm in arm to the vehicles, Whitmore nodded his head at the two men in begrudging approval. "Not bad," he told them, as if they'd just taken a test and scraped by with a C+. But the next moment, he was grinning from ear to ear, unable to hide his admiration for all that the two heroes had accomplished. "Not too damn bad at all!"

He congratulated Steve with a handshake, then turned to the lanky MIT alumnus who had punched him in the nose years before. "You turned out to be even smarter than I thought you were," he said as they shook hands. "And a hell of a lot braver than I ever gave you credit for. Thank you, David."

"What I would like to know," a loud voice interrupted, "is how come Mr. Healthnut is suddenly smoking one of my disgusting cigars?"

Julius was relaxing on the bumper of the Humvee, his legs not quite long enough to reach the ground. David let go of Connie long enough to wrap his father in a rowdy bear hug, lifting him off the ground.

"Oy, now he's a pro wrestler."

David set the old man down and eyed him suspiciously for a moment. As Julius composed himself, straightening out the hair and clothing his son had mussed, he asked David what he was staring at.

"How did you do it, Pops?"

"Do what?" the old guy asked. "I don't know what you're talking about."

"You know exactly what I mean," David kept at him. "First, you got us to Washington, then to Area Fifty-One, and just when I was about to quit, you gave me the idea for the virus. I suppose you'll tell me it was all just a series of accidents, right?"

For a split second, Julius let a cunning grin play across his face before returning once more to an expression of mock annoyance. "I don't know what happened to you out in space, but I'm thinking those aliens maybe did something funny to your brain."

The two men smiled warmly at each other.

Steve was kneeling down beside Dylan, getting his welcome home hug, when General Grey stepped forward for a word with him. "Well, soldier, you've had quite a weekend."

"Yes, sir, I have," the Marine pilot agreed.

"And you did one hell of a fine job. We're all proud." Grey offered a salute, which both Steve and Dylan returned.

Triumphant, the group began to load into the Humvee for the ride back to Area 51. As they were doing so, Patricia Whitmore pointed up to the sky and yelled, "Hey, what's that?"

The group turned in time to see a fireball, orange and red, streaking overhead like a falling star. Then another trail of light, this one bright yellow, ripped across the aqua blue sky. Wreckage from the exploded mother ship was raining through space and burning itself up at it entered earth's atmosphere. The colorful meteors would go on bursting in the air all through the night.

Steve lifted Dylan into his arms and looked skyward. "You know what day it is?" he asked.

"Yup," Dylan told him, "it's the Fourth of July."

"That's right, son. And didn't I promise you fireworks?"

THE BATTLE OVER Area 51 had ended in a relatively clean and painless victory. Fewer than three hundred people had died. But the situation was far different in other parts of the country and around the world. Humanity had survived, but only at a staggering cost. Millions were dead and millions more were injured. Many would never recover from the wounds, both physical and emotional, they had sustained during the invasion. Even as the survivors began digging themselves out from under the debris, thankful to be alive, they felt the dread of the months and years of rebuilding which lay ahead. The howls coming from the victory celebrations echoed out over a collapsed and blighted world. In most places, the destruction was so severe that the living envied the dead.

More than a hundred of the world's largest cities had been obliterated, among them ancient, irreplaceable treasures such as Paris, Baghdad, New York, and Kyoto. Gone too were the world's finest museums and libraries, its major airports and factories, food processing plants, markets, office buildings, and one out of every three human homes. Refugees, hundreds of millions of them, without shelter or means of feeding themselves, wondered how they would survive. The situation was most dire in the southern hemisphere, where it was the middle of winter. Mass migrations to the temperate zones of the earth began immediately, further taxing already strained ecological resources. The earth's water, land, and air were all heavily polluted in the aftermath of the short but cataclysmic war.

It seemed that everything had been lost and that only one thing had, perhaps, been gained: a wider frame of reference. Along with the certain knowledge that humans were not alone in the universe, the murderous squabbling over petty differences of race and nationality suddenly seemed to be petty foolishness. In the wake of the attack, the people of earth finally realized the things they shared in common far outweighed their subtle differences. There was a worldwide recognition that the human imagination had been fundamentally altered and there was no turning back. In a sense, the species had grown up the hard way, being shoved unwillingly toward maturity. There was also an awareness of a new interdependence: the world would have to prepare for the possibility of a similar invasion in the future. Whitmore's hope had come to pass: July Fourth would no longer be merely an American holiday.

It was a new future, and leaders like Whitmore were anxious to help shape the new world that would be built upon the ruins of the old. They knew the direction and character of this rebuilding would be determined early, within the first few months. There was every possibility for America, one of the most violent and divided nations in the world, to tear itself apart in a struggle over scarce resources, but there was also the possibility of people coming together, cooperating with one another in a spirit of community that would set an example for others around the globe. Before the dust of the battles had settled, Whitmore would be on the campaign trail once again, making essentially the same call to service and self-sacrifice he had delivered during his run for the presidency. But this time the scope would be international and the risks much higher. What kind of world would he pass on to his daughter?

As the rebuilding began, one fact quickly made itself abundantly clear: the human spirit, like the supple, tenacious weeds already beginning to push their way up through the ruins, would once again reassert itself, tougher, smarter, and more unified than ever.